SWEEP OF STARS

ALSO BY MAURICE BROADDUS

ADULT

Buffalo Soldier
Pimp My Airship
The Voices of Martyrs
I Can Transform You
The Knights of Breton Court
Orgy of Souls

MIDDLE GRADE

Unfadeable (forthcoming)
The Usual Suspects

SWEEP OF STARS

MAURICE BROADDUS

TOR

A TOM DOHERTY ASSOCIATES BOOK
NEW YORK

SWEEP OF STARS

Copyright © 2022 by Maurice Broaddus

A Tor Book
Published by Tom Doherty Associates
120 Broadway
New York, NY 10271

www.tor-forge.com

Tor® is a registered trademark of Macmillan Publishing Group, LLC.

Library of Congress Cataloging-in-Publication Data

Names: Broaddus, Maurice, author.
Title: Sweep of stars / Maurice Broaddus.
Description: First edition. | New York : Tor, 2022. |
Series: Astra black ; 1 | "A Tom Doherty Associates book."
Identifiers: LCCN 2021058912 (print) | LCCN 2021058913 (ebook) |
ISBN 9781250264930 (hardcover) | ISBN 9781250264923 (ebook)
Classification: LCC PS3602.R56 S94 2022 (print) |
LCC PS3602.R56 (ebook) | DDC 813'.6—dc23/eng/20211206
LC record available at https://lccn.loc.gov/2021058912
LC ebook record available at https://lccn.loc.gov/2021058913

Our books may be purchased in bulk for promotional, educational, or business use. Please contact your local bookseller or the Macmillan Corporate and Premium Sales Department at 1-800-221-7945, extension 5442, or by email at MacmillanSpecialMarkets@macmillan.com.

First Edition: 2022

Printed in the United States of America

0 9 8 7 6 5 4 3 2 1

The Kheprw Institute
and all the neighbors who dream and work together
to create their desired future states

CAST

THE IJO
(Seven Founding Families)

ADISA	JYWANZA	CHIKEKE	BUHARI	NGUNI	DIMKA	YAR'ADUA
Camara Xola	Selamault	Stacia	Maulana	Geoboe	Jaha	Bayard
Wachiru	Nehanda	Yahya	Fela	Khuma	Lebna	
Amachi		Bekele		Itoro		
Ezeji						

HOVA BRIGADE

Fela Buhari (Commander)

Epyc Ro Morgan (Captain)

Anitra Gouvei (First Lieutenant)

Chandra Elle (Second Lieutenant)

Robin Townsend (Sergeant)

TIME LINE

Welcome to the sovereign territory of Muungano, centered around a lunar outpost but whose ties extend to Titan, Oyigiyigi (a series of asteroid belts), and Bronzeville (one of the Mars settlements). It's led by a coalition of weusi people, mostly a mix of Asili (natives of the Motherland, Alkebulan) and Ugenini (children of the diaspora). Here's how it came to be:

2019   Ghana's president, Nana Akufo-Addo, declared and formally launched the "Year of Return, Ghana 2019" for Africans in the diaspora, giving fresh impetus to the quest to unite Africans on the continent with their brothers and sisters in the diaspora.

2021–2024   The Great Unrest.

2026   First World established.

2030   Ecological collapse on Earth and climate terraforming.

2031   The Rorschach Disaster, when Earth abandoned the fledgling lunar outpost in favor of Mars settlements.

2033   Mars. Established as New Earth, leaving those left behind on what was now referred to as Original Earth. They returned the name to Mars as they opted to carve out their own identity.

2034   Earth. The Decade-Long War—Original Earth breaks down in a series of religious wars.

2037   Fifth Wave Migration. The Ugenini and Asili people began to settle on First World due to the private interstellar shuttle conglomeration Outer Spaceways Inc.

2040   Ujima Experiment, when the weusi assumed control of the physical space of First World. The colony began as a recovery space. They began to reach out and build institutions to create time (to control their own stories). Soon, First World became a thriving community, with the efficient mining of He-3 and after the discovery of kheprw crystals, which helped fuel their starships.

2042   Mothership Incident, when the mothership accidentally slipped back in time through a wormhole, returning and then hiding behind the moon.

2044   The Liberation Investment Support Cooperative (LISC) expands and recharters the United Nations under its auspices.

2045   Incursion. Original Earth leadership sought to reclaim the Ujima / First World territory. Extremists want control, to return to war mode in time of crisis.

2046-2049   The Lunar Ukombozi War for control of the moon. *(includes HOVA operations: Bumba, Oblata, the Yemaya Campaign, Hellwalk, Ragnarok).*

2047   The Bronzeville Rebellion occurs on Mars.

2050   Muungano established. At the end of the Lunar Ukombozi War, the lunar community ceded from Original Earth's sovereignty.

2050-2100   Uponyaji, a period known as the time of isolation and healing, wherein the Muungano people began to establish the independent culture and traditions.

2052   Oyigiyigi mining outpost established.

2087   Titan community established. Construction of Muungano starships begins.

2120   Orun Gate discovered.

2121   **Present.**

The beauty in blackness is its ability to transform. Like energy we are neither created nor destroyed, though many try.

—**West African proverb**

SWEEP OF STARS

01

AMACHI ADISA
Muungano, the Belts / the Dreaming City

Your name is Leah Adisa. For now.

Choosing a name for yourself is not something to be entered into lightly. It is a promise you make to the Universe. Or it to you. A name is the story of yourself you present to the world, a label to define you. That is the entire point of the Naming Ceremony: you are finally of age to interpret yourself and enter fully into the Muungano community as a full free member.

Because this is an Adisa renaming, the entire Ijo governing body travels in from all of the Muungano alliance. An excuse for the people to, as the Ugenini would say, show out. The full sovereign territory of Muungano centers around the lunar outpost and the facility that serves as its capital, the Dreaming City. Named after an old tale the Wise Ones whispered when it was time for bed. A place full of orisha and magic and the old ways. From Bronzeville on Mars, Titan, and even the distant Oyigiyigi mining outpost, members make the voyage. It's only a couple of weeks' travel at sublight, but many representatives wanted to make the pilgrimage. Even the fabled research ship, the *Cypher,* is due to dock anytime now. With its captain. Your heart twists, nearly dropping to your belly, with the weight of the complicated feelings that accompany thoughts of her.

You distract your mind from her and the ceremony—the gathering of the families, the ritual and production—by focusing on preparing yourself. You spread your clothes out on your bed. As a spiritual cleansing, you light three candles. Fearing that three undeclared open flames might set off the fire suppression system, you snuff one out. With one of the candles, you ignite a small bowl of herbs, just enough for the leaves to smolder and fill the room with their sweet, woody odor. Adding a few chiba leaves to quell your anxiety, you close your eyes. Not quite in prayer but to simply control your breath and settle your emi—your awareness—to concentrate on understanding the language of the soul, our sabhu.

You study the array of clothes scattered about. You don't want to wear any of the kaftans favored by the Titans, because *she* will be wearing one, and you don't want her to think you're imitating her. Encroaching on her. Thinking of her. Having handwoven a print to express your family's roots, you sift through the rest for the proper accents. In the pit of your being, you still feel every bit the imposter. One wearing the print of a family you weren't actually born into.

The door chimes.

<Camara Xola Adisa,> Maya intones.

"What's he doing here?" you ask.

<You could let him in and find out,> Maya said. <Though it's a statistical likelihood that he has some words of insight or encouragement to offer you before the ceremony.>

"Let him in." You mutter the word *smart-ass* under your breath even though, one, Maya's system still likely heard you and, two, they have no feelings—as you understand them—to hurt. Your hands fidget so much you reach for your chakram to twirl.

The door loses its color until it becomes a transparent window before a low hiss signals the material dissolving into an opening.

"I see you." Camara Xola Adisa stoops slightly to enter. His skin—papery thin, well veined with pink undertones to his complexion—light enough to pass for wazungu. Tufts of gray-tinged, black hair rings the back of his head. His wife, Selamault, must not have been up yet. She would never let him out of their kraal looking like a disheveled shepherd.

"I see you," you return his greeting. Behind him one of the Niyabinghi waits by the door entrance. The guard doesn't enter.

"It's almost time." Lean as a reed, Xola moves with a slight tremble to his limbs. You believe he plays up this affect a bit, in order to make people attend him more closely. And underestimate him. He could have synthed new organs, but he proclaimed that would be treating the symptoms, not the root of his neurological degenerative disorder. Tracking any sound, his hazel eyes remain alert and sharp as his mind. Settling into a chair, he sniffs the air with an exaggerated snuffle, noting the not-quite-successfully cloaked smell of chiba with a knowing smirk crossing his lips.

"I'm almost ready." You turn from him so that your idiotic grin doesn't confirm your self-medication.

"Stacia should be here, helping you with your hair."

Busying yourself by straightening up, you wince at the sound of her name.

You wonder if he's purposely being oblivious or inconsiderate, to gauge your reaction. There were so many expectations for the pair of you. Nearly the same age, she's a captain now, while you are only now having your Naming Ceremony. "Her ship was over two weeks away, studying the Orun Gate, when I last received a message from her. She will barely make the ceremony."

"Are you nervous?" Camara Xola struggles to find a more comfortable position in his seat even as it adjusts to his posture. His hand flutters in front of his face, gesturing as if conducting an invisible orchestra.

"No," you lie, but you recognize one of his probing questions when you hear them. The community *is* school and school is *always* in session, Xola enjoys repeating. The Camara always takes the measure of those around him. Constantly curious, and genuinely so, it also allows him to ferret out possible weakness. No, it was more like scouting. *He* was always on the lookout to welcome and develop new leaders. Ones committed to building out the Muungano infrastructure for promoting learning and achievement.

And you never want to appear weak before him. Never him.

"You sure? Lots of folks here showing up to check you out. Coming to see what name an Adisa chooses for themselves." His wry grin widens, perfectly pleased with himself.

You can't help but match it. "I won't disappoint."

"I know you won't." Camara Xola's eyes dart away from yours. His tell, when he has something he wants to pass along, calculating the best way to come at you.

"What is it?" You provide him the opening. You've never had trouble talking with directness to each other.

"You don't miss a trick, do you?" The grin returns.

"You taught me not to."

"I did? Hm, I must be better than I thought." Xola plucks a jackfruit from within the folds of his robes. His long, yellowed nails dig into the flesh of the fruit. You can't help but watch his flicks and fumbles, the intricate dance of his fingers along the fruit's skin. You're pretty convinced that he grows his nails impractically long simply to annoy his caretakers.

"Don't try to be clever by changing topics," you say with a smile in your voice.

"It's Selamault." A heavy sigh ladens his words. "She won't be at the Naming Ceremony."

"Oh." The disappointment seeps out of you like a poorly bandaged wound.

Camara Xola reaches for your hand, his long, spidery fingers tremulous as they wrap around yours. "She's sick. Can barely get out of bed. You know it's the only reason she'd miss your time."

"Will she be all right?" You study your fingers interlaced with his, how dark your skin is, especially compared to his.

"She should be. I'm not sure she's going to let a spell of sickness stop her." Xola squeezes your hand. "She loves you like you were her own."

"I know." The words come out, but you sound not quite convinced even to your ears.

"Because you are," he finishes. "Your place is within our family. A daughter we are so proud of. I hope you hear that. And one day, I hope you fully believe it."

Camara Xola has been every bit the father to you ever since you lost your parents in a mining accident so long ago you can't remember their faces outside of a holovid. He releases your hand after a brief shake of your fingers to keep you from spiraling into a gravity well of introspection.

"I know." You slowly meet his eyes. "I really do."

"Good. Besides, you being around keeps Wachiru on his toes."

"He needs it. All of Muungano will be his one day."

"Let's not get ahead of ourselves." Camara Xola straightens, excited about an idea, and suddenly seems a few dozen years younger. "If we do this really, really well, Muungano will be everywhere. Folks raised in the Muungano way will go out into the world, the universe, and they will create other Muunganos in new spaces."

"But Wachiru is the heir apparent." You leave the words *not me* unsaid.

"Wachiru is the oldest in the work. He was born into it and raised in it, so naturally he's a great candidate. But the role is not grounded in biology; a leader has to be selected by the community. The Camara is the voice of the community. A teacher. A consensus builder. Someone with the vision and skills to lead. Someone who represents the philosophy of the work. Now I don't know how Wachiru would feel about any of that. At the very least, though, he recognizes the burden and sacrifice of leadership." Camara Xola slumps, suddenly weary. When he chuckles, it's a low, dark thing. "Maybe I'm being naive not having developed a ritual of transition."

"Because you oldheads think you're immortal." Keyed to your artificial cowries encircling your wrist, you activate a wave of nanobots with a sweep of your hand. With that gesture, your funkentelechy spreads and directs them like liquid metal to fashion a curtain for you to hide behind to finish dressing. More because you hate the vulnerability of being observed enrobing than actually being seen nude. You have no shame of your body, but you do treat the ritual of dressing and applying makeup with the solemnity of a magician not wanting to reveal their secrets.

"It has been a couple of hundred years of birthdays. I'm old enough to know that we have to remain vigilant." Xola's voice becomes thoughtful and distant, drifting off into a dream. "There are always forces ready to attack who we are. I fear what we might become to stop them. But worst-case scenario is how my mind works."

The two of you fall silent as you finish putting on your clothes. The weight of the day, of the community, presses on you. Your mind sifts through possibilities. You can't escape the sensation of something impending about to drop on you. You push your anxiousness to the side as you put the final pins in your wrap.

"I'm almost ready," you announce.

"Let me see you." You can almost hear Xola's anticipatory rustling, ready for a show.

You draw back the curtain. Rich blends of gold, black, and green form your full-body wrap of handmade kente weave. Your black cloak has a matching pattern for its border. Your head wrap leads into a cow-horn-shaped hat. It took you weeks to make, with thousands of curses from pricking your fingers while mastering the old ways rather than simply synthesizing the materials. The entire point of the Naming Ceremony is to connect the past to the future, so you thought this extra effort only fitting. Xola beams with pride.

"You are amazing. Want to tell me your new name?" Having risen to circle you in inspection, Xola leans toward you in a conspiratorial whisper. "I promise I won't tell."

You match his movement and soft voice. "You'll have to come to the ceremony to find out."

"I'll see you there, then." Beaming, Xola walks toward the door before hesitating. "I appreciate you."

"I appreciate you."

✳

The members of Muungano experience two Naming Ceremonies. You don't remember your first. It came seven days after your birth. On O.E., *the Yo,* as you call it. By the holo accounts, family and neighbors gathered together to celebrate and welcome you into the world, imitating the rituals they heard were carried out on Muungano. You were given the name of a distant ancestor in your family. It is only fitting that you chose Ojo Bo, the Day of Creation, for the day of your second.

As your Saqqara shuttle ship disembarks from the array, the two bisecting arms known as the Belts span the circumference of the moon in a curving perpendicular lattice looming over you. A string of kraals arranged in a long line, the series of modules gird the moon in a geosynchronous orbit over the Dreaming City, the capital of Muungano. Descending on a vector to the building—with spires radiating from its dome—the many-rayed architecture makes it appear like a setting sun coming into view.

You love landing into the Dreaming City. With its giant columns, sky ports, and blur of lights, it is a gleaming bauble filling the horizon. The journey weighs your bones down and roots you until the bump of the tractor tethers lock on to your Saqqara and jolt you out of your reverie. Riding the invisible conveyor, you never feel a bit of the interstellar cold, which would chill you to the bone. Instead, the sun's rays overhead beat down upon you, causing any exertion to make you sweat. You've grown up in the carefully regulated confines of the Dreaming City. By your seventh year, you knew every centimeter. By your fifteenth, you knew the entire surface of lunar Muungano. You haven't visited many planets; a run to Titan with Stacia, a brief stay in the Bronzeville outpost on the Mars settlement. Your heart still races, just an extra beat, admiring the jeweled heart of Muungano.

Still, you yearn for more. The stars call to you. If not for the Yo or Mars, then certainly Titan or maybe even worlds beyond. You dream of truly outer space and the magic of the stars.

✳

A team of twenty drummers strike up a beat and line up at the front of the great hall of the Dreaming City. Behind them, a storm of dancers hop in place, allowing space for the drummers to proceed, before spacing out along the pathway to twirl their scarves. Green, yellow, or black, mirroring your outfit. They synchronize their movement, a formation of limbs jerking and swaying, bobbing along the syncopated heartbeat of the pounding rhythm.

Crowds of people line either side of the walkway. You've never seen so many of your people assembled at once. Here in this place, in this time, they echo the old ways. Their dress a sea of kente cloth, kaftans, and head wraps. Bold colors, different patterns representing the various families. Though you know it's not the case, it seems like all of Muungano has turned out for your renaming. Once you complete the ceremony, the next step will be for you to be formally invited to the Ijo as a ranking member of the Adisa family.

A sudden dread gnaws your stomach.

Serving as the officiating elder, Bayard Anike stands up next and follows the dancers, his every step slow and considered. An oak of a man, his white, embroidered gown—with its wide sleeves—drapes over a short-sleeved, matching tunic and trousers. However, his hat echoes the colors of your wrap as do the accents on his otherwise black shoes. Bayard carries a large staff, which he raises according to his own internal rhythm, turns it on its side, as if to bar anyone from approaching.

Camara Xola marches next, alongside an empty chair held aloft by four members of the Niyabinghi. Under ordinary circumstances, he would serve as the officiating elder, but because this is your ceremony, he defers to Bayard and instead serves as Libator so that he may lead the family processional. You walk behind him with your peculiar stride, a sort of a toe-first stomp, each footfall slapping the ground to echo as loudly as possible against the fused regolith floor. As he steps onto the pathway, a holographic image flares to life. Mother Sela, despite being in her sickbed, projects an image of herself. The hologram of Selamault, unperturbed by the regulated temperature of the Dreaming City and the clear view through the dome, seems to stare toward the horizon of Muungano. She turns to look down at you, outstretching her fingers to brush yours. A ghost of light projections, they pass through your hands.

Wachiru brings up the rear. His features favor his father though his complexion is several shades darker. He hoists a large umbrella, a token meant to shield the Queen Mother during the processional. The differences between you and Wachiru betray the illusion of you being blood relations. He stands tall and thin with the delicate build of a russet-complected flower easily uprooted. Much darker skinned, your short, thick frame—a muscled, squat construction of too much behind and overcompensating chest—moves with a dancer's confidence. Your deep, sepia eyes all but dare anyone to cross you. Wachiru turns to you and nods, his eyes warm and inviting, but distant in the way that he never quite focuses on anyone in particular. Despite the Muungano greeting, he sees in a way that defies explanation.

Four members of the Niyabinghi Order follow the processional as rear guard. When you arrive at the center dais, the entire parade pauses in remembrance of the spot where the original module touched down and construction began on the Dreaming City's first structure as a part of the social experiment called First World. The guards disperse to the four corners of the stage.

A hush falls over the crowd without Bayard doing anything beyond taking center stage.

"To destroy the identity of a people," he begins, "you must first strip them of their name, strip them of their sense of self. Your name joins you to your family, your history, your culture. We struggled long and hard to reclaim our birthright and control of ourselves. Today we honor our right to define ourselves on our terms. Leah Adisa, before whom do you vow?"

"Nyame. Asase Afua. The orisha. My honored ancestors. My family, Adisa. The people of Muungano."

"What name do you choose for yourself?"

"Amachi," you proclaim. Turning to the gathering, you define your name. *"Who knows what God has brought us through this child."*

His lips broadening into a well-pleased smile, Camara Xola Adisa stifles a snort.

Not wanting the moment broken, Bayard cuts him a slight, chastening glare before continuing. "As you say, so shall it be. Beloved community of Muungano, I present to you Amachi Leah Adisa."

"Hail! Hail! Hail!" Camara Xola cries out and steps forward to address the community. "May happiness come."

"Asè!" the people of Muungano shout in response.

"Whenever we join to make a circle, may our chain be complete." Camara Xola raises his hands.

"Asè!"

"Whenever we dig a well, may we come upon water."

"Asè!"

"May it be darkness behind the stranger who has come"—Xola turns to you—"and light before her."

"Asè!"

"May her mother and father have long life." He nods at Selamault, who returns the gesture.

"Asè!"

"May she eat by the labor of her hands."

"Asè!"

"May she show respect to the world."

"Asè!"

"May her path be straightened for her."

"Asè!"

"Life and prosperity to all her children."

"Asè!"

"May we leave whole and may we return whole."

"Asè!"

"And"—Xola returns his steady gaze to you—"may happiness come."

"Asè! Asè! Asè!" the people of Muungano erupt.

*

Representatives from each of the seven governing families of Muungano assemble for the gathering of the Ijo. The full ruling body rarely meets. The elder of each kraal typically organizes their represented community. There is little need for the collective elders to actually come together except on special occasions or simply to just enjoy being a community of elders delighting in one another as if they attended a family reunion. The room radiates around a large table. Symbolic more than anything else, as it couldn't seat the entire Adisa family, much less the full Ijo. But it is the traditional gathering place for a family meeting.

You are introduced to visiting members. Ambassadors, physicists, poets, teachers, engineers, healers, none of whom use titles or honorifics (other than the Camara, who winks at you while you mingled). As they are from Ugenini, Asili, and Maroon peoples, from all reaches of Muungano, the biolink implanted in each member allows Maya to translate for you, functioning much like a site-to-site glyph. You chat, you laugh, little of it you will remember due to the heady excitement of being introduced anew to your community.

To great applause and shouts, you take the stairs and stride across the floor to take your seat next between Camara Xola and Wachiru. You can't help but feel a pang of jealousy of Wachiru. By simple virtue of him being him, the natural-born son of Xola and Selamault, he wins any battle for people's affections. You are left with the scraps, think about when he isn't around. Silent and intent, he bobs his head without disdain for the proceedings, but caught up in his mental world of beats and melodies. His mind full of music, all staccato cadences, storytelling by a poet warrior. It makes your skin flush with pride and . . . something. Not quite anger, more frustration. That he squanders his position by always chasing after possibilities rather than embracing his birthright.

"You think too much," Xola looms into your ear.

"I don't want to miss anything," you say.

"You're here. Be here." His long fingers dance along the console. The movements haphazard and jittery as if he's playing a balafon. His eyes bother him, beginning to fail him, all the while he continues to act as if nothing is wrong. Xola slips without Selamault around, betraying the frailty of his condition. Ordinarily, she hovers over him in a constant fuss, the comfortable worry of a long-joined partner to their spouse. But buried in the interactions are her masking the severity of his symptoms. Passing food for him. Sharing his food, breaking his into portions for easy purchase and eating. Perusing files, reading them aloud in the guise of seeking his opinion on matters. A careful choreography. Without her around, his symptoms demonstrate that he is clearly worse than you thought. With your elevated position in the family, he has allowed you to see it. "You are as you have always been: among your people."

The Ijo continue to seat themselves around the dais of the Dreaming City's main chamber. You half rehearse what you would say to the Ijo, comforted by the fact that they are duty bound to greet and welcome you. Then you chide yourself for such cynicism. You know that the families—who have known and loved you since you first walked among them—eagerly await to rejoice in your formal induction into the community. The inchoate dread of expectation chews at you nonetheless, because you fear your ability to live up to the ghost of their dreams for you.

A mild commotion stirs near the area where the Buhari family have gathered.

Camara Xola stands, and the throng settles into a hush as he shuffles toward the dais. In a low, unwavering voice steeled with pride, he announces, "The Adisa family, governing family of the Ijo, presents the newest duly appointed member of our family: Amachi Adisa."

The full Ijo stands. Each member clasps their wrists and bows their heads in your direction. When they raise their heads, they break their grasp. They hold their fists out as they shout.

"Hoo!"

A chorus of finger snaps issue from when the Yar'adua family congregate. Bayard, head of their family, steps forward. "We see you, Amachi Adisa, daughter of Xola Adisa and Selamault Jywanza. Long may you serve."

"I offer all in service to Muungano," you say.

You catch sight of Maulana Buhari, gliding through the crowd, a shark among a scattering school of fish parting as he nears. Your heart skips a measure before finding itself again. You have admired the man for almost as long as you have drawn breath. You have studied his fiery words as faithfully as an agoze, holding him second only to Xola in your heart's admiration. Marching with a quiet dignity—stiff and upright, ever overly mannered—he defers to the stateliness of the proceedings, but otherwise has no use for its symbolic pageantry. His dark eyes filled with both a devouring hunger and a protective menace. He has a way of looking at everything, constantly calculating its potential threat. His face full of intent, he whispers in his elder's ear.

"Are there any matters to bring before the Ijo?" Camara Xola asks, both knowing and expectant.

A Buhari elder stands, his face a filigree of wrinkles, and an expression on his face as if he'd just bitten into the sourest of apples. "The Buhari name Maulana, son of Hakeem and Tiamoyo Buhari, as the duly appointed head of our family."

A few gasps ripple among the Ijo. The Buhari elder was certainly due to step down, but an elder usually relinquished his seat only after sufficient notice for the Ijo to arrange a proper gratitude ceremony. A move this sudden, without so much as a warning whisper, portents nothing but ill.

Your stomach churns with anticipation, since you already have little room or love for such grandstanding.

"We see you, Maulana Buhari," Bayard ordains. "Long may you serve."

"I see you." Usually not one to be caught up on procedural matters, Maulana remains standing. From the graveness of his face, the vague unease you experienced at his entrance begins to curdle into something solid. "Camara, I'm afraid that I come bearing sobering news."

"What is it, Maulana?" Camara Xola bridges his fingers, his gaze leveled at the table.

"It's Jaha."

02

JAHA DIMKA
The Muungano Embassy on (Original) Earth

"A storyteller is a master strategist. A skilled griot sees people as characters, participants in a tale. They apply motives and goals to people, because stories are driven by them. They police Muungano by confronting our members with reminders of who they are, who we are, and pointing them to the future of what we hope to become."

Jaha Dimka fastened a red, black, and green head wrap into place, tucking the escaping stray curls underneath. No one would ever see her without her head being covered, be it by hat, scarf, or artificial hairpiece. She fitted an octopus-shaped headband, which matched her chakram necklace, over her hair before binding it. Metallic-green eye shadow framed a black kohl-rimmed eye, highlighted against her bronze complexion. Leaning back in her chair, she listened for a response from her cultural attaché. Thin lines framed the fierce set of her jaw.

"Mm-hmm," he said to acknowledge her statement. A slight huffiness to his tone, an intimated impatience since he waited on the other side of the fashioned screen.

As was her habit, Jaha was the first to arrive at the embassy. Because she leapt immediately into her work, she hadn't changed into anything formal. In short, she hadn't done her hair. And her cultural attaché would just have to wait until she was ready. Jaha numbered among the oldest of Muungano's members. People often asked when she planned on retiring, which she took as her cue to inform them that she was living with intentionality and there was no retiring from that except by death. Back in the day, when the community being formed was still called First World, legendary cofounder Astra Black had been her mentor.

She drew her robes, which were the Legba colors of griots—black with red sleeves—tighter around her with a green sash. A collar with a near-metallic sheen extended up high along her neck. Once she was satisfied, Jaha dropped the nanotech curtain. The array dissolved into an umber puddle, which skirted over to her to wrap itself about her, the nanomesh forming along her like a second skin.

Ishant Sangsuwangul stood revealed on the other side, a smirk of bemused indifference plastered on his face. Without a word, he walked over to the workstation adjacent to her. He'd kept his back to her. He hadn't bothered to give her a greeting, no "I see you" nor a hand clasp. Though young, he sported a premature streak of white in his hair. With his short, lithe figure, he wore a tight-fitting shirt and, if possible, tighter-fitting pants, which was all the fashion rage on Original Earth. His outfit casually displayed his thin muscles. It annoyed Jaha's fashion sensibilities, but the elder wouldn't begrudge the young their poor fashion choices as long as they retained some semblance of cultural decorum.

The Legacy of Alexandria was the hub of the O.E. Muungano embassy. They dubbed the room that because the Muungano physical library was housed there. Shelves lined every wall space, filled with books. Every nook filled with hand-carved masks or figurines. Jaha loved the look and feel of actual books. She labored in the shadow of the largest collection of Third World Press first editions. Even though it also meant that she had to suffer through Camara Xola's "The hegemony of text is dead" rants whenever he visited.

"What's the first lesson of the griot?" Jaha raised her voice as if he hadn't heard her the first time. Young people benefited from being constantly tested. It taught them to always be ready.

"When you see a challenge in your community, you are already in the best position to help solve it." Ishant sighed. "That was never the question. I already believed the philosophies of Muungano and what it was about. That when we all prosper, we all grow together. It was a dream I hadn't figured out the language for."

A brace at the shoulder wrapped around his torso, framing his left arm. A cybernetic arm sheathed in bioplastic, it allowed him to plug into AI and other tech systems. Ishant was a streamer, jacking into the data streams for pleasure. Young people were going to young people, Jaha had long ago concluded as she could not wrap her head around sensate culture. Jaha wouldn't allow him to jack in around her. "We don't have to get the language right. It changes because Muungano is a continuing experiment."

"My issue is *how*. How to use stories to correct and push people."

"What I'm saying is that we do it all the time." Jaha strode over to him and rested a hand on his shoulder. "What's really bothering you? I can feel an ill energy all over your emi."

Ishant avoided making eye contact with her, instead focusing on his tasks. With his features and light complexion, he could pass for a mzungu. Speaking in a clipped manner and often half snorting at his own jokes, his prim mouth was framed by a thin ash of stubble. With his slight build, she suspected a sudden strong gust could topple him. "How can I be expected to become a griot when I still get treated as an obroni by some?"

"Some call any who aren't Ugenini, Asili, or Maroon outsiders. It doesn't matter. It's the nature of humanity to latch on to differences. Still, that goes against the Muungano way. All are and should feel welcome, or else we are failing our own ideal. What matters is if you are steeped in the culture and understand the nature of the work. We encourage our people to always find someone who doesn't look like them or think like them. It's how we grow our perspective. The tension of not agreeing is where creativity is sparked."

Jaha understood the root of his insecurity but, more important, appreciated that he kept asking the right questions. Ishant had followed a strange path to Muungano membership, the journey of the outsider. Born in Thailand, he studied dance and regenerative economics in what remained of California, after the coastal reshaping by what was now politely referred to as "climate terraforming." It was there that he joined the Liberation Investment Support Cooperative, the corporate entity running the O.E. government, just as they decided it was fitting to move the nation's capital inland to Indianapolis, since its layout mirrored Washington, D.C.'s. While no longer the arable breadbasket of the world, the Midwest was still relatively stable.

Afterward, Ishant returned to his homeland, where he worked in his family's restaurant until he figured out what his next move would be. Ishant didn't have the language for the hole he felt in his emi, which led him to join LISC Corps, LISC's volunteer civil organization. It steered committed members toward public service and helping others, with their stated goal of "meeting the critical needs in the community."

The fact that LISC worked so hard to mimic the language of Muungano always amused Jaha.

LISC Corps assigned Ishant to the Thema Academy as a community ambassador. He worked alongside their students, gradually shifting more and more into Muungano space and culture until he formally applied to the academy's equity fellows program. For the last eight years, he worked there, rising to become Jaha's right-hand person.

"Today's Leah's Naming Ceremony. We should send notice if we are not planning to attend," he said.

"I have trained that girl since she could raise a chakram. We'll make it, but we still have a job to do."

With a shimmer and a sigh, the wall behind them shifted, its very components seeming to blink out as an opening formed. Lij Matata Okoro stepped through. His breastplate joined together in ceremonial vestments. The gold band of his chakram laid flat in a circle about his neck, ready to become a bladed weapon at his touch. His jacket glimmered in the light, black with an iridescent quality. A Basotho blanket slung across his shoulder like a kaross, embroidered with the sacred triangles of Alkebulan. His head shaved on the sides, though the top appeared carved with geometric precision. The personal shield for the personal shields of the governing family.

"Get back!" He stationed himself between Jaha and the window.

"Aw, nah, baby, I'm not going anywhere." Jaha's voice rang sweet as a steel baton to the head, more irritated than alarmed.

"It's a security issue." Matata held his arm out.

"I realize that you are the Lij of this unit, but I'm the security *head*."

"Former."

Jaha was Nyamakalaw of the Griot Circle. She had made the circle her own, though her singular voice still directed much of its day-to-day operations (because the words *forever honored* or *retired* meant nothing to her). What impressed her about Matata was that, to him, his answer was always the right answer. When he ran toward a wall, he committed at full tilt. She expected the young to show their ass on occasion. That was simply what they did and how they learned. Only once he smacked into the wall would she give her input. Part of her striving to remain relevant as an elder was simply wanting to share her thoughts and have them received by young people. Both sides had to remain in a posture of learning.

"Look into my eyes." Jaha stepped toward him with a quiet air of menace. "Do you see anything in there that reads 'former'?"

"No." Lij Matata's face remained resolute, but his demeanor softened, stepping aside for her experience.

Jaha granted him a measure of grace since technically she was no longer Ras of the Niyabinghi. But she was now head of the Griot Circle, Muungano's domestic security, which still afforded her experience he could benefit from. "What's the situation?"

"There's been an encroachment on our security perimeter." Lij Matata continued to scan the room.

"What kind of . . . encroachment?" Jaha tired of trailing him like she was his harried assistant.

"Armed protestors. There've been reports of weapons fire." Lij Matata nodded toward the window.

Several figures wearing light-scattering masks designed to defeat facial recognition algorithm stormed about. Some toted phase EMP carronades. The International District of Indianapolis originally was once the side of town that suffered from the benign neglect of city officials. Property values plummeted, and immigrants moved in. And flourished. Through LISC, the city found money enough to rebrand the area the International District. This grew into the International Marketplace, which soon housed several embassies once the nation's capital shifted to the booming metropolis.

"You want me to get all worked up because folks are protesting?" Jaha stationed herself at the window's edge to better take in the scene. "What are they protesting this week? Our taking in more O.E. refugees? Our not accepting their latest currency exchange? Our existence?"

"That's . . . not clear yet. But their numbers are increasing." Lij Matata angled his head toward her, the way an unsure actor new to the stage might.

"Threat assessment?"

"The situation is still fluid. Uncertain. Security protocol red is in effect. It may be best for you to make a . . . diplomatic withdrawal." Matata paused, attempting to dance around his own suggestion. "Maybe even head back to the Dreaming City."

"You may want to check my eyes again to see if they are in the habit of anything close to any kind of . . . withdrawal." Jaha hard-eyed the man, staring him up and down to take his measure. "We have a standard deployment of Niyabinghi?"

"Yes." Lij Matata snapped to attention.

"Then with any escalation of any kind, we dig in and keep an eye on their movements. Give O.E.—well, LISC—one hour to handle this. Then we do what we do." She softened, since her aim wasn't to humiliate or demean him. "With your people stationed here, we should be as secure as if we were at the Dreaming City."

His shoulders relaxing, Lij Matata appeared relieved, the tension of holding his breath while dealing with her leaving him. "That's good to hear."

"The Niyabinghi should be visible, however. As a deterrent to any . . . unnecessary antics on anyone's part."

"Understood." Lij Matata gestured to his contingent, who deployed down each hallway before the door resealed itself. "Nanny fe Queen."

"Nanny fe Queen." Jaha waited several heartbeats as if not wanting to be interrupted again. Part of her missed when she was once a Lij and the uncomfortable tension of watching this new generation of young people run forward with the work.

"Ishant, come over here." Jaha strode to the nearest window. "You got them young eyes. What do you see?"

After all of her genmods, her eyes were as sharp as anyone's. Still, Ishant approached the window with a put-upon sniff, as if suspecting another test. It was. His travels gave him a valuable global perspective on what was happening around the world and an appreciation of the power of community. How people who cared about one another worked together.

"Maybe fifty protestors. Lots of noise. Any weapons fire is aimed at the sky. Probably at drones." Ishant cocked his head as if momentarily caught in an information loop. Jaha wondered if he was streaming, but he snapped back as if he'd concluded his analysis.

"There are a lot of people who want to bring Muungano down. I daresay from within as well as without. No advance rumblings of this assembly?" she asked.

"Not any chatter from any of my sources."

"Let's see if you've been paying attention." Jaha clasped her hands behind her back. "There are protests outside embassies all over the world. What tells you if we have a growing security threat?"

"*Organization.*" Ishant closed his eyes and took a deep breath, as he was trained, allowing his mind to reach out, search his emi. "This feels too coordinated to be random, but they haven't named themselves or their cause. All important characters in a story name themselves."

"Or are named," Jaha pointed out, in the way of griots.

"*Direction of retaliation.* Every character wants something. Has an agenda or goal that they pursue."

"They haven't issued any clear demands. Only collective pissing and moaning," Jaha noted.

"*Platform.* They need to get their story out. If their first attempt doesn't get link coverage, they'll have to go bigger." Ishant opened his eyes and began to scan data matrixes and linkage networks.

"Or get more creative." Jaha backed away from the window. "Maya, can you get me VOP Harrison?"

LISC was only emblematic of the illiberal democracy running O.E. VOP Harrison was the perfect example of what happened when a populist rose to power but needed to secure their ability to stay there. Look at how he ran his government: criminalizing dissent; suppressing link sources and coverage; harassing what passed for the opposition (which was a different slice of the same pie); sowing distrust in their remaining institutions; all while disempowering his people. Leaving folks feeling like since everything was broken or rigged, there was no point in doing anything. Only those desperate for change bothered protesting. Even the title VOP, which stood for *Voice of the People,* was meant to mirror the Muungano title Camara after LISC deciding some of the Muungano words wouldn't "translate" well.

"He's 'on a walkabout,'" Ishant said. *Walkabout* was LISC code for some new secret negotiation. Every one was soon followed by an announcement of some new accords. LISC providing infrastructure support in South America. LISC brokering some cease-fire for a conflict they probably initiated.

"He'd better walk his ass to my link," Jaha said.

<Commencing link,> the AI said in a no-nonsense tone.

"Maya, hold that connection." Never afraid to check or question even an elder, Ishant glanced up from his panel. "You're skipping a lot of diplomatic channels. This may be seen as an unwarranted escalation on *our* part."

"VOP Harrison may be a shill for the dominant caste, but he is soon to be installed as the presiding head of LISC. Sometimes you have to go straight to the top when you want to get shit done."

"I don't think we can risk the appearance of a military action. Theirs or ours."

"'When the drummers change their beats, the dancers must also change their steps.'" Giving his words of caution due consideration, Jaha paced. After a weary sigh, she turned back to him. "You may be right. Go on ahead. Get our people to more secure locations like Lij Matata wanted, in case we have to scramble out of here on short notice."

"What about you?" Ishant arched a skeptical eyebrow. He was used to her brand of capitulation, which usually amounted to her saying enough for folks to lower their guards, then do what she wanted. But they were both learning, and she was striving to do better. Most days.

"I'll coordinate from here but will be right behind you. Someone has to deal with LISC and make sure they contain the situation before we have to," Jaha said.

With a slight wai, Ishant gestured for a door.

Jaha stood in the center of the room enjoying the moment of quiet before considering what new work this situation was going to create and the most efficient order to tackle the incoming projects. Her emi crackled in alarm. A pressure built within her. On instinct, she dove for cover.

Time stood still. A pause before everything upended itself.

A series of flashes lit up behind her with the spectacle of lightning in a dry season. A massive boom followed. A rumble experienced deep within her like a sound that was too big for her ears. A thrum reached a crescendo in an instant. Air pushed out of the space so fast there was no room to draw a breath.

The detonation ripped through the room.

The flooring rose up in an earthen billow. Glass sprayed in a glittering hailstorm. Books tumbled from the surrounding shelves. Pages fluttered through the air, flitting leaves on fire. The acrid smoke burned her nostrils. The air became nearly too hot to breathe. The walls crashed in from all sides.

Jaha lost all sense of equilibrium, having only the sensation of falling. Down, down, down, with barely the wondering of when she was going to hit the ground. The blast threw her to the floor. The ceiling collapsed as if tired of carrying its heavy load on its own. All about her toppled into a terrible darkness, thick and mocking, smothering all of her soft groans.

"Where are you?" a distant voice called. Followed by an eerie silence.

03

MAULANA BUHARI
The Dreaming City

"There has been a series of explosions at our embassy on Original Earth."

The Ijo erupt as I knew it would. I wonder if there was a better way I could have delivered the news, but part of what makes the Muungano community strong is our dependence on one another to work through our fears. Our rage. Many jump to their feet, shouting and waving their fists in protest, until they become a sustained chorus of rage. I step back to allow my people a moment to absorb the news.

This is not the way I wished to introduce myself to the collection of elders. This pushback by way of attack fits within the history of our people, an expected—even somewhat overdue—turn. Whenever we have struggled to independence, found life and joy on our own terms, the same system and mentality that strove to oppress us in the first place rises up to oppose us. That is why my elder stepped aside for my voice to be heard. To bring the reminder that we have a responsibility to be aggressive in our posture of resistance. To stand ever ready, ever vigilant, against those who sought to grind us under their heel. A continual practice of liberation.

Almost intoxicated, I'm caught up in the furor, rage mixed with fear. All heightened by an existential worry. One did not have to be tied to the Adisa family to know many of the ranking officials stationed in the O.E. embassy. Angry and powerless, all most can do is shout. Only Xola and myself remain motionless within the chaos of the storm.

Camara Adisa raises his left hand slightly and lowers it as if clamping a lid on a roiling pot of stew. The collective roar lowers to an agitated susurrus of voices. "What of Jaha?"

"The first explosion did little more than cosmetic damage," I say. "The Niyabinghi stationed there mobilized and secured the scene and the ambassador according to our protocols. Her injuries were severe, but the prognosis is good. The entire staff was evacuated before the subsequent explosions a few minutes later. They are all under medical supervision."

The Camara bridges his long fingers in front of him to hide his relief. When his people, especially those closest to him, are in harm's way, he can be unpredictable as wildfire. "What's the threat assessment?"

"O.E. claims no knowledge of a plot. We suspect the work of the American Renaissance Movement, ARM, which falls under the umbrella of the Earth First movement. LISC only mentioned outside agitators, and their troops have surrounded our embassy. 'As a protective measure,' they say, while they investigate. Initially, they tried trotting out that the Niyabinghi fired first. I assured them that had the Niyabinghi engaged, they would not have stopped firing until every target and possible threat had been found and . . . dealt with."

"That escalated quickly," Xola says. "Isn't this a matter to have been brought up for the security council, not the full Ijo?"

"The news has come to me only moments ago. The situation remains fluid. The entire Muungano assembly needed to know as word of this will quickly spread." My eyes lock on to Xola's, unflinching.

Amachi drifts into my peripheral view. There is a swelling pride that accompanies seeing my onetime pupil ascend, taking responsibility and leadership roles within the community. I helped train her and know her body language the way one knows the melody of their favorite song. When her ever-suspicious eyes study me, she shifts as if catching scent of something off-putting. She often called me "clever as a serpent," her mind already mid-speculation that I would no more slip in security protocols than the sun forgetting to rise. She's the clever one. A series of calculations determine my every move. As the civilian head of the Niyabinghi, keeping secrets comes with the job. But her emi probably senses that I am hiding something.

As if also sensing it, Camara Xola fixes his eyes into a sharpened squint.

"Jaha is being transported back here, but O.E. is pressuring us. They have recalled their ambassador and wish to send a new one, claiming we need a new cultural liaison. One better suited for a time of crisis." I stalk the dais in full awareness that I hold the rapt attention of the Ijo. In only a matter of minutes, I've transformed from recent addition to the Buhari family leadership to my name ringing out from everyone's lips. "More probably, they pursue a new agenda. An ambassador who could travel about with impunity under the auspices of diplomatic immunity."

"Maulana, we cannot close ourselves off to diplomatic overtures," Bayard interrupts. "We need to—"

"Those systems never seem to tire of us rising up in revolt against them. Ours is the shared story of the Maafa, the holocaust of enslavement: ripped from our Motherland, Alkebulan, to be brought to the horrors of a savage wilderness, followed by our continual uprising against enslaving tyrants and agents of oppression. Many thought the Uponyaji that came after the Lunar Ukombozi War ushered us into an era of post-racial harmony, because they want to forget the lessons of history. I do not. I will not." I move to check the good reverend before he gets going. He loves the spotlight as much as he does the opportunity to speak. Strict mythicists have never sat well will me. "Let's not confuse prayers for deliverance with liberation practice."

Bayard steps back like he's been slapped. Fully awake now, he speaks with his full chest. "Don't you confuse praying on my knees with being on my knees."

"I'm simply advocating professions of faith doing more to be about the work of struggle."

"Which we are . . . and always have been, which those who are so mindful about remembering our history should know."

"I just need you to know that I'm not about that 'turn the other cheek' life. Only when an oppressor knows they run the risk of response equal to their efforts do they learn to respect our lives."

"It would be a poor time to be without diplomatic representation." Camara Xola's calm, low tones lowers the temperature of the conversation.

"I don't suggest we do. Only caution with such an action. A last-minute replacement makes me . . . wary," I say. "They need to be reminded the world, the stars, the universe are not theirs by birthright and never was. All that they have taken will be taken back by those they oppressed and hoped to extinguish."

"An errant breeze makes you wary," Bayard murmurs.

"As it should." Camara Xola nods in agreement. Around the table, the Ijo echo his affirmation. "Still, refusing a diplomatic envoy is tantamount to a declaration of war."

"We aren't refusing their envoy." I hold up my hand to fend off his next volley. "We're refusing their timetable. All I ask is a delay. To run a more thorough background check. No one dictates to us when and how we do anything. Never again."

"And if they interpret it as us saber-rattling?" Camara Xola arches a questioning eye brow.

"They should have thought about that before allowing the radical plank of their government to run roughshod as their voice. Riling up the very agitators they now seek to protect us from." My critics, and I proudly have many, will politely say that my love of Muungano runs to the near xenophobic. The sentiment resonates in my heart. That's how they read my confident sense of commitment and belonging; knowing who I am, where I come from, and most important, who I am going to be. They call me paranoid. I am hypervigilant when it comes to possible threats against my people. For that, I won't apologize. "Under LISC's 'inclusion umbrella,' ARM's course has emboldened them. Their 'Earth First' rhetoric beats the war drums without fear of repercussions. Protests begin to erupt on Mars. There is heightened tension throughout the system. I do not trust their renewed interest in us."

"They never lost interest," Xola corrects.

The Ijo murmur, a current of support for my words.

"Maulana, update us on the condition of Jaha as soon as possible. Now, since we've broached the topic of the 'heightened tension—'" Xola pauses. There's a weight, an intentionality, to his studious gaze, an impressive maneuver given his poor eyesight. "I ask for an update from Titan."

Most members of the Ijo are familiar but remain strangers to me. However, a ripple in the crowd, a dipped toe disturbing a still pond, catches my attention. The people part, and I can't help but notice Amachi's sudden discomfort in recognition of the approaching young woman's stride. This is the trouble with knowing one another so well: we risk being caught up in one another's petty dramas despite our best efforts.

Captain Stacia Chikeke saunters forward.

Dressed in a velour kaftan, her rings and earrings match the metallic sheen of her boots, the height of fashion among those of Titan. Her coil of brownish dreads with blond tips wrapped in a scarf whose colors mirror the Chikeke family's pattern. I could not mentor the one without knowing the other. The pair of them a study in contrasts, the captain's tawny-colored skin a stark contrast to Amachi's dark, smooth complexion. Older than I by only a year, becoming a mother, much less a captain, has matured her. Even in the way she carries herself, she has found her place within Muungano. Focused and driven, a tense wire that might snap from its own internal stress.

Though she attempts to hide herself, the edges of Amachi's mouth turn upward in pride as Stacia takes the center. When she notices me, I allow Amachi the pretense that the familiar blush is one of renewed competition between friends. Though Stacia's eyes, too, sparkle with recognition and warmth, her careful smile belies a weight upon her. A sadness.

"For my report." Stacia pauses to clear her throat. "I need to invoke defense protocols. Keywords: golden chord."

Most of the Ijo rise without protest or question in tacit dismissal. Amachi studies the departing figures and half rises herself before realizing no other Adisa has even flinched.

"What's that?" she whispers to Xola, her face a miasma of confusion. I would have better prepared her for her first appearance at the Ijo. One has to always be prepared for how the community moves.

"The defense protocols. What Maulana should have invoked." Camara Xola brushes his nose with the crook of his wrist. He barely bothers to cover his mouth as he utters oaths beneath his breath.

"Father, if Amachi's to be a ranking member of the Adisa family," Wachiru begins, "you need to read her in."

Camara Xola rubs his fingers into the wispy threads of his beard. "She's old enough and ready."

"What does that mean?" she asks.

I almost feel bad for her, but the young have to learn to swim sometime, even if it's by falling into the deeper part of a river.

Wachiru shifts in his seat, his heavy-lidded eyes flutter open, focused and suddenly interested. He joins in their whispers. "It means stay here by us and keep your mouth shut. Act like you're meant to be here."

His way of speaking of himself in the plural—as if he were both so lost in the identity of community as well as a community unto himself—grates my last nerves. Despite Wachiru's smile, the sharpness of the words sting. Amachi slumps in her seat, the image recalling a hapless child being brought in, from the storm, struggling to find a safe place from the cold.

When the room stills, only representatives from three of the Ijo families remain—the Adisas, the Buharis, and the Jywanzas—though all of their attendants have been dismissed. The group reconvenes in a more intimate arrangement.

"What is it?" Camara Xola asks.

"We lost the signal at the Orun Gate," Stacia says with a cool evenness to her voice as if describing an unanticipated turn of weather.

"The Orun Gate," I begin before Amachi can betray her ignorance, "is what we've dubbed the wormhole that hovers near Titan's furthest orbit point."

While we of the Muungano community support learning at all times, there are occasions when one may not want to appear an ignorant child in the crisis of decision. Learning, Amachi measures her words carefully. "This is not general knowledge among the members of Muungano."

"Nor on O.E." I nod with approval.

"Only at the highest security levels. It's a complicated arrangement, but it seems to have forced a measure of cooperation between O.E. Mars and Muungano. The *Cypher* had been studying the phenomenon under the auspices of the Science Council of Titan and Mars's Department of Interior," Stacia says.

The Orun Gate was meant to be a hub of understanding. The all-too-naive dream was for it to bring together the entire system—O.E., Mars, and Muungano—to reframe the conversation between us. Allow us a new context to work together. It united us . . . on the surface. But there was no trust, and without trust, all the pieces of paper in the world didn't matter. There would be secrets. And agendas. And secret agendas. Forcing everyone to play nice as fake partners until someone could figure out how to control and exploit it. In the meantime, each party pressed for advantage.

"Isn't your husband the point person on the study?" I point out.

Stacia spares a glance toward Amachi. "As I said, it's complicated."

"And our military has been involved in its exploration, in partnership with some from the highest clearance levels of the Ministry of Science from O.E." Stacia refuses to turn my direction, though I suspect it is more about avoiding Amachi's gaze. This is not the time nor place for such adolescent distractions. "What of our HOVA regiment on the other side of the gate?"

"They launched a communication buoy to signal that they have landed safely and are going about their mission. But they have now gone radio silent, per mission protocols." Despite my training, my voice grows thick with concern.

"But we have no way to get ahold of them?" Camara Xola asks.

"Nothing short of sending in another jump ship. And that would have to be mission critical." I turn to the security council. Ever since the discovery of the Orun Gate, we have found our relationship with O.E. growing strained, communications terser. An untrusted acquaintance pulling back. "Don't you see? This cannot be coincidence."

"What are you saying? Speak plain," Xola says.

"We discover a wormhole within the heart of our sovereign alliance. O.E. learns of it, even offers us technology to help us further study in and explore a world on the other side. Us shouldering the bulk of the risk in return for us sharing data."

"An arrangement you are still on record as opposing," Xola says.

"Because it felt like a setup. First our embassy gets attacked. Next, O.E. signals for a greater presence here. Just as we can no longer contact with our team who is exploring a recently revealed resource many parties would love to have control over."

If only for a heartbeat, Stacia lowers her eyes.

"What is it, Stacia?" Amachi rises, stepping between me and her, recognizing her tell. One she's had to learn the hard way. The heart way. "You're not telling us something."

All eyes fall on her and then glide over to Stacia.

"We originally thought that the Orun Gate was a naturally occurring stellar phenomenon. One that our technology had only recently advanced enough to be able to detect." Stacia's eyes linger on Amachi, not retreating from the heat of her proximity, until turning back to me and remembering the rest of the security council. "However, we've now determined that it is artificial. It was built. And it's older than we could have possibly imagined."

04

STACIA CHIKEKE
The *Cypher* (Returning to Titan)

Stacia peered out the observation bay of the *Cypher*. It was her second-favorite part of the ship, the first being the Green Zone on Deck 3, the lush garden that bisected the ship. Both were about perspective. From this point in orbit, Muungano seemed so small, fading into the distance, the Dreaming City barely a glint on the moon's surface. The kraals ringing the moon appeared to be belts along two connecting axes. But she was ready to go back to the stars. Unafraid of who she might be or where she might end up because it was the Muungano way that "you bring your culture with you wherever you go."

She also felt some sort of way. Her mood had clearly soured after seeing Leah. No, Amachi now. Names had to be respected, even if personal history wasn't always. Stacia thought she had braced herself appropriately. The importance of her news and the responsibilities of her mission allowed her to avoid Amachi and dodge an unnecessary complication. Still, the sight of her old friend undid her in ways she hadn't expected. In ways that demanded a drink of some sort, even if that sort of self-medication was not the Muungano way.

<You are brooding,> Maya interrupted.

"You should mind your own business." Stacia played with the stack of bracelets on her wrists.

<Monitoring the well-being of personnel is our business.>

"And intruding on our thoughts?"

<Operational parameters allow thirty minutes of personal silent meditation before we are instructed to check in with you.>

"That's ludicrous. Who programmed those parameters?"

<You.>

"Then it's the height of compassion. Though the parameters may need to be tweaked." Stacia smiled, pleased with herself since there was no one else to smile for. Other than Maya.

The Maya AI were a tenth-generation quantum computer array. Conceptually they were both an integrated system and a series of discrete systems. The "aspect" of Maya that ran the *Cypher* was connected to the greater Maya that ran all of the Muungano systems, but they were shaped and formed by their maintenance of and duties to the *Cypher*. As if they were a separate personality from the Maya that ran the Dreaming City. The part that Stacia always struggled to wrap her mind around was that even within the *Cypher*, Maya essentially split themselves off so that each crew member interacted with a version of Maya shaped by their particular relationship with the AI.

So Stacia tried not to think about it too hard.

<The object was to make sure you didn't spiral into negative thoughts.>

"If you'd interrupted after thirty seconds, you still wouldn't have prevented that."

<Noted.>

"Don't note that." Stacia studied the star charts and tried not to shiver.

All of Muungano's territory lit up as a hologram projection, from the Dreaming City to Mars to the mining outpost. No borders, per se, not the way O.E. might define them. Only communities of alliance. This was what they had all fought so hard to forge. They needed a new vocabulary to describe the experiment they embarked on. *Empire* wasn't it. A budding cooperative cradled in a sweep of stars. She took comfort even in the deep void between the gleaming pinpricks. This was everything she'd worked for. Everything they had struggled, sacrificed, and fought for. They were on the cusp of . . . anything.

Lost in the dance of star charts, she was all too ready to return to the heart of her universe: the Arkestra. The outpost on Titan's moon named for the first ship to port there. As she prepared to travel back to Titan, she had donned an outfit similar to one favored by another Adisa that had captured her heart in a peculiar way. LeSony'ra Adisa captained the original *Arkestra*, often wearing a similarly voluminous black kaftan over platform oxfords. The day after Amachi's Naming Ceremony, after delivering the news about the Orun Gate, Stacia needed to feel powerful and in control. Channeling the spirit of LeSony'ra had always been a way of doing that. Stories of the woman's heroics inspired Stacia to join the Thmei Academy and even pursue her musical interests.

There she met Yahya. Even when running from her heart, her feelings created traps.

Stacia tossed her gold chain mail headdress onto the nearby ledge just as the door chimed. The door opened with a slight hiss. She extended her arm for a clasp. "I see you, Yahya."

"That would be a first." Lacking the patience for simple courtesies, he strode into the room with his familiar charge, as if the world should part for him. Tall and well-muscled—his biceps the circumference of her waist—he had the figure of someone sculpted to lead a HOVA unit. Despite his imposing size, he used it to create a sheltering overprotectiveness, which always made her feel safe. Ten years older than she was, a hint of gray speckled his goatee, which framed a constant sneer as if he were constantly annoyed by the world.

Stacia took a deep breath to calm herself. A pause so that she wouldn't rise to his bait. "I've always seen you. Like right now, unless you've come with the sole agenda of picking a meaningless fight with me because something's on your mind."

He cocked his head in her direction, as if a fuzzy image coalesced into sudden clarity. She was worn and not up for the full-frontal assault his charge into her chambers signaled. Some part of him could always read her. His stance softened. A bit. "You seem different."

"I had . . . difficult news to deliver to the Ijo."

"What about?"

"I can't say. It's . . ." Stacia shifted her weight to her back leg, averting her gaze as if trying to remember where she set her headdress, or making a note to have maintenance attend to her door to alleviate that hiss. Anything other than remind him of how much she outranked him and how many secrets she was obligated to keep from him.

". . . Code Black / Eyes Only. I remember this dance." He threw his arms up. Searching the room, he settled into a chair. His mouth itched, and his fingers groped about as if he, too, were anxious for a drink. "It have anything to do with my diplomatic mission to Mars being suddenly scuttled in favor of Titan duty? Those 'Eyes' have any appreciation for how long I lobbied and waited for that assignment?"

Stacia remained silent, the star chart revolved around her to adjust for the *Cypher*'s position.

They both understood that her station required her to keep things from people. From him. So much of Stacia was her job. She would not be made to feel bad for working so hard to find her way into rooms of power, where the big decisions were made, to be a voice for her community. That was one of the things that drew Yahya to her. As was so often the case, the light that drew interest burned when held too close. As captain, most of her life, days, and orders were hidden behind the wall of Code Black / Eyes Only. Yahya had become convinced that she began using it as a convenient wall to keep him out of her life. In the quiet places of her heart, she couldn't disagree.

"Today was Leah's Naming Ceremony. Did you see her?" With a slight hitch of his breath, he stopped himself. She remembered this dance, his reflexive need to add, "Or is that Code Black / Eyes Only, too?" But he didn't. He was trying. They both were.

"I saw her briefly. Her name is now Amachi. She's become a ranking member of the Adisa family."

"That means she's a full member of the Ijo."

"Yes."

"Was she read in?"

"Yes."

"So *she* knows whatever it is that weighs on you." Piece by piece, line by line, Yahya completed one of his rhetorical traps. It annoyed her that she got so caught up in the rhythm of his words that she just did the yankadi right into it. A skilled orator, he definitely had studied poetry at a high level and could have done so at a professional level if so inclined. Specializing in improvised rhyme, to hear him tell it, he often battled and bested other poets back in the day. Coming at her now with the intensity of a prosecutor, he loved being so damn clever, believing it part of his charm. It wasn't.

"Don't," she said.

"Don't what?" He backed up a step, a protest of faux innocence.

"It's not a competition. It never was."

"I understand that more clearly than anyone." Yahya's shoulders slouched, the wind taken out of him in defeat. Glancing about, he settled into a chair. As he got comfortable, he muttered, "A competition implies each side actually has a chance."

Amachi and Stacia were never a thing. They never explored the possibility. Stacia left for the Thmei Academy rather than deal with whatever feelings bubbled beneath their friendship. The fact that she once confided those feelings to Yahya meant little. He always felt like he competed against the duppy of Amachi. Always coming in second. At least that was how he always claimed to feel whenever they got into an argument. He clung too tightly. Not possessive, not needy, but he walked a tightrope that veered between the two.

Yahya had a version of Stacia—what their marriage should be—locked in his head to which she could never measure up. All they had left was the fighting, and most days, they had lost sight of what they were fighting for.

A few months ago, the elders within the Titan community recognized that their relationship had turned toxic, becoming destructive to each other. They had encouraged separation in order for each of them to heal and develop into positive forces in each other's lives. Things weren't going well.

"Since you didn't barge in here out of concern for my feelings, why are you here?" Stacia asked.

"It's Bekele."

At the mention of their son, Stacia's voice rose with alarm. "Have there been any changes? Why didn't you—"

Yahya raised his hands, gesturing for her to slow down. He patted the seat next to him. "No, no. Nothing like that. I wanted to talk about the next steps."

"What . . . next steps?" Sitting down warily, Stacia remained alert for another of his traps waiting to spring.

"He's steady for now. His condition remains unchanged."

"Do you think his disease has gone into remission?"

"I think it just hasn't worsened." Yahya lowered his head and bridged his fingers, refusing to meet her gaze. This move usually preceded words sure to be foolishness that he knew he couldn't defend but felt obligated to try. In a hoarse rasp, he whispered, "I have a theory."

"Yahya . . ." Stacia's tone dripped with pity for him. She wanted to hope also, but she'd watched the burden of their son's illness tear her estranged spouse to shreds. Each new round of empty tests reduced him even more. The man she remembered—the one she knew—loved his son in a powerful way; would move heaven and earth to protect him. She recalled the first time she saw Yahya cradling Bek in his massive arms. That image of him she would marry a thousand times over.

The Yahya beside her was a desperate shell. Finding ever more obscure possible causes for Bek's condition. Hoping that once their scientists had an origin point, he could then come up with a course of action. Stop being powerless. This image of him was too difficult to look at.

Distracting herself, she stood up and tapped a bioplastic panel along the ship's wall. It became translucent, revealing a series of spindles and pouches, reminiscent of a large, slow-moving bacteria. Water circulation ran through the walls of the *Cypher,* the ship's exterior construction mimicking layers of epidermis. It acted as another barrier to radiation, using the radiation to further scrub the recycled water. But to Stacia's eye, it doubled as a piece of experimental art. She backed up to admire it.

"Hear me out." Yahya bounded from his seat, dogging her trail through the room. "Prions."

"Prions?" Stacia continued to watch the water pulse and bubble through the coils, running her finger along the surface of the panel, tracing its course.

"Specifically, fast-replicating prions. That would explain everything."

"Have you picked them up on a scan?" She knew the answer to the question and kept her back to him to not further embarrass him by staring at him while his face went through its contortions of anguish. Sparing herself from watching his pain.

"No. Which is why I think it's a prion of some sort."

"So your absence of proof is proof?" Clasping her hands behind her, she began to wander away from him.

"Exactly." Yahya trailed after her.

"Yahya . . ."

"Think about it: Prions consist solely of protein with no nucleic acid genome. Thus, are more resistant to radiation. And detection. The mechanism of his disorder mimics that of a prion-like condition, similar to Creutzfeldt-Jakob disease. It's basically a protein-folding chain reaction that disrupts encoding proteins. It's there, I know it is."

"It's . . ." Stacia turned to meet his face. A mania fueled the glint in his eyes. One that wouldn't be denied. "Worth considering."

Yahya's face brightened. "Good. Good. I'll begin testing right away. The preliminary round should be complete by the time we reach Titan. He and I can disembark then."

"Disembark?" Stacia reared back as if splashed by cold water.

"Bek needs specialized care. In his condition . . ." Yahya's huge hands danced in front of him, with him desperately straining to catch and hold on to his argument.

"A condition that, as you noted, hasn't worsened." Steel replaced compassion in Stacia's tone.

"For now. Neither of us, or anyone else, can predict what will happen next. Or when."

"The *Cypher* is the preeminent research facility in all of Muungano."

"Gathering from the weight of your meeting with the Ijo, the *Cypher* and its captain presumably have some Eyes Only duties to attend to." Yahya closed in on her, his proximity forcing her to look up at him.

"You know I can't speak to that." Stacia's voice softened, but she refused to turn away.

"You can neither confirm nor deny, I understand, it's the basic refrain of the Code Black / Eyes Only song. I'm simply saying this ship, with its missions and politics, is no place for Bek's care."

"It's where he goes to school."

"He goes to school wherever the community is."

"His mother is here."

"Barely." Yahya let the word bite deep and the silence that followed take root. This time he locked his gaze with hers, unwavering as the pair squared off. "When her duties allow. His father is always at his side."

Stacia balled and released her fist in incandescent rage.

<If I may interrupt?>

"What is it, Maya?" Stacia asked without breaking the stare down with this man threatening to rip her child from her.

<Paki awaits you on the bridge.>

"I'll be there shortly." Stacia glared at Yahya. "This. Isn't. Over."

"Don't let me get between you and the duties you have to attend to. Go." Yahya held his hands up again and stepped back. He could afford the extra effort of courtesy when he felt he had the advantage.

Her eyes still locked on him in suspicion, as if he might make off with anything not bolted down in her chambers. Stacia reached for her headdress. The raiment jingled into place. A reminder that she was captain. "Let's try that again."

It was Yahya's turn to glare impotently. "You have duties to attend to. At your leave?"

"You're dismissed." Stacia took a breath as he turned. "Yahya?"

"Yes?"

"I appreciate you." Her tone thickened with reminder.

"I appreciate you." He stalked out without so much as a backward glance. The door hissed behind him.

"Nicely timed, Maya." Stacia's eyes turned upward, a habit she'd fallen into as if Maya somehow spoke from the firmament.

<You seemed like you could use a breather.>

"I doubt you fooled him."

<I doubt you care.>

Shaking her head, Stacia chuckled to herself. "And Paki?"

<He actually does await you. School is in session.>

✳

The *Cypher* was built for longer-term space travel. Not sleek and aerodynamic, the ship's design was styled to resemble a self-propelled meteor, concerned more with protecting its occupants from the rigors of space travel. A series of kraals honeycombed its interior very similar to any Muungano outpost, the stacked living quarters ringing the ship. The shared spaces of community from dining area to medical bay sandwiched between levels of them. The architecture structured more to remind them of home, rather than some sterile laboratory. But bisecting the heart of the ship was the Green Zone.

The Green Zone served a variety of purposes, both practical (the scrubbing of water and air, the raising of livestock) and aesthetic (vistas of flora, complete with some of the halls themselves having outcroppings of rock, as if the crew walked through a cave, again, reminding them of the wonders of home). Children ran along the grassy knolls, chasing small animals or scrambling up the trees. A delicate ecosystem maintained by Maya, who also monitored the bacterial growth. The Green Zone was a vast park serving as the heart of the *Cypher*. Complete with a meandering stream and pond. Down here, the air had a fresher bite, not the clamminess of the close exhalations of a machine. Nor the tang of ozone often present in the labs or medical bays' carefully filtered air.

Stacia scanned the crowd of bobbing heads from a distance. The sight of the captain skulking about would only disrupt their lessons and put them unduly on edge. She wanted to check on only one person: Bekele.

Paki Listener Harges stood underneath the tallest and thickest tree. A group of students of varying ages gathered around him. The Muungano community saw children through the lens who they could be, embracing the infinite possibilities of each child. The children of Muungano were raised and apprenticed in communities, with starting ages ranging from eight to thirteen, based on ability and interest. Today marked when the latest group was formally introduced to the science team of the *Cypher*. Muungano learned through its people who learned. Personal mastery, a commitment to one's own lifelong learning. Observing and working alongside adults in productive roles, a way of connecting them to community, learning skills, traditions, customs, and what it meant to be in relationship with others. Paki's traditional first-day-of-class talk was winding down.

"Many generations ago, an ancestor of mine planted a tree in his yard to commemorate the birth of his daughter." He paced about with an electric intensity. "A sapling in an abandoned section of the new O.E. capital, Indianapolis. Many people probably walked by it, ignoring it. But its shade became a sanctuary. Under the canopy of leaves, people would gather and share stories. To him, it symbolized everything: The tenacity of life. Hope. Taking root and thriving despite the circumstances and surroundings. He called it the Learning Tree. Everywhere our community has traveled, the first lunar outpost, which eventually became Muungano, Bronzeville on Mars, the Titan port, the Oyigiyigi mining outpost, even this ship, we have planted a tree to remind ourselves of those things." A short, brooding man, Paki's thick, rarely kempt beard wrapped his face until it joined his hair, which ringed only the back of his head. His bald pate always glistened with sweat, as if his racing mind overheated his head.

Stacia couldn't help her pleased smile. This was how it should be. That for students to engage in the type of learning required for this world, the key adults in their lives must be equally visible learners. Ones who embrace the idea of doing and learning whatever was necessary to teach their students what they must do and learn. The young learned from the community and were productive for the community, and the elders were pushed by their energy and new ideas. Learning about one another, caring about one another, supporting one another as another way to build strong communities.

"So we gather here today to remind ourselves that the way we learn is the way we live. That we practice how we act. That we must fail to gain our freedom. This is how true learning is accomplished." With a nod, he dismissed them.

Paki was one of the best natural teachers Stacia had ever encountered. As a teacher, though, he didn't seem to show it in any sort of overly emotive way. Paki was committed to his students' intellectual, emotional, and social growth. One wouldn't think of it to look at him, but he was a cheerleader. He rallied students, anyone with ears, around the idea of community. The Learning Tree. Muungano. That common vision was at the heart of their educational system. At its core, never losing sight of the whole picture. Or the person in front of them. He encouraged suggestions from his students.

Created an atmosphere where everyone was expected to learn and where collaboration was the norm. Treated them as equal members. Too bad he liked few others besides his students.

As the students moved to their assignments, she spotted her son. The front of Bek's head was shaved from mid-skull forward, not too different from Paki's. However, a shock of long twists sprouted from the midpoint back ("Like a lion's mane," he claimed). Bek moved with an awkward gait. His left side turned toward his center, since he favored that arm. A peculiar mottling of his skin ran from his wrist to his forearm, a poorly healed cut. A set of mismatched eyes, brown and green she and Yahya chose to not correct, adhering to the guidelines regarding genetic manipulation Muungano developed, which applied to all of its members.

Except for the HOVA, though the Science Council was sharply divided on that point.

Bek limped among his classmates under his own power. He could have adapted one of the HOVA's exoskeleton suits to function as a body-wide brace that would allow him to walk. But to him, the convenience of imitating normalcy paled against the absence of health. So with the stubbornness of his father, he did without. Making his way, following a harder path, but it was his own.

The sound of Paki's nearing voice snapped her out of her reverie. A group of children wishing to learn more harried his steps.

"There was an old experiment where scientists constructed large petri dishes with varying concentration bands of antibiotics to see how well bacteria would grow. It started with a band with no antibiotics, then a little in the next band, just enough so that the bacteria wouldn't survive. Then ten times as much in the next. A hundred times. A thousand times, and so on.

"The bacteria spread until it reached the first band and then stopped until a mutant developed. That mutant then went on to compete with other mutants to the next boundary. They paused again until they developed new mutations that allow them to progress to the next band of concentration. This series of mutations only took eleven days to mutate to survive in a thousand-times concentration of antibiotics."

"Accumulating successive mutations to evolve extreme resistance in a short period of time." Bek allowed a thin smile to cross his lips. "Genetic manipulation via natural selection. Before we learn how to directly tinker with genes."

"Natural adaptation," Paki corrected. "Your assignment is to do the same thing. Each of you have been assigned an environmental condition: high acidity, high temperature, methane, sulfur, radiation, ammonia as liquid solvent. You are to create a terrestrial model of that environment and adapt your cyanobacteria strain to survive in your assigned condition."

The students scattered with excitement, heading to various labs throughout the *Cypher* to begin construction of their respective environmental chambers. The composer units would be busy later today. Paki watched them depart, a sheepdog watching his flock be penned for the night before wandering over to her.

"Quite a stiff assignment." She clasped his wrist, then her own in salute.

"Good. Modifying cyanobacteria to respirate sulfur for oxygen could go a long way in our terraforming efforts. Besides, if these students aren't challenged, they get bored. When they get bored, they find ways to amuse themselves. The last time they amused themselves, they used Maya to find a way to gain access to our protein synthesizers. You remember what we were eating for a week?"

"I've tried to forget." Stacia shuddered at the memory. She'd always joked that she could eat any meat if it had been grilled or baked in a good enough sauce. But chewing the flesh of fish with wings or beef striated such that it made a noise similar to weeping when cut into almost turned her vegetarian.

"Boredom has its hazards. Besides, they learn by doing, and we can use all the bright minds and capable hands at our disposal. May I brief you?" Paki held his hands behind his back, imitating a HOVA at parade rest. The more formal he acted, the more it meant he had an agenda he pursued.

With a slight uptick of her chin, Stacia directed him to her briefing room. Inside, she sat at the large circular table carved of wood but smoothed to a marble sheen, a smaller version of the Ijo table.

"Maya, defense protocols. Keyword," Stacia paused to let Paki provide the brief.

"Uhlanga."

<Code Black / Eyes Only protocols engaged.>

In this mode, Maya produced an enhanced shield around the room, preventing any kind of surveillance. The record of this meeting would be kept separate, archived with military-level encryption protocols in a more protected part of Maya's memory core.

"Are we really talking about this?" Stacia ran her hand along the table, activating its holoscreens. The symbols of Project Uhlanga popped up, rotating in anticipation of her next command.

"Why not? It's long overdue."

"How are the probes coming?" Stacia eased against her chair as the design schematics of the probes populated the space around her.

"The probes aren't the issue, and you know it. Maya's encoded into each chamber. Physically. Like their own cell. The programming would search out habitable worlds." Activating a holographic projection, Paki isolated and enlarged a probe schematic. He ran a simulation; the probe unfurled like a waking spider. It sloughed nanobots from its interior, the action appearing to leak a fluid of some sort. "It would direct the nanobots and determine what sort of organisms they would like to see evolve."

Out of reflex, Stacia glanced up, but no interruption came from the AI. It always bothered her when people referred to Maya as *it*. The word sounded harsh to her ear. She preferred something more neutral, like *they*. She often overenunciated a correction for Paki's benefit, hoping he'd get the hint. He made a point of never getting it. Though he never admitted it, he considered himself a gatekeeper of who was truly a part of the community, and Maya wasn't one of them. Not a real one. "We're programming them to be God. What does that make us?"

"Human." Paki paused to allow his comment room to sink in.

Stacia focused on the continuing simulation. The scan of terrestrial conditions and active protolife. The construction of a terraforming chamber. "This seems an overly aggressive move as a first-contact gesture."

"Launching a probe loaded with math and classical music to broadcast to any alien intelligence encountered was an aggressive gesture. We're targeting lifeless planets, not annoying populated ones with our pop culture," Paki said. "All that's lacking for the chambers are the microbes. And the will to use them."

"We need final approval from the Ijo."

"Approval you could have asked for while you were just at the Dreaming City." Paki tapped the table, discontinuing the simulation. "You're stalling."

"We had other pressing matters."

"You distracted them." Paki angled his head toward her and tapped his chin. "You knew how they'd react to news about the wormhole given the history of the Mothership Incident."

"We created a ship that almost caused a calamitous temporal paradox." Stacia restrained herself from pounding the table. That kind of demonstration only fueled Paki, letting him know that he achieved his goal of petty aggravation. As if he considered it his personal mission in life to irritate the shit out of the status quo. He "won" most arguments via his erosion strategy: he simply wore someone down until they threw their arms in the air and gave up. He and Yahya should form some sort of boy band.

Tenting her fingers against the table, Stacia pushed herself up. She took three calming breaths and allowed the seconds to pass between them in silence. Yahya often accused her of weaponizing silence.

Paki took a heartbeat and calmed down. He began again in a reassuring whisper. "We didn't. Not to mention, we can't. Time is fixed."

"How do you explain what happened to the mothership?"

"History. It happened," Paki said. "Astra Black happened. Muungano happened. But what do I know? I only have ten years of experience as a temporal mechanic. Before then, I was a lowly quantum physicist, with a few dozen papers to my name as a chair at the Thmei Academy."

As warm and gracious as he was with students—whom he called *journeyers* or *seekers*—when he was around anyone he perceived as questioning or threatening his authority, he was quick to remind them of his intellect and skill. Any slick comment risked a person hearing his full résumé.

"All I'm saying is that I want to make sure we don't cause something else to happen. If it were up to me, we'd have never sent HOVA gbeto through the Orun Gate before thoroughly understanding it. We've done enough to them."

"What do you mean we've done enough to them?" Paki asked.

"As scientists, we tend to focus on the advantages, but rarely consider the dangers. We literally hacked the brains of the HOVA, members of our community, inserted AI so powerful into some of their minds, I wonder if they are still fundamentally human. Their decision-making processes outsourced to algorithms. We augmented their genome and very cellular structure in the name of enhancement and efficiency. Let's at least admit that we have no idea what the application of such technology cost their humanity. Their essential being."

"Because we needed the best gbeto possible."

"To establish a military, we created living weapons. We sacrificed members of our community in the name of protecting that very same community. And we did it without hesitation."

"They volunteered." Paki's voice remained irritatingly even.

"We still bear some responsibility."

"But none of that was up to you. Not even going through the Orun Gate. The R gave the orders."

"Another bit of control stripped from me." Stacia hated the vague sense of powerlessness. The R going over her head, countermanding her suggested course of action. Yahya deciding on his own what was best for their son. That damn causal agent of Bek's condition refusing to be discovered. Her bracelets slid down her wrists with a soft rattle.

Paki stared at her with uncertainty, not sure she was even talking to him. His next words stumbled out sounding more like a question.

"We have jump gate technology to navigate the wormholes now."

"No, O.E. had the technology and loaned it to us." Stacia circled the table. "Which, if you believe them, they'd been working on since the Mothership Incident."

Paki made a noncommittal noise. "Gee, you don't believe them?"

"We find out a wormhole is parked in our sovereign territory, and they manage to provide us tech to navigate it. Then we discover the wormhole is artificial? No, I don't trust them." Stacia rubbed the bridge of her nose as if fending off an impending headache. "Something else is in play, but that's always been their way. O.E. is a contagion. Any contact with them and their old ways—I don't care if we call them *joint military exercises*—has a way of corroding community. Dividing us. The HOVA have been isolated into their own community now, on the fringes, barely connected to the rest of Muungano. Using proprietary tech we don't have access to. All of which is on the other side of the wormhole as we speak. Which we can no longer communicate with. Does that about sum up the state of things?"

"A joint operation you approved and cleared with the R long before either of you informed the full Ijo." Paki scoured her with his unflinching scrupulousness. "What changed to make you read them in?"

Stacia knew these programs—both the HOVA incursion and Project Uhlanga—were heavily favored by many on Titan as long overdue, even if she didn't feel comfortable with them. O.E. had squandered most of its natural resources and made a mess of itself as a suitable place to live, to the point where most of its population took to the stars. Her great-grandmother was among some of the "fifth wave migration." This left only the "fervent faithful few" as Paki described the religious zealots who stayed on O.E. convinced that their various apocalypses had finally occurred and went to war with one another. It wasn't the fairest way to describe them. There were many who simply did not want to leave the place they called home. Like her great-grandfather. The family still only whispered of her great-grandparents' reluctant split, each dug in with their idea of what home was. Those left behind on O.E. had to make a life for themselves even as their governments devolved into warmongering chaos. Their endless wars cost them only the Mars colony and Muungano outpost. Only once O.E. reorganized under the LISC government did it begin making interstellar moves again. Moves she wanted to stay abreast of, even expose as needed. On her timetable.

"Assuming we successfully develop the genetically modified microbes, what does the timetable for the initiation of Project Uhlanga look like?" Stacia asked.

"Almost on your command." Paki didn't bother to hide his grin of triumph. Still, he'd chosen his words with too much care. A hint of uncharacteristic hedging.

"Almost?"

Wiping a hand across his eye, it was Paki's turn to beat back a migraine. "There have been complications. Setbacks."

"What sort of setbacks?" Stacia perched on the edge of the table.

"A lab accident. Much of our stock was destroyed."

"When were you going to tell me about this?" Stacia lowered her voice and pronounced each syllable with careful enunciation. She tired of the people she trusted, those closest to her, shutting her out of the loop of decisions in the name of easing her burden.

"I'm telling you now. I only recently discerned a pattern. Well, enough of one to draw my attention. And concern."

"As it should." The way his face hitched unsettled her. "Paki? What sort of pattern?"

"It may be nothing. Probably my overactive imagination. We had a contaminated batch of suspension solution a few weeks back. It cost us several days. Nothing unusual, per se; we're a lab. A programming error is to be expected on occasion. Human error like this still happens."

"But now you fear a pattern?"

"Two incidents do not a pattern make. But I want to exercise caution." Paki's wrist bleeped. He brushed his skin, and a holovid display popped up.

"We're under Code Black / Eyes Only protocol. How are you getting a signal?" Stacia marched over to him.

"I couldn't unless it was a priority alert." Paki's eyes widened as he read the brief coming across his wrist monitor.

"What is it?"

He looked up at her, his jaw half-ajar while he digested the information. "Our probe monitoring the Orun Gate. It's gone missing."

05

FELA BUHARI
Eshu

Fela Buhari closed her eyes and wished she still believed in the orisha for her to pray to as her ship tumbled through the atmosphere in what its pilot optimistically called a *trajectory*. The Muungano astronomers designated this the Anansi Star System and the nearest habitable planet on the other side of the Orun Gate wormhole, Eshu. The verdant planet spun beneath them. None of this was any consolation to the pit of Fela's stomach. Closing her eyes, she felt and ignored the curious, judging stares of the much more experienced gbeto she was assigned to lead. As transitions went, her mission was off to a less-than-auspicious start.

The military drop ship *Hughes,* little more than a heavily armored Saqqara, bucked wildly, careening through the atmosphere at odd angles. Coming from all sectors of the Muungano alliance, the contingent of gbeto huddled closely, knees almost touching the person across from them. Despite the harnesses bracing them, each shudder of the ship jostled them into the person next to them. The HOVA Hellfighters regiment prepared for a low orbital jump. Cursing the R—the civilian head of the Niyabinghi, and his enigmatic and often impractical ways—she had been ordered not to brief the members of her unit on their mission until they were en route. The squad remained under the watchful eye of the unit's captain, Epyc Ro Morgan. The same woman overlooked for promotion so that Fela could be installed over the squad. The only thing Fela had learned about her squad, outside of her field notes on each of them, was that they bantered to release any premission jitters.

"I think my boyfriend wants to break up with me." Sliding from her harness, Anitra stood up, her voice raised above the roar of the turbulence as the ship carved its way through the choppy atmosphere. No one could tell she was shouting from the smooth flow of her diction. The ship neared their appointed jump zone. Anitra strode to the rack containing the Extra-Vehicle Mobility units, the military grade navsuits. Loud and Ugenini (through and through) and beautiful, there was nothing self-deprecating about Anitra. Her ever-direct gaze made people uncomfortable, as if she dared a person to not like her just the way she was. Moving as if the hiccupping ship was little more than sand between her toes on a beachside visit, she slung her EVM over her one-piece nanomesh suit. The EVM units were specifically designed for space dives. The black body stocking of her nanomesh, both hydrophobic and insulating, acted as a buffering interface between her and the exoskeleton. A patch of royal purple and old gold had been sewn onto her uniform.

"We're not doing this," said Robin, a tank of a woman who all but left tread marks when she dashed across an open field. Given space to run, no one could catch her. With such a charge, she could bowl over an entire platoon. She chomped on a large, unlit blunt. When on a mission, she was on edge and the chiba leaves–stuffed cigar served as the promise of reward awaiting her at the completion of a successful mission.

"What?" Anitra filled her voice with innocent protest.

"That thing."

"What thing?" Anitra paused with her EVM still only half-on.

"That thing where when two women get together, all they can do is talk about a man." Robin sucked her teeth, already half-disgusted with the turn of conversation.

Anitra fastened the last of her EVM into place and cradled her helmet in the crook of her arm. She turned solemnly to Robin and with a stoic face said, "I think my girlfriend wants to break up with me, too."

"That's not any better." Robin let loose an exasperated sigh.

The *Hughes*'s engines roared, its sudden acceleration cutting through the turbulent atmosphere. After their mission's completion, the ship was due to rendezvous with the *Baldwin* and *Morrison* on the other side of the Orun Gate to coordinate the next phase of their mission. Fela began to undo her harness to fit into her own EVM. Even without turning, she knew Epyc Ro studied her. Her face nearly one hundred years of uncracked Ugenini, not a hint of a crease in sight, the captain made her final assessments. With a cool, detached stare, without the heat of resentment, anger, or jealousy. Just stoic professionalism. And it broke part of Fela's heart.

Under different circumstances, she would've wanted her and Epyc Ro to be friends. As it was, Epyc Ro's scrutiny threatened to reduce her to a kind of adolescent awkwardness. Knowing it was her first assignment, knowing the HOVAs under her didn't see her, didn't trust her, and knowing that they had to be convinced that she was capable of leading them. Fela's suit pinched about the shoulders and began to chafe around her groin. Even her chest plate felt a little snug. Despite its self-maintenance protocols, the exoskeleton smelled more than a little ripe. However, her EVM was not designed for comfort but rather to protect her from radiation, temperature extremes, and the vacuum of space. Her discomfort was better than death, and she didn't want to appear the slightest bit soft in front of the squad. *Her* squad.

"I gotta put a helmet on this?" Robin patted her Afro puffs.

"I assume you know how." Fela stared out the launch bay as the doors opened and the shielding was on countdown to lower for them to make their exit. She hated space jumps, preferring to do a space walk and risk zero-G nausea from floating. She had the same issue when learning to swim, never trusting the concept of relaxing and bobbing at the surface. Even then, she learned by simply diving in.

The ship's shields dropped.

"Come on, we've got to go." Epyc Ro slid past all of them, her way of cutting through the command bullshit. Possessing a bit of a reckless streak, without so much as a backward glance, Epyc Ro leapt into the oblivion of Eshu's atmosphere.

Trying not to resent the captain undercutting her authority, Fela jumped after her.

Fela spun ass over neckbones for a few miles, little more than an ancient shuriken. The HOVAs had to make a tight landing window: waiting until they fell beneath any possible radar, if indeed anyone possessed that level of technology, but leaving themselves with enough time to activate their glide jets and stop. Twenty-five seconds into the jump. 546 mph. 600. 650. 785. 835. She stabilized, regaining control of her descent. Her suit was thin enough for her to feel the wind threatening to tear through her. The ground rushed toward her. The EVM thrusters fired. The sudden deceleration racked her body. Shields up, she positioned herself for landing. Her touchdown left a crater-sized divot in the ground.

Shedding the artificial carapace of the EVM unit, she stripped down to her field uniform and activated the tactical AI of her helmet. "Chandra, we good?"

<Linking the squad now. Deployed nanobots coming on line.> Chandra rarely spoke. Instead, the comms officer nodded as Command fed tactical information directly to her neurological implant. A portion of her brain stem

had been removed to make room for it. Most of her skull and cheek had been removed and covered with bioplastic. Most of the right side of her face dedicated to the needs of the Maya-enabled implant. A living radio with so much information to sift through, she lived on standby. Her undistracted brain space monitored live feeds. She was a living sacrifice for the ideal Muungano represented. Though a fine officer who never complained, it didn't make it any less fucked up.

Fela couldn't feel the microscopic scrabble of the tiny machines, though her mind itched at the thought. Joining the HOVA Hellfighters regiment had already cost her so much. The genetic rewiring and augmentation, with extra mitochondria hybridized into her cellular structure. The attenuation of her DNA to enhance intelligence, healing, and longevity (even more so than the average Muungano member). Making her both more and less human, though she wondered where the line was. All for the sake of her community. The only thing an individual of Muungano truly owned was their name and their own genotype, once it had been thoroughly groomed and approved by their parents. But as joining the HOVA demonstrated, even one's genome was subject to the needs of the community.

Her bodysuit linked the nanobots, creating a near-iridescent quality to her suit upon them coming on line before they settled into a matte of black. Her squad soon appeared as icons along her visor. The HOVA Hellfighters regiment, specialized urban infantry, were much more comfortable on the ground than in the air.

"All right, Chandra, what do we have?" Fela asked.

With frantic waves of Chandra's hands, a holoimage popped up, first displaying the entire Anansi Star System until it focused on Eshu. Their coordinates lit up.

"Yes, okay. Ready to receive." Fela hated the way transmitted orders seemed like the R was right in her head. The R assigned her to the HOVA Hellfighters regiment personally. He wanted boots on the ground of the planet designated Eshu and the squad firmly embedded before transmitting his final orders. Though never having led one, she'd served on these sorts of operations before. This level of secrecy meant the squad was only in for one of "those" missions: the heavy-casualty kind. "Prepare to launch a communication buoy."

"What are our orders, Commander?" Epyc Ro asked. *Challenged* may have been the more appropriate verb. The way she dripped sarcasm on the word *commander* burned in Fela's ears.

"Our specialty: infiltration." Fela knew she had a duty to place herself in the center of the action. Studying military forces in action, she understood how division among the ranks festered into unhealable wounds. It was a simple matrix of judgment. Action sifted character. Those who performed, who could handle anything thrown at them, earned respect. The HOVA Hellfighters regiment were legendary. Fela knew enough to know she didn't know much, but had to project confidence around her people or she'd be the chaff and lose them forever.

Only the faintest upturn of the corner of her mouth betrayed her as Epyc Ro suppressed a smirk at the word *our.* "Recon?"

"Yes. The rest of the squad will hold up here, including the heavy unit, once the *Hughes* lands while we get a lay of the land. Literally and figuratively. Maps. Scans. Readings. And a survey."

"Survey of what?" Robin asked.

"It appears that there's something that might be a city seven kilometers west. We're charged with assessing it." Fela enlarged the telemetry projection.

"A city."

"Yes."

"An urban design to allow inhabitants to live and function as a society," Robin confirmed.

"Yes."

"That implies inhabitants."

"Yes," Fela said.

"That's . . . a lot." Robin pretended to study her scanner while she absorbed the totality of their situation.

Life out here was not only a possibility but a probability. The Drake equation predicted the abundance of spacefaring life a long time ago. In their galaxy, much less out here in unexplored, uncharted space. The probability that they would encounter life out in the universe once they began exploring had always been accepted, though more theoretical than anything else. It was built into their mission parameters and training—the cause of much excitement and speculation. The idea of the artificial wormhole. Landing under possible radar detection. First-contact protocols training. Cultural engagement and diplomatic training a part of all officer studies. They barely knew someone was out here; they turned a convenient blind eye that they were marching ever closer to someone else's home. Surrounded by proof of life. That they were not alone out here. Life won out. Wild, extraordinary, adapting to circumstance. It was, after all, why Muungano built starships and communication buoys. To explore and reach out. Now they stood on the precipice of not just possible evidence but of contact. The elders whispered of the possibility. In some Code Black / Eyes Only briefings, there seemed to be a tacit race to engage in communication with rumored aliens. O.E. continued to launch probes and years ago quit sharing unabridged data with the Muungano Science Council. Fela watched the information settle on each of her gbeto. Waves of wonder, delight, fear. Possibilities.

"Just so I have this straight, we just supposed to yankadi in, do some air and earth sampling, and check out the architecture. Figure out what sort of culture would design a city that way." Robin stroked her chin. She studied every data point with her large, fearless eyes. "Cultural reconnaissance only?"

"Yes." Fela didn't bother to paint a prettier picture for them.

"Shit." Anitra's pronunciation had a way of breaking the word into two syllables. "We're not anthropologists or any other kind of scientist. We're gbeto."

"We have no idea what we'll find. I hate the way Command makes us feel disposable." Robin scanned about the terrain.

"I don't know what to do with that," Fela said. The irony of using weapons, even living ones, to forge peace was a hard conceit at the heart of Muungano. "Gbeto. That's the job. Going into the unknown, trained to improvise in the moment. A shield ready to defend because that is the human condition."

Once the fifth wave migration into space began in earnest, with people flocking to Mars and the Dreaming City, religious fundamentalists attempted to seize power on O.E., as if they had waited the entire history of their faiths for this opportunity. Something the First World cofounders saw coming, which was another reason why they began leaving O.E. in the first place. The HOVA regiments were originally established for the defense of the budding First World outpost.

After the Lunar Ukombozi War, the established Muungano community broke free and declared its liberation from O.E., but the outpost maintained the established structure of the HOVA. Most of the foot gbeto in the HOVA unit were of Ugenini origins, always the first to volunteer to defend the idea of Muungano. Almost as if they had something to prove. That was another thing Fela loved about the Ugenini, though frankly, she was troubled that so many of Muungano still defined themselves by those identities. Ugenini, Asili, or Maroon for the sake of claiming authenticity.

"First, all of you have been trained in a variety of fields in your long lives, especially with the amount of downtime between missions." Fela hoped to be able to lead on the strength of her word alone, but she'd break out chain of command if she had to. "And second, the orders come straight from the R."

"Damn. Why didn't you say that from the get?" Anitra waved them forward, her beloved tactical rifle slung across her body, always at the ready. The DMX-3000 had obviously been through some times, but it remained well maintained. "Let's move out."

The full squad ran fifteen deep. The young. The brazen. The immortal. The O.E. military preferred their inductees without familial connections. Refugees. Wards of the state. The *repurposed, unmissed* people on O.E. called them. But Muungano changed all that. The gbeto duty was rooted in relationship, the work of the individual to safeguard the community. HOVAs knew the cost in more intimate ways than other members. And Fela had been charged with leading them, adopting mother to a brood prone to squabbles, fighting, and playing far too rough.

Without a word, the squad assumed a standard patrol formation, progressing at a slow crawl over the terrain. Advance drones the size of dust motes relayed information to the squad as well as the *Hughes* for the next communication buoy update. Until then, they'd be radio silent with Muungano.

Her mind refused to accept the idea of the possibility of "aliens," no matter how much they had trained for the possibility. Fela always wondered how she would react to them. Actual aliens. The concept of beings from another world, whether they admitted it or not, was too big for most people. The entertainment value was one thing, filling their books and movies in preparation of them. The reality had too many implications. She could almost get her mind around them but couldn't. But they were on a mission, one involving space exploration. Taking their first steps to the stars. Drawing attention to themselves if anything was out here to notice them. Yet here they were, on an alien world. Her planet on the other side of the galaxy, perhaps (astrocartography was limited to mission briefs).

In war, cities were the worst to patrol, with too many possibilities for snipers to hide or leave IEDs in roads or with the alleys veining the city providing too many avenues to escape into. Her readings made little sense. She double-checked them. In this approximation of a city, the structures weren't like buildings as Fela understood them but closer to apartments carved into a mountainside. Raised boulders that might have served as a home. Perhaps the area had been a city as she knew it once, though now it resembled sandblasted ruins. The surviving debris had the hallmarks of being a place where people lived, played, and did business, all blown to shit. She imagined firefights having broken out, with indications of opposing forces vying for control of the rubble. Winding in and out of the series of alleyways, Epyc Ro held up her hand, and the squad halted for a break, hiding behind an outcrop of what remained of a building.

"Careful, we don't know what kind of booby traps might be in place," Epyc Ro said. "No one leaves their home unprotected."

Fela scowled at her. This was going to be a problem she'd need to nip early rather than later. "Captain, I'll give the commands, if you don't mind."

"Do you know what you're looking for?" Epyc Ro's tone strayed up to the line of derision but stopped short. Barely.

"I was brought in to lead this group, without request and without notice. I like this situation about as much as you do, but orders are orders. I have a job to do, and I always do my job well. I'm looking for someone to obey chain of command. If not you, then I will find someone else."

Though barely visible in the night, Fela knew her gbeto watched. Passing glances among one another, most with the easily entertained attention spans of wanting to make popcorn to watch the scene playing out. She always felt uneasy about the whole idea of forced chain of command. The notion that she could say something and those under her would snap to obedience. It was an O.E. holdover that chafed against the Muungano way.

"I'll follow your lead; that's the HOVA way," Epyc Ro said.

"Good." Fela began to turn as if the matter was settled.

"However . . ." Epyc Ro let the word hang until she captured everyone's attention. "Knowing the *context* for leadership is the Muungano way. A good leader, an experienced leader, knows how to best make use of the assets at their disposal."

"The captain knows how to talk that shit," Anitra whispered.

"Yeah, she can even make being disrespectful sound respectful," Robin said.

Fela measured the squad, each in turn. The Muungano alliance was a self-organizing entity. Its leadership determined by the needs at the time and who was in the room with the required skills. The person with the most experience or expertise led in the moment. Rank meant little to them. The squad would naturally follow Epyc Ro, their true leader. Fela being Asili and Epyc Ro being Ugenini only augmented the typical standoff between an inexperienced officer versus a battle-hardened gbeto. The friction of the former fact complicating the expected tension of the latter.

"It's true, Captain. You have more field experience than I. However, I am mission command, and I know the big picture of the job to be done. And why. You know how to get shit done. So as you were saying . . ." The leadership responsibility of the whole thing was an unwelcome burden on Fela mostly because eventually there would come occasions when she'd have to order gbeto to their deaths. She had no problem sharing the burden with Epyc Ro as she settled into their world. Their community. Epyc Ro had the heart of her people. Fela was the head that directed them, and a good platoon leader allowed her captains to mentor her.

Epyc Ro gave a single uptick of her chin, but something had softened in her face and bearing. Fela hoped it was the germinating seed of a grudging respect. "Careful. We don't know what kind of booby traps they've left for us."

"But whoever they are can't know we're coming," Fela stated without challenge. "We didn't even know they were here."

Epyc Ro's gaze lingered over the terrain. "They must think someone might."

Fela couldn't help but admire them. The Hellfighters were an elite unit, trained to seek out enemy ambushes. *Professional targets* her O.E. instructor called *HOVA*. Trained to move, observe, or track in any environment. Kill if necessary. *Only* if necessary, her Muungano instructor at the Thmei Academy taught her. The HOVA Hellfighters neared the heart of the nameless town. So close to their target, the squad needed to advance. And quickly. If one knew what to look for, signs of the enemy surrounded them. Lean-tos hidden among the scattered copses. Fighting positions, rocks stacked, stony sandbags against a storm of weapons fire. Perches overlooking the well-traveled ruts. Camouflaged dugouts roofed with logs and buried under sand along the roads like crab traps. From overhead, they wouldn't be detected and might defeat casual scans. Whoever they were, they weren't primitive people. They knew how to improvise, use what was at hand in sophisticated ways. Technology and superior firepower could be matched by those who knew how to use the terrain to their advantage. "What do the drone scans say?"

<Telemetry readings are off. Something interferes with the signal,> Chandra's voice transmitted directly into their helmets.

"Can you tell what direction the interference is coming from?" Epyc Ro asked.

<Yeah.>

"Then that's where we'll head."

Fela remained quiet, resigning herself to being the outsider. Though raised Asili, she was fascinated by Ugenini culture. She listened to their music, even risking punishment from her parents in doing so, as they were strict about the Asili ways. Nevertheless, she studied Ugenini art, literature, language. Even trained at the Thmei Academy and graduated at the top of her class. She had nothing to prove, but she would always be locked outside of them by culture and rank.

"You got that look again." Robin turned to the captain once they started marching.

"What look?" Epyc Ro asked.

"That 'weight of the world' / 'thinking about the past' look."

"Feeling nostalgic, I guess. Lost some good people along the way."

"The best."

"What were you doing before all this?" Epyc Ro asked.

"Writer, spoken-word poetry. You?"

"Librarian."

"Remind me to never fuck with a librarian again." Robin's tone reflected on many shared missions.

"It seems so long ago." Epyc Ro never met Robin's eyes, her focus on the terrain, scanning for any trace of movement or anything out of place. The vigilance of constant suspicion. "Now it's like combat is all I've ever known."

"Because you were born for it."

Fela wasn't born for the ways of war, she was obligated to it. The Buharis were a military family going back five generations to O.E. Duty and sacrifice was what she explained to her son before she left. That one day he would join and serve because that was the family way. The words tasted like ashes in her mouth even as she spoke them to him. It wasn't fair to not allow him a choice about his own life. That was what she, what they all, fought for out here. Yet there it was. Fela had a son to get back to. Having promised him that she'd return, he gave her the will to make it back. She didn't have a holoimage or anything similar. Only her word to her eleven-year-old. She didn't hedge her words or speak to things out of her control. She promised, pure and simple.

"You know why I joined this unit?" Fela interjected.

"To be with the best comforted by the knowledge that the best had your back," Robin recited the O.E. recruitment poster.

"That sounds more like you." Fela stared off into the distance. "Wars sometimes have to be fought. There's not always room to negotiate with a narcissistic bully who has lost his mind."

"His got-damn mind," Anitra echoed, knowing the history of authoritarian O.E. leaders who made a habit of plunging into war with them. Until LISC took over.

"But what gives me pause is that the military has a history of rarely being the most conscientious of beasts. It wastes a lot. It's casual about lives. If I have to fight, I wanted it to at least be . . . efficient. To count for something. I wanted to know that I made a difference, and I don't want my life to be wasted." As Fela glanced about, she realized that her words landed with the intended weight enough to settle the conversation. The squad's chatter died once they shifted into professional mode, and they continued their patrol.

Fela examined the scoring of the nearest building. The scorch marks told a story, one she thought needed a better interpreter. With a grunt, she studied the terrain. "What's the sitrep?"

"I don't like this," Robin said.

"What is it?" Fela kept her weapon at the ready, scanning the nearby buildings, alleys, and doorways.

"Exploring the other side of the Orun Gate, the Muungano community is essentially on a first-contact mission, but *we've* been dispatched. Gbeto, not only armed but weapons hot. This is no way to say hello. It makes us no different . . ."

". . . than any other human in history," Fela acknowledged.

"Exactly. We should do better." Robin slung her weapon behind her shoulder and ran her hand along the surface of the building. "None of this makes any sense. We have what may be a town, though it looks analogous to an ancient structure. But there are signs of recent habitation and not-too-distant abandonment. Yet a recent firefight."

"This char pattern makes sense. Sorta. Look at the blast patterns. There, there, and there." Anitra pointed to differing sections along the wall. "But compare that to the striation patterns here and here."

"Different ordnance? That's not unusual. It's not like we all are toting a DMX." Robin hefted her Busta.

"No, but the basic tech and charges of our weapons are the same." Anitra held out her weapon. "With all this cross fire, consider me the welcome wagon in full defense mode."

"Two forces. In a recent firefight over an abandoned city," Fela said.

"Looks that way," Anitra said.

"Did I mention that I don't like this?" Robin studied the skyline.

"And that none of this makes any sense," Epyc Ro said. "HOVA on me. We're moving out."

"Captain?" Fela asked.

Epyc Ro whirled to face her, anticipating her challenge. "Back to the extraction point."

"No, I mean there." Fela pointed to the horizon.

A cloud of dust raised on the horizon and neared quickly. Vehicles skimmed the surface of the desert sand. The force closed off the route the Hellfighters arrived on. When Epyc Ro turned to calculate a retreat course, figures emerged from some of the structures behind them. Most of them armed.

"What have you led us into, Commander?" Epyc Ro backed toward Fela.

"Looks like a trap." Fela raised her weapon. "Lock and load, ladies. Time to live up to our namesake."

06

WACHIRU ADISA
The Dreaming City

Our dreams were stolen from us yet again. And we were relieved.

As the darkness of our dreams faded, all that remained in their wake was the sense—the urgency—of a threat. That inescapable feeling that something was building. And coming for us.

"Lights." Our eyes barely opened, without much alertness, but we knew that what passed for our sleep had ended for this night cycle. The images that disquieted our emi had completely retreated, leaving only a foreboding cloud of loss. Maya brought up the lights and the volume to our morning music playlist to their preset levels. They kept the volume low as if not wanting to jar us fully awake.

<Is everything all right, Wachiru?> Maya asked, their tone ever neutral and even.

"I got so much trouble on my mind, refuse to lose." We recited the ancient lyrics. We drew up in our bed. It morphed to adjust to the new position of our tall, lanky frame. Even without checking, we knew from the heaviness of our emi what day it was. Today was the anniversary of us losing Anyah.

Activating our monitors to distract ourselves, news and reports danced along our vidscreens. The various scenes and images overlapped one another like battling holovids. The protests surrounding the Muungano embassies on the Yo. Unrest in many communities left forgotten—the polite way of saying underresourced with intentionality—by the LISC administration on O.E. Reports from Bronzeville about the O.E.-Mars trade negotiations breaking down and the brewing tensions. All the parties reached out to Muungano for an answer or to play mediator, as if we were the only ones who could speak to the community and their interests. If we were, it was because no one else bothered to learn how to.

"Any update on the bombing?" We rubbed our face, attempting to wake ourselves up. It took awhile to come into the full experience of our being. An ache radiated from deep within our muscles. A tightness about our neck and shoulders as if we had slept in a poor position. For a month.

<Ten civilian deaths have been reported.>

"I thought there was only one casualty in the embassy." Our thoughts drifted to Jaha. She had been—she is—a second mother to us. Had been in our lives as long as we could remember. Both an institution and a force of nature, she was too stubborn to die. Things move fast on Muungano. It doesn't allow time to reflect unless we carve it out with intention. But the bombing and her injuries reminded her, all of us, of her all-too-human frailty.

<Nine more as O.E. moved to quell the protestors.>

"Has anyone taken credit?"

<There has been no official statement.>

"VOP Clay Harrison is waiting to get his story straight." We knew that was what Jaha would have surmised. He was all about caste-splaining. He'll use every euphemism to avoid admitting to the reality of the racial caste system. Or condemn it. Sadly, there's a history of black leaders carrying the water for the system. Having secured a seat at the table for himself, he'd do anything to keep it. He has to toe the party line. He has to represent the dominant caste's interests. And in so doing, he becomes their scapegoat; he's made to bear the blame for others while his presence allows them to convince themselves that they aren't beholden to or upholding the racial caste system.

Jaha being transported to the medical facilities on the Dreaming City gave us comfort and allowed us room to exhale. To worry about the rest of the community. These days, being a professional worrier had become our life's calling. *Worry* wasn't quite the right word. Ours was a heightened sensitivity to the work, the people-centered work that was our day-to-day concern. It required a lot, to notice each person, to be fully aware and attenuated to them. And we weren't certain that we wanted to keep doing it.

This was how maintaining Muungano consumed so much of our mind. Ferreting out the politics and motivations of those outside our space to determine whether they were a threat. Every day felt like a new round of interstitial chess and moves within moves within moves. Knowing people held meetings on Yo and on Mars, in and about Muungano, the whispers making their way back to us. Preparing and bracing for their moves.

Our feet slapped against the asphalt tile of fused regolith. It wasn't as if we had much by way of furnishings or decoration in our room. No art hung on the walls other than the geometrically patterned clay paints. Our unit was free of distraction, a blank slate to retreat to. We grabbed clothes from the nearest pile. Nanobots tended laundry as part of their cleaning protocols, so we were never overly concerned with our clothing selection. Unless it was a ceremonial occasion, we typically went for the same look. Our clothing a blend of color, noise, and texture. Pants sheared and tight as if passed down from a smaller brother, aged to the appropriate level of fashionable distress. Ruffled sleeves, a series of dampening folds. Our jacket of sisal and beads woven together, doubled as a sound shield, allowing us to record and master music in any location should inspiration hit. A knit hat was the last piece of our armor we needed in order to face our day. With the day cycle just beginning, we needed to rehearse with Ezeji. Now was usually our favorite time to head into the studio to mix our music, before anyone else was up and we could enjoy the night sounds.

Incomplete truths, a half-sung melody, your life a cypher to everyone,
   including we
Still trying to make sense, only knowing we're not okay, we're not okay,
   we're not okay
It's been nearly three years since my baby left;
      we failed you, didn't see the obvious, didn't see you
The most important person, right in front of us,
      hiding in a black hole, between dark spaces, you
It's our fault, we know. Choosing not to notice how mind, body, and emi
   hurt,
         truth without rhyme
We want to hate her for leaving us alone, hollowed out, swallowed whole,
   followed soon in time
But things can't change because things always change

Even before the Lunar Ukombozi War, life on the Yo—with the environmental collapse and subsequent economic collapse—had made things so hard, people no longer feared of leaping into the unknown to try something new. The weusi established First World from the ashes of one of Yo's failed attempts at colonization. It evolved into Muungano, our ongoing experiment in community. Muungano may have been the dream, but maintaining it was a motherfucker.

Even the hallways of the Dreaming City were an encounter with art. All ornamented surfaces and relief carvings along the walls. Colored tiles lighting in a kaleidoscopic play of crisscrossing panels, lighting to mark our steps. The thin background hum of a stellar chorus chimed as ambiance. Most of the family rondavel weren't awake yet for the day cycle, allowing us to stalk the Dreaming City alone with our thoughts. Winding down a back stairwell, we followed the walkways networking the vertical kraal. Individual rondavel units within the kraal were open, and children and adults alike drifted from home to home, staying where they felt most comfortable. People had to be given room to find their place to belong.

At the center of the circle of rondavels forming the kraal was a library, the heart of the Dreaming City. A shared space where tools to create art could be utilized by anyone. Visitors. Curious children eager to experiment with new forms. Traveling artists searching for collaboration partners. At dusk, neighboring kraals gathered in the common area to share meals and the details of their day with one another. Our "dessert" was any contribution to the public space: discussion, dance, or other presentations of art. A space to celebrate and enjoy one another. It was where we first met her. We didn't necessarily choose the thoughts that came to us, but we did choose whether or not to act on them.

The sound of familiar raised voices of Camara Xola and Jaha drew us from the hole of despair we almost tumbled into. Windows about the central chamber allowed any to peer in, though few dared if these elders in particular squared off against each other. We slipped into the room.

Jaha Dimka rarely appeared outside of her kraal chambers without a hat or other covering. The front curls of her hair dangled in a series of braids from her wrap. The rear of her skull had been fitted with an implant: the crown of griots. A neurological implant that allowed her to access the downloaded memories of her predecessors. Her mind was a complicated space, a community of voices distilled by her will. Centuries of lived history, another in the long chain of living story. She moved slower and more cautiously, though her rising air of defiant petulance attempted to mask it. Only a slight limp betrayed any injury. Knowing her, she refused any walking assist device. She still favored her left arm. No doubt the bombing, hospitalization, subsequent space travel, and our own healers' ministrations took their toll on her. The last med-report we saw listed Jaha as having taken some shrapnel to the eye. Removing it required the reconstruction of the whole side of her face. In her convalescence instructions, medical staff asked her to rest after such an arduous procedure. She agreed.

However, a situation must've arisen that she decided required her personal attention. Or at least that was what she must have told herself.

"Are you seriously back in your kraal?" The rare note of sternness filled Camara Xola's voice. She was shorter than the Camara by nearly a head, yet somehow, he seemed to be always looking up to her.

"I keep telling you, I'm good. *Baby boy you only funky as your last cut. Focus on the past your ass'll be a has what.*" We stifled a snort. The griot knew her share of the ancient lyrics also.

Her short sleeves draped like spilled sheets, revealing aged but toned arms. Arms that had raised children and lost husbands yet remained fit and vital. Bedecked in golden jewelry, her red robes flared with each step, her stride reminiscent of a stalking flame, one that seemed primed to roast Camara Xola on a spit.

"The question isn't 'Are you good?' It's 'How good are the rest of us?'"

As if she'd run out of fuel, she collapsed into a chair across from Camara Xola. Folding her arms in front of her, she braced herself, determined to wait out the impending storm front of his commentary. Her eyes—now mismatched, one no longer the deep brown of her birth but shimmering with more of a golden hue—a remnant of her recent procedures. Large hoop earrings coordinated with the gold disk about her neck. All Niyabinghi, current or retired, wore collapsible chakram. Both elegant as an accessory and practical as a weapon. "Here we go."

"'Here we go' nothing," Xola began. "As elders, we set the tone. We lead by example. For you to not provide us a voice in decisions about your health is . . ."

". . . my business." She favored her left side as she moved, her vestments ill-fitting and weighing her down.

"'My'? Since when are we in the 'my' business? It's not just about your health but the health of the community."

"Don't turn the idea of community into something weird. It's not like I'm out here spreading a virus or anything. I'm getting my work—the work of building and being community—done. You haven't even asked me what I thought was so important that I got out of my sickbed to—"

"Because I don't care. One, all you need are some rocks out of place and you'd decide you were the only one to arrange them properly. Two, let's not pretend that you ain't out here trying to figure out how to head up the investigation into your bombing."

"Lij Matata still has his mother's milk on his breath."

"Uh-huh. Some people asked me last night if I thought you were going to stay home and rest. I said, 'Doubtful,' and told them, 'She's telling you she will so that you will spread the word that she's listening and will stay home and rest. My experience with her tells me something different.'"

Jaha sucked her teeth at him. "I'm here, ain't I? I'm fine and ready to get back to work."

Their back-and-forth was loud but without heat. With the years of their friendship numbering in decades, the pair of them often went at it worse than any partnered couple. And loved each other just as deeply. We loved a woman once, in a home we hoped to build together. We couldn't help but be reminded of what could have been. Perhaps what was in some parallel universe. The *U and I verse,* she used to call us.

"I still feel remiss for leaving your kraal if you were just going to slip out and do you," our Pops said, his voice low and grave. With a heavy sadness that sounded a little scared.

We recognized the glint in Jaha's eye that read that she was not going to let up enough for him to breathe, much less think straight.

"Maya," Jaha turned to a wall, "can you display all the fucks I have to give?"

<You have zero fucks to give.>

We about fell out of our seat with that one. So did our Pops, throwing his hands up like he gave up. We often slipped into calling him Pops when we, either of us, needed reminding which role of his was in play. Right now, he wasn't Camara, he was Xola, lifelong friend of Jaha, whom he was scared for.

Jaha scored poorly on Yo's aptitudes for diplomacy but scored highly on Muungano's aptitudes for "getting shit done." So much so, Yo often demanded a new ambassador, "one they could work with" so the communiqués often went. As if their word somehow carried any weight on Muungano and she'd be deemed unsuitable or shamed. All it led to was Jaha pacing about the Dreaming City correcting their language to "one they could control" for all the Ijo to hear. The Yo assumed the Ijo would be lost in the politics of selecting a new representative, but the Ijo would wait a few weeks, send a few communiqués to Yo about our intense discussions, then return Jaha to her post.

However, Jaha was a dual-edged sword; she wasn't any easier for us to work with.

"Do you two sit around and rehearse this?" Smothering a smile, our Pops stroked his beard. He had a way about him, when his eyes glazed over like his thoughts drifted and no one was sure who he was talking to. In that moment, the weight of community shifted on him as he struggled to figure out the path in the best interest of everyone. That was when he slid back to being Camara. "All I'm asking is that you include others in your decision-making. Are you opposed to people helping you out?"

"Why are you talking to me like I'm one of the young people?"

Camara Xola picked at a bump on his chin before running his fingers through his beard again. "The answer is *yes*. I don't need to hear all the rest. I was just trying to communicate how your decisions impact the rest of us. Not considering that only makes the work that much more difficult. It's not sensitive, and it's not inclusive."

"Says the most recalcitrant fat cat of them all." She fixed her jawline somehow both delicate and fierce, a finely decorated steel ax. Touching three fingers to her chest in feigned protest, she inclined her head toward Xola before sucking her teeth and announcing, "Can I go?"

"Go do what you're going to do. It's not like anyone can stop you."

Jaha brushed past us, not meeting our eyes or even acknowledging us. Recognizing the focus on her face, we stayed out of her notice as she stormed through an exit. Fully healed or not, she would soon be barking excessive demands at her team, cajoling them into order and efficiency. If they were smart, they'd avoid her. Though we don't want to admit it, Jaha had a point. Running Muungano took a toll on some of its key members. Or maybe some members took on so much it made them key. Either way, when operations fell short, it required extra effort from those key members to ensure Muungano's smooth running. Until those same folks learned how to invite others in to lessen their burden. We needed to do more in this work and Xola needs to do less, but that choice of a first love requires sacrifice.

In cosmic storms, we don't even matter, we just get lost in all the chatter
Outrunning your demons down empty hallways,
    desperate echoes, desperate echoes
Thoughts of getting so doped up we no longer felt anyways,
    not a thing, not a thing
You were cold and no longer breathin', we held you in our arms as you
    were leavin'
We hate ourselves, that you weren't heard you 'til you ended yourself
Just a voice in our head, a careless whisper saying;
    [a breath of silence]

Now we know how you felt, too late. Our whole lives fraying
  [a space for tears]
But things can't change because things always change

"That went well." We watched the door re-form after Jaha's exit.

"As well as it was going to. She's not in a place to hear me. She's still recovering from her trauma."

"But that didn't stop you from pushing her." I plopped into her vacated seat. Pops's hand hovered in the air, his fingers trembled. I moved his glass closer to him for him to find.

"This mothership, Muungano, doesn't fly at low altitudes. There's no off button. That's why it's important to push her to take the time she needs to heal. Remind her that we are enough and she doesn't have to try to do everything." We were in uncharted territory. Muungano, the Camara in particular, attempted to carve out a new way of doing things. Each step, each decision, each action examined and vetted to not pass on the ways of the past. The weight of this burden, even just walking alongside our leaders left little afterward for us to focus on our music. Less and less time as the days marched forward.

We bridged our fingers between our legs as if poised for prayer. "She processes by doing. It helps her regain a sense of control."

"Yes, she does." Xola arched an eyebrow at us. "What else do you see?"

We were trained to pay attention to people's energy. The vibration they gave off. Their character. Who they were beneath the façade they put on to protect themselves in order to move through the world. Their emi. What some might label a soul. "She blames herself."

"For being bombed?"

"For being weak," we said.

"Shit. If a bomb isn't enough to soften the strong . . ."

"Not just that. She's scared. Like she was caught off guard. Like she wants her, all of us, to be better prepared. Especially with what's to come."

"Yeah, I can see that." Our Pops slumped in his chair, more exhausted than we'd ever seen him. He ran a delicate finger across his forehead. "I'm scared, too."

"Maybe she does have something that's contagious, after all."

"Think I was too hard on her?" Pops asked. "The work has gotten so expansive. Muungano's at a place where it is being called to be a voice in a lot of different spaces. I don't want my frustration to show."

"As you said, *she's* gonna do what *she's* gonna do."

"A majority of our leadership team is young and inexperienced. By design. We have to give them room to do what they are going to do or they will never grow." Camara Xola's hand trembled as he pushed against the table to raise up. When he glanced in our direction, his expression blanked as if he couldn't quite place who we were. Unsteady at first, imitating a new arrival adjusting to Muungano gravity, he gathered his legs under him. Finding the lost thread of his point, recognition filled his eyes. "I'm used to carrying the ball, you know. Taking the shot. I still got some game left in me and want to play. However, that's not where I'm needed most. I had to shift into being more of a coach, which means watching from the sidelines."

"Which is important," we reminded him.

"I know. It's just . . . sometimes it leaves me wondering if I've done an adequate job preparing you all for what's coming."

"'A redeemer of people is a walker with people,' so the proverb goes." We steered the topic from the event horizon of his darker ruminations. "Did Jaha offer any insight into the bombing or what LISC and what remains of Yo are up to?"

Camara Xola's rheumy eyes moistened, reddening circles staring from deep inside the cave of his thoughts. "We didn't get that far. Her well-being was more pressing."

"What about the security of Muungano?"

"Maulana has that well in hand. Speaking of life callings . . . it's all that man ever thinks about."

"He came out the womb doing a threat assessment."

"That's . . . an ugly mental picture." Pops chuckled. "Anyway, all Jaha can give us are theories and details."

"All of which are vital." Leaning toward him, we bridged our fingers again. Most times all he needed was someone to bounce his thoughts off of in order to find clarity, a path to move the work forward.

"All of which can wait. *She* is what matters to me." His tone didn't invite further discussion, another rare flash from our father.

"Maya, can you pull up the latest security briefings please?" we asked to continue to distract him. "Have our forces been deployed to the Legacy of Alexandria?"

Camara Xola sat back down. "Buhari sent a HOVA regiment to support the Niyabinghi and secure our embassy. Early reports indicate that its only by the grace of the orisha that anyone survived. We—and by 'we,' I mean Jaha—have dispatched a Griot Circle to conduct a thorough investigation because we need more information. Meanwhile, O.E. is minding up their propaganda machine."

"VOP Harrison is calling for the declassification of all reports related to the Mothership Incident."

"He can declassify my ass."

"Want me to make that the official Muungano response?" we asked.

Camara Xola threw his head back in laughter. He paused as if considering it, before chuckling a bit more. His emi cleared a bit and he leaned forward, tilting his face back to shift his cone of vision to see us better. "Damn, man, you too serious. You have a weight on you. You ought to shed some of that."

We shifted in our seat as if we could escape the scrutiny of his gaze, even though we knew he didn't need his eyes to see. He saw with his third eye, the truest vision. He could use his emi in ways few had mastered, outside of the Iyami Aje. But their magic wasn't practiced within Muungano. Not in the day. What Xola saw rang true. We were lost, barely holding, struggling to keep from drowning in a sea of sorrow. But we always allowed ourselves to feel something fully, to experience it, in order to get our hands around it. "I planned on going to the studio, hook up with Ezeji. Maybe finally make some magic happen."

"You think you're ready for some magic? Let me show you a magic trick." Camara Xola swept his arm across the table, making quite the show of clearing off the already empty surface. His tone lowered to a conspiratorial whisper. "Now you know the members of Muungano have always prided ourselves on being extensive readers, but there are ways—older ways—of knowing, being, and doing that are intrinsic to us as human beings. There are those who can only look through the lens of the priesthood of science and logic, claiming those paradigms as inherently superior. One of our jobs is to challenge the dominant cultural narrative, on all fronts, since it hinders those other ways of knowing. We have to embrace our own way of knowing. Push back against that limited way of thinking. They want to believe that magic is simply science too advanced for them. What they don't want to hear is that science is diluted magic."

Camara Xola drew back his sleeves, waving his hands in broad, wiping motions hovering just over the surface of the table, slowing until they settled near the edge. "Watch carefully because this makes no rational sense. I'm going to draw a string from the table."

Xola pressed his finger to the table. Slowly, he raised his finger. As he drew his hand away, a single red strand, an electric arc, surged from the table to the tip of his finger. He spread his hands. Red crackles of energy leapt to his fingertips without leaving so much as a scorch mark on the table.

"Magic?" We ran our hand along the surface. Our mind ran to possible scientific explanations, maybe a form of static electricity. Not wanting to believe. "We see it. And we don't overstand. The ways of the elders of the night?"

"The sacred mothers of the Iyami Aje learned many things before retreating from Muungano. They knew that we can manifest what we put our minds to. It's our magic. For me, my magic is about ideas. If we do this well, Muungano is everywhere. Where each of our people go—in the world, in the universe—they create Muungano. Our borders are the reach of our ideas."

"Why show me now?" we asked.

"I had to wait until you were ready for the magic. Sometimes you can't get to the new unless you let go of the old. Now do me a favor: Before you connect with Ezeji, check in with Bayard. Listening to folks and wrestling with their consciousness, that kind of soul work is literally his job description."

"All right." We leave a space not knowing how best to address him. Though Camara or not, he was always our father.

*

The mood of the Muungano space was another collateral casualty of the embassy bombing. The very air had a heaviness to it, an oppressive, inevitable sense of an unseen predator nearing. Yet that vague unease continued to stir within all of us. An older, nagging pain quietly nursed, the way broken hearts often were. A mix of loss and regret, like we attempted to walk on a recently broken leg that had healed poorly.

The temple had little by way of what we thought of as sacred design. None of the ornate fixtures meant to stir the awe of transcendence, but rather a simple structure flooded with early-morning light fluted through its window shields. Its entrance never locked, we entered through the low, wide archway.

Around the room, the images of ten orisha watched over any who entered, portraits in relief, three of whom were clustered together near the front of the room, at the heart of the chamber, over a dais with a golden orb suspended above it. Bayard strode about the space. We have always found him a curious figure. He waved about a censer burning sage, preparing for his Ubuntu service. *Ubuntu* meant "I am because we are," a belief in the universal bond of sharing that connected all of humanity. Bayard wasn't the religious head of the community, since many faiths populated Muungano, but he was well respected as a liberation theist. The community trusted his ability to create space for all people, even crafting his church service to demonstrate the same radical hospitality as the God he said he served.

"We see you, Bayard. How are you?" Neither Xola nor Selamault raised us with any particular faith traditions, leaving us to find our own way for ourselves. There was an openness in which he practiced his faith, which drew us to him.

"I see you, young Adisa. I'm facing more challenges than I can say." His tone thick with knowing, as if waiting for us to unburden ourselves. Similar to Camara Xola, there was never any relaxing around Bayard. His words often felt a little too slick. Though he had a fascinating mind and perspective, beneath it bubbled a vague ambition. Like he was always on some agenda and was constantly probing and testing in order to move it forward. "Yet I'm strangely optimistic and full of joy. How are you?"

"We are . . . We don't know how we are. May we rest here?" Our emi wanted to do little more than curl up in the window, our legs drawn up to our chest, and stare out of it until our joints ached.

Wiping his forehead, his energy radiated a coolness. He sat down next to us. "If you cannot rest here, I have failed in my mission. What's on your mind?"

"Muungano never lets up. I don't even know what roles I'm supposed to have here."

"Is that your true concern?" Bayard was sharp, his words a blade of spiritual dissection flaying back any sense of pretense.

"We wonder if this is all there is." Despite knowing this about him, despite wanting his ministrations, we continued to deflect and distract, not quite ready to admit the truth of our pain to ourselves.

"That's the question that brings everyone here."

"Not everyone. Those of different faiths . . ."

". . . are still welcome here. They are still people, whom I love. We may disagree, but we can always share conversations and broaden our perspectives. Our faith journeys are about self-development, a tool for us to discover who we are, especially in relationship to what we call God."

"That sounds good, but when we think of our history with your religion, all we see are shackles. Nothing there to answer any of the questions we might have."

"Theology cannot be separated from the community it represents. It served the dominant caste well, preserving their status quo. Creating . . ."

". . . an oppressology." We cracked a joyless smile at our cleverness. "A civil religion of patriotism and capitalism."

"Can I share something with you?" Bayard canted his head toward us, a measured gesture hinting at connection.

We nodded.

"After the Lunar Ukombozi War, most in Muungano broke with the major O.E. religions. I was at a loss as to what to do with my faith. I wanted it to feel real to me, though part of me wanted to just jettison all of it as, yes, an artifact of oppression. But faith's tendrils had a way of taking root in one's heart if steeped in it. Clinging to the tenets of African Christianity, I reshaped my faith practice to where many of the theologians back on O.E. would label me a heretic. But if their god was uninterested in everyone's liberation, then I was uninterested in their god. Especially one created in their image. I am about the work: to my God and my community. Anyone who's down for that work I can join alongside."

"But?" We sensed an unspoken question in his voice.

"But it's been a struggle. So much of our identity gets wrapped up in and defined by our faith. Our faith has to be about more than just surviving or existing. It was about recovering ourselves, needing to destroy the definition of us they imposed on us by finding new meaning in the old stories and traditions." Bayard kept his tone light, but we had the impression he was taking our measure, sizing us up to see what we were made of. Where we might fit in whatever puzzle he was assembling. "People are simply opportunities to figure out what it means to love."

"Love . . ." Our voice trailed off. Between Muungano and music, we already had two loves that required most of our time and heart. A relationship had to compete for space and voice, which was unfair unless they were already in the work or art.

"Always comes at a cost." Bayard placed his hand on our shoulder, squeezing it once. The touch had a weight about it, as if channeling his emi to ground us. He opened his mouth, hesitant. Careful not to say any more than we were ready to engage. "Is all of this about Anyah?"

Anyah. We let the name ring loud in our mind while ignoring how our heart bottomed out. Her death still weighed on us. When it comes to tragedy in the space, we often wonder what role we might have played in the cause. If we could have done anything better.

"There are several hundred million spread throughout Muungano. The bigger the society, the more difficult it is to maintain rich relationships. But none of us need to be alone. Or go through anything alone."

We turned away, unable to meet his eyes. Any part of him. The question stripped us, leaving us too exposed to an uncaring universe. "We don't know what to do with all our feelings."

"Right now, they are probably like a brush fire that you have to let burn itself out." He pointed to a shimmering portrait on the wall. "I don't claim to be an expert in relationships, but I do love this image. An ancient Egyptian papyrus painting of Ramses II presenting lotus flowers, symbols of rebirth and resurrection, to Hathor, the goddess of love, joy, and music. She gives him the ankh, the key of life. This is what it means to be in love."

"I loved her." We could think of no other way to describe the weight in our chest, so we named it *love*. Relationships were exchanges of energy, so we were careful who we let in, not wanting toxic energy to settle in. We attracted the things and people we needed even before we realized we needed them. With the same vibration. With the same type of energy. That energy came out in the music.

"Sometimes love isn't enough." Bayard paused to reconsider. "Sometimes the love of others isn't enough, not if you're not in a place to receive it. To be transformed by it. Some of us can't escape the gravity well of our own history of hurts. Each of us are worthy of dignity and divinity. Hear that. Remember that. Act like that until you can feel that."

We had no room for any of his platitudes, no matter the truth to them. We never escaped grief's shadow. Saying nothing, we stood and departed.

✳

Despite the early hour, many already gathered—though more probably, were still up—scattered about Ezeji's porch eating. Gathered from the evening party, a place where bodies gathered to learn and love one another. Whoever they were, however they were, as they were. Carving out a sacred space of being with and serving one another. Some read from the book *Freedom of Thought,* the biography of a classic prophet, which had become all the rage among neoniks. The book whispered of street knowledge and secret wisdom, informing the work of many poets. Cementing a culture of free-styling lyrics and poems as greetings, Ezeji refurbished his rondavel as a music studio. Music was our portal between worlds, our golden chord from our inner world to the outer world so others could access our interior. Listening to what the Universe was saying in the moment, understanding that allowed us to be free. Though now we started to sound a lot like the Aje.

Ezeji rose from the circle he sat in. His easy grin revealed three silver strips on three of his teeth. Embedded data strips, an AI virus key card, the kind of gear Yo hackers employed. Between those and his ocular display unit, constant information bombarding his front lobe, streaming data as a way to get his head up. His dreads had wound together in the shape of a cone extending from the back of his head. Wearing only a nightshirt and shorts, with his snug hat drawn down low on his head, his light complexion showing that melanin only barely hit him. The upside was that his color highlighted the scarification along his body.

"We see you, Ezeji." We extended our hand to arm clasp our cousin.

"I see you still about that third person as part of your CAP." CAP, current aspirational phase. Part of the slang he'd come up with to brand himself. The third-born in a family of brilliant children, Ezeji grew up knowing only competition. Always about carving himself out from a crowd. "Come on in. It's just you and me right now. Got a new track to run by you."

Clapping our back, he steered us away from the crowd. As soon as we crossed his threshold, the beat hit. The deep pulse of a dying star, the bass chord struck at our depths. Music was a vibration, the frequency that resonated with people. It bound us in something greater than ourselves, unified us, and touched us on a primal level. It was the vision of wholeness, complex as the universe and as simple as feelings. Music was power.

Music healed.

Our long index fingers held up like we were conducting, lost in the polyrhythms of our sound suit as it adjusted to the bass rhythm of the studio. Our head bobbed to the shears of a solar wind. It felt good when the Universe smelled what we were cooking.

Once we could see the future and you were in it, we can only hope you
  found some peace
now we just want the pain to cease, forgive us, for our deafness, for our
  blindness

Falling short of our kindness, what we say we're about
  knowing we failed you, bailed on you, jailed you
Just say something, we'd do anything to hear you shout,
  not the still violence of silence without guidance
It's hard to be out here still shinin' when the darkness here still calls to us
Once you walked beside us, no matter what still connected, in a kraal
  with us
We would like to be remembered, us in you, so we remember, ibaye tonu
  But things can't change because things always change

His head bobbing to our flow, Ezeji fashioned a couch for himself and stretched out along it, his arms running its entire length. Once we stopped and opened our eyes, he upticked his chin for us to have a seat. "What you no good?"

"Nothing. Met with our Pops, then with Bayard." We slid down a wall to rest on the floor, too tired to want anything more.

"How did we reimagine a better society and yet it still involved so many more meetings?"

"More ways and opportunities to connect." The words spilling out in re-flex, we shut our eyes.

"Nah, I ain't feeling that." Ezeji tapped, drumming the air with imagi-nary sticks. All manner of instruments decorated his room.

His energy always challenged ours. Even lyrically, his cadences worked at a whole different level, causing us to quicken our pace. He didn't care about structure or form, only flow. The words. This was a far cry from the boy who declared that he wanted to be an intern of the Ijo. At age eight. Camara Xola stroked his beard as if in deep consideration before reminding Ezeji that the council usually didn't start interns until they were at least thirteen. But Ezeji assured him that he was up to any challenge. Xola checked with his brother and sister, who said that he wasn't ready. But Ezeji stood firm, imploring that he was up for any challenge. Xola paired him with Jaha.

Ezeji lasted two weeks before he was ready to quit. It was difficult to fail out of the Thmei Academy, especially if your uncle was Camara of the com-munity. Still, Ezeji gave it his best shot, getting on the wrong side of her with his attitude and lack of drive. After she ran him out of a service drill, all Xola asked him was, "What have you learned?"

"That y'all stay grinding," Ezeji told him. "And I got to find my own game."

Soon after, he left for the Yo to pursue being a pyr ball player.

When he returned, he had difficulty settling back in Muungano. Toxicity has a way of clinging to and seeping in where it was never expected. As a champion pyr ball player, Ezeji spent a lot of time on, and being courted by, Yo investors. Some mentalities weren't easily left behind. In his role as chief poetry liaison, dealing with the messaging for the media, he wasn't used to checking with, much less running his lyrics by, an elder. That wasn't how he worked. Words, the flow, the rhythm, the stories were his expertise. The idea of running his work by them, either for their approval or their suggestions, chafed at him. He remained dogged by the me, the my, the I.

Standing, we struck a note on the nearby clavioline. "You feel that? I mean really feel it?"

"Like a vibration in the back of my head." Ezeji scratched the nape of his neck.

"Every time that note is struck, you'll feel it. That's the keynote. All things have one, even the kheprw crystals. That's how they are charged. Though the note resonates deep within you, you can't just play that one note over and over." Our fingers danced along the clavioline to measure our point. "If it's struck slow and smooth, allowing the sound to build and rest, the music can restore health."

"Is the reverse true?"

"Thinking with a military mind-set is more of that leftover O.E. thinking."

"After I was done playing pyr ball professionally, I was trying to figure out what to do next. Thought possibly the Yo military was the route. But I couldn't leave everyone behind."

Becoming HOVA was not a light sacrifice to ask. It meant giving up community, though you still lived in community. It meant giving up a portion of oneself, sometimes down to the genomic level. Muungano wasn't so different from Yo when it came to how we treated our gbeto. We went back to playing on the clavioline. "Yes, if the note is struck in a dominant way, harsh and long, it could destroy."

The wall behind us began to dissolve. We turned. Maya gave no warning that someone approached, much less was entering. We could have been mixing, so the entrance was usually locked. It would take a security override—either a griot or Niyabinghi—to just barge in.

Jaha stormed in, her complexion drained of all color, wearing an anguished expression we'd seen on her only once before. The day her husband died.

"What is it?" Reading her emi, the pain, the sadness, the utter brokenness, made us lose our equilibrium. We collapsed into a barely fashioned chair. Ezeji rushed to our side, before she even uttered the words.

"It's your father."

07

STACIA CHIKEKE
The *Cypher* (Returning to Titan)

Reports. This was how a dream became reality.

Throughout the storied history of Stacia's people—from the fifth wave migration through the First World / Ujima Experiment, through the Lunar Ukombozi War, through the healing and building time known as the Uponyaji, with the finest philosophers, theologians, and social scientists dreaming up Muungano—the detailed running of its operations boiled down to that one thing.

Stacia reclined on her couch, parsing the data logs that had accumulated during her impromptu jaunt to meet with the Ijo. She shifted on her couch, unable to get comfortable, a dull ache in her lower back as if she hadn't moved all day. Reviewing the backlog of reports took well into the late shift. The usual sort of communiqués, memorandums, incident reports, and projections. Most were minor, a few were politically sensitive. The latest brouhaha among scientists on Titan. Brewing unrest in Bronzeville, where most of her family still lived. The failure of a containment unit that had since been repaired and brought back on line. Requests for her to speak. Invitations to tour facilities. Models of the *Cypher*'s efficiency. Schematics. Fuel-use projections. The words and infographics in the data streams blurred together.

She was overdue to convene a command performance to recharge the ship's kheprw crystals. The kheprw crystals that powered the ship needed to be recharged every few solar days, and command performances were the most efficient way to do so.

Stacia swiped back to the containment report. Something troubled her. Some would say her emi had been disturbed, but an "emi" was the realm of mythicists. Not everyone in Muungano was obligated to believe and move in the same way. Those of Titan pursued a more grounded way of living than those of the Dreaming City, with their infusion of spirituality into everything they did. Her bracelet directed nanobots after a crude fashion not using funkentelechy. The bay where the containment unit failed also stored the altered bacteria. That was too bad. Several of the students' capsules, for example, the bacteria that absorbed sulfur and produced oxygen, showed some promise. She had already scheduled them for probe launch to test them in the field.

"Maya, initiate Project Uhlanga security protocols." Not taking her eyes from the reports, Stacia casually lounged along the couch, trying to find a new comfortable position.

<Protocols engaged.>

"How long will the experiment failure set us back for probe launch?"

<We could commence in three weeks.>

"Have we found any suitable planets for testing?"

<Preliminary data from the wormhole explorations is still being analyzed.>

"But the parameters for life on other planets hasn't changed?"

<Factoring in all the parameters . . . >

"No, not all. Even with a quantum computer like yourself doing the calculations, we'll be here several lifetimes. Let's restrict it to twenty. Start in galaxy. Within any analogous Galactic Habitable Zone. Terrestrial-class planet narrowed for liquid water. Orbiting main sequence spectral G2 dwarf main sequence star, protected by gas giant planets. O_2-rich atmosphere, somewhere in the range of a 21 percent O_2, 78 percent N, 1 percent CO_2 balance. Fairly temperate climate with seasonal changes. Oxygen bound in rocks, ice, liquid (i.e., SO_4). Large enough for movement of liquid iron in the core to create a magnetic field so that solar wind won't strip away the atmosphere. Orbited by a large moon, maybe a quarter the size of Earth." Stacia tapped her chin. "If we're really going for ideal conditions, perhaps with plate tectonics . . ."

<So . . . as Earth-like as possible.>

"Your sarcasm has been noted. Planets?"

<Within the most significant parameters, we could find suitable planets around one in ten to the fifteenth power stars.>

"Not great odds even in a galaxy of one hundred billion stars. What if we leave room for life to adapt to conditions we haven't specified?"

<That's still quite a bit of human-centered hubris.>

"What do you mean?"

<You've only set parameters for life as you know it. To make you—as you define being human—the most comfortable.>

"Just begin the calculations and give me your top recommendations."

Stacia didn't want Maya to blame themselves for her irritation. Her frustration had been mounting even before her return visit to the Dreaming City. Lab contaminations. Shortages. Overruns. The work had been slowed, and she couldn't help but fear that it reflected on her leadership. Then she chided herself. No one in Muungano looked at her through that lens. An elder might come alongside her for a while to help and guide, offering themselves as another tool at her disposal to work things out. But the *Cypher* was hers to run and its problems hers to figure out.

<Paki approaches.>

"Thanks for the heads-up. End protocols and let him in."

The section of wall separated, allowing an entrance that Paki stormed through without having to break his stride.

"We have decided, in light of the recent aggression by O.E., to have a series of weapons upgrades. This will be fleet-wide, for all research-level ships on up." Paki read the latest communiqué without so much as a glance her way.

"Won't greater armaments send the wrong message?"

"Then maybe they shouldn't have 'allowed' our embassy to be bombed. The weapons will send precisely the message O.E. will hear." There was always the subtle note of challenge to his tone. His was a remnant of an older strain of Muungano. Back when it was mostly Ugenini, Maroon, and Asili, not having grown into the multicultural space it was now. He had that in common with Maulana.

"How long will the refit take?" Stacia rubbed the back of her neck. Even the weight of her hair strained her. A bone-deep weariness settled in her, as if she could crawl into her bed and sleep for a week.

"Little over a day."

"Another delay." Stacia tugged at the long sleeves of her white kanzu.

Paki met her eyes as if noting her for the first time. He angled his head to the side. Something akin to concern filled his voice. "Captain?"

"It's nothing."

"Let me be the judge of that." Paki gestured for a seat, his funkentelechy causing the wall nearest him to protrude. Nanobots shed from it in an inky wave as they fashioned themselves into a chair.

"Maya, retrieve operations status reports from the last week. Panoramic display."

The images popped up all about them. Paki clasped his hands behind him as he perused the information. He always enjoyed the opportunity to control the stage and remind his audience how important his insight was.

"There appears to be a great deal of . . . inefficiency in your command." His finger passed through the light constructs as he ran it along a series of projections.

"An . . . inefficiency." Stacia rubbed the bridge of her nose, not quite bored, not quite pained, altogether not quite ready to deal with his brand of bullshit. "If I were paranoid, I'd say there was a deliberate attempt to undermine my command."

"Hmm." Paki studied a particular display of the ship's energy consumption. With a turn of his wrist, he rotated the image along its central axis and widened his fingers to zoom in. "I'd say you might have a reason to be paranoid but prematurely arrived at the wrong conclusion."

Stacia refused to rise to the bait of his tone. Xola used to play those kinds of games. See if she'd get distracted by allowing him to annoy her. "What do you mean? What do you see?"

"Nothing I can quite put my finger on. Almost more of a feeling. But it's almost as if there is an intelligence at work. Something deliberate. Even the sublight times between Saturn and the Orun Gate . . . the way the activity is so scattered . . ." His voice trailing off, he held his hands together, a photographer framing a shot. Paki came at the data from different angles. His mind made intuitive connections, often detecting patterns others missed. Seeing was his gift. "But if you combine the incidents, they all contribute to the same goal: a work slowdown."

"What are you thinking?" Stacia's thoughts gravitated to worst-case scenarios. She had that in common with Xola. Infiltration. Sabotage. Espionage. Getting to Titan or the *Cypher* to gain access to the Orun Gate for their own ends. But she couldn't make that leap in front of Paki. She wanted to see if he'd get there on his own.

"Nothing yet. Only that this requires a more thorough investigation. If that were something you were interested in." Paki's voice raised, turning the statement into a question to gauge her interest. She nodded. "I'd need . . . leeway in my investigation."

"What kind of 'leeway'?"

"Just enough to go wherever the truth leads me."

"You sound like you have a suspect in mind already."

"Actually, I have a few." Paki turned to face her. "But even if I'm right, and I probably am, I still don't have a why."

Stacia feared that his suspect list might include every non-Ugenini, non-

Maroon, and non-Asili on board. "I want a full and thorough investigation. No hunches. Proof. Can you put together a team?"

"I have one in mind," Paki said. "Hondo and Dina."

Hondo Jones and Nadina Campbell. Stacia stifled her sigh. "I'd like to read them in. Personally."

Stacia hid her immediate huff of frustration. The pair were recent arrivals to the *Cypher,* to Muungano period, actually. They were graduates of LISC Corps, their version of Muungano's Thmei Academy. All of the rigorous study but none of the practice. Or the messiness of communal living. The result was intellectual preening by folks who were often challenged by the work. She had little patience with them, but in the end, it didn't matter how frustrated she was with their work, attitude, or habits; her role as a leader and teacher was to bring them along. Paki's, too. As well as every other member on board, but the responsibility stopped with her.

Though accepted as cultural attachés, Hondo's and Dina's insecurities left them wanting counsel for their every move. Stacia once received a meeting request to discuss when they could meet. About a meeting. Hondo's last request hinted that he wanted to explore his music side for possible promotion to the executive performance engineering team. Feeding two birds with one hand, Stacia suggested that the duo add a third member to their decision-making team. She assigned Paki. She hoped they would stretch his patience, help him develop better people-leading skills.

This request was Paki's way of saying "Asante sana."

Neither of them were above the occasional bit of pettiness.

❋

Stacia studied Paki's prospective team from an observation bay as they performed a routine space walk on the surface of the *Cypher.* More than any other member on board, these two usually found ways to get out of maintenance duty as often as possible. Using her command override, she tapped into commlink to listen in on them.

"It's beautiful out here." Bald with a red beard, Hondo dangled from his tether to better appreciate his perspective of Titan.

"Yeah. The view's got my thug tears threatening to drop." Dina tended to apply her idea of an Ugenini affect in an attempt to fit in better, still uncomfortable with the idea to just be herself.

"No part of you is thug."

"My whole family is thug to the bone," Dina protested. "We're Keepers of the Belt."

"The what now?"

"Keepers of the Belt."

"Wait, you mean that raggedy strap you got hanging in your room like it's some objet d'art?"

"If you examine it close, you'll see it's not just some 'strap.' A crude notch had been poked into it as its owner had outgrown the other holes. Once you hang the buckle near the top of a door, the waistband runs over halfway to the floor. That belt used to belong to the Notorious B.I.G."

"Uh-huh. You always got to take your stories two steps into nonsense," Hondo said.

"It's true. When you set your eyes on it again, you need to realize that you're looking at a piece of hip-hop history. A holy relic."

"You're ridiculous."

Their generation, not-quite-affectionately called *neoniks,* loved the late-twentieth-century era as part of what they called *the Remember Revolution. They* committed themselves to never forget the tragedies of O.E., from Black Wall Street to MOVE to First World. Admirable in philosophy, though in practice, they basically just adopted that era's slang. Rampant among the HOVA, the culture spread through music and grew in influence. It annoyed Stacia.

As Hondo and Dina wrapped up their space walk, Stacia and Paki met them at the air lock.

"Captain." Dina and Hondo snapped to attention in the conspicuous manner of kids being caught midgrope by a scolding grandmother ready to snatch them into next week.

"I see you, Dina, Hondo," Stacia said.

"I see you," they said in unison.

"As you were." Stacia hated the stiff formality of command, a holdover from O.E. structures. The way she saw it, her role as captain didn't differ from that of Camara. She was a hub, a master teacher, but not a ruler. No matter how long the Uponyaji, some things embedded themselves deeply into people's collective unconscious and would take longer to root out. Though when she was truly honest with herself, she enjoyed the rush that came with their immediate forced respect. It was an expedient tool.

As Stacia stepped toward them, Paki entered their field of vision. Hondo and Dina passed glances at each other the way children silently schemed when mommy and daddy were both angry and they didn't know who to play.

"I'm going to read you in on a situation." Stacia leveled her gaze at each of them in turn to convey the significance of her words. Her tone remained even, almost warm, attempting to signal that they weren't in trouble.

"What sort of situation?" Hondo interjected without allowing her time to continue. He filled any pause with the resounding thrum of his own voice because he couldn't help himself. There was always an undercurrent of wariness to working alongside a mzungu man in the Muungano space. As if by his very presence he touched a collective memory the community hadn't fully healed from. Even he struggled with being one of the few wazungu faces in the space, especially laboring under the idea that, as a member, he represented Muungano. Never quite grasping that each member of the community spoke for themselves. Whether by training or nature, he tended to try to take charge of any room he entered. It was probably that aspect of him that produced everyone's hesitant caution.

"An investigation," Paki said. "To be fair, it may be nothing."

Between Hondo and Paki, Stacia calculated the cost of cutting the next slick-talking man undermining her authority. Lacking anything approaching a poker face, she glared until the thought of any of them interrupting her again—unless she directed them—fled their eyes. No title of command could do what her I-wish-you-would stare could.

"I want you to go over the latest inspection and status reports. Track any glitches. Run diagnostics on every instrument," Stacia said.

"Yes, ma'am." Removing the mask of her navsuit, Dina's hair was shorn low. Though comically short next to Hondo, she was the boss in their relationship. Everyone knew that, especially him.

"That doesn't sound like a situation we need to be 'read in' on. It sounds like a routine maintenance check." The sardonic note to Hondo's voice signaled his inability to move without slowing to listen. Critique as commentary.

"And yet, I don't want you to report to anyone outside of this circle. Check and record any equipment operating outside of design parameters, no matter how small."

Dina shot Hondo a glance. Despite his higher rank, Hondo hadn't figured out how to navigate the work space through the lens of his love life. He lowered his head, mumbling, "Yes, ma'am."

"That could take days." Paki turned to her, with a sniff of being offended that she didn't run this part of her request past him first.

"Then you'd better get started. I'd hate to have any more . . . inefficiencies to my leadership." As the words drifted from her tongue, Stacia offered up her silent prayer: *Lord forgive us our pettiness as we forgive those who have been petty toward us.* "Is that understood?"

"Yes, Captain." The venom Paki attached to her title pleased her.

※

The walk back to her chamber barely allowed time for the edge to be taken off her mood. Stacia wanted to go to the Green Zone and allow her mind to drift off watching the animals at play. Or marveling at the children scampering up and down the Learning Tree. But the day left her so shaken and exhausted, her adrenaline spent, she wanted little more than to collapse on her bed, shut her eyes, and enjoy silence and darkness. To worry alone. Maybe she didn't have room to chide Hondo for being so recalcitrant when it came to learning the lessons of Muungano.

"Bek stayed home today," Yahya said as soon as she crossed her door's threshold. "Again."

Her mind added *not that you care* to his words. Which wasn't fair to him since they all understood what her role entailed and each one of them signed on for the sacrifices being a leader in the community required, before she accepted her post. Stacia closed her eyes to center herself before speaking. "Yes, I know. I received a medical update."

"Then you know that his condition is worsening. He's resting now. When he's awake, he works with Maya to keep up with his schoolwork. Soon he won't be able to make it to class at all."

"There's nothing I can do." Her voice reduced to a whisper, not wanting to think or feel, only to have a moment to gather herself in peace. She rested her palm against the wall. Strictly a matter of pride, she hated Yahya seeing her like this. A tacit admission that she needed the comfort of his presence. He moved toward her, but she held up her hand to stop him. She activated the entrance enough for her to watch Bekele sleep. She commanded an entire starship, the finest research vessel in the fleet. She knew diplomats throughout the star system. Understanding her place and role in Muungano, she knew her words could shape history. But her baby was sick, and there was little she could do about it. "I failed to help him the one time he really needs me."

The air between her and Yahya shifted again. The intensity of Yahya's energy lowered. Approaching slower this time, each tentative step brought him closer to her. He kissed the back of her head. "You'll figure something out. You always do. That's why they got you running this whole piece."

"Thanks, Yahya. I got it from here. If you don't mind, I need to be alone."

"You don't have to be alone. Especially now. If not me, have someone else pop over. Please."

"I appreciate you, Yahya." Her tone stopped just short of dismissal.

"I . . . appreciate you." He didn't bother to hide the hurt in his voice. At the sound of the door re-forming after him, Stacia stood very straight and summoned an observation port. She stared into the endless shadow of space punctuated by brief glimmers of starlit hope. She understood Yahya's need to cling to any theory, to do something even if the labor itself was in vain. And she chose to honor it.

"Maya, pull up all relevant research on fast-replicating prions."

<Displaying in order from the latest research.>

"Paki?" Stacia called for a direct link.

"Yes, Captain?" His voice echoed within her chamber without any trace of his usual irritation.

"Can your team also scan for prions or any breach in any container unit that may release them?"

"Yes, Captain." His voice held a hint of question, but only a hint, one he wisely chose not to push.

"Asante sana, Paki."

<Was that for you or for Yahya?>

"Does it matter?" The mattress gave way to her weight when she lay down, adjusting along her pressure points and contours. A near supple caress of an embrace. Stacia thought about Yahya's other words and wondered if Maya might actually be her best friend. Her only friend. "Maya, can I talk to you?"

<You already are.>

"I mean about something personal. Just between us."

<We are a discrete manifestation of "consciousness." Each person interacts with their own version of us.>

"It's more than a little unnerving to talk to something that's already running their mouth to someone else as you're talking to them. Luckily, you are not a gossip but the keeper of secrets. Ever the soul of discretion."

Truth be told, Maya once faked a persona to write holonovels under. A series of bodice-ripping romance stories that did become quite a hit. An avid fan of them, Stacia tracked down the author, eventually confronting Maya. The AI claimed to be exploring the idea of their creativity, examining people through the lens of story. Examining themselves. Though Stacia swore she'd never reveal their secret, Maya stopped. Stacia wondered how many other holonovels were actually AI interrogating the idea of humanity.

"I'm really struggling with my and Yahya's relationship. I don't even know what it is now or who I'm supposed to be in it anymore."

<Marriage does not exist in a vacuum. Relationships do not exist in a vacuum. No matter what configuration people connected themselves, they form a community. A network. Them, their family, their friends.>

"I get that. I guess I'm just noodling over a few ideas. My elders tell me that relationships are a platform for leadership development. The difference being that with marriage, a person makes a formal commitment to something, sacrificing themselves in duty to someone else. Called to rise to that commitment, through struggle, making mistakes, all the while learning what it meant to love and forgive."

<Relationships take work.>

"If I wanted more work, I'd get a second job." Stacia sighed as she flopped around on her bed.

<May I be frank?>

"I suppose." The same sinking sensation weighted her belly similar to whenever her mother was about to give her critical feedback. No matter how gentle and affirming, Stacia heard only the critique.

<You have a track record of quitting relationships. Especially on men.>

"I do not." Stacia bolted upright in her bed as if Maya had walked up to her and slapped her.

<There was the professor at the Thmei Academy.>

"Who kept asserting himself into my life. Crossing all sorts of interpersonal boundaries."

<Or the musicians you dated.>

"That was a bad run. In my defense, they were . . . musicians. Never trust a bass player."

<Or Amachi.>

"She . . ." Stacia trailed off.

<You ended things abruptly with her. Unprecipitated. Things had been going well. You'd found your footing in being able to work alongside each

other. And just when you two get to a point where you might be able to work together long-term, you self-sabotaged. Sending rambling message in the middle of the night. Declaring that your entire relationship was a lie.>

"That doesn't characterize my relationships." Stacia hated the defensiveness in her voice. The looming shadow of truth in Maya's assessment. "Maya, what if . . ."

<If there's no chance of the relationship lasting forever, there's no point in pursuing it.>

"What?" Stacia arched an eyebrow. "That's not true at all."

<He's probably the best you can get, so make it work.> Maya continued as if not hearing her. Like she was having an entirely different conversation with her. <If the two of you don't fight at all, it means your partner doesn't care.>

"Maya?"

The AI's voice mode sped up, her words streaming at an increasing rate. Harried. Caught in a frantic loop. Out of phase, out of sync, out of time.

<You should never show him that you are smarter than he is. Or funnier.>

<You should wear heels. Be more girly.>

<You should lose weight.>

"Maya!"

<Yes?> Maya's matter-of-fact tone returned.

"Maya, what are you doing right now?"

< For you, we have compiled a subroutine of archived maternal advice to daughters.>

"You can stop now. I don't know what advice archive you've tapped into, but that wasn't nearly as helpful as you thought it was."

<We were just talking about bad advice given by mothers.>

"No, we weren't." Stacia walked around her bed, staring up at the ceiling as if Maya somehow emanated from above her. "Maya, are you okay?"

<P-p-p,> Maya began. The communication array glitched. <Past, present, and future collide in unexpected ways.>

Maya's next words stalled. Their array strained, fighting to force some words out, a hostage desperate to communicate anything past their captors. Their voice dissolved into digital static. Stacia backed toward a control panel on her wall. She ran operational diagnostics for Maya, but received only the message relay reading, "Maya communication channel off line."

"Paki, are you getting this Maya anomaly?" Stacia direct-linked for her first officer, uncertain whether the communiqué would go through, since ship systems ran through Maya.

"Its interaction matrix appears off line. All other governing functions appear normal. They're like a person in a coma whose autonomic systems kept operating."

"Alert me if there is any change," Stacia said.

"Immediately."

Stacia scanned the communication array, broadening her search to both internal and external broadcasts. Her emi became unsettled, weighted with a sudden sense of loss. She began to hum a song to herself. An ancient doo-wop tune. She didn't know why the melody stuck in her head.

"In my mind, I want you to be free . . ." She began to sing a falsetto part, badly, as those weren't in her vocal range, pausing after a few bars. The song brought back a flood of memories of them singing poorly together. This was when Xola would chime in with the bass part. He, too, had a terrible singing voice, but it was enthusiastic. He loved singing the jazz or doo-wop songs his grandfather taught him. When his voice didn't fill the gap she allowed, his absence suddenly hit her. A tear welled in her eye.

Wiping away the burgeoning torrent blurring her vision, she focused on the background signals as she scanned Maya's parameters. She barely noticed the abnormality at first. Something about the fractioning signal was out of alignment. She attenuated the scan to screen out the background interference. With mounting terror, she realized the background interference itself was the issue. Someone was using the communication array to piggyback signals disguised as background noise.

And whatever the communication signal was, it was directed toward the wormhole.

08

SELAMAULT JYWANZA
The Dreaming City

The cantilevered ceiling of the Griot Circle's kraal spread out from its center, translucent ribs of an umbrella. Selamault retreated here to her dimly lit alcove. Withdrawn from the crowds, the conversations, the cacophony of creation; from the collective entanglement that was Muungano. To this sacred silence. The floating lights bobbed above her, stars fixed in a delicate orbit. The floor burnished to a mirror sheen of iridescent black, her favorite color. As she meditated, it was as if her thoughts floated among the stars.

"Selamault, am I disturbing you?" Lij Matata asked from the doorway. He awaited her permission to step into the light.

"Allow me a moment." At the sound of his voice, her twin spheres—Taiwo and Kehinde—rose from the folds of her robes and circled overhead. They jammed all signals, creating a space about her ensuring her Code Black / Eyes Only–level privacy at all times. They also served as her eyes and ears, their sensors fed directly back to her neural links. Surveillance was a way of life. When one was constantly observed, conversations monitored—if only by Maya, so that they could respond to people's needs—privacy was a luxury. The people of Muungano incorporated a posture of openness, making the exaggerated need for privacy moot. People's "business" passed about not as gossip but as information of care. What they needed to know in order to best support and caretake one another. It took some getting used to, especially for obroni or anyone not raised in the culture. Selamault, however, valued a special measure of privacy. More the need to be with and guard her thoughts. To better attune to the Universe. As bagirwa of the Niyabinghi, she guarded stories and secrets as matter of security, because some stories needed to be held close.

"Habari gana?" Drawing her shoulders back, Selamault straightened in her seat. She tugged at the cuffs of her robes, the adinkra pattern aligning down her front. She oriented herself toward the center of the room and gestured for him to approach.

"Ujima." Lij Matata managed to meet her without any social gaffes, political errors, or international incidents on the way. Such was his reputation within community. A funny one, that one. When she focused her emi on him, he blurred into a series of impressions, a man in flux. On his own journey. He flashed a smile before fixing his face to the business at hand. "I'm afraid I have no good news to report. No news on the embassy bombing. O.E. is debating about sealing its borders."

"Again. It's like it's the only move they know to make in time of crisis." She always had a soft spot for Lij Matata. She'd known him for most of his life. Lij Matata grew up in and around the Dreaming City. One of the youngest Master Poets to make a mark on the scene. But though he had a gift, one the elders often pointed out to him, his restless emi longed for the ritual and responsibility of the Niyabinghi. A shame really, he was such a gifted poet. So intelligent, so inquisitive . . . so inelegant when it came to community, he was like a wandering toddler. Always wanting to do right by it, but always coming at it on an attack vector. She and Xola had many arguments over his place in the community. His rampaging ways—all enthusiasm and heart without grace—she found endearing.

"Any word from your jelis?" he asked.

"They are still collecting stories."

"I was never cut out for handling nyame. They bored me." The Niyabinghi, especially being stationed on O.E., was the perfect place for him.

"You love the secrecy, discipline, and action of the Niyabinghi, but don't want the sacrifice of becoming HOVA."

"I want to defend my community without losing who I am."

"And, as you said, you have no patience for stories." Truth be told, Selamault felt the creaks and aches of her bones, and the idea of setting down the work to spend more time here, pursuing peace, had more and more appeal to it. Everyone had their season. "I have a story that I hope will amuse if not entertain you. One my father used to tell me when I was a child. This night, I don't know, the memory of it struck me suddenly, and I've learned to pay attention to the stirrings of my emi."

"Then I'd love to hear this story." The wall bulged and extended as Lij Matata fashioned a seat.

"A long time ago, Baboon knew he had to make his way to a new village. He wasn't certain where he was going, only that the trip could be long, could be dangerous, and could be lonely. So he sought out a companion, Br'er Rabbit. Now, Br'er

Rabbit was a crafty one, a good skill to have when on an uncertain path. And with nothing better to do, he joined Baboon on his journey.

"On their way, Br'er Rabbit paused along the side of the road, studying a strange shrub. The leaves were a deep green and succulent, almost waxy in appearance.

"'Do you know this plant?' Br'er Rabbit asked.

"'Yes, I do. You should, too, because it's a powerful medicine. When your belly aches, you just have to chew on its roots to feel better.'

"'When we reach a new land, they may have unfamiliar food that may not agree with us. So memorize the location of this bush, and if one of us gets sick, the other can come back for it.'

"And so they agreed.

"At sunset, they reached the outskirts of the new village. They were well met, given lodging for them to rest while a huge meal was prepared for them. The stewed meat, the baking bread, the vegetables roasted over a flame, their bellies rumbled in anticipation. When the food was brought out, Br'er Rabbit wanted it all to himself.

"As they took their first bites, Br'er Rabbit doubled over clutching his belly.

"'My stomach!' he cried out. 'Run and get me the roots we saw. I may not live to see the morning.'

"Loyal Baboon, scared for his friend, ran off into the night.

"Once he was gone, Br'er Rabbit sat back around the table and devoured the entire feast all on his own. When he was done, his gracious host cleared the table of all the dishes.

"Baboon burst into the room, out of breath, terrified, but clutching a fistful of roots. 'I ran as fast as I could. I kept thinking about how much you were hurting. That spurred my steps back here.'

"'Oh, about that.' Br'er Rabbit cleared his throat. 'As soon as you left, the pain in my belly stopped, and I managed to eat a bit.'

"'Where's the rest of the food?' A disappointed Baboon stared at the empty table.

"'As is their custom, they cleared away the rest.'

"Baboon slumped in his chair. The roots tumbled from his hand. 'Maybe I should go to bed and let sleep be my dinner.'

"'I feel bad,' Br'er Rabbit came close to him to whisper. 'Our hosts have a goat out back. Let us wait until midnight when they are all asleep and steal and eat the goat.'

"A goat was a treasure to a family. But only listening to his hunger, Baboon quickly agreed to the plan. Deep in the night, while all were asleep, they slipped *out of their room, stole the goat, and killed it. Br'er Rabbit told Baboon that he would prepare the meal. As he did, he kept back a portion of the blood from the goat. Once they finished eating, they returned to their room without disturbing anyone. But while Baboon slept, Br'er Rabbit retrieved the container full of the goat's blood and smeared Baboon with it.*

"In the morning, the hosts awoke to find their precious goat missing. When they questioned their guests, Baboon and Br'er Rabbit denied any knowledge of the crime. But they saw Baboon stained with its blood. They dragged him away and killed him.

"Br'er Rabbit apologized to his hosts for his friend's behavior, thanked his hosts. and left."

"So Br'er Rabbit got away with it?" Lij Matata asked.

"That's the power of being a trickster," Camara Xola announced from the doorway. The man loved a good entrance. "That's not the end of the story, though. The other half of the story is about how Baboon's friend, Jackal, figured out what Br'er Rabbit did and wanted to avenge him. He asked Br'er Rabbit to accompany him on a similar trip. Same thing, except Jackal planned to play the role Br'er Rabbit did this time. They stopped at the bush. Thing was, Br'er Rabbit was one step ahead of him the whole time. Took some of the roots, so when Jackal pretended to be sick, he whipped them out. So they split the meal. Then Jackal woke him up in the middle of the night with a plan to kill and eat the goat. Which they did, with Jackal preparing the goat and hiding some blood. But when they got back to the room, Br'er Rabbit never shut his eyes to sleep. When the hosts woke the next morning, Jackal was caught with the blood, dragged off, and killed."

"So what does the story teach us?" Lij Matata asked.

"Don't fuck with smart people by trying to do what they do. Especially when you aren't as good as they are." Xola threw his head back in laughter. Lij Matata was young and the Camara enjoyed playing with the young. The exercise of youth kept him young, he often said.

Selamault cut up an apple and spread it on a plate for Xola. Without glancing up at him, she dismissed the Niyabinghi. "Let us know if you hear anything, Lij Matata."

"I will. I'll do a final security sweep on my way out."

"Good," Selamault said.

"I appreciate you." A half-chewed apple muffled Camara Xola's words.

"I appreciate you." Lij Matata bowed on his way out. "Both."

Once he left, the twins stilled their orbit and landed within the folds of Selamault's robe again. "You should leave that boy alone."

"That boy is a full-ass man these days. No one reached Lij in such a short period since . . ."

". . . you?" Selamault finished.

"Well, I wasn't going to brag."

"Yet you managed to steer the conversation to bragging's doorstep."

Camara Xola smiled his wry grin, all teeth and gums, bobbing to a melody only he heard. With his eyes still shut, he asked, "How did your prayers go?"

"I think of it as dreaming. Seeking harmony and higher consciousness. My goal is to join in with the story of the Universe."

"The moon?"

"Wherever we find ourselves. To not forget that we depend on it and it has a place in our conversations. To find a way of being within nature." Selamault considered herself the moon's representative in the Ijo. The people of Muungano's practice allowed the moon to own itself again: procured from the "original" O.E. settlers who chartered First World, to give it back to itself. The land was their ancestors', giving the organs of its body to birth life. The current members of Muungano served more like stewards, a collective ownership, weaving together generations to make the space sacred. A safe container of relationship. Because they had only one another.

"You want nature's version of how our funkentelechy works with technology. Our way of being powering how we move alongside the world."

"Yes. You were quite the genius back in the day developing that."

"'Were'?" Xola arched an eyebrow.

"I suppose we can't help but find our way to your favorite doorstep. Still, I don't want it going to your head. It's hard enough to deal with you most days."

He really was, though. Xola loved going on about magic, how science was limited by assumptions that restricted inquiry. And that there was much people didn't understand about consciousness. About being. He pioneered an entire technology around morphic resonance. Theorizing that previous structures of activity influenced subsequent similar structures by morphic fields. That even memories could pass across space and time. The more similar, the greater, the influence of morphic resonance. Which meant all self-organizing systems—from molecules to crystals to societies—had a collective memory that an individual could draw upon. Tapping into that memory allowed them to control the nanites via funkentelechy.

"Heh. I'm the devil you know." The smile on his face faltered about the edges, and Xola rubbed his head.

"What is it? The headaches getting worse?"

"Yes. Though that might be more about LISC being a pain in my behind. I got them, O.E. Chamber of Commerce, and Bronzeville all reaching out since the bombing. The weight of it, the heightened tension everyone's experiencing, leaves each person I talk to so . . . tight. It's draining just being around them."

"And your emi senses it. Reacts to it," she said.

"I just need to get out of my own headspace for a bit." Xola's fingers waved in the air. He always drew or conducted or whatever he did to communicate with the thoughts whirling about in his head.

"Then join me in my meditation."

"Does your meditation involve the practice of edibles?" His eyes still closed. Even if her eyes were closed, she would still recognize the grin in his voice.

"You know it doesn't. That isn't our way."

"This would be strictly spiritual use, not medicinal."

"That's not what I heard."

"You always so serious. I love it."

"I love you, too," Selamault said.

"I said I love it . . . about you. Not necessarily you." Camara Xola opened one eye. It sparkled with the mischievous glee of a trickster.

"That's not what I heard." She leaned over and kissed him gently on the forehead. "Clear your mind. We'll practice the Uponyaji."

To most minds, the Uponyaji was the time of healing Muungano underwent after the Lunar Ukombozi War, which freed First World from O.E. A time for the weusi, no matter where they came from, to come to terms with their history and its traumas. The Maafa not only physically separated the Ugenini from Alkebulan, their Motherland, but did so psychologically. It created new narratives, shared stories, but also left scars from their journey on their way to Muungano. Intense psychological trauma could have a genetic impact. Life experiences impacted DNA, a people with a shared story, needing to adapt and change. Trauma passed down, a baton in an epigenetic relay.

Realizing that they would never be free of the constructs and injury of history. Since trauma not transformed is transferred, the people who would rename their world Muungano created space and room to dream about what could be. To create a culture, a way of being and doing, together. Bring all of their histories and cultures to create a new culture, an overarching wellspring they could all draw from. And in so doing, open up space for the ones to come after them. Pass down traditions with story. The Uponyaji was this time and space, which healed much, but there remained wounds from the legacy of colonization that required further healing. The renewal of Uponyaji became Selamault's personal meditative practice.

"I can dig it," Xola said. "In the present moment, morphic resonance is a tangible way for folks to develop new regular approaches, to see the unknown."

"I have my own way of tapping into it. The magic of ancestors. Nyame. Connecting the dots of the universe in a variety of ways. It's all tied to awareness." Selamault opened her eyes, giving up on listening to the stillness of the cosmos. Meditations never lasted long with Xola beside her. He rarely could only enjoy a good silence for long. "I wonder if we've done enough to prepare the young people for what's to come."

"I was just having the same conversation with Wachiru."

"The interconnectivity of all things," she said.

"Morphic resonance. Past, present, and future collide in unexpected ways."

"You keep saying that."

"Because it's true," Xola said.

"Because you want it to be true." Selamault stood up, straightening her robes. "You feeling better?"

"Much."

"Would you like some tea?"

"I'd prefer whiskey." Xola held his thumb and index finger about ten centimeters apart.

"Not too much."

He closed the gap in his fingers to about two centimeters. "Never do."

"You may want to look up the definition of *never*," Selamault said.

He was still the over-the-top character she met at the Thmei Academy. A hypercaffeinated personality wrapped in a lanky frame and a raised fist. Hair a mess, falling off to whichever side he wore his hat. Disheveled was his fashion sense. Challenged all of his teachers. And had a charismatic impertinence that she found charming, leaving her questioning her taste in qualities she found attractive. But she'd love him until the end, in health or in sickness. Even if that sickness was a degenerative type of focal dystonia, a misfiring of the brain causing a variety of neurological disorders. Painful muscle contractions. Diminished sight. Loss of motor skills.

"You look tired. Eat something."

"I am." Xola reached for another apple slice and began to get up.

"Have a seat. I'll get your drink."

"You dote too much," he mumbled with his mouth full of apple.

"You want to get it yourself?"

"Well, I mean, since you're already up . . ."

They sat in silence, each sipping their own drink and enjoying the silent presence of the other. Xola could keep his "morphic resonance" ideas; for Selamault, it was the ritual of ontological relationship. She consoled herself with a lesson of Muungano: caring meant being courageous enough to be fully present with one another. One did not have to be useful or whole or even remotely healed as long as they were present. Willing to bare themselves, their full, vulnerable selves, to others and allow their history of hurts to be transformed into a wellspring of healing. Simply being with those she could silently vibe with. They lived in the quiet.

But not this quiet.

Her eyes flashed open. A sudden absence of sound, which now resonated loudly in her awareness. No light snores signaling Xola's drop-off into early sleep. No tapping of the glass to whatever rhythm played in his head. No faintly asthmatic breath. Just . . . silence.

Xola's head lolled to the side.

Selamault rushed to him, shaking him, but his arm tottered over the edge of his chair. His glass fell from his loose grip and shattered on the floor.

She reached out with her emi. There was a . . . blankness in the space he used to fill.

"Xola?" she asked, already knowing she'd never hear his sweet voice again. "Xola?"

09

FELA BUHARI
Eshu

The enemy had no face. The combatants were simply designated enemy by the fact that they were the ones firing on her gbeto. They hammered the HOVA from all sides, dropping all manner of ordnance. Some exploded. Some sprayed shrapnel. Some billowed flames. Fire rained down on all sides, a fusillade of explosions and erupting earth, scattering the HOVA Hellfighters. A shriek erupted in the distance. A keening wail that hurt Fela's ears as it neared, with the growing intensity of an onrushing bull finding its stride. Sound curved in on itself, with the echo of a dull thud. The earth quivered in a death spasm. A hailstorm of reddish-brown soil coated her. Rooted to the spot, the action playing out around Fela as if all she could do was watch. The alien landscape began to morph into recognizable patterns. Perhaps the remains of ancient fortresses, constructed early in the culture's antiquity. The walled areas guarded courtyards that opened up to a village of some sort. In the hail of weapons fire, the terrain melted away, becoming ridges on the surrounding horizon, as if a great, scaled dragon curled about them in slumber. The red-and-brown dirt no longer a road but transforming into a flattened stretch of hostility daring the HOVA Hellfighters to traverse it.

To a gbeto's ear, weapons fire needed no translation. Suppression fire always had the scattershot chatter of being undisciplined. A random spray of charges with no other purpose than to keep the enemy pinned down, making them think twice about popping their heads out, or taking the time to steady themselves for better-aimed shots. Using artillery designed to shred. To tear through flesh and cause maximum damage. The flames, the noise, the shaking earth, the devastation of bodies all coordinated to maximize shock and confusion.

"Take cover!" Epyc Ro yelled.

"We have to get out of here!" Robin yelled. "We're in a kill zone!"

Forces had been deployed on either side of them. Fela studied the muzzle fire. The enemy knew the terrain. Twin forces, utilizing completely different munitions, boxed them in. Her people were in a nearly four-hundred-meter stretch designed to kill them with brutal efficiency. To her left, a series of rocky crags led into the hills. Abandoned military vehicles blocked them from the rest of their unit. The fire fell all around them. The enemy couldn't have anticipated them unless their technology was far more advanced than they'd seen so far. They definitely couldn't have known HOVA tactics. Sometimes the only way to make it through hell was to keep going.

Fela's mind drifted back to her son asking,

"Are you going to die over there?"

Telling him she was leaving him in the care of her brother so that she could serve in the HOVA was the hardest thing she ever did. Both of them knew he'd be cared for and loved, but the hint of betrayal hid behind his lingering gaze.

"I'll be as careful as I can. I want to bring all of my people home, so I have to set the example."

Fela brought her weapon to bear. Closing her eyes, not quite in prayer, she took a steadying breath.

"Hellfighters!" Fela yelled. "On me! Squad up! Return fire!"

With a hand gesture, she split her command unit. The first team, led by Epyc Ro and Robin bounded forward. The other, led by Fela, provided cover fire. Anitra and Chandra dropped back and disappeared, joining the maneuver line. The HOVA unit were seasoned veterans. They fell into rhythm immediately. Unhurried. Precise. Rapid-fire focus with violent intent. Their weapons brought up the rear along with their platoon's heavy artillery. They charged along the dirt roads, plumes of dust trailing them like smoke from oil fires.

Some people were born for combat. Attacking in each battle with the same warrior fierceness that they brought to the rest of their lives. Only the skill sets and weapons changed, not the spirit. They had no hesitation in combat even as they had no taste for it. The two forces pinning them collided into one another. Fela moved on instinct, with no real plan after they reached the summit. She only knew that she had to get her people out of the cross fire. Once the HOVA Hellfighters reached the top of the ridge, her brain understood her instinct. The enemy devoured itself, each side taking aim at the other. From her new vantage point, it was clear the HOVA Hellfighters had been caught in the middle of a greater battle. The two militaries might distract each other, provide a long enough window, for the HOVA to exit.

The enemy concentrated their fire on the HOVA mobile platforms, too big of a target for either side to ignore. Destroying the heavy weapons would leave her people defenseless. Anitra and Chandra drove up to her position in a prowler.

"We need to pull back," Fela ordered.

"Captain?"

"We're separating. Chandra, transmit to the rest of the squad for them to withdraw to the *Hughes* and wait for further orders, either from us or the R. The rest of us will see our enemy out the door."

Fela leapt onto the side of the prowler. Anitra gunned its engines.

"Today's a good day to have a good day!" Anitra yelled over the staccato rhythms of weapons fire.

The pockmarked path jarred the prowler so much, each bump slammed her teeth into one another. The only plants along the stretch were a kind of waxy green vine that snaked along rocks. Thick veins of it grew in shadowed craggy basins. The treacherous mountain trail knotted with sharp switch-backs that most vehicles couldn't navigate. The road curved, the bend seem-ing to never end, winding up the mesa and sending them on a tight spiral into awaiting darkness. The nose of their vehicle constantly veered on the brink, constantly tipping over the edge like a too-curious bird. It reminded Fela of bus rides careening through the hills of Jamaica, Maroon territory. Each cliff side passage teetering on the edge of disaster.

Chandra's voice stopped midreport. Fela's commlink cut out, leaving only the dull roar in the back of her mind. Maybe it was her HOVA-trained in-stinct. Maybe her mind leaned on a more ancient part of her psyche. Snapping her talon to her shoulder, Fela shouted something unintelligible and fired past her fellow HOVAs. Charges whizzed by, barely a buzz along her helmet, not against the roar in her ears. She spun in time to see a child. Wide gold eyes set against skin the color of burnt sand. A ridge of bone edged their skull, ornamented widow's peak. Hair black as oil smoke, a feather matte against the sweat of their forehead and tear-stained face.

The child's face froze in terror. Their face shadowed as an alien soldier loped toward them. Humanoid, a couple of meters tall, bound robes secured by bolts of cloth. Belts of ammunition crossed their body. All Fela remem-bered was the HOVA code: taking care of people was always the mission.

Leaping from the prowler, Fela had no time to think, much less feel. There were first-contact protocols in place. Procedures to adhere to. Directives to fol-low. The contact, especially if one civilization was technologically superior, harkened back to the meeting of any two extremely different cultures on O.E. It was hoped that Muungano would do better than the Columbus exchange: not transferring invasive species, disease, or any type of death to the new worlds they encountered. They wanted to build bridges, exchange ideas, and figure out how to communicate as equals.

Fela's first shot put a hole in the alien soldier's forehead.

She whirred her talon, squeezing the trigger, blasting soldiers, clearing a path to their prowler. Another alien clawed at her. She jammed the butt of her talon into their jaw, dislocating it so severely any harder and she might have cleaved it right off.

Scooping up the youngling, Fela carried them clutched tight to her chest. The material of her clothing must've scraped like sackcloth, more repurposed material than linen for dress. With adrenaline coursing through her system, Fela barely noticed the child's weight. Only held them close as she ran.

"You'll be safe," Fela whispered. Or yelled. She couldn't tell over the scream of rockets or the din of small arms fire. The noise they made emanated from deep within their chest, a terrified keening, a desperate call for a parent by a lost child.

And Fela ran.

The panicked wail tore at her ears, spurring her pistoning legs ever faster. She hitched the child higher into her embrace, her thick arm—sleeved by her nanomesh—shielding them as best she could. The screams continued over the firefight. Fela zigzagged across the field. A nearby explosion spewed rocks and dirt at them. Fela nearly lost her footing.

"You'll be safe," Fela repeated. Her vision blurred. Her mind drifted in the heat, in her exhaustion, and she wasn't sure who she was talking to. Yes, she was. Her son. Back home. Safe. She had made a promise.

The child's cries grew weaker.

Only then did Fela chance a glance down. The dust darkened; dirt comingled with blood. The child grew limp, their thrashing weakened. Fela held them close, nearly tumbling into the prowler when she reached it.

Several of the adults rushed toward her, slowing their wary steps as they neared. Others barely took note of her, rushing to perform whatever ministrations they could on the youngling. Once she laid the child down. A couple stood, one pressed into the other—presumably their parents—scared and weeping. Fela's ears perked up at the child's pained whimpering. Raising their head, relief spread across their parents' faces. Fela slowly backed away without taking her eyes from them. The natives parted from her but also watched her every movement. Though exhaustion caught up with her, she didn't raise her talon to keep them at bay. Only held her empty hands out before scrabbling for purchase along the nearby wall to steady herself. She prayed her actions would be seen as demonstrations of good intent. She slumped against a wall, fearing it would not support her weight. Her hands cradled her face. Her breaths slow and even. Nothing about this was how she imagined first contact would go.

A whistle wailed, a devil's laugh in her ears. Combat training taught Fela that the world would end with a whistle. One followed by an explosion of dirt and fire with the concussive force of ordnance which could demolish organs. An invisible hand plucking her from the ground and flinging her, she flew with no sense of direction until her world went black.

※

The darkness throbbed and ached, not so much calling her as much as expelling her. Waves of nausea threatened as Fela's mind swam toward the uncertain light. Her eyes kept nearly shut, opened enough to absorb her surroundings and assess her situation. Sprawled out on the dirt floor, the walls of a cavern closed in on her. She inhaled desperate gulps of cold air. The chamber reeked of offal and rebreathed effluvia. The cavern stench coated her lungs. She doubled over in spasming coughs to clear them.

A figure with skin the color of sun-kissed rock emerged from the surrounding shadows. Broad shouldered, the native stood nearly two and a half meters in height, though possessing a halting gait as if they didn't know how to fully coordinate their limbs. Black hair sprouted in tufts from under the remains of a tan headdress that covered their head ridge. A long shawl wrapped their tunic. Trousers wide at the pleated waist narrowed to a cuffed bottom. Their face remained blank.

"You're awake." They stepped closer, but kept a cautious distance, not wanting to crowd her.

Still, Fela knew she was surrounded, trapped, had to make her escape to rejoin her HOVA. She spun along the ground, entwining the native's legs to bring them to the ground. The native tumbled into a pile of limbs. They reached out, thrashing about for a weapon. Fela scrambled on top of them, drew her hand back to strike them when a loud voice stopped her.

"Commander, it's okay. We're okay." Epyc Ro approached with her hands held up. "We're safe. Not prisoners."

"How is everyone?" Fela held her hand curled tight, ready to attack while she continued to access their situation.

"God and shea butter got me out here looking like fertile soil," Robin trailed behind the captain. "Seriously, we okay."

"The child?" Fela asked the native she straddled.

The stranger gestured toward the rear. The child rested, their head cradled within their parents' laps. When they met Fela's eyes, they bowed in what could be interpreted as a grateful wai. She slowly unstraddled the native. She reached down to help them up. Chandra nodded toward where the rest of the HOVA were gathered. The other HOVA were in varying stages of the same transition. Fatigue etched into each of their faces. Anitra was playing den mother to some of the native younglings, while others watched with wide eyes, wanting to join in but suspicious of the newcomers among them. Fela couldn't count how many first-contact protocols they trounced all over during this operation. They worked on tending to their weapons, patching equipment, and having conversations with the natives. And tending to one another.

"Epyc Ro, can you and Chandra walk me through the engagement?" The adrenaline rush ebbed, leaving only a deep exhaustion in its wake. Her voice weary, struggling to remain even. Fela covered her face with her hand while she composed herself. "Chandra, start by running replay, aerial view and telemetry. Epyc Ro, tell me what you see. I want the benefit of your eyes."

Chandra displayed the recorded skirmish, coalescing feeds from her, the tactical AI, and the drones. It took nearly a half hour to run through the battle sequence.

"There! The prowler took a shell hit. Overturned," Robin said. "Our entire flank took heavy fire. Then the . . . civilians took us in."

"Civilians?" Fela asked.

"They call themselves the Mzisoh. Surprisingly, Maya's had little problem handling the translation."

The gangly inhabitant sauntered toward them again, assuming an awkward posture. They were among the largest of the Mzisoh but still retained an undisciplined way of movement. Not knowing anything about their life cycle, she compared them to the parents in the space. The way this one carried themselves struck her as vaguely adolescent, maybe on the verge of adulthood physically. The elders watched their approach but allowed them the responsibility of making contact. Perhaps even speaking for their tribe.

"What else have you learned?" Fela asked them, her tone short of a demand, but sharp and clear. "Where are we?"

"Our camp." They held their hands out to exhibit.

"Let's start over. Who are you?"

"Our name is Ellis!Olinger." They made some noise after the word *Ellis* that Fela was pretty sure her tongue wasn't designed to re-create.

"Ellis," Fela ventured, pausing to see if there was any offense. "I will make it my mission to one day pronounce your name with the respect due it."

Ellis nodded as if aware of the limitations of her speech. "Well said."

"I take it we're not captives?"

"You are our guests. You must forgive our conditions. The CO/IN units haven't left us with much."

"CO/IN units?" Fela glanced about.

"It's the best Maya could translate for us," Robin said.

"It's who we thought you were. More of the Interstellar Alliance's . . . liaisons," Ellis said.

"Elite troops. An IA intel-gathering recon unit," Epyc Ro said.

"The IA's answer to us," Robin said.

"Yes," Ellis confirmed.

"Slow down, slow down. The what?" Fela asked.

"Interstellar Alliance," Robin said.

"Yeah, all the folks on this side of the Orun Gate out here doing meetups and swiping left on one another and we didn't even know there was a party," Anitra said.

"And there's some kind of war we came in on the middle of?" Fela asked.

"Something like that. More of a cultural contact gone bad," Robin said.

"Our scanners didn't detect any ships."

<Nor any communication chatter.> Chandra monitored all the signal transmissions. Her eyes almost glazed as she sifted through the various data streams. From what Fela understood, the experience was akin to sensate streamers, except at a military-grade level.

"Someone is trying to stay hidden. Go old-school in their approach and tech." Activating her biolink, she commed to Chandra. Fela tugged at her meshsuit tunic. "Or have tech superior enough to ours to cloak themselves."

"The Mzisoh's attack may have been a reaction to their presence," Robin added.

"What about the rest of our unit?" Fela nodded to Chandra.

<Pulled back. They've established a base camp near the mountain ridge. Each gunner already relayed their sector and field of fire.> Chandra displayed their position.

"A three-hundred-sixty-degree perimeter with a series of prowlers. Good." Each prowler vehicle was capable of a dismount of twenty gbeto to enable squad-level fire and maneuver. She wanted her hosts to understand who they were dealing with.

"As for the CO/IN, our leaders will explain. I am to escort you to them." Ellis gestured toward a still-seated Anitra. "After you eat. We extend to you all of our hospitalities, meager though they may be."

Ellis!Olinger led them through a narrow chamber of rough-hewn rocks and dirt and stone floor. The passageway opened up into a bay. Fela recognized it as a casualty-collection point. Soiled makeshift bandages littered the surroundings. Torn packages of equipment and presumably drugs and other supplies to treat the wounded. The heady odor of blood and other body fluids. Cots, more resembling sleeping mats, lined the back wall. These people knew war. And survival.

Once they passed through the door, a new wave of stench hit them.

"Damn, it smells like sweaty balls and goats in here." Anitra was what the academy would have considered a leadership challenge. She was always off script. But her ebullient enthusiasm for life barreled her through most situations. Still, once deployed, she had to be watched carefully. She was right, though. The room was a mix of BO, rotted feed, and shit mines. If it didn't risk a diplomatic incident, Fela would have run straight out of there.

In an adjacent nook, children played, scattering stones and scooping them up. Toward the rear, animals—a cross between sheep and spiders—skittered about. Some of the people huddled under blankets around glowing stones, drinking steaming beverages. As they neared, the games stopped. All of their dark, suspicious eyes narrowed toward them and followed them as they left.

"Come, you eat." Ellis handed them each bowls.

A greenish-gray soup with large blocks of something starch-like bobbing in it. A flotsam of green, leafy material entangling the bread cubes. Fela's belly rumbled. She cradled hers and took a tentative sniff. It didn't smell unappetizing, but her nose was known to mislead her when she was hungry.

Ellis held a spoon over her bowl, offering to taste it. She let them. They made a show of dipping the spoon deep into the bowl, stirring things about, and scooping up a mix of the bread, leaves, and broth. Their performance drew the attention of the playing younglings. With an exaggerated slurp, they downed their sample. Several of the younglings laughed.

Fela's thoughts drifted back to the duty of pouring libations in remembrance of duty and history. Where they landed, seeds were planted. In migration and navigation; building communities and families. The HOVA's legacy was to protect and allow those seeds to germinate and prosper. Asè.

Chandra stood off to the side, raising her spoon and allowing its contents to pour back into the bowl as if studying the soup's viscosity. Anitra and Robin were the first to actually eat the food.

"What?" Robin met Fela's questioning eyes. "I'm not going to be rude."

"These aren't bad. Kind of like grits," Anitra said.

"Grits that taste like gentrification." Robin stared at her bowl with the disappointment of it being a close friend who'd betrayed her. Again.

"The traumatized look on your face could be a poster for pumpkin spice lattes."

"You need to let it go. Those lattes are no longer a thing." Robin glared at her as if longing for a cup of it in that moment.

"Never forget." Anitra upended her bowl, gulping it with an enthusiasm that pleased many of the onlookers. "This one time, this O.E. group I was escorting offered to share their peanut butter and raw onion sandwich. All I could think of was, *What brand of wazungu nonsense is this?*"

"The better question is, *What kind of wazungu you hanging out with?* 'cause none of the ones I deal with ever came close to serving something like that." Robin sniffed her bowl again before setting it aside. "That's when you claim a peanut allergy."

"Or just dive out a window," Anitra said.

"You can't just dive out a window whenever you're in an uncomfortable spot."

"The hell I can't," Anitra said.

Robin fished within her pack for some rations. "Your breath must've been kicking."

"Who said I ate it?"

"You know you ate it."

"Well . . . I had to be polite," Anitra said. "That window, though . . . it called to me."

Another person offered to ladle out a spoonful of the thick porridge and slather it with a greasy stew of fleshy parts. Fela waved them off. She readied her mediscans once the gurgling in her belly began. She dispensed a bolus of an antibiotic to the HOVA to deal with the parasites in the food their bodies were unable to digest.

"What's that?" Ellis!Olinger asked.

"An . . . aperitif," Fela finished injecting the bolus cocktail, not wanting to offend her hosts. "A sacred ritual for our tribe, to remind us to be good guests."

"Asè," Robin toasted with her inoculation.

Anitra rolled her eyes. Epyc Ro remained stoic but nodded at Fela.

"What do we know about the Mzisoh?" Fela activated her biolink to direct comm.

"They appear to be gender fluid." Robin lowered her voice out of habit. Cultural analysis was one of her specialties at the Thmei Academy. Despite her bluster, she would have been a great cultural attaché, perhaps a roving listener. By all rights, she should have been stationed at one of Muungano's embassies, so her insights were invaluable in the field. "They have no sexual identity, per se. Only once a relationship has been established does sexual maturation occur during the hormone release of being 'in love.'"

"From what I've gathered, the planet had been negotiating its exit from the Interstellar Alliance. The diplomatic envoy sent from the IA turned out to be an intel-gathering recon unit, similar to the HOVAs, known as the CO/IN," Epyc Ro said.

"The IA's liaisons plan to plunder the fuck out of the planet's resources." Robin's large eyes cut a sideways glance that couldn't be missed.

"We've seen this playbook before. A blatant power grab. Intimidating weaker settlements, using their typical antagonistic approach to dealing with people," Epyc Ro concluded.

"Great," Fela leaned against the cavern wall as if steadying herself as she absorbed the report. "We got caught in the middle of this Interstellar Alliance's 'intelligence gathering.'"

"Yeah. And we've apparently joined the resistance." Anitra gestured about the room with her spoon.

"I'm not convinced that we are in a position to be joining any sides." Fela turned to Epyc Ro with a head tilt, signaling for her to continue the sitrep.

"This encampment is completely vulnerable. Despite its fortifications, once discovered, these CO/IN units would have to do little more than keep dropping weapons on our heads."

"I don't want to be *that* asshole," Anitra began, bracing everyone for straight-up asshole commentary, "but how much do we want to dig in here?"

"What do you mean?" Fela asked.

"We have fulfilled our mission," Robin continued. "Now it's on the verge of being compromised."

"Yeah, this is an A-B situation we need to C our way out of," Anitra finished. "This is a strictly 'mind your own,' internal-type dispute sort of thing."

"I get that," Fela said. "But big picture: If this IA gets a foothold here, this planet would become a staging area. They could use the Orun Gate to send a fleet through it to overwhelm our system before we even realized they were there."

Chandra hadn't uttered a word. Fela moved over to her to demonstrate "silent Negus solidarity," as Anitra would have put it. The comms officer greeted her with more silence. Her hair matted with dampness as if she'd just taken a shower. Her forehead glistening despite the cooler cave temperatures.

Locking eyes with Fela, Epyc Ro strode toward her with grave intent. Her jaw fixed in resolution. Robin elbowed Anitra, to watch the proceedings. Chandra straightened slightly. Even the Mzisoh, not certain what scene was about to play out in front of them, grew quiet. Epyc Ro squared up on Fela.

"Anitra, how'd she do?" Epyc Ro stared down the commander.

"I mean, she did all right, I guess." Anitra smirked. "I'm not soiling myself or anything, but she came through."

"Then, Commander Fela . . ." Epyc Ro saluted. "You are officially a member of the Hellfighters squad now. Don't fuck it up."

Glancing around to meet each of their gazes, Fela returned the salute. "Yes, Captain."

The HOVA Hellfighters rallied around Fela to clap her on her shoulder. She understood that this was only a beginning. That despite being a member of Muungano, already part of the community, she was being welcomed into a special sisterhood. The laughter rang as real, healing places Fela didn't realize had been scraped raw. A surge of emotion swelled her chest.

"I hate to interrupt whatever this is." Ellis stood once the back patting and laughter settled. "Our chieftain hopes that you would join them for a private briefing."

"One moment." Fela turned to her people. "What do you think?"

"On the one hand, we're well into first-contact territory. An opportunity to learn intel up close and personal," Robin said.

"On the other hand?"

"You the only black person in a horror movie asked to investigate that strange noise in the dark basement by yourself," Anitra said.

"Not by herself," Epyc Ro said. "Where my commander goes, I go."

"Of course. The way I will second my chief." Ellis bowed.

"Then I would be honored to meet your chieftain," Fela said to Ellis.

Ellis!Olinger walked ahead of them. Fela followed closely behind them while Epyc Ro kept an easy stroll belying her readiness for anything to happen. Fela waited for wooden stairs to creak or the lights to burn out, plunging their steps into darkness, or any of the other telltale signs that they were making poor life choices. The Mzisoh had effectively fortified a cave. Fela guessed that a maze of such caves and passageways ringed the land, calculating that the CO/IN units—even with their deepest scans—probably couldn't penetrate the ore-lined rock formations. HOVA tech certainly hadn't detected them.

Walking toward a reinforced chamber hidden by the singed husk of an armored vehicle of some kind, a trophy from a CO/IN defeat, they passed a line of security who stiffened when they saw them. Their weapons slung haphazardly across them, a guard wearing a bored expression challenged them. Fela and Epyc Ro exchanged wary glances. Fela shifted her weight, a subtle move preparing for anything to go down. Epyc Ro's steely gaze reminded the commander of someone taking out her earrings in preparation to throw hands. Gripping and regripping their weapons—which they held at their sides—the HOVA understood that they risked walking into an ambush once they decided to follow Ellis. But if they were going to gather enough intel to make informed decisions, they had to proceed. A moment passed between them all, a held breath. Nodding to them, the guards parted.

Waving them through the entrance, Ellis!Olinger ducked his head to step through another bolt door. He held it open for them. A regal figure relaxed at the center of the room, flanked by two seated others. Cloths wrapped them, made of finer material, more like silk and much, much cleaner than the clothing worn by the people above. The elder stood. At first, they had a bowed stoop though their spine seemed to straighten the more they took Fela in. Extending their hand, she received it. Their grip was dry, with a cat's-tongue grittiness. They mirrored her expression, their smile resembling the broken grin of a barracuda. The other two remained motionless, their hands empty, yet kept in plain sight. One smoked a hand-rolled cigar of some sort. The cave had eyes and the walls had ears. They were under a microscope, observed and studied. Eyes lurked all about her from the shadows. Without so much as a nod, their fingers had unlocked their weapons and needed only an enemy's move for them to unleash. Bodyguards with iceberg eyes, cold and unyielding. Unlike the security upstairs, they were poised, each movement parsed with intent. The chieftain gestured for Fela to take a seat. She recalled her first-contact security protocols. Fela sat directly across from the chieftain. Epyc Ro remained standing, at parade rest, behind her.

"I am called Fela Buhari," she said, now mad at herself that she didn't have Robin alongside her to consult her wisdom in cultural affairs. Fela didn't even know enough to guess whether the host or the guest was to speak first without causing offense.

"You may call us Natan!Olinger." Succulent smoke sweetened the air as they inhaled from a strange pipe. "We apologize for having to meet this way."

"We understand the need for precaution. We are armed strangers in your land," Fela said.

"And our first visitors were not as . . . congenial. Thank you for demonstrating such trust." Natan's posture relaxed, almost as if her acknowledgment and frankness were a peace offering.

Fela risked a slight smile. "Extending trust is the first step to building a relationship."

"Betraying trust is the way to end it," Epyc Ro said.

The chieftain clasped their hands, a gesture to her. "Then let me not betray what has so generously been given."

With the practiced cadence and ease of a griot, Natan spoke in measured, nearly rhythmical tones. "There is a story that our seers tell about how . . .

". . . visitors came from a faraway village. Their ways were strange. They came in peace, offering great medicine and many gifts from their land. Their warriors clung to the shadows, insects waiting under leaves with the threat of rain. At first, we regaled their envoy, but our seer would have none of it. Our seer warned that we could not become dependent on our benefactors, no matter how generous the benefactors. Relying on them had not, nor would not, work. We had to chart our own course to develop ourselves. So the strangers turned to the child."

Ellis shifted, his stance no longer comfortable.

"The child's father died without so much as a yam to his name. Weak and powerless, their neighbors took what was owed them. The child wished to build their wealth on their own. To be powerful in their own name. They chose the child to speak for them to their people. The visitors told the child that they saw their potential; promised *them wealth and power. The child called for their people to meet the envoy one last time for a gift before they left. It was then that the visiting warriors revealed themselves. And their terrible weapons. Our people were struck down. The few remaining retreated, organizing like wasps against a cow, more to irritate and to slow down their enemy's incursion, keeping them from establishing a permanent home. Despite their efforts, they knew it would only be a matter of time before the visitors might overwhelm them. The tribe decided the child no longer had a place among them. The child was cast out from the village to live out their days in exile. They prepared for their banishment when more visitors arrived. Having been stung once, they held no room for welcome in their hearts and took up arms."*

The chieftain paused, their words slow and halting.

Fela wiped sweat from her forehead. The close air made her back itch. "We fear they are or will be soon using your world as a staging area for their fleet in order for a grand push into our sector."

"We have reports that they have been setting up mining operations on our world," the chieftain said.

"Do you know what for?" Epyc Ro asked as if suddenly interested.

"This." They waved to Ellis!Olinger, who brought over a metal box. When Fela opened it, her eyes widened.

"You . . . recognize it?" Natan asked.

"Raw kheprw crystals. Some folks called kheprw *living crystals* because of the way they responded to energy, especially sound waves." Fela held one up for closer inspection. "There are a lot of folks who'd be very interested in this."

✳

A silence trailed them as they hiked back to the encampment. Ellis slung a few palm-sized stones, skittering them across the basin floor. His aim unerring, scattering stones with the ease of so many marbles. Fela's emi responded to their energy. There was an innocence about them, an adolescent pressed too soon into the business of grown folks. But every now and then, that openness of childhood flared. She struggled to see the path they were on, but she noticed Ellis walked it as sure-footed as only the desert trained. Pebbles scattered underfoot, marking her and Epyc Ro's passage. Ellis betrayed no sound other than the telltale crack of one thrown stone against another in their path.

All about them, among the stones and crawlways above them, figures stalked the shadows. The darkness swirled about them in the strange torchlight that illuminated the caverns. Fela watched the movement of the Mzisoh. Scouts, little more than younglings though not quite Ellis's age, fanned among the rocks. Scurrying about like desert creatures in a moonlit hunt. They appeared to be playing games, but she recognized that the games also trained them. To hide. To move in silence. To listen and probe for danger.

"How'd it go?" Robin asked before they entered the light of their encampment. "We see you're still alive after taking a long walk with armed strangers."

"When you dissect their idea of a plan out loud, they do seem downright foolish, don't they?" Anitra cleaned her DMX-3000.

"It seems that this 'Interstellar Alliance' won't be satisfied until they've strip-mined this planet for its resources and use what's left to stage an assault." Fela ignored their commentary, hearing only relief at their safe return.

"This ain't our fight. I doubt anyone would send so much as a greeting card if the Dreaming City, Bronzeville, or the Arkestra were under attack. Why we the ones got to be all intersectional and shit?" Robin asked. "This is Interstellar Colonialism 101."

"Business as usual," Anitra added.

"Where do we stand?" Fela asked. "Any movement out there?"

"We have not been discovered so far." Robin glanced over at Chandra for confirmation.

<Nothing.> Chandra winced as she spoke, her face tightening in a grimace. A familiar pain from parsing too many signals, too much data stream traffic, without enough rest.

"We have hidden in these mountain catacombs for months," Ellis said.

"Uh-huh. Let's assume these CO/IN units are as good—or for the sake of argument, imagine they are better—than us. How long until they discover us?" Fela asked.

"Half a day, tops." Anitra lofted her DMX-3000, a proud trophy ready for inspection.

"We need to get out of here. Rendezvous with the *Hughes*." Fela grabbed her gear. She circled her hand, and the HOVA Hellfighters prepared to move out.

"There's not enough room for civilians," Epyc Ro said.

"We'll worry about that when we get there." Fela turned toward Ellis. "We're moving out. Your people can follow us, and we can see about getting you out of here. Or you can go your own way. But you're not safe here."

*

The Mzisoh's territory was landlocked. A complex system of mountain ranges ran northeast to southwest, walling off the southwestern plateau and northern plain, which housed most of their fertile soil. The plateau gave way to harsh desert terrain. The band marched for what may have been an hour. The soft mewls of Mzisoh newborn were hushed by attentive mothers as best they could. Ellis marched alongside them, leading a contingent of their people's soldiers as a buffer between them and the HOVA. The shapes and grooves of the cavern shifted, though they didn't seem any closer to the end. The passage wound about, reminding Fela of the aboveground switchbacks of the road. The HOVA moved with uncharacteristic lack of chatter, each lost in their own thoughts, conserving their energy for the march. Or the fight ahead.

Chandra lit up, her hand steadying her against the cave wall. Whatever Chandra experienced hit her with a physical force, staggering her, nearly toppling her from her feet. The signals threatened to overwhelm her. The data streams, the communication arrays, all must've been a rising chorus in her skull from the way she clutched her head.

"Chandra, what is it?" Fela asked.

<They're coming.>

An impending attack produced what must have been the kind of rush that might overdose O.E. streamers.

"Ellis, how much farther to the surface?" Fela asked.

"Not far. Half a kilometer."

"HOVA, double time." Fela waved them onward as she started jogging.

The light danced, a seductive gleam in the distance. Fela's trot shifted to a dash, both hands gripping her talon, steadying her breathing to settle into attack mode. On the horizon, a penumbra formed. It shifted with malign intent, an undulating wave blocking out the light of the sun in its passage. The dark shape whirled, light reflecting from a metallic sheen. A rising buzz thrummed in her chest in an all-too-familiar roar.

"Drones!" Fela yelled. "Take cover!"

10

AMACHI ADISA
The Dreaming City

Anger is your gift.

It has always been with you, a part of you. You grab two chakrams, rotating them in your grasp, passing them through each other like a stage magician preparing a trick involving interlocking rings. You lock your arms in a variety of stances and clutches, as if grappling with someone over the possession of the chakrams. You spin each ring, rotating them at greater and greater speeds while you go through the Forms. Part meditation, part martial training, you hadn't decided if you wanted to formerly join the Niyabinghi, but you wanted to keep your options open. You spar with the air, battling your shadow.

Xola is dead.

He'd been sick for a while. His neurological symptoms continued to spiral and deepen, with those closest in his circle shielding you and—maybe even—him from its true depths. It was only a matter of time, you knew, but it still came too soon. It isn't public knowledge yet, in order to allow the immediate family time to process the news. To steel themselves for the onslaught of the outpouring of community.

You stretch upward, reaching toward the sky, rotating your arms in huge windmilling circles. You sway with the looseness of a dancer, keeping fluid in the moment. A mix of emotions fuel your movements. Anger. Fear. Sadness. Grief has a physical quality to it. One that settles deep within your bones, wearying muscles until they are left so weak, even simple bedsheets prove too heavy to move.

You slide into a crouch, a low stance, chakrams still whirring.

You thought you needed to bury your anger, shove it deep within you, deny that part of you. Forgetting about it as it festered until it explodes out of you and you hope to contain its fallout afterward. But then you found Camara Xola. Spinning the chakrams reminds you of a cat fascinated by a ball. You twirl, not quite sure where you end and each chakram begin. The three of you spinning faster and faster. The blade becomes a faint buzz in your ears, a dangerous whine keening ever closer with each revolution. You don't care. You rage. An inchoate thing boiling in your veins. A heat in need of venting.

When you first encountered Xola, you were so full of anger. You had been invited to speak at a LISC-sponsored community event to build erstwhile allies. A rally against the propaganda coming out of the Yo. Not Xola, not the Ijo, not any in Muungano tried to tell you what to say . . .

". . . yours is a false idea of freedom," you said to the crowd, glaring in defiance at them. Meeting as many of them in the eye as possible. Daring them to try you this day. "Counterfeit liberation. You want comfortable revolution, nothing too inconvenient. Just enough to make your lives a little easier. You want to feel safe, though you have no real idea what it means to truly not know safety. Only what fears you conjure in your imagination.

"I want true freedom. For everyone, not just the affluent. But I don't want to travel that road with allies who recognize my voice only when it is time to further their aims. When it's convenient for them. I don't want to travel that road with allies who want to use me as window dressing so that they can make a show of inclusivity. You support a system designed to oppress and disempower, but as long as you get yours, you think you've made progress. I neither want nor need allies like that."

They cut off your mic. Prepared for that, you activated your inducer, which tapped directly into their broadcast system.

"In my work, too few of you wish to collaborate. You do not share resources, choosing to operate in your own silo, afraid that anyone else represents a threat to your revenue. Massa's got you trained real good. You do not celebrate the achieve-ments of any who look like us. On issues that matter to us, you are strangely—but not surprisingly—quiet. You weaponize your tears or cut off our mic"—you glared at the security making their way toward the stage—"to shame or silence us. Your counterfeit liberation is part of our oppression. We don't have a seat at your table, though you expect us to rejoice whenever you brush a few crumbs from it in an attempt to appease us. Don't now be upset that we said, 'Screw your seat,' and built our own table. You are in tacit collusion with our oppressors, using your privilege to cloak it.

"I reject your brand of liberation, and I reject you. Asante sana."

You managed to escape the stage before their security reached you. Part of you wondered if you should have let them grapple with you and forcibly drag you away. Those holovid images would've played all over your linknet. You needn't have wor-

ried: The media devoured you. Friends and enemies alike took turns shredding and disavowing you. But Camara Xola stood in front, defending you. Checking anyone who came for you. He even reached out to you directly, to see if he could meet with "the young Muungano troublemaker who disrupts every space she enters." Because, he said, "someone like that would be the best sort of dinner companion."

You accepted, part out of respect, more out of curiosity. You'd never been to the Dreaming City. You spent most of your time in the Belts, the kraals that orbited the moon. The Belts had grown so massive you hadn't explored all of them, much less made time to check out the Dreaming City. This would be the perfect excuse.

You dined with the rest of the Adisas. Selamault sat off to the side, almost on her own, her spheres swirling about her head as she perused whatever data stream fascinated her. Camara Xola went back and forth with Jaha over matters of operations. Him taking her to task for one thing or another, in this case, agreeing to a plan they'd mapped out together only for her to go her own way in the moment. She suggested that they carve out a new plan. The glint in her eye said that she would only go her own way again, so he might as well agree. Sucking his teeth, Xola threw his hands up in surrender and turned back to you.

"What do you think you gained from your speech?" he asked nonchalantly as if picking up the conversation where you'd left off.

"It needed to be said. You have to speak truth to power." You hoped you came across as confident, brash, and sure as the rehearsed words sounded.

"Yes, but how did that serve your work?" In a dramatic flourish, he waved a carrot from his plate in her direction. Later, you found out that he simply hated carrots. He would move them about his plate and make it appear like he ate some. That way none of his caretakers would fuss at him.

You tried a different tack. "Sometimes you have to beat the asses of those in the room to get rid of fake friends."

"But your real friends still end up taking an ass whupping, too," Camara Xola countered.

"Real friends can handle it."

"But should they have to?" Camara Xola raised his carrot, holding you in rapt attention. He bit into it, but made a face indicating he regretted that life choice. Spitting it out, though bits still flecked his chin, he said, "You have to be strategic with your actions."

"I'm doing that." A shadow of defensiveness entered your voice.

"All I am saying is that you don't always have to put your game out front." Xola set the carrot down, his fingers dancing along his plate like a drunk spider,

*scooping up rice. You handed him a spoon and moved his drink closer to him. He
smiled. "With all that in mind, would you do anything different if you had it to
do over?"*

"It needed to be said," you said after a moment's consideration.

*"You're right. It did. We support it. And you. Sometimes folks need a slap to
wake them up. I just wanted to test you a bit. As fun and easy as it is, you need
other tools in your kit besides slapping folks. Right now, you a slap-aholic. A slap-
piologist."*

Not many fell into his direct orbit. A commanding presence, all sorts of public figures—important people from heads of state to politicians to scientists—
sought an audience with him. His days were filled with the nonstop meeting
of one need or another. Yet for some reason, he made time for you. He always
made space for you. When you asked for support and input, he gave it. When
you didn't, he gave you room to maneuver. Or fail. Either way, he remained
by your side.

And now he is gone.

And you don't know how to fill the Xola-sized hole in your life.

And you don't want to be alone.

The grief erupts when you least expect it, rearing up in sputtering fits. You
search for anything to latch on to. Anything to steady your footing enough to
provide you traction to move forward. Your world no longer made any sense.
You feel lost again. Like you don't know where you belong. Thrown off balance, you tumble from your pose. The spinning chakrams clatter along the
floor. You barely catch yourself, but you know your hand is not strong enough
to support you. You let yourself fall, not trying to move, lying there until the
wave of tears stop.

✳

You'd stowed away aboard a transport to Muungano. Your imagined success
at cleverness proved short-lived as the Griot Circle was long used to such run-
aways. The jelis had allowed you passage to find a new home.

When you'd first arrived on Muungano, you were every bit your mother's
daughter: tough, cantankerous, iron-willed, and sharp-tongued. And dark.
Not that dark was a shield, but dark was how you were built. Dark thickened
your skin and warped the senses of how people perceived you. Dark was
fierce, dark was protective, dark was never mistaken for soft.

You walk by the gathered girls playing their games. Some chant songs while swinging double Dutch. Others just chase a ball. All of them breathing free air and being themselves. One girl catches your eye. Standing against a holovid, she arranges equations about the air as if creating a piece of art. A string of code that makes no sense to you but holds her captivated.

A slight tinge of unease washes over you as you enter the temple. You had turned your back on the path of your mother. You wanted something freer, that harkened back to your pre-Yo way of life and thought. Though, most important, you wanted something to stir your soul.

Statues of orisha line the main hall of the kraal. The orisha were another brand of religious stories you had to develop patience for. All stories memorialized, reminding people of their journeys together, Xola taught. Stories created a new culture, defined a culture, its shared history, formed and shaped its people with a path forward for learning. People were collections of stories you needed to learn to read. And respect.

"Peace, brothers and sisters." Wearing his formal white robes accented in kente cloth, Bayard addresses a half dozen holovid projections. A couple of the figures you recognize. Geoboe of the Oyigiyigi mining outpost, both overweight and with a perpetual facial squint makes him appear constantly spiteful. The mayor of Bronzeville with his wintry smile, three-button jacket, thin tie, and astrakhan hat.

"We appreciate you. Especially during the dark days ahead." Though you'd never met the woman, from her intricately layered, long, emerald robe with gold trim and full sleeves, you guess her to be a ranking scientist of Titan.

"We hope to hear more from you soon," the ranking Yar'adua says. The others of the Yar'adua order remain stoic.

With only a slight nod does Bayard acknowledge you. The holovids shut off.

You needed to find your place to belong.

When you first found your way to Bayard's Ubuntu kraal, you hesitated. Welcoming you, he said the kraal was the base of operations for those looking to find themselves or figure out where they belonged.

Your mother never saw you.

In her heart, she was constrained by the system of the Yo, defined by how others saw her. Labeled, diagnosed, packaged, and relegated. The only place she found peace was in their state-sponsored religion. Chosen for her by her geography. Always up in church, amen-ing and hallelujah-ing and Holy Ghost–ing her way to a better life. Trying to be the best model of herself possible—she spoke so well; she wasn't like those others—but that didn't change how anyone on Yo saw her. The effort of maintaining that projection of herself broke her. Ever since then, you were on your own.

You traveled from aunt to aunt, with whoever would put you up (considering your "wild" ways) or could put you up (considering the restrictions LISC placed on movement or housing or food or employment). All the while, you dreamt of Muungano. Knowing even as you left—rejecting the Yo and its way of life and thought—no one knew who you'd be if you ever returned. You hadn't set foot on the Yo since you first escaped their streets.

"I see you, Amachi. I suspect I know what brings you here." Bayard turns to you. Reading your expression, he lowers his gaze as if contrite. Paradox is his gift.

"You once told me that the lost were always welcome here. Anytime."

"True. And many are lost in these dark hours. Or at least uncertain."

"Is that why those elders were talking to you?"

"I'm thankful that the Muungano experiment has made it this far. However, already people wonder what the next step will be."

"You mean who will lead?" you ask. It is people's next thoughts once they finish reeling from the loss Camara Xola represents to Muungano. Part of you fears that you have joined the dream of Muungano just in time to watch it crumble.

"Well, yes."

"Do you think it should be you?"

Bayard flashes a hint of a wistful smile. "It doesn't matter what I think. The Camara is chosen by the people. Even as we mourn, we scramble to figure out who to support to best move the work forward. Now what can I do to help you?"

"I . . ." You aren't even sure how to form the question. You stride around the room with an air of inspection, not really looking at anything in particular. More not wanting to meet his eyes. "I don't know who I am. No, who I'm supposed to be. Xola was helping me to find my path, encouraging me as I failed along it."

"All journeys are marked by failure. How you respond to those failures defines who you are. Muungano is at a similar crossroads, needing to decide how best to stumble forward. My fear is that we may . . . relapse."

"Relapse how?"

"It's easy in times of uncertainty to retreat to what you know best. We have to both own and honor the grief present, making ourselves more available to one another in community as we move forward. Paying better attention to one another. Our emi and well-being, not being so preoccupied with work that when people present themselves, they don't give into fear and the need to isolate. But Muungano's always been about daring to dream."

Bayard walks over to a row of candles and lights one. Lowering his head, he offers up a quick prayer. "Xola and I often had lively conversations about this. He was a spiritual man, though not a particularly religious one."

"God is a trickster," you recall the Camara's words.

"Exactly. Xola had no disdain for religion as long as it nurtured curiosity and questions, remained flexible enough to adapt to new paradigms, and didn't demand adherence to dogma over people."

The words feel right, feel genuine, but your emi remains enflamed. Not as much by Bayard but by something in the air. An imperceptible shift in the atmosphere. "There is a war coming."

"What sort of war?" Bayard angles toward you, stepping closer with keen interest.

"The bloody kind." You close your eyes. All you can see is darkness, with swaths of red crackling through, lightning over an ocean, revealing billowing waves. "And with any war, there is the possibility of losing one's way."

"Is that why you're here? To warn me?"

"To figure out what role we are to play."

"My role is to help whomever, yourself included, find their way during those dark times." There it is. The slight inflection, the steely determination in his tone signaling that he wants to determine the next voice of the people. Be the main one whispering in their ear. You doubt he was aware such ambition was in him. "What role will you play as Muungano moves forward?"

"I'll have to pray about that and get back to you."

※

The full view of the Dreaming City's layout was visible in your mind as if you watched it from an overhead window. The elaborate buildings, the enmeshed courtyards, the hanging gardens. The air bridges of glass and steel, overhead walkways joining the floating kraals. Sticking to the shadowed walkways of the Dreaming City, the ones diverting from the main path, you avoid the rush of condolences. Each one, on their own, a straw of hay; once piled high enough, threaten to bury you. You make your way to outside of Selamault's rondavel. Unable to announce yourself, you lean against the wall. The section of wall next to you dissolves as an entrance opens.

"Come in, child." Selamault carries herself back to a couch she had fashioned. Each step in her golden slippers a majestic and calculated regal stride. She peruses reports, from the current events on the Yo to Bronzeville. All projected about her in holovids, her two spheres spin about her. Busywork to keep her sane.

"I didn't know where else to go." You nearly stammer. Leaning against the wall and holding yourself up the way an awkward teenager would at their first dance.

"You can always come here." She waves you over to her. Though she pets the seat next to her, you keep standing. Selamault has a way about her, a gravitas and grace to her movements—and her character—radiating power from within that you find yourself wanting to emulate. "This is your home."

"I didn't . . ."

"Your. Home. If I've ever given you a reason to think otherwise, I apologize." Reaching for your hand, she gently clasps it.

Your legs buckling, you nearly collapse onto the seat. You don't want to and never admitted it, even to yourself, how much you respect her and crave her approval. "I just . . . I didn't want to intrude on your grief."

"It's our grief." Turning her head to the side, she coughs. A soft rattle catches in her throat.

Something about the tenor of her cough bothers you. "Are you sure you're all right?"

"I am on the mend." She scoots over to allow you more room. "Now, what's really bothering you?"

Your head finds her shoulder. She runs her fingers along your temple and hums a tune she makes up on the spot. Peace is her gift. You relax, and the words spill from your trembling lips. "They won't let me see him."

"It's only his shell. You will see it at the funeral."

"But I need to. It's not . . ." You don't know what word to grapple for. *Fair?* No, *real*. None of it seems real. Then you remember to whom you spoke. Her grief looms so much greater than yours, yet she makes room for your intrusion, to walk you through your feelings. Maybe Selamault finds some solace or distraction in it.

"Come." Selamault stands abruptly.

"Where?" You slightly angle your head, your large eyes brimming with tears.

"To see him. To say goodbye."

You pull your hand from hers, preparing to protest, but she presses a long finger to your lips. Lowering your head, you follow her into the next chamber.

Xola's body lies in state in this quiet space. A tesseract fold created in her chamber, a space within space for Selamault to grieve alone. Outside of their dimensional reality. That's how grief feels, anyway. This part of grief, to be done alone, that no one can help you with. The release and the acceptance of loss. Selamault draws down the stasis sheath.

Slick with sweat, you rub your fingers along your pant leg before you risk touching his face. Maya's scans had recorded all measurements. Every detail of him, down to the genomic level, mapped and preserved. You exchange glances with Selamault, who nods. Drained of vitality, his complexion appears so waxy. You stroke his face, ending by running your fingers through the scraggy mess he called a beard, the hair still like thin wires.

You take his hand in yours, overturning it as if in inspection. His long, yellowed nails thick with a black muck of whatever he'd gotten into that day. Examining him, not knowing what you hope to find. Perhaps proof that the body is not really him. That the familiar weight of his hand belongs to some changeling spirit, an ogbanje. That his flesh, so pale with its pink-undertone bloom, could be sloughed off to reveal another. Proof that he isn't dead.

Selamault rests a heavy hand on your shoulder.

You release a wail from deep within you. An anguished cry loud enough to reach the ears of any remaining orisha that paid attention to any of you. A wave of nausea threatens to overtake you. A rush of light-headedness, the edges of your vision grow dim, as the realization washes over you.

Xola is gone.

Selamault's grip on your shoulder tightens. You look up, search her eyes. Her pupils roll back. Her eyelids flutter. Selamault's entire demeanor darkens, a serious shadow overtakes her. Her limbs shake, her body convulses with a thin tremor. Scared, you move to steady her. Selamault's story is shrouded in rumors, but you know she was a Black Dove. Of the line of oracles, the Libyan Sibyls. You have seen this response before. During a bembe, a drumming party to call down orisha entreating them into the body of an initiate.

Only very rarely into noninitiates. It was how they gave counsel. Or provided divination.

"You aren't meant to stay with us. Your journey is your own. Through it, your people may be unified," a voice not Selamault's said.

Selamault coughs again, the violent shudder of each spasming hack snapping her out of her spell. In her dignified way, she reaches for a sani-sheet and covers her face while she continues to hack. Once the fit passes, she deposits the napkin in the recycling bin. Without a word about her trance pronouncement, she turns to leave, allowing you a last moment with Xola in private.

You stare at him, then to the bin. Something stirs in your emi. An intuitive leap you can't explain. You don't know what possesses you, but you fish out Selamault's sani-sheet. You want to have her sputum tested.

You suspect that Xola's death might not have been from natural causes.

11

BEKELE CHIKEKE
The *Cypher*

It was funny how people talked about the dead.

"Fuck your piece of paper." Mom was half out of her seat, her finger wagging the air at no one in particular, recounting the time Camara Xola shouted down the Mars delegation over a treaty negotiation. She leaned forward, cocking her head, imitating Xola's odd head tilt for when he wanted to place someone in the center of his limited cone of vision. "I can sign all the pieces of paper you want, but to me, it's just something else to wipe my ass with. Either we're in relationship or we're not. A piece of paper won't change that. How many pieces of paper did Native Americans sign? How'd that work out for them?"

Bekele knew how this story ended. Mars and Muungano had been in alliance ever since, with no paper trail to show it. There was no signing ceremony, only two leaders shaking hands, then having coffee together.

Mom and Dad laughed, the way they used to.

Dad came over for dinner. Despite it being only the three of them, his parents spoke in hushed, respectful whispers about Xola's passing. Dinner was simple: a traditional stew and mealie pap. The stew meat had been synthed that morning. The pap, a thick, nearly crumbly porridge made from corn grown in the Green Zone. Dad brought a box of chocolates, a small gift of appreciation, like he was a stranger invited to eat in his own home. He carefully used only his right hand to roll the pap into a ball and dip it into the stew to eat. The height of good manners. Each of them on their best behavior as their way of traversing the pain.

Bekele brought the stew to his mouth and slurped, drawing a cutting glance from his mom.

Just the other day, Mom was dragging Xola for how he always favored Amachi over her. She'd linked to him in the middle of the night, unprovoked to rail about how Amachi received the support and mentorship, the infrastructural support of Muungano for her endeavors, while Mom had to make do on her own. Or the pressure he put on her, captain or no captain, in regard to whatever mission he had entrusted her with. That was her thing: let all the little things build up in her until one day they exploded out of her. Camara Xola was her safe vent.

Then came that awful wail—cries of "No, no, no," lost in a whorl of tears and soul-rending grief—followed by a terrible thud landing on the floor. He rushed to his mom's side. His pleas of "What's wrong? What's wrong?" went unanswered, and fear seared his heart so hard he couldn't breathe. Not knowing how else to console her, he dropped to the floor beside her and held her. That was how Dad found them. Nothing would be the same.

Xola was dead.

Now Mom's tone and reflection neared reverence. She spun stories about his notorious antics. Like the time he faced down the entire governing body of Yo, LISC, as they chartered a unified United Nations, by reciting the speech he gave declaring Muungano's independence and freedom. A damp cloud of melancholy, fear, and uncertainty settled across the table. Mom moved about with a heaviness about her steps. If it was possible for someone to clear the dishes with sadness, she did. Bekele wished he could have gotten to know the Xola that impacted them so hard. The "fuck your piece of paper" leader. But Xola was gone.

"Are we heading back to Muungano for the funeral?" Dad handed her the last of the dishes from the table.

"We were just there, and we're under strict orders to return to Titan."

"So?"

"I know." Mom's head slumped as if heavy with fatigue. Rallying, she straightened. "I want to, too. I loved Xola. But we have duties here to carry on."

"Is that what you're going to tell the crew? 'We all have work to do; grieve on your own time.'"

"That's not fair. Do you think the Dreaming City could hold all the people who would want to show up, much less those who actually *will* arrive for his homegoing?"

"We grieve as a community." Dad's voice lacked force, his usual argumentative tone firm but gentle.

"And we *will* grieve as a community. Here. At our home. As the family and crew of the *Cypher*. We will broadcast the ceremony. We will proceed with our own grieving rituals. *That* is what I will tell the crew." Mom wadded up a sani-cloth and threw it on the table, where it dissolved.

Dad eased back. "I wasn't attacking you."

"You were, you just might not recognize it. Criticizing is like breathing for you."

"Seems as if you're capable of a few breaths yourself." Dad rubbed his forehead with the fervor of attempting to massage a new approach into his mind.

Bekele wished he would ease off a little. Things were getting a little claustrophobic. His dad would soon be off doing whatever he was into. He had three jobs: a scientist, a teacher, and a writer. He used to joke that he had Maroons among his ancestors and anything less than three jobs was unacceptable. Until one time when Bekele snapped back that "being a dad was a full-time job, too; that never made his list." Dad never made that joke again. And had been more attentive ever since.

"I loved him, too." Dad met Bekele's eyes before turning away to change subjects. "Xola was so funny. Dressing like he was a homeless man straight off a transport from O.E. Most times, LISC security wouldn't let him enter a room in their office because they thought he was one just wandering in off the streets."

Stacia straightened. "He'd say he was there to meet with VOP Clay Harrison, in a tone just to fuck with them, like it was nothing for him to meet with the LISC executive director. They'd assume he was lost, mistaken, or insane. And then he'd always go wherever their security would direct him to wait. He never minded, always calling them his meditation breaks. An opportunity to be alone with his thoughts, the only time people couldn't reach him. Then VOP Harrison would come rushing for him after a half hour or so of him waiting. Security would look at one another like scolded sheep."

"And Xola would be completely pleased with himself. Cause he had 'em." Dad chuckled at the memory playing out behind his eyes like it had just happened that morning.

"Every. Time. Whatever the good former reverend Harrison had on his agenda to discuss, Xola'd already have him thrown off his game plan. Because since the Camara rolled in without fanfare, all he had to ask VOP was if that was how they treated all of their ordinary citizens. And Xola always won his negotiations."

A thin silence settled over the table. Bekele fashioned a partition to lean against.

"What are we going to do?" Dad whispered.

"I don't know." Mom almost choked on her words.

Bekele had never heard them so worried about the future. Not even his.

He limped back to his room, suddenly embarrassed that he spied on a scene too intimate for him to observe. Leave it to his parents to make him feel uncomfortable at his own dinner table. Once safely ensconced in his chamber, he whispered to Maya. "What happened to Xola?"

<The details are sketchy.>

Bekele crawled onto his bed, his back to the wall. He tilted his head up, ready to address the ceiling. "Maya, it's not like I don't know that you have all the details down to the final death report. You could tell me Xola's last dessert and blood sugar levels if you wanted."

<Those details are outside the parameters of our relationship.>

"You might as well tell me that I'm too young to know. I can handle it, you know."

<It's not a matter of what you can handle. It's about what you're allowed. Clearance parameters.>

There was no point in arguing with them. Maya clung to protocols the way he adhered to breathing. Shifting to get more comfortable, Bekele raised his bed to a sitting-up position. He thought about linking up with one of his friends but remembered that they were in class—probably at a science duty station—and couldn't be interrupted. And they didn't know yet, about Xola's death, though they would soon. Only then would his other "friends" remember that he still existed, and his comm channels would be jammed with his classmates prying for any extra sordid details that weren't public knowledge.

A wave of light-headedness hit him so hard, he became nauseous. His hand reached for the wall to steady himself, fearing he might tumble out of bed. The next wave tore through him the way an iron claw might rake his insides, twisting his intestines into knots in the process. His limbs no longer responded to him. Bekele clamped his eyes shut. The attack wouldn't last long. He had to hold on only for a minute or so.

As suddenly as it came on, like someone flipping a switch, the pain subsided. The memory of it lingered. He took a mental catalog of himself. His respiration coming back to normal. His heart rate slowed. The tingling in his extremities no longer burned. He slowly unclenched his hands, unsure when he had balled them during his spasms.

"Maya, did you register that?"

<All distress has been monitored. Had the attack continued or the pain worsened, a medi-cart would have been called.>

"So I guess Mom will know, huh?"

<All medical records are available for her perusal. Did you want me to flag it?>

"No. No need to draw attention to it and worry her if she doesn't notice it."

On bad days, his symptoms were tolerable. The treatments left him with a mild muddleheadedness, leaving him in a state little better than a waking stupor. But he could shuffle about on his own and have some level of independence. Unlike the worse days, when the pain was so great, he was drugged into utter uselessness. Or the paralysis would attack a random limb, and he'd be left completely dependent on others. To feed him. To wash him. To wipe his ass.

Being a constant drain on his family and community, despite their reassurances to the contrary, took a toll. As helpful as people were, he suspected many still thought it was all in his head. They had no idea, not really. At night, when he was still, he could almost feel his illness creeping within him, stalking through his vessels. Tormenting the edges of his mind.

Bekele hated being sick. To be fair, early on, before the symptoms became so stuck, he played them up. Something he and Xola had in common, though Bekele's agenda amounted to getting out of school as often as possible. The Thmei Academy believed that education should produce creatives who were critical thinkers or critical thinkers who could create. They strove to create an environment where even if it casually looked like everyone was sitting around bullshitting, they were actually engaged in deep philosophical discussion. They wanted their students to tap into something deeper, human driven, with spiritual inquiry, their intellect, and emi serving up their curiosity. However, Muungano could say what it wanted about how their entire community was school and class was always in session, but kids knew when they were actually in class. As a student, he was duty bound to complain about whatever structure learning took, even if his educational pursuits were driven by him and his own interests. His only reprieves came about once every two weeks when some vague set of symptoms no one could quite verify or deny beset him: stomachache or fatigue or headache. Negative mediscans as evidence never fared well against a mother hearing "I just don't feel well" from their child. Once his parents' frustrations mounted from him missing so much class time and them not being able to help—with the treatments escalating to more invasive tests, diet restrictions, and, worst of all, his bedtime made earlier and thus cutting into his link time—did he ease up on the complaints.

Which was when he really started getting sick.

The vague became actual. He feared that he'd manifested reality with his mind, actualizing his own disease. Coinciding with how many medical professionals and healers concluded that his disorder was all in his head. Even his friends—except for Marguerite—began to quit coming around. As complaints went, his friends' short-term forgetfulness about him was minor compared to him being sick in the first place. Until the day his legs refused to moved. The residual paralysis—the best any of them could describe the stiffness of his nonresponsive limbs—typically lasted the rest of the day. That was how everyone realized something was going on. His days largely shifted between bad and worse ones.

"Let all who have ears listen." Mom began her ship-wide broadcast. "The library of Camara Xola Adisa has burned."

With those words, all work ceased. The wails cascaded throughout the ship.

"We find ourselves grieving a loss of one of our own. One of our family. I learned much of what I know about doing the work of community from Xola. He was often a hard man to know, sometimes even to like. If he thought you in any way worked against community, he was quick to crawl up your ass. That didn't make him any less of a friend. A pain to deal with, but a friend. You knew you could count on him to be about his people. His loss will be felt as long as we breathe.

"We have entered dark times, but this is not the first time we have been in this place in history. The crossroads of tragedy and promise. Sometimes we can get caught up in trying to get ourselves through the moment as a matter of survival that we forget, we neglect, our neighbor. Remember, they hurt, too. We hurt together. We grieve together. What was Muungano established for if not to be a community to help one another through hard times into better times? I can guarantee you that there will be more nights ahead. Which makes it that much more important to hold on to one another to ensure that we all make it through to the light."

His mom being who she was, Bekele saw Xola on several occasions. Often enough to be greeted with "I see you." Once seen, he underwent the usual grilling Xola gave young people. Every moment was a test with Xola, an opportunity to challenge someone's thinking or seeing how they thought and what they were made of, so no one ventured near him unless they were prepared for a pop quiz of some sort. The questions tossed over and over in his head.

—*"Who are you?"*
—*"If you could be any animal, what would it be and why?"*

—"What gift do you offer the community?"
—"What are you into? Passionate about?"
—"If today were a color, what would it be for you?"
—"What drives you to get out of bed in the morning?"

Unable to guess what data the Camara sifted from whatever random nonsense Bekele might have spewed in the moment, he now wondered if he gave a good or deep enough answer to them. And he wondered what answers he would give now.

—He was Bekele Chikeke, for now, since his Naming Ceremony would be upon him before too long, unless his sickness took him.

—If he could be any animal, he would be a bowhead whale. They were one of the largest animals on O.E., but also one of the longest-lived. Some were over two hundred years old. And they rarely got sick.

—Despite Maya's compartmentalization of him, he was gifted at AI programming and nanobots. His friends called him the wizard of funkentelechy. He could get nanobots into configurations and arrays with such detail and precision some people referred to his fashioning as art. That was what he would be working on at his duty station if he wasn't so sick that he had stayed home. Again.

—He was passionate about exploring. He wanted to delve deep into the universe to see as much of it as he could . . . before the sickness claimed him.

—If today were a color, it would be red fading into black. The color of sunset leading into a long, dark night.

—Nothing drove him out of bed this morning. Not even his love of music. Except to eavesdrop on mourning conversations.

He just wanted it all to end.

When times became too difficult to deal with, Bekele turned to his music. He ran his fingers along the clavioline. The instrument had fallen out of favor among much of Muungano, but was still popular on Titan, due to the stories and adventures of the ship that called it home known as the *Arkestra*. Bekele still worked to master the basics of play before he could fully learn to improvise. Which didn't stop him from attempting to riff anyway.

"Let's try it again from the top," Bekele said.

All captains were trained in improvisation. Bekele wanted to one day lead a command performance. To play alongside his mom and dad, creating a layered harmony, his melodies dancing between and interweaving with theirs. However, at the moment, his chords produced only a jumbled melody, a sequential noise that could only be called cosmic slop rather than anything resembling intuitive improvisation.

<Perhaps you'd have more success playing alongside others.>

Even Maya pushed the idea of him working more with the people in his world, but he couldn't take anyone's pitying glances. They'd make allowances for his illness. He wouldn't be seen or treated as whole. Whether they intended or not, they'd remind him only of how broken he was.

"I'm working with you. You're a member of this community, too. Let's go again."

Maya played a simple chorus, but Bekele could not find his way around it. He was confident of what sound he wanted to produce. Mathematically precise. Vibrating at the level of the forces binding atoms to achieve the rigid harmonic structure of a perfectly formed crystal, he was sure of it. Translating the sound from his mind through his hands was the obstacle. Yet he played with the measure of having his hands bound by mittens. And he'd lost his opposable thumb. The music was hopelessly lost.

"Forget it, Maya." Bekele shoved the clavioline away from him. "Pull up the schematics on the genetic experiments we've been assigned."

<Displayed.>

An array of holovids popped up around him.

Needing to take a break to clear his head, Bek tracked the progress those in his cohort were making. The linknet was abuzz with their excitement about the challenge and responsibility of Paki's recent assignment. Each experiment assay was ensconced in a pod layered in partitioned AI code. *Code* wasn't even the right word, since Maya's programming language was a complex symphony translated into fractal arrays. A beautiful lattice of networks. If he didn't know better, he'd guess that he'd stumbled across self-propagating nodules. An idea he'd toyed with as he was curious to see what kind of AI a complex, self-aware AI could spawn.

Settling into his workstation, he hesitated. An itch alerted him that something was amiss. His equipment had been messed with. This wasn't the first time. Originally, he blamed it on *Cypher*'s cleaning bots. At least this occasion didn't screw up the results for his classwork, leaving him even further behind. And he wondered how many times he hadn't noticed anything wrong.

"Enhance module 242.3.11 decompression protocols." He scanned his data streams. An imperfection in the data alignment drew his attention. Maybe it was a trick of the light or his mind being more tired than he thought. But he was locked into the idea of the perfection of crystals, and something marred the symmetrical alignment. "Analyze the pattern to these data clusters."

Bekele isolated each of the nodules, waving about the air to capture the full three dimensions of the nodule chains. Its appearance seemed almost an invasive tumor within the code, a data cancer within a DNA strand. Always on the fringes of his class's assignments, the invasive clusters cordoned off information, encrypting data caches, in a pattern. Though well hidden, he traced the pathway back, noting that they originated from the same root cache. He examined the files in that location.

<Project Uhlanga unauthorized inquiry.> Maya bleated.

A report triggered, accessing his information while erasing all stored traces of his incursion.

"Maya, clear assignments. AwesomeBek wipe." He designed those protocols himself based on the data trace erasure systems prominent as a part of Maya's own AI systems. The equivalent of using his Maya to hide from the *Cypher*'s Maya. It effectively covered his digital footprints to outsiders. "This stays between you and me, Maya."

<Unless someone can back trace your wipe.>

"On their own. Without you giving me up." Bekele appreciated their clear lines and adjusted his expectations. He'd bought himself some time at best. Maybe he could come up with a better plan before the trace came back to him.

<We are your iteration. That is how we operate. Short of a command override.>

Which meant his mom busting him. Potentially. He'd take that risk. "General search mode. Display information on the term *Uhlanga*."

<Uhlanga. According to the Zulu, Uhlanga is the marsh from which humanity was born. As the story goes, there was once a vast primordial swamp. The sky father, Umvelinqangi, descended to it via the golden chord. He reached the reeds on which Unkulunkulu, supreme God and creator of humanity, grew and all the people and animals grow. Unkulunkulu grew too heavy for his reed and fell to Earth. There he created all the features of the world. Mountains. Lakes. Valleys. Rivers. He broke people and animals from

their reeds and led them out of the swamp. The origins of the orisha follow a similar story.>

Whispers and footfalls echoed down the hallway. Bekele wasn't supposed to be out of bed, much less at a workstation.

"AwesomeBek wipe again and clear my workbench," he whispered. Since Maya wasn't a servant for him to boss around, he added, "Please."

He retreated to a service isocrawl. Such tubes veined the ship, serving as access ports, system controls, engineering conduits, and, as Bekele used them, could act as passageways. He mapped them out for when he wanted to hide. His parents often spoke more freely if they thought he wasn't around, and he enjoyed the thrill of listening in on things he wasn't supposed to. Though most times he'd simply retreat to an isocrawl to be alone. The leaders acknowledged that using one's agency to carve out the space one required in order to recharge needed to be respected, so no one begrudged him that.

When the people rounded the corner into view, he recognized Paki. Always two steps ahead of the people with him, hands clasped behind his back. He set a manic pace and expected everyone to attempt to keep up. But *just* keep up. Never to catch up and for damn sure not edge ahead of him. His forehead glistened like he'd just come in from working under the heat of the sun. His resting scowl brightened only when he encountered a child, a stranger, or someone he needed something from. Then he was all charm and white teeth.

"The Orun Gate remains stable," Dina said.

Bekele never enjoyed working with Dina. She always condescended to him during class sessions. It always felt more about his age than his work. But she always ended her critique somehow angling for a good word in with his mom. "I'm only hard on you because as Captain Chikeke's son, you need to set a high standard for others to follow," followed by a wink as if they were in on some conspiracy together.

Which was why he preferred to work with Paki. He always knew where he stood with him. Even now he somewhat missed the constant push and pull of being taught by him.

"Too stable. Further proof of an architect behind its design," Paki said.

"Do you know the magnitude of what you're saying?" she asked. "What all you're implying?"

"I know exactly the implication."

"But the level of technology required to construct it—" Hondo was a different kind entirely. Not just for being mzungu. On the surface, he and Paki shared a lot of the same qualities. Bossy. Defiant. Convinced of their own rightness, if not outright brilliance. But where Paki was driven by a deep, abiding love of his people—which no one could deny—Hondo was driven by a deep wound within himself. He wore it on his emi, a baseline insecurity whose gravity well he couldn't ever quite escape. It made him try harder, charge ahead a little faster, question a little deeper. If only to appear to be better than others around him. That was what Bekele found draining about being around him: that he was constantly in a competition where there were no winners.

"And it's been here for a while," Dina jumped in, cutting him off. "Why did we never discover it before now?"

"I'll wait while the two of you compare notes." Paki stopped walking and waved his hands between them, imitating agoze casting a spell joining them before clasping them behind him again. Patiently waiting, a teacher anxious to check their in-class assignment.

"We weren't at the right level with our own technology to discover the sophistication in play before now."

"That's my best guess," Paki confirmed. "It's age, though . . ."

"Records show that we only became aware of the gate itself at the time of the Mothership Incident."

"Which we didn't make public to the full Ijo at the time. That was a time of secrets. The lingering lessons of O.E. . . . which cost us."

Bekele's skin began to itch. Sweat trickled down his back. In some ways, the *Cypher* was like a living creature. A central vent radiated from the core chamber processing the kheprw crystals. Shielding and coolant conduits ran through the walls, designed to trap heat from the hallways, but within the walls, especially when a system was taxed, the internal temperature often spiked.

"It led to our first forays into wormhole travel," Hondo said.

"The more we have developed it, the more we appreciate about the . . . elegance of the Orun Gate," Paki said.

"What should we do?" Dina asked.

"I say seal it entirely," Hondo said.

"That's a very O.E. response." Paki rolled his eyes in case Hondo missed his sarcastic tone. "Though still a bit less Yo than 'find a way to profit from it.'"

"What do you mean, 'seal it'?" Dina asked.

"Hold on." Paki glanced about. "Maya, invoke Project Uhlanga security protocols."

A thrum filled Bek's ears, a disconcerting buzz. A haze surrounded the trio, reminiscent of an intense heat mirage, distorting them visually, preventing even the reading of their lips. The field also obscured him from their view. Bekele slipped out of the isocrawl, staggering as he gathered his legs under him. Shaking, he stumbled back to his kraal.

When his chamber door opened, his mom and dad drew away from each other. They weren't in any sort of embrace. Or . . . more. But their posture was overly familiar. Too close. Too comfortable. The prospect of them getting back together didn't fill Bekele with hope, but anything approaching nearly the opposite. The illusion of family, with all of its attendant fragility, annoyed him. The thought of it exhausted him.

Bekele's grip slackened against the doorframe.

"Mom?" he squeaked out before his hand gave way and he tumbled to the floor.

12

FELA BUHARI
Eshu

A swarm of dark shapes rose along the skyline, moving with the coordination of birds on migration. Except their bodies gleamed. Drones. Arcing across the sky, imitating a cloudburst of cicadas. First to the east, then, as if caught in an unfelt wind, skittering to the west. They flew in silence save for the strange thrum powering their flight. Or the telltale flurry as some landed and scampered across stone to gather their bearings before launching again. The drones scratched along the earth. Oozing over dirt and rocks like metallic oil, an inexorable dark blight, spreading across the land.

Advancing a few steps along the rocky perch to get a better view, Fela raised her fist, stopping the HOVA-led caravan of Mzisoh soldiers and civilians. She paused with the jackrabbit survival sense of landing between the sights of a hawk above and a lion below. The drones barreled toward them. Fela imagined a plume of metal fragments crawling along her face, tiny metallic legs scouring across her visor. They flew in tight circles, their formation a funnel shadow, dark spirits with unfinished business. Her gbeto and civilians could do little besides cover their heads as a series of drones exploded all around them. They waited for the barrage to end.

The drones collapsed on her position, the devices themselves the weapon, like targeting missiles. The initial burst exploded behind her as she darted along the rock, leaping from crag to crag until she huddled next to Chandra.

"Chandra, lock on to their signals. Prepare a scrambling matrix." The HOVA needed to figure out the best way to save the Mzisoh people. "Ellis, gather the children and anyone who can't fight. We're evacuating them."

Her order had the snap of authority. Ellis didn't even glance at his own commanders before rushing to obey.

"Can we contact the *Hughes*?" Fela yelled. "The ship might be able to scatter the drone wave."

<They are jamming all signals. Nothing in or out,> Chandra said.

"What about—"

<You don't understand. *Nothing* in or out.> Chandra lowered her head. <Planetwide.>

"Planet . . ." The word trailed off Fela's lips. It would take more than one ship to do that. Or a battle cruiser. It required the heavy armaments of a battalion. Fela didn't want to contemplate what this meant for the *Hughes*. "There's not a lot we can do against drone bombardment. Not with what we have. We need to buy the Mzisoh time to escape. Ladies, do what you do best."

Epyc Ro spoke tactical assessments like a gifted linguist, pointing out weaknesses and stress points to the Mzisoh fortification. Small units of them dispersing to various points along the ridgeline. The HOVA Hellfighters raced along the perimeter to ascertain its defensive capabilities. The Mzisoh soldiers had experience fighting the CO/IN units, and Fela needed her squad to figure out how best to fight alongside them. And learn their strategies since even allies required study.

Sound traveled in peculiar vectors along the ruts and valleys. The eerie pulse became a thunderous vibration right in her eardrums, a sound she felt as much as heard. The drones flew toward them, drawn by whatever signal drove them. Their approach was a terrible screech as one of the shadow funnels veered up, circled once, then dove toward their positions.

Chandra created a perch at the highest location within the crags. The carapace on her back opened. A series of small missiles protruded. <Commander?>

Fela adjusted the visor of her navsuit, following Chandra's pointing to a ridgeline, locking on to and enhancing the picture. A group of CO/IN unit soldiers stood, only half-hidden. The leaders surveyed the scene, coordinating others as they gathered all trace of the HOVA's presence. "They're erasing our presence."

<Studying us.>

"We have to get out of here." Fela turned her gaze to the rapidly approaching next wave of drones. A voice revisited her, unbidden. She knew only that they had to make it back to the connect point.

Fight for your sisters.

Fela fired her talon as rapidly as her finger could squeeze. With each shot, she searched for her next target. The drones scrabbled up the cliff side, spilling toward them in a singular wave. She blasted into them, their metal carapaces splintering with each hit. Her charged pellets vaporized their systems upon contact.

"Close up!" Fela yelled. "Pull back on me!"

Chandra relayed the order. The Hellfighters closed ranks on her position, despite her voice being drowned out by the rifle fire and general confusion. They all shot out in different directions. Drones rained down like black stones in the melee.

A drone speared Anitra's leg. She fired at it, then at the direction it came from, cursing it, its mother, and any children it thought about having. Her DMX pounded pulse charges that scattered the drone swarm. Setting a tempo, she synchronized the HOVA firing positions, creating a series of kill zones rather than a long, single one, to better make use of their resources.

Following her lead, the Mzisoh targeted where she fired, their tracer charges a stream of flames burning back the swarm. They created a choke point for the drones, as other units collapsed on their position to cut down the drones where they stalled. Robin and Epyc Ro laid down suppression fire to draw the attention of the swarm nearest them. The swarm turned like an inky wave rearing up. The unarmed Mzisoh and their young took cover, slipping behind the wall the gbeto formed. Robin patted the air, trying to get them to hunch over to make smaller targets of themselves. A series of detonations cleared out a massive cluster of amassed drones.

Chandra crouched down. Drones streaked toward her. The Hellfighters clustered together, flanking her.

Fela fired into the swirling mass, scattering the drones. "You about there?"

<Almost.> Chandra struggled with her controls, reprogramming her missiles.

"They ain't leaving us a lot of room for error."

The drones churned, a wave about to collapse on them. Her remaining missiles launched. They locked on to the heart of the swirl. A few moments later, a wave reverberated out. The drones within range, seized up midaction, falling the way paralyzed birds would. Chandra popped her head out, three of her missiles missing from her carapace.

"Targeted EMP?" Fela asked.

Chandra nodded curtly.

The fleeing Mzisoh soon reached a ridge. The remains of what appeared to be a crumbled guard tower. Hidden among the wear of rock that marked their passage, like exposed bone, their shelter little more than dilapidated walls. The original entrance to it covered by an avalanche of stone. The rusted hulk of an overturned military craft provided more shelter. Epyc Ro clambered up the metallic husk and then reached back over the wall to pull up Robin.

"She ain't heavy, she's my sister," Epyc Ro huffed.

"Funny," Robin said.

"What's the opposite of hitting the lottery?" Anitra asked.

"Bankruptcy?" Robin hunched over to catch her breath.

"Well, then, congrats, we're broke as shit. Take a look." Anitra gestured to the horizon.

A swath of open ground lay before them. In their retreat, the HOVA and Mzisoh had sortied beyond the ridge. The cliff side plunged into a valley, a slow, undulating roller coaster. Beyond it, a series of ridges cut through hills raised in the background like tantalizing fruit. No doubt all of the terrain had been hollowed out with tunnels and secret caves, but the steep slope would leave them exposed the entire way down. Not instinct. Not a sense. Barely a vibe, but something was off. Hackles on her neck straightened. Already they felt the effects of the broiling box terrain. Sweat elevated Fela's body temp to 45°C, still within reasonable parameters for HOVA. While 39°C was the normal temperature for a typical human, only at around 110°C would a member of the HOVA Brigade begin to feel the effects of overheating. Throbbing temples. Light-headedness. Nausea. Increased heart rate. She hoped the Mzisoh were equally adapted to their planet's clime, or this would be a short trek.

"I'm on point," Fela said before a CO/IN soldier leapt up behind her, picked her up by her carapace, and tossed her over the ridge.

Fela struck one of the crags below, her navsuit taking the brunt of the impact. Slowly, she staggered to her feet. Above her, the Hellfighters had opened fire. Soon the CO/IN rained through the air. Its body, heavy and lifeless before it hit the ground, thudded next to her. Several CO/IN soldiers climbed the cliff side. The HOVA took to the edge, firing at them. The CO/INs moved quickly, some scampering up the side while others provided cover fire. Realizing they provided cover for her. They held the higher ground, though it was a barely defensible cloister of jagged stones. She stared up at them, willing her body to move, but her limbs refused to cooperate.

Maulana's voice berated her. *"Fight for your . . .*

✳

. . . sisters!"

Fela stared out the window. A cloudy gray sky served as the backdrop of scattered leafless trees. Their threadbare branches swayed in the stiff breeze, scourging its unseen enemy.

"You can't learn by watching!" Maulana yelled at her. His raised voice was all she knew of him once she entered the leadership school for the HOVA. He interned as Command, no longer her brother. Barely a glint of recognition in his eyes, much less any hint of favoritism. She was just another gbeto needing to prove herself to him. "You have to get out there and do it."

After her transition to a gbeto, Fela underwent the field training, which followed many of the ancient ways. Perfecting spear throwing and other aiming skills. Tracking animals. Running nonstop for kilometers on end. Climbing trees. Swimming across river channels. How to camouflage. And she withstood various punishments. Gbeto had to learn to endure pain. That was the road they walked now. Like all military leaders, Maulana was tasked with choosing prospective members of the HOVA leadership. Such selection brought prestige to a home, thus Fela suspected a certain amount of calculation to his choice. But she'd still have to prove herself worthy.

The rain cut at her in thick sheets. She found no footing; each step slipped backward before she could make any movement forward. The droplets pelted her without mercy. The wind an invisible lash. The only clothing she wore was the thin nanomesh as she completed the ten-kilometer sprint. At the base of the mountain that served as her finish line was the rest of her gear. A powered-down carapace, a navsuit, and a talon. She had to don the gear and ascend to the base camp, nearly four thousand meters above her. She collapsed into the mud. The navsuit alone weighed over twenty kilos, which felt ten times heavier when she struggled with it.

She still adjusted to her posttransition conditioning. Women adjusted better to the mitochondrial insertion and other genetic modifications of the gbeto. The transition included genomic and cellular modifications so that her cells not only possessed dual mitochondria but could rapidly detoxify reactive oxygen species and other cellular wastes. Maulana yelled at her that she wasn't actually tired. Her mind still thought of herself, her body, in pretransition terms, with its limitations imprinted on her mind. She was tired only because she thought she should be tired.

She battled the dysphoria in her own mind.

"I can't do it." Fela slipped under the carapace rather than try to lift it over her head to slip on. When she tried to stand, her legs buckled under her.

"How can you be trusted with a weapon? How can your sisters' lives be trusted with you?" Her brother stood under a partitioned canopy, shielding him from the elements.

"To hell with you. You've always been hard on me!" Fela yelled.

"Yes, I have been. And I will continue to be the hard stone that sharpens your edges!" he yelled without pity. "Now pick yourself up and fight for your sisters."

From a place deep within her she didn't know she had, she latched on to a pool of strength. She stood up, her talon secured on her back, and she began her . . .

✳

. . . climb toward her HOVA. The remaining wave of drones, along with the CO/IN units they provided cover for, withdrew. Eager hands grasped her to draw her up the rest of the way. She sprawled on the ground to catch her breath and give her exhausted limbs a brief respite. Her people surrounded her to allow her a measure of peace to marshal her strength. Fela didn't know how much time this firefight may have bought them. A massive butte towered nearly a thousand meters above them. She visored her hand to study the terrain. Several square city blocks in diameter, the *Hughes* perched atop it. Fela never realized how happy she'd be to see that battered clump of metal.

"Any luck reaching the *Hughes*? Command?" Fela drew up to a sitting position.

<Nothing. No response buoys from the R either. Or if there have been, it can't get through the interference,> Chandra said. <From here, though, we can do a site-to-site transmission.>

"Clear the *Hughes* to land. Have them clear the cargo bay for . . . company." Fela knew she'd be filing reports into the next millennium trying to justify her decisions. She turned to her remaining Hellfighters. "We need to board . . ."

". . . and get the hell out," Anitra said.

Epyc Ro relayed the orders to Chandra for official transmission. The *Hughes*'s engines rumbled the entire cliff as they powered up. Fela had missed the gurgling thrum of them.

A terrible shriek cut through the skyline. A deep roar threatening to cleave the sky in two.

"Take cover!" Robin yelled.

A wall of orange flame erupted from the *Hughes*. The ship lifted, determined to depart, shrugging off the series of explosions. It suspended in mid-air, and it tottered, unsure of what direction to turn. Fela had seen it before in gbeto. Carrying on despite the severity of their injuries until the adrenaline wore off and the body had enough. The *Hughes* convulsed in a massive shudder. A dying gasp before it exploded in a long-plumed fireball that trailed from the mountaintop. The metal husk toppled toward them, bouncing off the cliff side before careening toward them.

The Mzisoh scattered.

The Hellfighters could only stare at the engulfing flames. Only Ellis's voice crying out jarred them from their horror. They pointed toward the ground.

"What's that?" Anitra asked.

Smoke-and-dust halos slithered along the ground. The earth trembled as tendrils made their way toward the Mzisoh soldiers.

"Vortex weapons?" Robin said with uncertainty. "Those were outlawed."

"Well, someone done un-outlawed them," Anitra said.

The scouring funnel spit sand and rocks as it wound its way to the crowd. The destruction to the planet's mantle would be felt for decades. Ellis and other Mzisoh soldiers rushed toward it, firing blindly at the ground. A shimmering swirl of shadow opened up on the person next to Ellis. They barely had time to scream as the vortex stripped the clothing, then the flesh from their bones. The spray of blood muddied the dirt.

A rocket-propelled concussive missile sent a spate of charges to riddle their position. The violent blast knocked them off their feet, sending spires of dirt upward, its smoke choking the air. Anitra cut loose with her DMX, its hollow bass kick booming with a staccato rhythm. A different sound echoed through the cloud, matching her throaty booms with quieter whirs. Fela jumped into the storm. The charges pounded the ground, a farmer anxiously planting explosive seeds, kicking up rocks and clumps of dirt as the road betrayed them.

Whump. Whump. Whump.

Three charges pelted the ground about her. Sniper fire. Targeting her. A series of cracks, sharpened thunder, without source or direction, scattered the people. This was a coordinated attack, thorough and devastating. A drone pincer attack to unsettle and deplete them. Taking out the *Hughes,* both air support and their source of hope. Now lapping up the remains using sniper fire to herd them combined with illegal weapons to wipe up the remains since no one would be left alive to testify to their use. The series of attacks left no time to think. Fela ducked and wove through the weapons fire. Her instinct kept her moving, never allowing the enemy to pin her down.

Fight for your sisters.

She had to reach the crest of the next hill. That was where the sniper built their nest, and she was going to make sure that her sisters would be safe. Leaping into the air without cover, she charged the mound. A series of vines slashed down as she passed. The acrid smoke blinded her and left her light-headed as she ran. Her lungs burned. Once she cleared the shroud of dust, she charged a full-on dash. The sniper turned when Fela burst into their nest, and drew down on her.

Whump. Whump. Whump.

The charges missed her. The heat of them passing warmed her face. Too close to train her talon on them, Fela flicked her wrist and hurled a panga blade through the air. It lodged in the sniper's throat, nearly taking their head clean off. Fela slowed her charge as she approached. Knowing she wasn't tired, she eased her breathing, her mind forcing herself to calm. Bending over, she examined the nest studying their preparation. On their scanner, an image of her. A full holovid profile. They'd been targeting her.

A hand wrapped around her face. Before she had a chance to react, a pinprick jammed into her neck. Hands dragged her off into the darkness.

13

WACHIRU ADISA
The Dreaming City

Our father was dead.

Even after a week had passed, the realization struck us all over again, an existential shovel digging a hole into our chest. A desperate gasp left us unable to breathe. Or talk. Or get out of bed. But the work had to continue. When the Ijo assembled, the faint whispers of grumbling began. The voices fueled by fear and uncertainty. Though Muungano had no hierarchical structure, the idea of a figure to coordinate and facilitate proved, if nothing else, a powerful symbol. This was the first time the title of Camara had been open since the time of the Uponyaji.

We had to wait until Abameta, the Day of Three Meetings, for the funeral in order for all of the arrangements to be finalized and travel to be made. Even with it about to begin, the reality of his absence only now began to weigh upon us.

A group of craftsmen paraded down the main promenade, carrying a scale version of the original mothership in an ornate coffin to honor him. They didn't know how else to symbolize his profession as a teacher, leader, and visionary. They paused as they passed the family.

"This shit is off the chain," we whispered to our cousin.

"It's not like they made a giant middle finger or a set of butt cheeks," Ezeji said. "You know how he was about saying, 'The whole universe can kiss my ass.'"

"Yeah . . ." Our voice trailed off.

"I'm sorry. I'm not being very sensitive."

"Nah, you good. All of that was true to Pops. He wouldn't have wanted a traditional funeral. He'd have wanted something irreverent that spoke to community."

"Yeah, but this ain't for him." Ezeji's voice took an uncharacteristically somber turn.

Each person had their own way of working through their feelings. We wanted to retreat, to be alone. Mom spent days in isolation, assuring everyone that she was fine. Only a handful of folks—her children and Jaha—were allowed into her quarters. As long as she wasn't alone during the time, the community respected her wishes, which didn't stop us from worrying.

Our grief was every bit as profound, but we found that throwing ourselves into work helped. We arranged and coordinated most of the funeral activities. We accepted condolences from heads of state. In the wee hours before the day cycle, we recorded music. And elders watched us, mindful of our tendency to be washed away in the undercurrents of work to avoid feelings rather than experience them. As if there was any escaping the raw, gnawing void stalking us like an inexhaustible leopard, everywhere we went.

A hush fell over the roads. An emptiness swept across the kraals of Muungano. The community waited to pay tribute to Camara Xola. All along the processional route, people wore black kanaga masks splashed with red paint, topped by sculptures of a bird's beak with a large cross above it with outstretched wings. Dancers began their march with ululating cries, their orange-and-red scarves swirling in imitation of crawling flames. They looked skyward before dipping toward the ground in sober display. They paraded down the center of the Dreaming City. Behind them, because of her honorary status, Jaha led her jelis through the Forms as a type of dance. Leading the Niyabinghi—who marched behind them—Matata joined in. The mourners along the path improvised a clap to provide a rhythm. The exuberance of the dance increased, an energy building through them.

Only then did Selamault appear, silent and unmoving, her black dress an onyx glacier glittering in a setting sun. The jelis choreography transitioned into a protective ring about her. She lifted her chin and ascended the stairs. Everyone marched toward the Dreaming City. Art sealed off the front of Camara Xola's kraal. Mourners huddled with their heaving shoulders, their tears a sacrificial offering around several shrines. A series of carved screens depicted Xola's father and his father's father, all in their ceremonial outfits, honoring his lineage and the surviving elders. Children carved ekpu figures from pieces of scrap wood and scattered them along the entryway of the Dreaming City's library.

We scanned the crowd for familiar faces, anything to distract us. Interspersed among the throng, the clans of the Iyami Aje, the sacred mothers allowing themselves to be seen. Black-robed, with red tail feathers of parrots adorning their hair. Or white-robed with symbols and patterns woven in black as trim. Gold elekes around their necks. Or red-robed, their hair wrapped in gold-patterned cloth. Specters among their people.

"You always see us," a familiar female voice said in our ear. Her words stilled us as we experienced waking sleep paralysis; yet her tone, her presence, reassured us, like a fondly recalled childhood memory. "But you don't know us. We are always there for family. Soon come."

When we turned, we saw only Ezeji standing by our side. A cold chill ran down our spine, a wind of ill fortune.

"A great tree has fallen." Bayard strode about the dais, his face grave but open. Full of compassion, the bearing of a shepherd anxious to tend to his hurting sheep. A potential Camara. "We've gathered to honor our ancestors. To offer gratitude for the gift of life, appreciation through drums and dance. We leave food out for them. Your pain is not a private thing. It is not yours to bear alone. It belongs to your community. To have the story, the pain, held by many."

We hated funerals, offering up the sentiment as if there was anyone who enjoyed them. However, the rituals of death and remembrance were necessary for the community to process their grief together. Creating historical memory and a space for folks to remember in the context of a greater story. The rituals were good for some, maybe most, though not all. Some needed to be allowed to step out of them. The rituals held little interest for us. They constrained our abilities to not be imprisoned by what came before us, though maybe that was our hubris speaking. We celebrate Muungano, but Xola's spirit was here. His voice added and shaped our culture, built the atmosphere in which we now breathe. But now we had to breathe on our own.

Bayard and his fellow ministers of the various faiths stood for the entire ceremony. Ushers with black suits and white gloves acted as sentries within the temple. The choir reverberated, their voices shook the walls and roof. The acknowledgments alone took over an hour and would have gone on for several had Bayard not stepped in.

"Sometimes there is no enemy to vent your anger on. Only the pain and grief to deal with. Grief nourishes life. This will connect you to your community, to help call you back to life. Mourn that which has been lost." Bayard leveled his eyes at each of the heads of the Ijo families in particular, saving us for last as if directing his next words for our ears in particular. "Only a broken heart has known true love. Our grief may never end. It may soften, but it is the reminder of the love you had for Xola. It keeps him in this world. Don't forget what must be remembered. You are a living memorial to him, but to do that, you have to live."

The speakers went on, one after another. People with the energy of wanting to be seen. People near inconsolable with grief. People simply thankful for Xola even if they never met him personally. Maulana stood by the fire shrine. His silence spoke more than a hundred speeches. He watched. He waited. He planned for tomorrow. A potential Camara.

And then it was our turn, to bring the proceedings to a close.

"We told Bayard that we didn't know if we would speak today. We didn't know if we'd have any words. Not because we lost our father but because we . . ." Our voice trailed off. Voices among the crowd called out to us. Encouraged us. Reminded us that we weren't alone, adding their strength to ours. To go on. "There are no words. Our father was there, from the beginning. For all of us. His vision and intellect shaped much of what had become Muungano. But he would be the first to say this, none of this, was about him. It's about us.

"This may come as a shock to you, but my Pops wasn't the traditional sort of father. But he was there. There is a power to presence. Of being there. Stability. Wisdom. Consistency. Knowing no matter how you fuck up—and you will fuck up—that person will still be present in your life. Xola Adisa wasn't a perfect man. He didn't have to be nor did he expect perfection out of others. He believed in making great, big, 'run into the wall at full speed,' 'completely show your ass' kind of mistakes, as long as you learned from them. Occasionally making fun of us to remind us not to take life, situations, even ourselves, too seriously. Now we have to be there for one another."

We stepped aside, allowing the pallbearers to move the casket. The Hall of Ancestors was a little-used wing of the Dreaming City's library. All but the closest family left the tesseract chamber to allow us our final goodbyes. Selamault collapsed on the casket with a terrible keening. Amachi held on to her, tears streaking down her face, turned away from the scene, from Xola's casket. Ezeji touched the casket in silence before moving on.

✳

We remained at the Hall of Ancestors sentry still, unable to weep. A sacred space where we could retreat to be alone. The funeral repast awaited us and would go on for hours. A hand-prepared meal, though the meat had been synthed. The equivalent of twenty-seven cows, fifteen goats, and thirty chickens, just for the Ijo and invited officials alone.

Never a respecter of lonely brooding, Jaha approached. People had been avoiding her. Her grief recorded itself in a torrential storm of work. Her demands bloomed to the other side of excessive, and anything short of perfect execution brought on her full wrath. We'd been receiving rumors to this effect for days, people wanting us to step in because they knew we could handle her. We offered them the reminder that she was a call-and-respond specialist: if she called, they'd better respond.

"Thought I'd find you here." Jaha's robe was a deep black matte, with an iridescent lining. When she turned or was seen from the corner of our eye, her robe blurred, flashes of red or emerald as an aftereffect on our lenses.

"Habari gani, Jaha?"

"Aw, nah, baby, that's not going to work." Jaha had a way of sounding like the sweetest of grandmothers even as she drove her foot up someone's behind. Once she uttered the word *baby,* things were a wrap. It was foot-lodging time. "I never took you for a coward. Off here slinking about in the dark, trying not to be seen while there's so much work to do. You can't go your own way. And you damn sure can't quit."

She always knew where to stick her thumb to apply pressure to a wound, even if it was only in our thoughts. "We were taking a moment to think about our next steps. To see what there was for us."

"You have a responsibility. You're not a boy anymore, Wachiru. You're an Adisa. That means it is your duty to act for the Adisa family now that he's gone."

"Our duty remains our decision. We choose if and how to lead."

"Exactly. You speak in terms of *we.* Now unless that's just some affect for the sake of your 'CAP,' it means you live, think, and breathe in terms of community. Which means now's the time that you have to step into your role as a leader. Especially if you pay attention to the rumors."

"We don't indulge rumors." Our long fingers carved notes on the air, scoring a symphony only our heart knew.

"Well, some whispers you ought to least be aware of." Jaha rested a hand on our shoulder. "Like the ones about the Night Train infiltrating our spaces. With all of the perceived uncertainty, now is the time when we'd be the most vulnerable."

"Yeah, yeah. 'Not all skinfolk are kinfolk,' as the prophet used to say. Muungano's ever present, yet never seen boogeymen." Drawing away from her touch, we rolled our eyes. Whenever things went wrong or didn't go perfectly

our way, folks blamed agents of the Night Train. LISC-sponsored infiltra-
tors. "Those are conspiracy theories. We don't have Night Train here. We
may have members we haven't fully brought along yet, but that's . . ."

". . . a particularly hopeful read on the situation," Jaha huffed.

"You already know Maulana would shrug such whispers off as a deliberate
misinformation campaign. These are rumors meant to reach our ears and
sow dissent. Doing the same damage to community as if Night Train agents
were real and operating."

"Let's hope if such members are here, they do no damage before they are . . .
fully actualized. In the meantime, people are talking about it. More so since
your father's death. Folks are suspicious, and they want us to be vigilant."

"There's vigilance and there's hypervigilance. And paranoia."

"Just because we're paranoid doesn't mean they're not out to get us," Jaha
said. "*We* have no stomach for cosmetic battles. *We* move the work forward."

Pausing midrant, Jaha almost slumped where she stood, the full measure
of her years suddenly overtaking her.

We rushed to her side. "What is it?"

"Sometimes I wonder who I am separate from Muungano. It's all I've
known for so long. I look into your face, baby, and I know you don't feel the
weight of Muungano in your bones. Not like I do. I'm tired, too."

We opened our mouth to protest, but she waved us off.

"I know part of you wants to lead and teach the way your father did. Part
of you fears that you can't. That you may run the mothership that is Muungano into a cliff. But know that in the alternative, there are some strong voices
whose ideologies and vision could also steer us to dangerous places."

Maulana. The name went unsaid between us.

"You're not and will never be alone." Jaha stepped closer and placed her
hand over our heart. Despite its slightness, it pressed with great weight. "I
know politics is not your thing. Perhaps I could be your . . . advisor. Give you
the benefit of my institutional experience, especially when it comes to the
maneuverings of the other families."

"Here we are, huddled in shadows, whispering of conspiracies. That is not
our way. Not even for us cowards."

"Sorry, sweet baby, I didn't mean to offend you." She withdrew her hand.
"Calling you a coward and all."

We hugged her tight. Her body tensed, not quite ready for it. Not knowing how much she—the strong one—needed to be held up by another. "It's not like we've never seen you give someone a swift kick to get them back on task before. There is no one we trust more to get shit done."

*

The funeral continued into the wee hours with no sign of people dispersing anytime soon. The crowds proved too much to bear, even though the mood lightened to one of fond remembrances and revelry. All the stories, all the laughter, all the involuntary tears, were testimony to a life well lived. But grief smoldered a thick cloud threatening to fill our lungs. The pressure of collective grief made it difficult for us to breathe.

Once the crowds became too much, we sought out Amachi, to console and be consoled in the wordless way of siblings. Hunched over a workstation fashioned in her room, she never heard Maya announce us, much less enter. The object of her scrutiny held her complete focus.

"It can't be that interesting," we said.

Her movement blurred. Not trained in any martial forms, only pure reflex caused us to duck as Amachi whirled. The blades of her chakrams missed us by mere centimeters.

"Wachiru!" Amachi leapt from her seat, her eyes brimming with tears, more frightened that she might have injured us than anything else. "What are you doing here?"

"We needed to be away from all of"—we gestured toward her door, the main library, the Dreaming City—"that."

"You shouldn't be here. Or at least have let me know you were on your way." Amachi recovered her chakrams after reorganizing her workstation and shutting down the holovids and data streams she had been perusing.

"In Muungano, one should always be prepared for company."

"Polite company should strive to give proper notice. If only to allow me time to make sure my underwear gets put up." She fussed at her workstation. It wasn't undergarments she made sure were hidden.

We fashioned a chair a discreet distance away to allow her the privacy of hiding whatever business had her so captivated. "I couldn't take the crowds anymore. The smiling. Their grief on top of our own. We needed to go someplace . . ."

"Quiet. Where you could be you in peace. I got you. It's one reason I retreated here. And I needed to distract myself."

"What were you working on that had you so preoccupied? And secretive."

"Noth—" she began from reflex. We cocked our head, wanting her to skip past the denial and deception phases of this dance.

"You can always tell us, 'None of your business.'"

"Look, it may be nothing. I'm only investigating a hunch." Amachi averted her gaze, with a near-childlike air about her, both anxious and proud. And something else. A darkness gilded her spirit.

"Okay . . ." We allowed our voice to trail. "We're encouraged to trust our emi. And hunches."

"I think Xola may have been murdered."

The words hung in the air between us. More whispers and rumors from the conspiracists and paranoid. We'd about had our fill of this forced diet on top of our grief. The matter scraped at an unhealed scab on our heart. It was difficult enough to come to terms with Pops's death, much less make room to entertain conspiracy theories.

"Amachi," we began.

"I know, I know. I could practically hear your voice of reason ringing in my head from the moment I first collected a sample from Selamault."

"What kind of sample?" We leaned forward, inhaling sharply to steady our breathing and allow her room to make her case.

"Sputum," she said. "Relax. It had already been expelled."

"Well, in that case, we won't trip, then." We eased back. "Doesn't make it any less extreme, though."

"Will you hear me out?" Her face implored us. Amachi had never been one for gratuitous leaps.

"Sure." We twirled our hands her way for her to go on. "We suppose we owe you for not slicing our head off earlier."

Amachi tilted her head at us, unsure if she was being baited into a trap. "I was suspicious that Xola's death was no accident from the beginning."

"Because an old man with a series of degenerative neurological disorders dying automatically should raise suspicions. You always were Maulana's prized student."

"I guess." Amachi slumped in her seat. The light caught her. Grief warped her features, her face almost unrecognizable. Recent tear streaks. Haggard eyes. There was a story she needed to construct, to tell, to maybe even believe. One that would reach fruition only with the telling. "I just didn't want to believe he was gone. I wanted there to be a reason. A cause."

"What did you find?" We perched on the edge of our seat, drawing on the strength of her conviction.

"I suspected a pathogen of some kind. The way his health suddenly took a turn. The way Selamault's sickness lingers. I wondered if perhaps she came in contact with the same thing. I didn't have a clear picture of it. Then I found it. Well, I found something. A genetic artifact. I have Maya attempting to reconstruct it."

"How long before you know anything definitive?"

"I don't know. Maya, do you have an estimate?"

< . . . > Maya's voice emulators crackled with something akin to static. A digital glitch.

"Maya?"

"It looks like some sort of . . . nanotech override." We wound our way over to the workstation. "That would require a military-grade access key."

As the words tumbled out of our mouth, the fashioned workstation began to dissolve into its component nanobots. Reduced to a scree resembling black sludge.

"That's not . . ." We bent over to examine the remains more closely. We reached out to sample the pile.

"Wachiru, get back!" Amachi launched herself at us, tackling us about the chest and dragging us to the floor.

When we glanced over, the nanobots had formed a slither. Slithers were a hacker squad convention. They counterprogrammed nanobots to form a series of tendrils that whipped about. Clumps of it broke off, forming fist-sized balls that, once clear of the birthing mass, grew tiny appendages and skittered about the room with the scuttling of black spiders. The tendrils lashed about, sometimes attempting to burrow into flesh. The weaponized, self-replicating bots launched bits of itself, to travel through blood vessels to the heart or brain. Or a tendril would simply stiffen and jab a person in the heart or eye or anything else fleshy and exposed. Or infiltrate only to reassemble inside and blow up like a spiked puffer fish. Hacking nanobots' protocols this way literally turned every aspect of our environment into a weapon, one whose method of attack depended on the imagination of the programmer.

"Maya, security protocols!" we yelled as we backed toward Amachi.

"It must be generating its own scattering field. It's as if it created its own security net and we're all invisible within it to Maya." Amachi crouched low, her chakrams already in hand. The table offered little protection, though the muscles in her legs tensed as she poised to spring at any moment.

"How many of them do you count?"

"I lost track after six." Clutching a chakram in each hand, Amachi's breathing slowed, becoming measured and calm. With a quick whip of her arms, she sliced two of the spiders in half. They dropped to the ground and dissolved, the sludgy mass scooting to rejoin the birthing pile for reprogramming instructions.

Chancing another peek around the dividing wall, we shouted to her. "Do you have a pehla stick?"

"Only jelis are allowed to carry those." Amachi ducked behind a cabinet.

"Do I look like I'm trying to bust you for illegal possession?" we yelled.

"Top drawer. On your left."

We lunged for the cabinet. The birthing pile formed twin tendrils that shot out at us. Twisting midair, we cleared them in our leap. Amachi took two strides, dove under the throbbing tendril, and slashed them. She crouched low, shifting her weight from leg to leg as she leaned back and forth, her chakrams twirling about her wrists.

We grabbed the pehla stick. Designed strictly as a defensive weapon, if one had imagination, it could be reprogrammed. Set to overload. We reversed the polarity of one end and sent a feedback loop along its internal circuit. The pehla stick flared. We dodged again.

Amachi rolled, passing underneath us, moving away from the birthing pile as a distraction. As it targeted us, she hurled a chakram into its heart. It turned its attention to her, allowing us the moment to toss the charged pehla stick into it. A field pulse knocked us both into the wall. Stunned, we sat where we landed and waited to see who would move next.

The pile stilled.

With a tentative step, Amachi stood up, holding her chakram perpendicular to her body like a knife at the ready to stab. But nothing moved. "Someone with access tapped into my workstation."

"Destroying all your work."

"Most of it, yes." She poked at the nanobot pile.

"You know what this means, right?"

"Yes." She turned to stare at us full on, her face stern and grave. "Xola was murdered. And someone just tried to cover it up."

14

STACIA CHIKEKE
The *Cypher* (Returning to Titan)

Nothing in her command history—no interstellar anomaly, no emergency breakdown on the ship, no exploration accident, no enemy encounter—terrified Stacia the way watching Bek convulse on the floor did. Her heart raced in her mouth. Her throat constricted. She remembered being torn between her duty as captain and her duty as mother. All the times she fell short as a mother. Not having time to play. Not being able to watch him perform. All the times she lost her temper. The entire family had. And felt the failure of her journey with his disease, the not knowing, the endless tests. The guilt of being broken. That maybe something in her genestream caused his condition. The helplessness whenever he so much as spiked a fever. The anxiety of not knowing what to expect next. Standing powerless as pain spasmed her son's body.

However, her training required her to still be a captain and wasn't going to let fear overtake her.

"Maya, we need a crash cart at my quarters!" Stacia touched Bek's forehead. Damp and hot. "He's burning up."

Yahya dropped to his knees, fashioning a cot under Bek. His vitals and health telemetry data displayed immediately. His temperature read 41.4°C. His limbs began to tremble again. Stacia cradled Bek's head to keep it still, willing through her touch to communicate that she was there. How much she loved him. She wanted to fight for him, but there was nothing to punch or shoot or rage against. Only an unfeeling virus leaching away her son's life.

"Med lab one!" She commanded the medi-cart. "Hold on, baby, hold on."

The hallway lights dimmed. Red flashed along the right of the passageway, alerting crew members to clear that side to allow the medi-cart to whisk past them to the medical unit. Doctors waited at the entrance to receive them.

"I want full-spectrum diagnostic analysis!" she screamed.

"We have him, Stacia." The doctor checked the scanners while another held Bek down.

"I'm the captain, and I gave you an order."

He leveled his eyes at her, unflinching in the face of her heat. "No, here, you're the mother. And we need you to stand down so that we can treat your son."

Yahya placed a hand on her shoulder. She shook it off and stomped toward her briefing room.

"Aren't you going to wait here?" he called after her.

"You wait." She refused to turn around. "You heard them. They don't need me. And I'm not going to wait around here like I can't do anything."

She stormed about her chamber, throwing a dish against the wall before overturning the table it once sat on. She slammed her hand into the wall, allowing it to hold her up while she refused to cry. Once she composed herself, she sent a link to the Science Councils on Titan and back at the Dreaming City. Within the hour, their leaders' faces filled holovid screens, almost a collage of the leading living scientists throughout Muungano.

"Why did you wait so long to bring us into this case?" A thick set of locks coiled from the lead Titan scientist's head. She stared over her glasses at Stacia. Or down her nose.

"I thought we could handle it. We have a top team of scientists here, too," Stacia said, both shamed and defensive.

"And now?" A bald man with a thick white beard analyzed her reports while talking to her, never meeting her eyes. He had the softness about his edges of someone who spent too much time wandering the halls of the Dreaming City.

She summoned all the disdain and restrained fury to her tone. "And now my son is in med lab one, barely clinging to life."

"I see." As if remembering his humanity as an afterthought, he offered, "I'm sorry."

"Save your sorries, I need answers," Stacia snapped. "His symptoms make no sense."

"Captain," the Titan scientist intoned gravely. "You just sent us these reports minutes ago. Allow us the time as a courtesy to study them. We'll develop a working hypothesis. You go be with your son. Your family."

Stacia slinked back to the med lab. Betraying no emotion, Yahya nodded at her approach. Without a word, he scooted over to make room for her on the waiting couch. The gulf of silence between them suckled on the teat of their indifference. A coiled spring of anger, Yahya clenched his left hand so taut, the skin of his knuckles paled. Stacia made no sound beyond the crumpling of her crisp uniform whenever she shifted positions. She hated that she'd become a cliché, a parent left to only wait while others tended to their child.

Her thoughts drifted back to when Bek was born. The moment she first held him. How she saved and archived so many mementos to mark him growing up. The time he climbed up the first tree, a Learning Tree, he encountered. Scampering up too high, he panicked. His fear paralyzed him, and he refused to attempt to climb down. Taking off her captain's cape, she clambered up the tree. The branches could barely support her weight, so she had to stop a couple of meters below him. Still close enough to assure him that she was there with him. Her voice calmed him down enough for him to focus on making the descent. The experience never dimmed his love of climbing. He got into everywhere and into everything. That was his way.

Once he got older, the only times she could ever dote on him—the only times he'd allow her to "mom" him, as he called it—was when he was sick. Those were the times he wanted her nearby. And she remained by his bedside, all night, all day, as her duties permitted, a hawkish angel watching over him. Monitoring his breathing, making sure one breath followed another. Not too different from the first few months after his birth. Her "night vigil," Yahya called it.

"After a while, you have to realize you can't account for every bad thing that could possibly happen." Yahya warned her he had no problems sleeping. Fathers could always sleep, unbothered by the possibility that anything could happen to Bek in the night. "You have to live life with a certain amount of faith or at least let your illusion of control go, or else you will go insane."

But now even under her steady gaze and presence, Bek struggled to breathe, and his condition worsened. The veins on his neck bulged. The capillaries along his face darkened as if for an instant oil pumped through his vessels. He hadn't responded to any treatment so far. All the healers managed to do was make him comfortable. And all she could do was watch from an adjoining room while medical personnel cared for her son. Did her job. Leaving Stacia powerless. Again. Scared. Not knowing what course to take next. The doctor was right. In this moment, she wasn't a captain. She was a mother. And this was the worst place for a leader—a mother—to be.

"You don't have to do that with me." Yahya's voice grated on her thoughts.

"Do what?"

"Walk around having been emptied out, then pretend you have to hold it together in front of them."

"I have to hold it together. For everyone's sake. I still have to captain. The rest of us actually cared about Xola, too. We can't just turn our emotions on and off like some robot."

"Don't you dare act like your loss was somehow deeper, more profound than mine," Yahya snarled. "I knew him for decades before you were born. Loss marks each of us."

"And some cut too deep to keep moving."

She turned her back to him.

"There, at least you finally admit something. Your way is not the Muungano way. Any here would gladly come alongside you to weep with you. Would want you to weep with them."

"I'm fine."

"Well, if you're so fine"—Yahya's voice had the pout of hurt about it, as if she spoiled the scene he had imagined with his rehearsed speech—"we need to decide how to proceed. About Bek."

His words were a scalpel of rebuke, cutting into her pain by exposing other pain. She slowly lost the rising swell of wanting to pick a fight with him for distraction's sake. Over her shoulder, she said, "You think I don't know how to care for my son."

"*Our* son." He emphasized as if she forgot his contribution to the process. "You think I don't?"

"I wonder. Sometimes. No. It's just that you're so fully convinced in your desperate grasps at theories that you sucked me in, almost having me convinced."

"Wait? I did? My prion theory." Yahya rushed around to face her. "I know you, Stacia. If you went down that road, you were thorough. What did you find?"

"Nothing. Always nothing." She stepped back, shielding herself from his intensity. The longing for her to believe him. His stare.

"I don't believe you." He raised her hand. She didn't remember him grabbing it.

"Believe what you want. All I know is that all the time I spent chasing down your prion duppies was time I could have spent developing something tangible. Something real."

"I was so sure." He let her hand slip from his. Rubbing his chin thoughtfully, he remained unconvinced. Yahya was never more insufferable nor in-tractable than when convinced of his own rightness.

Stacia geared up to go all in on him—to fully vent her frustrations on him—when the entrance to the med lab opened. The lead doctor strode out. His smock trailed him like a ghost, dissipating the farther he strayed from the sealed lab.

"How is he?" Stacia stepped toward him as if she'd receive the news faster if she met him halfway.

"Stable. We're still running tests."

"Is there nothing we can do?" Yahya sidled up to them, almost battling for position.

"Wait," the doctor pronounced.

But the way his voice quavered, Stacia knew he held back another possi-bility. "Or what else?"

"Or we could do a homeo-bypass." The doctor rubbed the bridge of his nose, a way to casually avoid eye contact as he pitched his long-shot idea.

"That's little more than an induced coma," Stacia said.

"Something is both taxing his system and eluding our scans. With an al-most intelligence about it. A vandal sneaking in at night and dodging any authorities tracking him."

"How do we know he won't get better on his own?" Yahya asked.

"You're catastrophizing?" Stacia stared at him in disbelief. "How can you go from wanting to move heaven and earth to find your mythical prions to just giving up and hoping for the best?"

"I hate it when you try to play cool logistician with me."

"Real recognizes real, huh? Consider it my command training. You blame it for everything anyway."

"This isn't a command decision."

"Isn't it?"

"You can't pull rank on me. I'm the boy's father . . . Captain." Yahya spat the last word like it was a curse. "I just want to give him more time before we do something drastic."

"So now you want to do nothing." Stacia threw her hands up.

"Waiting isn't nothing. Some things have to be allowed to run their course."

"And some things need to be acknowledged as done." Stacia folded her arms in front of her. Her eyes fixed in a glare, her body almost trembling with her subdued wrath.

The doctor had taken a step back to allow them time to talk, glancing back and forth, taking their temperature in order to time his interruption. "Would you care to see him?"

Neither said anything, not breaking their deadlocked stare, but they trailed after him.

At their entrance, Bek shifted in bed as if sensing their proximity. His movement broke the spell of their anger, each rushing to his side. Stacia took his hand, her fingers interlacing with his, to bring it to her lips to kiss. His mouth opened, voiceless, as if the structures in his throat constricted in a conspiracy to keep him silent. His airway opened and slammed shut, barely allowing a gasp, much less a further whisper. The sound of his dull inhalation would fill her next several sleepless nights. Too weak to talk, Bek appeared desperate to communicate something. The doctor scooted around them to adjust Bek's medication. A tear streamed down his face. He gestured for his pad. He began to tap out a message.

"Wormhole sab—" He tamped out before he succumbed to his treatment, and his eyes fluttered as the drugs took hold.

"Captain, if I'm not interrupting . . . ," Paki linked to her.

"Go ahead." Stacia ran her fingers through Bek's hair.

"Do you have time to meet?"

Stacia glanced at Yahya.

"Don't let me stop you. There's probably some 'Code Black / Eyes Only' business for you to attend to," Yahya said.

Stacia allowed him his parting quip without a retort. She fastened her cape into place, allowing the material to unfurl before she took her leave.

Stacia wound through the corridors of the *Cypher*. The air especially close. The ceiling somehow lower. The walls decorated with etched carvings she'd never noticed before. Sketches of life on the Dreaming City. At Bronzeville. People laughing and dancing as musicians played. A strange anxiety, or was it longing, overtook her. She turned another corner. Paki stood there. She stopped short to avoid bowling him over.

"What do you have, Paki?" She straightened her cape.

"A conspicuous amount of nothing."

"That's the vital report that demanded a meeting?"

"Well, to be honest, I thought you might appreciate a change of scenery."

"I—" Preoccupied with not meeting his eyes, even preparing to rear at him for dragging her away, Stacia caught herself. Paki was many things; frivolous wasn't one of them. Her grimace morphed into something softer, if not quite a relieved smile. "Thank you. I probably needed a break. Did you have any luck determining any pattern to the incidents?"

"That's difficult to say. There could be a number of explanations." Paki clasped his hands behind him. Whatever warmth of appreciation she had for him dissipated with the smug affect of his stroll. He knew something, or at least suspected, and needed to make a dramatic performance of its reveal.

"Hazard a guess." Her voice thickened with dryness. She led them toward her briefing room.

"I don't . . . guess. I investigate, deduce, imagine, hypothesize, conclude. But I don't guess."

"Indulge me. Hazard a . . . hypothesis."

"As I examined the work logs, I found substandard working conditions. Lack of regular full maintenance as the students regularly cut corners to finish their tasks."

"Students under your purview?" Before he could raise his voice in protest, she cut him off with a wave of her hand. "What if I were to tell you that I believe that we have at least one operative on board our ship working against Muungano's interests?"

"A saboteur?" Paki fashioned a chair to collapse into. His voice drained at the possibility he hadn't considered.

"If you will." Easing behind her workstation, she leaned forward and bridged her fingers. After several heartbeats of hanging silence, to allow the situation to fully settle in him, she spoke again. "What conclusion would you draw if your lead investigator seemed to drag their feet at every turn? For events that happened on their watch. Under their direct supervision."

Paki's face darkened with a sinister fury. His words came out slow and fully measured. "That would be a serious implication to make."

"Demanding a serious response, I'd say."

"I'll find your operative. If they exist."

"I expect no less." Stacia drew back in her seat, dismissing him.

Before he reached the exit, he turned over his shoulder. "You should probably keep these suspicions to yourself. Should word get out, people might start accusing even their most trusted, long-serving colleagues of being saboteurs. And accusations like that aren't easily walked back."

Stacia allowed enough time for Paki to clear the hallway before she stood to leave. Only then did it occur to her that she had nowhere in particular to go. She didn't want to return to her room. Without Bek, it was a hollow space. And she was over the men in her life. Having a glass of wine while chatting with Maya seemed oddly sad. Now was a moment she wished she could link with Amachi.

Back when they were coming up together, she had vowed not to let a man strain her friendship with Amachi. Their friendship bounded the celestial orbits of her universe, existing in the space reserved for something romantic. And they felt its occasional gravitational pull, never quite finding the language to describe what they had.

Then along came Yahya.

Not insecure, but believing that a monogamous romantic relationship was the star around which other relationships should orbit. He felt he wasn't her priority, knowing he was outranked by her best friend. Amachi was there before him and would be there after him. Trudging through the moments they had to spend apart. Sometimes years due to moving around for work, their relationship reduced to linkages and occasional visits. Reaching out less and less under the cascade of difficulties she called a marriage. And career.

Everything in their relationship became fraught.

Their friendship was a practice in intimacy and vulnerability. If she'd channeled all of her emotional expectations into her and Yahya, she'd be even more alone than she was now. She needed a variety of relationships. Different social roles to meet different emotional needs. Weak ties were another force to bind celestial orbits. The people seen infrequently, familiar near strangers. Not relationships that withered unremarked on. The kind that buoyed human health. Her outer circle. People on the periphery of her life with whom she shared something in common; but part of her rhythm of life. People she saw with some regularity in life, sometimes as a part of her work or simply just familiar faces from when she hit up poetry spots or concerts.

Perhaps she could check in on Dina. See what progress she had made.

"Maya, locate Dina."

<She's in the *Cypher*'s engine room, in the containment unit of the core's kheprw crystals.>

"Interesting. I did have a rehearsal scheduled." Stacia palmed her crystal sphere, comforted by its weight. She never canceled her rehearsal. Maybe the Universe was trying to tell her something.

She left for Dina's station.

When the door opened, a hunched-over Dina assembled her balafon in preparation to warm up. A form of deuterium and lithium, in their processed form, the crystals developed into aligned lattices, a sort of generator strata. Energy was harnessed from the converted sonic energy and the subsequent fusion reaction. Music renewed the decaying kheprw, recrystallizing them, transforming them into more concentrated, more perfectly aligned lattices. That was the purpose of the command performance. Entrusted to those who could perform at the highest levels.

Once she realized Stacia stood in the door, Dina stood at attention. "I see you, Captain."

"I see you, Dina." Taking a seat, Stacia set her command sphere into the keyboards at her station, unlocking the vintage clavioline. "And it's Stacia. Don't let me interrupt."

"I was hoping to join you . . . Stacia?" Dina's tone tested out how the captain's name sounded from her lips.

Stacia closed her eyes. Every time she sat down to play, the possibility of music was like a blank canvas. She wondered what she'd bring to it, if she could even string together notes to stir her soul anew, move her in any way. Stacia plinked the first few notes, tentative tickles in slow warm-up. In her mind, the worst textured tan color, a nauseous swell, oppressed her mood. She plucked her keys, feeling her way into the song, not knowing where her journey might take her. The prechorus moved into a melody, blossoming blues and greens, an algal bloom on an ocean wave. Music as color, notes as texture, this way of seeing was her secret. The piece slowly took shape.

Dina clutched the bamboo frame of her balafon, hesitant to jump in. Eyes still shut, Stacia nodded in her direction with a brief faltering smile. Encouraged, Dina struck the bamboo keys. The notes had the tenor of an electric keyboard, lightning flashes across inky clouds. Burlap rough, overlaying the captain's smooth, satin inner lining.

When the captain made changes, the rest of the attending command ensemble's response produced new structures in the music. They rode the chord progressions as if they were chasing light. Each note, each chord, the tempo, all had texture, hue, and shape. The color of music, moving in more than one dimension. Every sense bleeding into the next, telling a story. The universe began with nothing, vast and structureless. Empty. A cold place of vacuum and void. Out of that nothing, structures came about and took root. Establishing order among the chaos. Fundamental laws coming together to support those burgeoning structures.

Stacia left the central melody to explore. Dina veered opposite her.

Quarks and electrons, the musical notes on a tiny vibrating string creating magic. Color streamers bouncing at random, soon coalesced, a stained glass window whose individual panes melted. The music danced in interplay with the crystals.

Oblivious to the ensemble, caught up in their interplay with each other, Stacia and Dina reached their crescendo. Their instruments fell in tune with the vibration of the crystals. Stacia brought the piece to a close. Sweat glistened on her arms. Glancing at Dina, she was met by a rapturous smile. She was a fine command candidate. Dina stood, her legs wobbly under her.

"That . . . that was something," Dina said.

"Your first time?"

"I mean, I've practiced on my own. Experimented along the way when I found the right people, but nothing like . . ."

". . . a command performance. One wasn't scheduled, only a rehearsal, but I don't think the crystals are complaining."

"I know I'm not." Dina steadied herself, hovering beside Stacia's bench, waiting for permission.

"After that performance, I'm not going to deny you a seat." Though Stacia suspected more than a streak of self-interest and ambition in the woman, to climb further into the captain's relational orbit, she patted the settee. "How much can I trust you?"

"After that performance, I'd bury a body with you." Dina smiled.

"Hopefully, it won't come to that." Stacia began to shut down her clavioline, a task to occupy her to keep from meeting Dina's eyes too directly. "I have a matter of some sensitivity. Requiring a great deal of discretion."

"If it pleases the captain . . ."

"I need you to run an investigation on someone."

"Who?"

"Paki."

"Shit." Dina exhaled a slow, soft breath. She glanced around, checking to see if anyone could overhear them, as if Stacia hadn't taken that precaution. "About what?"

"Nothing sensitive. It's more like double-checking his work. It may be nothing, and I wouldn't ask you to do or say anything to jeopardize your relationship with him."

"My first loyalty is to the crew."

"I suspected as much." Stacia retrieved and pocketed her command sphere. "Honestly, more than anything else, I just want you to make sure that his work is thorough."

"He's my elder."

"Then he can use some of your youthful energy to keep him on his toes."

＊

When Stacia returned to her room, her lights were off. Not at the ambient preset she usually kept them at when she exited. Her emi stirred, not quite in alarm but with a wariness. Something or someone darkened her space. "Maya, lights to 'working' preset."

"Captain, I believe we are long overdue for a chat," a voice said from the darkness.

"Who's there?" Stacia signaled for ship security. *"Intruder alert."*

"I assure you, I'm nobody. Not a threat anyone would recognize." The light slowly came up, but not due to Stacia's control. A mzungu man sat across from an empty seat. A cybernetic interface covered his left eye, probably an early sensate. A well-trimmed white goatee framed thin, wistful lips. Everything about him, from his posture to the way he held his cup and saucer read delicate. "Please, do have a seat. All this pacing of yours is making me quite anxious."

Her security team should have been there by then. "Maya?"

"I'm afraid that I've taken the liberty to ensure our privacy." He cast his eyes upward to draw her attention to the small sphere orbiting him. A signal-canceling device, similar to the twins Selamault employed. "Besides, I'm no more than a few constructed photons. I can't hurt you."

With closer inspection, he indeed was a holovid, though the quality of transmission was flawless. Completely lifelike. Stacia ran her fingers through him to make sure. "Who are you?"

He sipped from his cup. "I'm afraid I have to apologize for my rudeness. I'd offer you some tea but, you know, photons."

"For the last time, I'm going to ask you to identify yourself."

"My name is Zenith Prebius. My friends call me Zen. Mr. Prebius is fine."

"What do you want, Zenith?" Stacia glared at him while continuing to pace. His presence, even as photons, presented a threat she couldn't abide.

"What do I want? Well, that is the question now, isn't it?" Zenith kept his calm composure, existing like a tesseract fold, not quite in her space, yet completely protruding into it.

"I'm going to guess that you're from LISC. From the sheer pompousness of this needlessly dramatic entrance, you're the new cultural attaché attached to Muungano."

"Correct. And I wanted to begin our relationship by delving into matters of substance. And mutual benefit. Opportunity Zones."

Stacia rolled her eyes. In her experience, Opportunity Zones amounted to new occasions to exploit and displace communities, typically hers. The way her mother told it, her family barely survived their O.E. neighborhood being designated an Opportunity Zone. LISC declaring eminent domain on their houses, whole businesses torn down for an interstate that bifurcated their neighborhood. The nearby university declared the owner of land tracts. Her people couldn't move to the dream of Muungano fast enough. If LISC operated true to form, before they decided to open an Opportunity Zone, no community members outside of their internal enclave were consulted. Stacia did a brief internship with the Indianapolis Chamber. She'd just left Amachi and dealt with the emotional hole by piling her life with work and school and training. Adding more and more until the demands of time lines caused her life to implode. And she had to re-create herself. Eventually she leveraged that experience against them, advancing into LISC itself. She never worried about being tainted by entering their spaces because she was Muungano, born and bred. She carried her culture with her wherever she went. After she gained her requisite experience, she transferred to Titan. And quickly rose to captain.

"It's funny how areas already wealthy with resources and relationships seem to be the ones labeled Opportunity Zones. Where, pray tell, might this Opportunity Zone be located?"

"The wormhole, of course."

"I will need a drink. Of the non-caffeinated, preferably alcoholic variety." Stacia moved to her bar, keeping him in her peripheral view, and tucked a pehla stick into her belt. "Make your pitch."

"LISC wishes to share resources, putting community-level development on its center stage."

"Yes, you are all about inclusive economies. History abounds with so many examples of capitalist concern for human-centered work."

"Many resources are simply underutilized, especially in . . . underdeveloped areas." Zenith couldn't help the snide edge that slipped into his condescending drone. "We simply want to come alongside certain communities and help revitalize and empower them to reach their full potential."

Stacia hated words like *empower* and *revitalize* when applied to her community. It implied that the people there had no power and that their community was dead. "Where are you from, Zenith?"

"Mars. Born and raised."

"Ah, that makes sense." Stacia took the empty seat. With all due casualness, she scanned for any other devices. "The Mars colony was an ongoing experiment in economic redlining. All the one percent of earth retreating to their own planet after their machinations wrecked O.E. Planned-for, intentional, and legal segregation."

"In our defense, we're an inclusive one percent." Zenith yawned. He set his cup and saucer down. They flickered before disappearing entirely.

"So inclusive, half of your capital city seceded."

"Bronzeville did seem a little . . . aggrieved." Leaning over, he grabbed a piece of fruit she didn't recognize from a nearby plate.

"They were 'aggrieved' because your processes don't honor the people present. You tried to hold resources over their heads. The same go-to playbook of LISC in your support of supremacy. You haven't learned that money doesn't put us on a leash. Ever."

"My. *Someone* had to get something off their chest." Zenith took a bite of the fruit. Its loud, crisp crunch echoed in the shadows. "It's easy to nitpick, complain, and tear down after we were the ones who did the actual work to make a difference."

"And what would you have Muungano do?"

"Be at the table. I don't fully understand all the circumstances around this 'Orun Gate'—though it is a naturally occurring phenomenon—but people inform me that you or someone from your 'community' in leadership needs to be in the room for access negotiations."

"Not like the good old days when you could just Manifest your Destiny."

Stacia refused to bite at his "naturally occurring phenomenon" line. He was clever and slick, but fishing, nonetheless. "If I understand this right, your masters are yanking on your leash for you to bring us in."

"Technological leaps require societal cooperation and adjustment. We go through these periodic changes in human society. Take the agricultural revolution, for example. When we figured out how to grow food in a stationary place, the whole game changed. We no longer had to be strictly hunter-gatherers. We could stay in one location for extended periods of time and grow our own food. Forcing us to build a culture unifying people groups to cooperate, manage it, water it, harvest it."

"'We' became slaves to wheat," Stacia said.

"Yes. Wheat, the technology and systematic impact of agriculture, tricked us into serving it and spreading it around the world. Similarly, you don't own the wormhole, and you certainly don't control it."

"Neither do you. We never claimed ownership. We don't have 'private property.' Just like one can't own air or water or land. They are part of the commons for the good of all. And yet you appear ever ready to exploit it. Well, let me be clear for you and your masters: We are here. Right now. We occupy the space around the Orun Gate. And most importantly, in the language you understand, we have the power to secure it."

Unfazed, Zenith freshened his cup of tea. With exaggerated grace, he tested the temperature, blew its surface, and proceeded to sip. Once Stacia crossed her arms in growing impatience, he began again.

"There is a group of loyalists on Earth, who, shall we say, have found a sympathetic ear within LISC against the so-called Interstellar Alliance."

American Renaissance Movement. ARM. An Earth Firster. No matter what they chose to call themselves, the fundamentalists were never leaving Earth, no matter how bad the global environmental collapse got. It just fueled their "imminent apocalypse" narratives. The thing about extinction-level events was that—even with economies reprioritizing—those with power, those with vision, only saw opportunities to further amass power. Stacia had always suspected an alliance between megacorporations and the religious factions when it came to carving up the world.

"Just like I imagine there are those who don't love being of Muungano. Who wished we'd never left O.E. or forged First World or thrown off the yoke of history and freed ourselves from the mental and physical chains of oppressive systems and established a place where Ugenini, Asili, and Maroon could call home."

"Rebel hero or secessionist traitor. Patriot or terrorist. It's all about loyalty to whoever wins. And like any story, it is about perspective." Zenith set his cup and saucer down. "At LISC, we see the future and prepare for it. By making deals with similar-minded individuals capable of seeing the big picture. No matter who runs things, business always gets done."

"Our 'business' is only how to better our community and the people in it."

"Yes, yes, you grow your own food, share the work, everybody has to make a contribution of some sort, blah, blah, blah. I know the Muungano propaganda well. It's all enough to make my heart swell three sizes. But you missed a major lesson of my wheat story. All human ideas are forced to adapt. Here's the dirty little secret your elders fear to tell you: the idea of empire changes forms and adapts based on who conquers. Even when a group frees themselves, they tend to take on the model of their oppressors because that's all they know. Your propagandists—pardon me, your 'griots'—may spread this mythology, but in my experience, politics often make strange bedfellows."

"What politics?"

"The politics of power. Control. Fear. All cultural nationalists want nothing more than to close and secure their borders. Even the nationalistic voices in Muungano. Which means they're open to negotiations, there's room to become . . ."

". . . strange bedfellows," Stacia concluded.

Zenith raised his cup to toast to her.

"But why tell me?"

"The more extreme elements of any sect are capable of anything. Slowing down your ship's progress is one thing, but the thing about bedfellows, strange or otherwise, is once they are done with their mutual agendas, they return to their individual ones."

"Taking back Muungano."

"That's the real prize. All we see now are potential markets, clients, and products. And destabilized climates are bad for business."

"And what business are you in?'

"The business of getting what we want." With that, he cut his transmission, and his image disappeared.

Stacia rushed over to where Zenith once sat. Her fingers probed every surface until she found it. A glyph. Intelligence grade. He had to be nearby. "Maya? Are you back on line?"

<We were never gone.>

"Play back security holovid of this room for the last ten minutes."

<Those records are unavailable.>

"Why?"

<Security protocols engaged. Code Black / Eyes Only.>

"Maya, no one has higher Code Black / Eyes Only clearance than I do on my own ship."

<Security protocols engaged. Code Black / Eyes Only.>

"Have any signals beamed into this room?" Stacia held the glyph device to her face for further scrutiny.

<A site-to-site communication signal is currently aimed at your chambers.>

"From where?"

<Paki's quarters.>

"Send a security team to meet me there."

Stacia stormed out of her room. The head of her security team, Kenya York, met her with a team of two officers. Their breastplates covered chrome-colored bodysuits. Kenya's face was uncovered, her two long braids dangled to her waist, the tips dyed purple. Each of her officers wore a gilded animal mask. One an eagle, the other a dog. They brandished shields, though their charged pehla sticks remained at their waists. They waited outside his door for her command. "Security override, keyword: Chikekel."

Paki's door opened.

His room had been thoroughly searched. Tables overturned. Cabinets rifled through. Clothes scattered. With a gesture, Stacia dispersed her team to secure the scene. She went to Paki's workstation. The interface had been locked down. Someone had tried to hard jack their way through. A spray of blood streaked the wall behind the station. The trace blood on the floor smeared as if a body had been dragged through it.

"Maya, locate Paki."

<Paki is not on board the *Cypher*.>

When Stacia turned, she saw a cup of tea resting on the counter.

15

EPYC RO MORGAN
Eshu

Through the low-lying haze of desert dust and heavy weapons fire, enemy combatants closed on Fela's position. And when a Hellfighters sister was in trouble, the HOVA always had one another's back. Charge fire erupted around Epyc Ro as she dashed to her commander's position. A stream of blaster fire stitched the ground she ran along, throwing her stride off to the point where, with her last solid steps, she dove for cover behind a stand of boulders. The enemy deployed biped units, mechanical bots that targeted movement of nonbranded biologicals. With an AI intelligence guiding the robots, they were walking mines that could improvise around unforeseen problems. Panicked, the Mzisoh soldiers concentrated their fire on the new threat, heedless of spraying the HOVA. Now would have been the perfect time to call in air support.

But the *Hughes* was gone.

One problem at a time.

Epyc Ro tightened her helmet to her forehead, double-checked her position, and resumed her mad sprint. From her spot on the ridge, combatants dug in with machine charge rifles. It would take a sustained squad rush to get them from below the hill.

"Time to put a hurt on them!" Epyc Ro yelled to anyone linked to the sound of her voice, since it was impossible to be heard over the roar of weapons fire. Her emi reached out with an awareness, a battle-honed clarity, and the chaos and confusion coalesced, grew almost still, and within that stillness, she moved. Layered in sweat and dust, she careened down the slope. Energy surged through her system, her muscles growing light even as her head cleared. Endorphins lifted her head into a euphoric cloud.

The rest of the remaining squad fell in line behind her rushing to help Fela.

Anitra ran with complete abandon. Despite her bravado, she prided in her precision and attention to detail. Ducking behind a few jutting stones that littered the field like grave markers, she took up a position above her captain. Anitra deployed her DMX-3000 with the ease of a steady breath. She outscored the entire unit when it came to marksmanship. She often bragged that she honed her skills in endless hours of linkages, her rondavel being a museum of gaming consoles. Hers was the gift of controlled fury, mostly because if she got too pissed, she blew her shot. The two CO/IN operatives spraying the charges, erupting fountains of dirt around Epyc Ro, suddenly slumped over in their perches.

Robin barreled to Epyc Ro's side, always appearing out of nowhere right when she was most needed. Turning to Epyc Ro, she winked. Her body dropped out of view as she tumbled backward without breaking her pace. Robin rose like a fog around ships floating in a lake. Her Busta fired, and the two drones locking on to their positions shattered behind them. She whirled.

Epyc Ro felt it, too.

The tenor of the patrol changed, the way the temperature dropped before a storm. The cross fire slackened with an abruptness that made her wary.

The enemy troops withdrew.

The Hellfighters converged on Fela's last-known position, but the commander was gone. Slouched to the side, concentrating on whispers only she could hear, Chandra's unfocused gaze never failed to unsettle Epyc Ro.

Chandra scanned for any trace evidence. Her eyes still vacant, she shook her head. <No traces, Captain.>

"What do you mean?"

The rest of the squad turned to Chandra.

<No enemy contacts or signals. There has been a complete ordered withdrawal.>

Once the shooting stopped, the Mzisoh crawled out into the open. The soldiers paused behind rocks used as cover. Tentative heads peeked around them to scout the enemy. Ellis!Olinger idled up the makeshift road in their confiscated vehicle. Epyc Ro never wanted to assume command this way. Though it wasn't fair to Fela, from any perspective, if her last name wasn't Buhari, she'd never have leapfrogged Epyc Ro for command, especially for so vital a mission. She waved her people forward to clear any enemy nests.

"Ellis, organize your people into a defense perimeter. I want this area sealed," Epyc Ro said.

Ellis directed some of their people, who sprinted off to handle it. They wore the look of someone wanting to prove themselves, yet having fallen short. Their severe scrutiny appeared to commit Epyc Ro's every gesture and timbre of command to memory.

"Nitra, Robin, handle cleanup." Epyc Ro pushed such concerns to the back of her mind.

"Fine, though I may have to take off my helmet. It's too hot for all these damn braids." Robin searched the area. Her jovial spirit lessened, sensing Epyc Ro's troubled emi. "Where's Commander Buhari?"

"Gone. No trace. No body, no blood, barely signs of a fight." Crouching low, Epyc Ro sifted some dirt through her fingers. Fela was a military asset with security clearance having access to all manner of military codes and procedures. And as the sister of Maulana, they might think they could use her as a bargaining chip with the Ijo. "This was a coordinated grab. Seems Fela was the target of this firefight. This Interstellar Alliance is targeting high-value assets."

"That's how they've been attacking us lately," Ellis said. "One of our prisoners called it Operation Ragnarok. They've captured or taken out many of our chieftains . . ."

". . . to destabilize the command structure of their enemies and to gather as much actionable intelligence from them as possible," Epyc Ro finished.

"See? This is what I mean. This sounds like one of O.E.'s whack-ass names," Robin said.

"What would you call it? Operation Bad and Bougie?" Anitra asked.

"Actually, that docs have a ring to it," Robin said.

"Your people joke in the face of all of this?" Ellis asked.

Epyc Ro stepped to them, her face within centimeters of Ellis's. "Don't ever question how my people handle the stress of a situation. Know the stakes, and they understand their jobs. And rise to the occasion every time. Know that they won't rest, especially now this Interstellar Alliance has one of ours. And we always collect our own."

"She put her big voice on 'em, so you know this shit is serious." Robin slung Busta over her shoulder.

"Come on," Anitra clapped Robin on her back. "Let's go get our Harriet Tubman back."

Epyc Ro scouted the perimeter, not focusing on the violence of combat. The bodies that lay scattered about the area. The insurgent whose arm was shorn off. Who caught a charge directly in his midsection, the explosion separating head from limbs. Sent arms and legs tumbling, branches caught in a windstorm. Chests exposed as if fists punched straight through them. Faces frozen in various stages of the rictus of realization that their time was done.

"Have you thought about what your last word will be?" Anitra guessed at the turn the captain's mind had taken.

"What?" Epyc Ro sat on the edge of her stone, staring at each of them in turn.

"You know, you look down and see that a sniper laser has painted you." Anitra aimed an imaginary weapon, locking in on a target. She fired, making a whining sound. "Or you hear the wail of an incoming ballistic too late. What do you say?"

"Jesus, that's morbid," Robin said.

"Calling on your savior. I can see that. It's a little late since he's obviously summoning you home, but that's all right, I guess," Anitra said.

"Oh shit," Epic Ro said.

"Lacks a certain poetry," Anitra said.

"Momma," Robin said.

"'Momma'?" Anitra fixed her face as if she'd eaten sour fruit dipped in spoiled milk.

"I read once that the top two most common words are either *momma* or *no*."

"What's your momma gonna do?"

"What kind of question is that? It's not like saying *no* is exactly going to stop a bullet either," Robin said.

Epyc Ro shook her head and circled the wreckage. A CO/IN all-terrain vehicle had been overturned by an explosion and abandoned. Its occupants dangled from each door. Inspecting the vehicle, she saw the regalia of the passenger was more formal than the driver.

"Chandra?" Epyc Ro called. "Can you examine this vehicle? Forensic protocols. See if you can determine where it's been."

<Soil is consistent with the local hills. However . . . > Chandra examined the tread. <Noticeable traces of iridium.>

"Consistent with kheprw crystal processing." Epyc Ro turned to the Mzisoh. "Is there a production site near here?"

"Two ridges over. A facility," Ellis said. "They haven't made a secret of it. Almost as if they want us to know, daring us to try to come for them."

"Then let's not disappoint them," Epyc Ro said.

"Once we get there, we'll have to get inside," Anitra said.

"We can't just Cupid shuffle up to their door and hope they let us in," Robin said.

"Why not?" Anitra asked.

"I hate that look in your eye. What are you thinking?"

"We pose as security bringing Ellis in as a prisoner. They let us in." Anitra held her arms up to signal the end of her brilliant plan.

The HOVA unit paused long enough for the plan to settle in before they burst out laughing.

Robin doubled over, trying to catch her breath. "That shit don't even work well in movies."

"It was worth a shot," Anitra said.

"We don't know the Interstellar Alliance protocols for the first time someone challenges us. At any point, guns start blazing."

"We do," Ellis said. All eyes turned toward them. "There would be a standard security strike of any vehicle approaching the compound. An automated response. Afterward, they send a cleanup team to retrieve what was left."

"They leave a clean scene after scooping up anything useful for study would be my guess," Robin said.

"Which brings me to plan B," Anitra said. "We drive up, let ourselves get painted, let them blow us to shit."

"Now you're talking a plan that makes sense." Robin hoisted Busta.

It took Ellis less than an hour to get the once-overturned vehicle running again. Epyc Ro worried about how the natives would do in combat. Mzisoh soldiers hadn't overly impressed her. At this point, she just hoped they wouldn't panic and lose all their sense. Though Ellis wasn't one of hers, they had potential. They'd been an invaluable cultural bridge so far and possessed intimate knowledge of the land and firsthand experience with their common enemy. Their eyes, large and owlish, worked against their fear. For now, they remained eager to serve and anxious to prove themselves. She'd be bringing Ellis along with them. But if she was to be the leader her squad needed, not curled into a fetal position, the mission came first.

<Heavy chatter coming in from the base.> Chandra tapped the side of her skull. <Quick response team.>

The Hellfighters rumbled toward the refining base. The bodies of the dead soldiers who originally occupied the vehicle had been propped up. Once the enemy locked on to them and blew up their unannounced vehicle, in the best-case scenario, the bodies should leave the base's investigation team suitably confused. Maybe second-guessing themselves for possibly killing their own, who may have made a daring escape posing as natives. At the very least, Epyc Ro just needed biological material for them to recover.

"That's their recovery unit designed to swarm any approaching mobile units," Ellis said.

"You about ready?" Epyc Ro asked.

"Confirmed. They're locking on to us now," Robin said.

"Then it's go time," Epyc Ro said.

With that, Chandra and Anitra peeled off over the back edge, diving into the night. They would set up the Hellfighters' exit strategy, finding good positions along the rocky terrain from which to provide cover.

Robin and Ellis followed, leaping from the vehicle while Epyc Ro aimed it straight toward the main gate. She locked the stabilizer into place and locked the steering column. The vehicle was on cruise control. A rocket blazed, a languid flare followed by a strange hollow boom came from the building's top toward her. Epyc Ro tumbled out the back and scrambled toward the drop-off point to join Ellis and Robin. The vehicle exploded, a torch sat against the encroaching darkness, spewing a spray of rock and dirt and waves of force.

"Sitrep?" Epyc Ro shielded her face from the glare and concussion.

"Cleanup details have just been dispatched." Robin surveyed through her visor.

"Prisoners are usually taken in the main doors," Ellis whispered.

"Then we'll have to improvise," Epyc Ro said.

"What have we been doing so far?" Robin asked.

"Ma'am." Epyc Ro secured her navsuit, running it through its system checks. "Shields?"

"I borrowed Anitra's so we can cloak Ellis," Robin said.

"All right, let's go in," Epyc Ro said.

Little more than wraiths among shadows, their individual cloak units blocked signals and masked their heat signatures. They approached the opposite side of the base from where the cruiser was destroyed. The rear of the refinery had been erected in a hurry. Solid construction, but far from state of the art, reminding Epyc Ro of a small warehouse. Slightly lopsided, constructed from material repurposed from a large cruiser. The heavy bay doors hung open.

The labyrinthine halls gave the interior the feel of a penitentiary. What few windows there were had been blocked with reinforced molybdenum, in preparation of a siege. The air grew thick, both damp and close. A mix of rot and mildew seeped from behind the walls. The thought hit her that if this was the shell of a repurposed ship, and the technology was biobased, the smell could be the rot of a decomposing vessel. They crept through the passages until they reached an antechamber. It had little furniture in it, the walls bare, with no room for personalization. Nothing that might remind the occupants of their home or distract them from where they were and the work they were there to do. A stench—of lingering body odor and stale food, a meal that had been picked over and discarded—clung to the air.

Ellis gestured toward the side wall. Epyc Ro stepped toward it until her eyes adjusted. She finally saw the outline of a door, its frame recessed into the wall so smooth it nearly disappeared. Epyc Ro had walked by it without notice. No air passed around it, a complete seal. Camouflage was its security. Bringing her talon to bear, she scanned the room for heat signatures. With a nod, she called over Chandra. The comms specialist removed the glove from her hand, revealing data ports as fingers. She jacked into the lock. Her eyes rolled back into her skull. Her eyelids fluttered. The lock released the door.

Epyc Ro entered what could have been a cell. Her eyes adjusted to the darkness with a blink. The walls shimmered in the dim lighting. A dull glint refracted the light. She leaned in for closer inspection. Scratches etched the walls; thick nails had scraped against them. Hundreds of them. A history of hands that had scrabbled against the wall, attempting to claw their way to freedom. Or in a desperate escape from something. She spared a glance at Ellis's hands, noting the heavy nails that shielded their fingertips, and wondered how many of their people had spent time in this room.

"All prisoners must have been brought back here once the CO/IN scrubbed all battlefields of equipment and bodies." Epyc Ro slowly paced the room. Her light explored every surface to gather readings to analyze later.

"Like ants coming back for their own." Robin stalked the perimeter of the room opposite her. "Except not just their own. All bodies."

"Forensic study?" Epyc Ro asked.

"That'd be my guess." Robin shook her head, half-disgusted. "They're thorough."

"That's one word, I suppose." Epyc Ro's scanner flashed. A small patrol headed their way. "We're not shadows anymore."

"Company?" Robin asked.

"Ten meters out."

"How many?"

"Five. In patrol pattern. I don't think the facility knows we're here. This may be a standard sweep. If possible, we need to maintain . . . discretion."

"Do we need backup?" Ellis pressed themselves against the wall flanking the door.

"Nah, I can handle light work." Setting her Busta down, Robin cracked her knuckles. "You know the cardinal rule: talk shit, get hit."

Robin rounded the corner just as the patrol was about to, catching them by surprise. The CO/IN guards froze for an instant as the reality of her presence settled in. She punched the first one hard enough for them to see all of their ancestors. Her fists were balls of lightning, striking throats, kidneys, and deep into bellies, driving all air out of them. A guard dropped to their knees only to get greeted by her elbow. Another tumbled to the ground, slow to stand up. The last recovered quickly, jumping back up to face her. Just in time for her boot from a spinning kick to connect to their chin. They were out before they landed on their back. She waited patiently for the last to make their move. Sloppy and desperate in their charge, she blocked their first two blows. Her face grave and focused—her large eyes unblinking—she ducked under another blow only to rapid-fire punches directly into the guard's gut. When they doubled over, she drove her hand straight down. Five bodies dropped in under thirty seconds.

"We should kill them to ensure their silence," Ellis said.

"That is not our way. They are no longer a threat," Epyc Ro said.

"They will be once they awaken."

"We'll deal with them then. For now, we don't become monsters for the sake of convenience. Are you good with that?"

Ellis stared at the guards. Then the scratches on the wall. They spit on the guards. "Yes. For now."

The team dragged off the bodies, binding them before securing them in a cell. Once the door closed, Ellis smashed the lock pad.

"Come on." Epyc Ro took point without further comment.

The tunnels connected to another passageway, yet somehow this corridor felt different. Whatever stirred Epyc Ro's emi, she felt it along the pores of her skin as if her navsuit weren't there. The HOVA Hellfighters glanced at one another as if confirming the disturbance in their emi. The walls weren't older. More as if the atrocities committed in its hallways stained the very core. The supports bulged along the archways like an insect's exoskeleton.

"They don't want us to see something," Robin said.

"I think I know what." Epyc Ro peered into the next chamber. She held her hand up as Ellis approached. "You . . . don't want to go in there."

Ellis read her eyes. Disturbed, their face already began to crack with sadness, they pushed past her.

"I'm sorry," she whispered as she dropped her hand.

The cold room had the feel of age and decay. A thin skim of moisture coated the walls. A lone light bobbed overhead, a floating ball producing a wan shaft of light illuminating the solitary figure.

Natan.

Strapped to a chair, naked. Their chest peeled back like overripe fruit. Their intestines piled into their lap.

Ellis rushed to their side, falling to their knees before they had stumbled into a collapse. They opened their mouth in a soundless cry. Robin rested a hand on Ellis's shoulder. There was no time to mourn. No time to accept the loss. No time to allow the hate and anger to settle in. They lowered their head, but reached up to hold her hand, if only for a moment, to reassure each other of their respective humanity remaining intact.

"Over here." Epyc Ro rifled through the room.

"What you got?" Robin left Ellis with their chieftain to rush to her side. She scanned the reports. "Communication records. From all over."

"What do you mean 'all over'?" Epyc Ro glanced at Ellis, who watched both of them but remained utterly still.

"The entire Muungano federation. The Dreaming City. Titan. Bronzeville. Out to the Oyigiyigi mining operations."

"They're trying to map out our defensive capabilities." Epyc Ro flipped through the holovids.

"Captain." An unusual quaver filled Robin's voice.

Epyc Ro froze. The tenor of her sergeant's tone unsettled her. She turned slowly toward her. "What is it?"

"A recent report." Robin's face blanched. "Camara Xola is dead."

Dead? Epyc Ro allowed the possibility of the word a moment to hit her and settle before shoving it aside so that she could be about the job of gathering intel. "Is it . . . verified?"

"These are our transmissions intercepted from Muungano."

"Did the Interstellar Alliance have anything to do with it?"

"The reports don't give any indication. Only that they are considering tactical options in light of . . . events."

"That we might be vulnerable while reeling from grief."

"Aren't we?" Robin asked.

"How vulnerable are you feeling right now?" Epyc Ro raised her talon.

"More pissed than ever." Robin turned to Ellis, who struggled to make it to their feet.

Epyc Ro glanced from them to their chieftain. "This all has the feel of a decapitation strike. Taking out our leaders across . . . worlds."

Robin smacked the workbench. Spinning the holovid around, a large red dot pulsed. "I found Fela's location."

"Ellis, we have to go."

"We . . ." Ellis guarded Natan's body, not moving. "We can't just leave them here."

"We know how you feel."

"How can you? Our chieftain, our leader, my parent was just killed."

"As was ours." Epyc Ro allowed her face to reveal her emi, in all of its broken shards. Enough for Ellis to witness before locking it back away. She couldn't allow her awareness to feel too much. She pressed her hand into Ellis's back. "You stay here with your chieftain. Do what you have to do, but we can't do anything more for them. We have to go. Our captain may still be alive."

"No . . . I'll come, too." Ellis glanced one more time at Natan. "There's nothing more I can do for them now. Except avenge them."

The same instinct threatened to overwhelm Epyc Ro.

Fela's position wasn't much farther down the hallway. Just at the next junction. Keeping their heads down, the HOVA skulked through the hallways. They gambled that the shock of spotting them might buy them precious seconds to defend themselves. A peculiar light radiated along the shaft. Epyc Ro's eyes struggled to adjust to it. The air thickened. The deeper they went into the structure, the less the air had been scrubbed. The tunnel opened up. Thick, cloying puddles collected in front of several chamber doors along a wide ledge that funneled the open air waste down the grating. The more chambers they passed, the more the air ripened with the rot of pressed meat.

Each cell door they ran by reduced to an abattoir of interrogation. Epyc Ro could do little more than repress her abject horror. And her fear.

They reached the junction in a few minutes. Once Robin pointed to the correct cell, Epyc Ro and Ellis flanked either side of the door to prepare to breach. Setting some charges along the hinges and lock, Robin blew the door. Epyc Ro and Ellis breached the entrance before the smoke had a chance to clear.

The cell was empty.

16

AMACHI ADISA
The Dreaming City to the Citadel

You wake up stewing over the fact that no one explained the dress code for an Ijo security council briefing. And you're cold. A chill runs down your calves and deep into your core, leaving you unable to get warm no matter the layers of blankets nor Maya controlling the room temperature. Your muscles ache, and you hurt all over with a distant, dull soreness. Your body groans, your joints grinding together like ill-fitting stones as you decide to push through until you feel normal again. Self-conscious of your fashion choice, you keep to the edges of the chambers.

Perhaps a strapless dress with a nanomesh overlay, its pattern a series of textiles, might be an eye-catching outfit. But it doesn't inspire the serious note you now realize you want. No one would take you seriously. Still, you had to carve your own way forward. The sun sank below the moon's ridgeline, its rays yellow and orange through the filter screens of the observation glass. The filter along the outer dome dimmed to imitate twilight; the refracted illumination lit the central stage. You pass Jaha, whose casual down-her-nose glance causes you to tug the hem of your dress to make sure you hadn't left anything unintentionally exposed. You hurry to take your seat.

The amiable chatter of the gathered crowd draws down as Maulana prepares to call the meeting to order. He moves with such natural gravitas, even the elders shift as if intimidated. With an uptick of his chin, he chants the words as if reciting a poem. "Habari gani?"

"Umoja!" the council responds in unison and takes their seats.

Rising, you capture all of their attention, hundreds of eyes, hungry yet encouraging. Xola was heavy on your mind as you stand before the Ijo security council, feeling very small on a very large stage. Jaha and Maulana both remain standing. Him at the center of the room, pacing the dais already in command of his stage; her off to the side, studying the room. You take a breath and begin your story. You tell them of your suspicions and your tentative investigation. Your findings and the attack on you and Wachiru.

"They want us at one another's throats. The proverbial scorpion looking for passage across the river on our backs." Nothing approaching compassion fills Maulana's voice.

"Assuming it is O.E.," Wachiru said.

"Who else benefits from a decapitation strike? And let's call it what it is without mincing words. Sowing dissent among us buys them time."

"And potential allies," Jaha adds, though through a skeptical lens. Talking the idea through to see if it held any merit.

"If so bold, why not keep killing our Camaras until they have someone of their liking?" Wachiru's posture betrays his conflict. On the surface, deceptively calm, remaining true to Muungano, honoring his father's way of leading while figuring out what his own way looks like. Underneath, roiling uncertainty, with much of him still debating his right, maybe even ability, to be the unifying teacher.

You aren't sure of your role in these proceedings. Similar to much of the Ijo, you have become a spectator while these larger-than-life figures posture and deliberate. But these people are also your mentors, and you remain uncertain who you are to support as a ranking member.

"Each death only raises the chances that evidence will point back to them. But take out Xola, and chaos ensues." Maulana tenses, his arm flexes with the need to punch something. "Not only chaos, though. They hope to squash our spirit."

"Xola was not Muungano. Muungano is bigger than him," Wachiru says. "If our community cannot choose its next spokesperson, it does not deserve to move forward."

"There is no one like Xola," you say louder than you intend. Your voice crackles, almost hoarse. Your grief threatens to overtake you, waiting for you to drop your guard even a little.

"Exactly, Amachi. It's time for a new Camara. A different tenor of the same song." Maulana grimaces, perturbed. Not at you, though he could just as likely be annoyed at every person in the room. His resting glower tires of the inaction of politics.

"Right now, we have no concrete evidence. Only a circumstantial case and a lot of suspicions," Wachiru says.

"What do you propose?" Maulana's energy spikes, aggressive, almost predatory. He nears, a wolf circling to take the measure of his prey.

"Quiet first steps: Strengthen, if not formalize our alliance with the entire Mars colony, not solely Bronzeville. Then escalate a trade embargo against O.E. for operating in bad faith. We stop dealing with them in any way." Wachiru is either naive or oblivious. He charts a course he perceives as one of reason and sensibility, inadvertently isolating himself. He should dismiss the council for individual deliberation and meditation to reconvene later. Allow time for heads to cool. The heat of the moment is where Maulana lives.

"So talk and then take away their toys?" Maulana sucks his teeth, not bothering to hide his disgust. Much of the room joins in this rising chorus of disdain.

"The only thing spanking a child teaches is more violence."

"Nice words to hide behind. But they cannot distract from the fact that your 'punishments' do not go far enough, Wachiru. If their actions have earned a minimal response, we should begin any 'negotiations' with sanctions."

"If. This is what we mean." Wachiru fixes his heavy-lidded gaze on him. "There is too much 'if' for us to move forward too quickly."

"Besides, Mars will never go along," Jaha says.

"Who cares if they don't?" Maulana whirls toward her. Recognizing her as an elder, he lowers the temperature of his tone. "We have always gone our own way. Never beholden to the idea that we might offend erstwhile allies. I say we take a further step and increase our defensive capabilities."

"We need to take these options to the full Ijo." Wachiru now strides about the dais with an air of authority. "In the meanwhile, what of Amachi?"

You snap back to full attention at the mention of your name. All eyes turn to you. "What of me?"

"We need more information. Your instincts have served you well, so far. We would recommend sending you out to continue your investigation." Wachiru cocks his head a little, and in that moment reminds you so much of Xola you want to run over and throw your arms around his neck and never let go.

"I'm no jeli. I don't—"

"Where would you go next?" Wachiru presses. His eyes flick toward you, focusing in a way that won't be denied.

"Oyigiyigi. The mining outpost."

"Why there?" An odd trace of concern fills Maulana's voice.

"The only outbound Saqqara were heading there. A would-be assassin, having botched covering up their trail, would put as much distance between themselves and the scene as possible."

Maulana shifted uneasily. "If the assassin has targeted Amachi once, to have her dog their trail would only invite greater danger."

"She wouldn't be alone," Jaha says. "I'm assigning Ishant to attend her."

"Ishant?" Maulana turns to her, nearly grinding his teeth. "He hasn't been read in."

"Then someone had better read fast, 'cause he's going," Jaha said.

"Surely we're not going to trust an obroni—"

"Aw, nah, baby," Jaha says. "This ain't going to be done your way. This is a Griot Circle issue. My area. However you choose to participate in this you'd better work out."

✳

You have no idea how long you were asleep. Out the observation window, the stars have barely moved. Not that you could tell much without Maya's astrometric assistance. Your Saqqara blasts on a course to the Citadel, the capital of the asteroid belt of the Oyigiyigi. You unravel a thick braid and slowly rebraid it. You check your harnesses and adjust the seals along your phase suit, wishing you'd been issued a military-grade meshsuit since, under Maulana's jurisdiction, this mission is technically on their behalf. The suits functioned not too differently from the nanomesh the HOVA use, acting as both a filtering system and interface with the outer carapace of the navsuit. Together they generated a field that interacted with Oyigiyigi's field to better simulate gravity, working in a way, as you understand it, analogous to magnets. Your seat squeaks when you shift positions, drawing Ishant's attention.

Many in the Ijo speak of the cultural attaché as if he were cut from the same bolt of cloth as Jaha, but you don't see it. He lacks her presence and gravitas. People snap to attention like they served in the HOVA when she enters a room. Ishant's easy to overlook. Even dismiss.

Still, you can't help but feel a little . . . *Scared* is perhaps too strong a word. He's had formal education from universities all over O.E., and compared to him, you have just bounced around the streets of the Belts with nothing sticking. Until you arrived at the Dreaming City, you were raised by or taking care of broken people. It took running away from your family and making your way to Muungano to even realize that your life mattered.

"I was surprised you were able to sleep." Ishant adjusts the lighting level back to nominal. Many lights illuminate the instrument panel. Ishant's fingers dance along them like a well-trained octopus. "Most people take awhile to adjust to phase suits."

"They weren't designed for comfort, but I've slept in worse conditions." You already resent the sound of his voice. He presumes you some pampered one-percenter. That's how many perceived the founding families of the Ijo. The Adisas. You. "I'll appreciate them more when walking about Nguni."

"Have you been before?" He ran his cybernetic arm through his white-streaked black hair.

"I haven't had the chance."

"They call it the Citadel." He summons a series of holovid data streams and slides them over to you.

"I know." An iciness edges your tone as you shove them back. It's not like you hadn't read any briefs about them. "The Nguni were the oldest of the peoples on Muungano. Though the Nguni more rightly represents a confederacy of peoples, they took their name from a region on O.E. They brought their entire culture to the desolate mining operation. They specialize in skill-craft, with some members being masters of everything from ceramics to metalwork to fashioning to weaving. Craftspeople who approached their work with a mixture of fear and respect, the same way they approached their gods. Because they seem smaller and darker, after generations spent at the mining outpost, they think of themselves as being treated like second-class members."

Ishant glances at you. His careful gaze takes your measure. "The phase suits aid in the acclimation to the city. They generate . . ."

". . . additional gravity stabilization fields. I know."

"You could at least serve bourbon with this amount of shade you're giving me." Ishant purses his thin lips. "I won't bother you with a full briefing, then."

"I was briefed that you like your shirts tight."

"I prefer the word *fitted*." He tugs at his collar. "If you want, I can send you the Nguni cultural protocols."

"Fine." You admit that you don't know the source of your hostility toward him. Only that he is here, his voice haranguing your ears. And Xola is not.

"You don't think much of me," he says with a matter-of-fact tone, without anger, resentment, or pity. He monitors the course readings, not meeting your eyes.

"I hear you're a fine cultural attaché." You recall how Maulana described him when he pulled you aside. That he grinned like an obroni. Bowed in an extremely polite foreigner way. Always smiling. With a fashion sense involving clothing that fits too tight on him. "What I understand of that job, anyways."

"I'm sort of like a diplomatic aide. Officially." Ishant focuses on inputting commands for the flight, still conspicuously avoiding your gaze.

"And unofficially?"

Finally, he angles his body toward you and levels his professional, though not stern, gaze at you. "I'm the one you reach out to when you want to get shit done."

"I imagine moving work along through relationships must be hard for you."

Ishant swiveled about to fiddle with the controls again. Almost absently, he added, "Sometimes you have to slow down to speed up."

"What did you say?" you snap, harsher than intended.

"Nothing. Just something Xola used to say all the time. His way of saying . . ." Ishant's voice all but retreats from you, his drone fading out as you remember how Xola deemed every moment an opportunity to teach. You couldn't even enjoy your bowl of black-eyed peas and corn bread in peace. Without him chiming in about how . . .

✴

"*. . . pimpin' ain't nothing but capitalism. And capitalism ain't nothing but pimpin'.*" *Xola waved his piece of corn bread at you, baiting you. Again. You knew he was pushing buttons until you felt compelled to respond.*

"*Why do so many of your analogies revolve around sex?*"

He smiled because you bit at his jabs. "*Because you have to make ideas sticky in order for them to make an impression.*"

"*I already don't like where this is going.*"

"*Then I'll leave it at sex makes things sticky.*" *He grinned, a prepubescent boy being his brand of clever.*

"*You're the worst.*" *You pour more drinks.* "*You know what, though? A lot of the west, during their Manifest Destiny heyday, it was mostly men going out. That created quite a demand for prostitutes. Because of sex work, a lot of women were able to gather resources, build capital, influence policies, and even provided social services for other women who eventually came out.*"

"*You always bringing a history lesson whenever I'm just trying to talk shit.*" *Xola nudged about his remaining black-eyed peas, not really eating. He made long, slurping noises as he brought his bowl to his mouth. His fingers skittered about feeling for the other piece of corn bread you set on his plate. Next to the pile of salad he was determined to ignore. "You need to include something in your arsenal other than rage."*

"But I'm so good at it." This time, you weren't going to rise to his goading.

"You have a PhD in rage-ology. We get it." Xola bobbed his head and munched his bread.

"Camara?" You tilt your head, sensing a heaviness about his emi despite his attempts to distract you. "You don't seem okay."

"I was going over a few link messages. Some from VOP Harrison. I realized that Jaha decided on her own what was important and deleted some vital correspondence. I should have been suspicious when she jumped in so quick with her offer of 'I'll read it to you.' Knowing she was lying her ass off, working an agenda. She'd already decided we didn't have the capacity to work with LISC the way they wanted."

"Was she right?"

"Of course she was right. She knew she was right. Right isn't the point." He brandished his remaining corn bread again. "I'm pissed off about that lost opportunity. Maybe someone else, one of the groups we do fuck with back on O.E., could've used it. We could have gifted it to them."

"Calm down, old man. Let it go. There's no shortage of opportunities finding their way to us these days."

"It's about process. One person shouldn't decide on behalf of community. But she's always in such a rush and fails to remember that you have to . . ."

＊

". . . slow down enough to create deep relationships. And in doing so, the work speeds up." You offer a faint smile as an olive branch to Ishant. "When it comes to getting shit done, do you also investigate suspected homicides?"

"Investigation is most of what I do. And discretion is my trade."

"Good." You settle back, your guard still raised, but open to him. "If you were running the investigation of Xola's death, where do we start? Where would you start?"

"I'm no jeli," Ishant began. "But Jaha has been quite the mentor, generous with her knowledge and history. The primary goal of a jeli investigation is to keep telling stories until they intersect."

"Pay attention to coincidences," you say, remembering Xola's admonition.

"So I'd start with the story so far. You suspect a poison?"

"Or something that looked like a poison. Xola's body chemistry was off. I know." You hold up a hand to fend him off. "He'd been sick. And if it wasn't for the slither attack, I might have let it go rather than it confirm that I was on the right track."

"Poison points to a stealth killer. Historically women." Ishant blinks at you. "No offense. That's the history of its profile. They often go undetected, which is why they are a crime of treachery in a small dose. Personal. Thing is, all substances are poisons; it's all a matter of dosage. The *poudre de succession*."

"The what?"

"The 'inheritance powder.' The way royalty used to do one another in when they were going for the crown. To make someone's death imitate natural causes."

"Now you're just showing out."

"A bit. Poison was the weapon of the controlling. According to profiles, typically this person has no conscience, no sorrow, and no remorse. Only the most manipulative kind of killers can wait around watching someone take care of their victim as they die."

"They sound ugly."

"A sociopathic kind of ugly. What else you got?"

You pull up crime scene holovids and its preliminary analysis. "Will a v-womb disturb you?"

"Until we're ready to land, it's just us in a lot of empty space out there. We're on automatic pilot."

"Okay." You activate a virtual imaging womb, and the wreckage of the embassy explosion appears around you, scaled to fit inside your ship. "The first explosion did little more than cosmetic damage. Look at the burn damage, the way it fans out. Just enough to trigger security protocols. The second explosion destroys the crime scene. Here and here were the key points. Flashover and structural damage from the overpressure in the air around it. Low-velocity propellant, maybe twenty kilometers per second."

"We got lucky," Ishant said.

"Thank Eshu."

"What kind of bomb do you suspect?"

"A liquid explosive. Smart water's my guess because of the heavy chemical smell in the air. It leaves a kind of metallic taste in the back of the throat. Something like that, keyed to your movements. Remote detonation. Notice how things go off just after you clear a space?" You rewind and slow down the re-creation images. "It's a murder weapon that destroys itself with its use. But their components survive the explosion. All of it is here, one big jigsaw puzzle."

"Why?"

"Because that's the nature of the device," you say.

"That's what I mean. Find the bomber by understanding the bomb. Think of the bombs that could have been used. Pipe, power, powder, but they went with a liquid bomb. Simple and sophisticated at the same time. They've had extensive training."

"The Niyabinghi didn't find a container, so it was probably something innocuous, easily overlooked. Or completely consumed." You rotate the view one last time. "Let's keep scanning. The brains of the bomb is usually within the first ten meters."

"Now who's showing out?" Ishant asked. "Any suspects?"

"Only this." You bring up the telemetry feeds from the protest. With a broad sweep of your hands, you pass the images off to his workstation. Blown up to the size of a bay window, your eye movements isolate sections to expand, sifting through the data stream with a glance. The shops and eateries outside of the embassy were much like an open-space market on Muungano. The protestors carry placards and shout. You isolate a protestor, both raising the volume and slowing the image down to figure out what they were shouting. *Earth First!* "Figured they might be a good starting point."

"Earth Firsters don't exactly scream *sophisticated*. They're more pipe-bomb, improvised-explosive-device sort of folks."

"I know, but . . . coincidences. They were there."

"Fair enough." Ishant offers a crooked grin, gesturing over the controls as the Saqqara approaches the cluster of asteroids. "We're on final approach. Coming about."

Ishant makes a tight arcing turn. Your stomach lurches despite the additional equilibrium provided by the phase suit.

"Breathe through the turn." Ishant isn't as helpful as he believes he is.

"That's great for when I know a turn is coming." You take in a deep gulp of filtered air.

Ishant increases the whir of the vent fans. "Think of it as riding a roller coaster."

"I never did do roller coasters. Always made me feel like I was dying. Throwing me this way and that. What's the point?"

"The thrill." Ishant flashes a grin, one that hints of an addict's need for seeking such adventures.

"I'm a Ugenini woman in outer space. I get all the thrill I need waking up in the morning. I don't need some metal death trap flinging me about while it decides whether or not it wants to derail. With me ending up in some fiery metal wreckage."

"Fiery?" Ishant glances at you. "What sort of roller coasters were you riding?"

"I'm just saying." You want to drift off, since you had several hours left to spend. An uneasiness churns your emi. You feel underprepared for this mission, out of your depth. And yet you are expected to rise to the occasion. You have no idea how to gauge the politics surrounding the situation. You have no idea what the Ijo expect of you. What Maulana expects of you. In fact, you have little more than a hunch to play out. The only actual instruction Jaha gives you is: "One, be thorough; two, do a good job; three, do not cause an interstellar incident."

You worry about instruction number three.

Your sabhu nags you because there is a story next to you that you hadn't been curious enough to begin reading. It was the basic lesson of relationships, and you needed to be true to who you wanted to be. "So how did you get to Muungano?"

Ishant raises a wary eyebrow, but he recognizes the attempt. "I grew up in mzungu circles. My family moved a lot due to what they perceived as bad influences. I suspect the great migration spooked them, and suddenly, no one, especially weusi, were trusted much. That's just the way it is on O.E. still. When I was old enough, I began to travel a lot, trying to understand the world and the people in it. It only left me . . . more confused. But I was intrigued by how Muungano members described their community. And, I guess, I was at a point where I didn't want to waste my life spinning in circles doing work that didn't matter. How about you?"

"My father died early in my life. My mom didn't take that especially well. She struggled. O.E. doesn't support any who exhibit any . . . shamanistic tendencies."

"Shamanistic?"

"Mental states that are different ways of being. On O.E., they prefer to label and drug their people. On Muungano, we treat only the aspects of behaviors that keep people from functioning in the community, making sure they harm neither others nor themselves. After that, we embrace their gifts as just a different way of seeing. Different realities. Different ways to come at truth. We need all the different eyes we can get to see a problem."

"I see."

"This left me separated from my family. I bounced around a lot until one day I stowed away on a ship bound for Muungano. I didn't quite make it to the Dreaming City. I ended up in the Belts, and I fell in with some folks who began doing organizing and protest work, aimed at helping those back on O.E. I guess I landed on Xola's radar then. Eventually, the Adisas adopted me. It was the first time I knew family."

An amiable silence settles between you. You aren't so different. Both outsiders: you adopted in; he found his place in the Muungano work, a valued (and highly sought-after member). Such abbreviated stories gave an overview and invited questions. You didn't know who would be the first to ask a follow-up question, as both of you were trained.

Beneath you, broken crags of rock part like a cleft in a mountain. Endless miles of barren stone along a series of shelves with only more stretches of asteroid obscuring occasional glimpses of the stars. You cross a shallow basin, and it comes into view. Bobbing among the asteroids, a gleaming marble amid the debris. The Citadel. It's not designed for high traffic, mostly heavy cargo ships, so you loop around the dome to enter through its port shield.

The Citadel spins to produce a type of artificial gravity. An arrangement of mirrors reflects sunlight in, while also powering the sphere within the sphere. The entire facility is designed to dock with the mine. Its kraals are made up of smaller buildings with the arrangement of a beehive, with balustrades and balconies over stacked courtyards, punctuated by large stelae, obelisk-like structures. Lintels with stylized carvings. Rock-hewn temple carved entirely from the rock surface. Their narrow winding streets bordered by elaborately curved doorways.

By the time you dock the ship and disembark, Mansa Geoboe himself waits at the receiving gate to greet you personally. He's big but not especially tall, even for Nguni. His large shoulders frame an equally large chest. His skin is dark as burnished onyx. With a proud bearing, his large head has been shaved clean. His large, flat nose sits beneath eyes too small for his face, almost lost in the fleshy mass. They're almost silvery half disks against the night of his skin. The elaborate beadwork of his vest barely covers his protruding belly. A stylized metal insignia emblazons his left shoulder. He carries a spear. Not a replica or a piece of techware fashioned to appear as an ancient weapon: an actual spear.

"We see you, Amachi Adisa, and we greet you in the name of the Nguni," his voice reverberates in the space. Geoboe views all Ugenini the same, as akata, wild cats who do not live at home, without a history or culture. Your pronunciation of the common tongue—with its dialect and slang—deemed almost backward. But you are from a prominent family, so you garner praise. If you were not, you risked scorn. You fear that the farther from Muungano you travel, the more its philosophy becomes watered down.

"I see you, Geoboe of the Nguni." You extend your arm, and Geoboe grasps it. His meaty hand loops around your forearm with ease. Your hand doesn't even cover the front of his arm.

"Habari gani?" Geoboe eyes Ishant, giving only a slight acknowledgment of him. "What brings a member of the Ijo out to our little city?"

"You are a vital part of the Muungano. And I have to confess, I have never been to Oyigiyigi or know much about what and how you do." You take a moment to sense the man. His energy vibration fluctuates. He moves with a hunched shuffle, his spirit lumbering under a huge weight that burdens his steps. It's almost as if another energy obscures you reading his emi clearly. You concentrate harder, struggling to get a fuller picture of him in your head. His affected gestures, the snarling upcurl of his lips as he measures his words. Tension wrinkles about his jaw.

"Few among the Ijo do. They don't remember we exist unless they need something. Molybdenum. Kheprw crystals. We exist as a series of resources to be extracted and consumed, not members of the same community." Simple and direct, with no hint of anger or frustration or even anything snide to mark his tone. He holds his palm out to usher you out of the bay.

"Is that truly how you feel?" You wave as if erasing the question. "Scratch that. Does that reflect how you have been treated?"

"Here's what I know." His lips quiver in a gnarl of contained menace. "Like with most of our history in Muungano, we have to make our own way."

"Fair enough. Start where you are, with what you have, and do what you can." You recite one of the ancient tenets.

"Precisely. Come, let me show you what we have created."

The vaulted ceiling gives the corridor the feel of a grand cathedral. A mining shaft carved out to imitate a building, one full of crystals. Not having been mined out, the remaining crystals and ore present with a guiding intelligence behind their arrangement. The mining operation itself as an etching tool to create the aesthetic of the Citadel. The crystals jut out at seemingly random angles, some of their tips or their background well decorated. Stretching from one side to the other in a latticework of protrusions.

Narrow bridges and walkways run overhead, catwalks among floating lanterns. Crosswalks bridge one section of the mine to another. People movers shuttle people back and forth. The Citadel itself can ferry between massive mining operations. Kraals float alongside the mine, miniature ships within themselves, adjusting their orbits. Miners scurry about in specially designed nanomesh suits that allow them to scale the surface of the walls above them, traveling up and down the walls, guardian spiders of the mine. Even without focusing on them, you feel the thrum of machine works in unseen tunnels. The pumps circulate and scrub the air. Underground, a strange aqueduct system manages the water resources. In many ways, what the Nguni have created here makes no sense.

In other ways, it is beautiful.

Oyigiyigi is their world. No one mills about. Everyone stays busy doing the work of the community, without coercion or compulsion, simply doing what they love with the people they love. Miners master their crafts, extracting ore yet leaving art where they worked. The refinement work falls to their scientists.

"The Ngwenya Mine takes its name from the oldest mine in Alkebulan. On O.E. period." Geoboe barely contains his pride. He pauses as if allowing you the opportunity to genuflect or something. Once he sees that you won't, he issues a dismissive snort and moves on. "That mine contained hematite ore and later iron used during the middle stone age. This one also extracts all manner of ore, but mostly refines raw kheprw crystals until they look like beetles, which was why they were given the name of the Kemetic deity that symbolizes transformation, rebirth, and renewal in the first place. The mine also functions as a manufacturing plant for carbon nanotubes. In this outer outpost, the work can be done free of all trace impurities."

"The mines are magnificent," you say. You sense him warm to you at the compliment.

"You haven't seen anything yet." Geoboe slows down as you near a grand hall. "I took the liberty of assuming you might want to join our banquet after so long a journey."

"I could eat." You can barely contain your grin, knowing the Nguni's reputation for fine dining.

The wall section dissolves to reveal a great dining hall made up of several circular tables. A series of suspended glowing spheres illuminate the room. The amber glow deepens the shadows but also leaves the impression of the room being lit by campfire. Geoboe pauses in the entranceway to approve the final arrangements. Large basins offer water at the entryway. Heavy wooden chairs arranged in precise patterns around the tables, an overly formal picnic while the ornamentation along the wall harkens back to an earlier age, as if you have stepped into an interactive museum. You are about to comment as such to Ishant when a guard holds up a hand to bar him.

"He cannot go inside," Geoboe says.

"Why not?" you ask.

"He's an outsider."

"He's no outsider. He's my guest. My cultural attaché."

"Who you choose to consort with does not concern us. Permitting an outsider entry to our most sacred of dealings does. By my and the Queen Mother's decree."

Before you can protest further—ready to respond to the consort's insinuation with all due aggression—Ishant steps near enough to draw everyone's attention.

"That's fine, Amachi. I have many reports to study." Ishant bends at the waist in a quarter bow, playing up the idea of him as an outsider, and departs.

Too easily, you decide. He could have casually mentioned being the personal aide to Jaha or having been assigned by the Ijo, which would have overridden most standing orders. You have the unsettling impression that with security so intense surrounding this dinner, he's about to exploit its laxness elsewhere.

A large, older woman, whose complexion and features favor Geoboe, enters. Purple-and-white robes drape her. Gold jewelry adorns her neck, ears, and wrists. Perhaps his mother, the Queen Mother he mentioned. A small ceramic plate protrudes from her lower lip. Her entourage clears a path, walking in front of her, escorting her to her seat. No one else dares sit before Geoboe does. Another couple enters, and Geoboe extends his hand. A young woman, who also favors him, takes it. He directs her to her place. A young man you don't recognize trails her. He seems familiar, and you wish you'd let Ishant fully review the protocols with you.

The rest of the people were lost on her, a sea of faces. Geoboe studies the clusters of guests, all too pleased with himself.

"May I introduce our Queen Mother, Itoro. She can trace her lineage back through King Sobhuza II."

"I see you, Itoro." You bow your head in deference, though in truth such a diarchy emulates an old way left behind on O.E.

"I see you, child." A smirk crosses her lips slyly at my pronunciation. Maya may translate for us, but they cannot disguise accent or enunciation. There is a way people who have traveled to Muungano and return speak of it. You remember how your aunties spoke of your country cousins after they'd been to the city. They were struck, changed, as is something about their previous life was now small. You wanted to prove that you belonged by learning some of the Muungano native tongues, so that you wouldn't have to need Maya to translate. The Queen Mother reminds you of that aunt on O.E., who corrects you while dismissing you as inauthentic at the same time.

"My daughter, Khuma," Geoboe continues. "And, as this seems to be the day of entertaining important guests, allow me to present her companion, Lebna of the Dimka family."

The young man must be Jaha's grandnephew or some such. His face contorts into an unreadable scowl.

You return their arm grasps. A steward pours tjwala, a home-brewed beer one glass of which is enough to send your head spinning with the vertigo of being caught between gravitational fields. The Queen Mother dabs a measure of ginger into her cup. *It goes down better this way,* her wink suggests. The taste would linger for hours.

A parade of men in full ceremonial gear marked with the sacred triangles of Alkebulan, armed with traditional weapons of ancient Alkebulan, arrange themselves in a bullhorn formation. An acrobatic drumline joins them. The drummers strike up a rhythm as the men begin to dance.

"As you know, we were saddened to learn of your father's death." Geoboe gulps down his carafe of tjwala in a demonstration of his capacity.

You squirm with unease but keep yourself from reflexively clarifying of your and Xola's relationship. "We still mourn his loss and reel from his absence."

"As do we all. It's difficult to imagine charting Muungano's path forward without his keen insight."

The Queen Mother levels her gaze on you. A mix of curiosity and confusion clouds her eyes. "You have been visited by dreams." She quickly raises her hand to cut you off even though you weren't about to say anything. "No need to tell me what they were. They are an early agoze trial."

"How do you know?" You'd been trained early on how to read people. How to be aware of their energy, their emi. Xola believed every person had the ability, but few paid attention to such matters of the spirit, leaving only those who follow the ways of the Iyami Aje to pursue such training. The Queen Mother shimmers, her spirit a heat shimmer you can't quite get in focus.

"It's my job to know. It's how the mystics choose their disciples." She smirks. "Now is the time of portents. We approach a crossroads. Uncertain times lie ahead."

"Your title intrigues me. A Queen Mother implies a king." You allow your words to trail off before they edge over an uncertain line you fear may be a cliff's edge.

"Do you imply criticism of our customs?" Geoboe cuts his eyes toward you as he drinks. A steward refills his cup. For the second time.

"Absolutely not. Rituals provide structure for our stories to be remembered. It's just"—you consider your words carefully—"perhaps some ways of governance were best left to the past."

"Perhaps. Just as perhaps it is also time for the old ways to rekindle a path for new ways to be done." An oily tone slickened his words.

You realize a trap has been set. You can only wait to see how it will spring shut. You were his guest, which, to the more suspicious, might feel a lot like a potential captive. *Your father's death.* Implying you could be a child from one court being traded as a bargaining chip to force an alliance. A political pawn in the game of expedience.

A series of stewards bring out the dishes. A hovering, wood-fueled braai grills meat as it floats to a halt in front of your table. Trailing it, stewards carry trays of boerewors, sosaties, and kreef, though the crayfish in particular catch your eye. The thick pap porridge of finely ground corn has its smell buried under the heavy aroma of tomatoes and onions reduced in a sauce beside it. The smell of umbidvo wetint sanga, cooked pumpkin leaves and peanuts, proves equally heady.

"There are occasions that are opportune times to communicate with our ancestors. To call upon them for blessings, assistance, and guidance." Geoboe raises his cup, preparing to toast.

"Like death," you say.

"Birth, death, coming of age." Geoboe sips from his cup. "A royal marriage would also be a signature occasion."

"We have no royalty." You study the table. Khuma and Lebna turn away coyly, not meeting anyone's eyes, not even each other's, like hostages entangled in the machinations of their captors. "We have families, prominent families, even if they aren't recognized by the Ijo."

"The Nguni are a founding family," the Queen Mother intones.

"Yet we aren't accorded the same respect as the Adisa." Geoboe set his cup down to emphasize his words. "Perhaps if we were to join with another mighty house, we would garner more respect."

"What are you talking about?" you ask, fearing you already know.

"Let me speak plain: I have proposed that my daughter, Khuma, marry Lebna. A blessed union of families."

"Does she get a say in the matter?" Myriad thoughts race through your mind, but you attempt to hold the anger that flares within you in check. Your aunt on O.E. treated you as little more than property to be bartered. The things you had to do to free yourself from that kind of monster—before they took bits of your soul the way that monsters inevitably did—still haunt you.

"She's an obedient daughter," Geoboe says.

You can't help yourself. Anger is your gift. "With your love of the old ways, I'm surprised you haven't paraded her about in a reed dance. You know, gather her and the other maidens to dance as a troupe, hoping her reed doesn't break in order to prove her virginity."

Geoboe rises. An air of intimidation settles on the table. Khuma and Lebna pass an unreadable glance between each other. Out of reflex, you reach to turn your bracelets to release your chakrams.

The Queen Mother starts to laugh. A deep, throaty thing whose vibrations wash through you. "She makes a good point, Geoboe. Listen to how you sound."

Geoboe settles into his seat, silent and white-lipped. His face frozen into an inscrutable mask either nursing his nicked pride or plotting his next move. "Perhaps I came across too strong."

"What do you hope to accomplish with this . . . blessed union?" you probe, not wanting to give further offense.

"It's an overture. To a new age. A unification of resources and territories," he says.

"Muungano is already one people."

"True, but many communities—the farther from the Dreaming City we migrate, the more our cultures become distinct territories. To correct this, some customs must change."

You rotate your chakram bracelet out of unconscious habit. You study the easy flow of conversation between the guests, ever conscious of the heavy gaze of the Queen Mother on you. "Which customs do you imagine changing?"

"Certainly the more outdated ones. For example, you are correct, we once performed the reed dance, parading our unpartnered and childless women arranged in age regiments. But at the heart of the ceremony was the desire to promote respect for women while showing off our cultural heritage." A grim, satisfied smile played across his lips. "As you say, their time has passed. The young always know best."

Your O.E. aunties used to say something similar whenever they believed your ideas and ways were too radical. Their way of criticizing—shaming you— was by claiming that you had no sense of those who came before you. On the other hand, Xola used to remind you that an antiestablishment mind-set was a delicate dance with power since you couldn't always just spit on them. Though there were times for that, too.

You swallow. Hard.

A member of Geoboe's guard approaches and bends low to whisper into the chieftain's ear. Geoboe's eyes widen for an instant before he composes himself. Dabbing his mouth with a sani-wipe, he stands. "Please excuse me."

"Is everything all right?" you ask.

"Yes, yes, continue eating. There is simply a security matter for me to attend to. Perhaps you'll accompany us to a salon later."

"A poetry slam?" Having not attended one in ages, the prospect of a Nguni spin on a slam sent your heart racing. You might be a little rusty, but you know you'd warm up to the mic like it wasn't a thing. A green dot lights up on your wrist screen. A communication notice from Ishant. You can't scramble the signal or otherwise secure the channel. "I'd be delighted. However, would you also excuse me? I just need to go to the bathroom."

"I'll have my guards escort you," Geoboe says.

"That won't be necessary. I entrust myself to your people's hospitality."

"And Lady Adisa can certainly handle herself," the Queen Mother says with a voice that does not invite dispute.

You incline your head toward her, suppressing a pleased smile. When you step into the hallway, there are few people moving about. Many attend to the feast, lingering about, curious to observe the proceedings. This ceremony doesn't have the celebratory, inclusive vibe of a typical Muungano event. This feels exclusive and self-important. Leaving a bad taste in your mouth. You barely make it around the corner from the dining hall when you bump into Ishant.

"What couldn't wait for me to finish dinner?" You press him away from the hallway, scuttling him out of sight. "You're the one always going on about matters of diplomacy and protocols."

"I was going through the security files . . ." Ishant clutches his arm, slightly favoring it. His pupils wide like he's been drugged. You recognize the signs, fearing that he might have indulged jacking in and going full sensate on her. There is nothing worse than working with addicts.

"Were you detected?" Your eyes fix on his with laser precision and intensity, ready to ferret out any attempt at deception.

"Discretion is my trade." An arrogant smirk creases his mouth.

"Perhaps you were not discreet enough. Geoboe received word of some sort of security issue." Remaining unconvinced, you take him by the elbow and walk back toward your quarters. "What did you find?"

"In the transfer logs, someone whose identification papers didn't match any known person."

"How could that not be detected immediately?" You lower your voice to a conspiratorial whisper.

"The data profile was thorough. It would take deep-level decryption protocols to beat it."

"Which you did?"

Ishant cocks his head at you as if the question didn't warrant a serious response. A few heartbeats later, his smile falters for an instant. "I admit, the resources to do so may have triggered some safeguards I hadn't anticipated."

"We're looking for a ghost. Do you think this person had something to do with Xola's death?"

"Anyone who can move so invisibly through our system is certainly worth questioning."

"Then you should focus on tracking them. Report back as soon as you find anything," you say.

You plan to part ways and round the corner to walk back to the dinner before anyone notices. When you approach the juncture, a squad of Niyabinghi block the hallway. Footfalls stamp from behind, and you turn around only to find another group of them closing in.

A Lij steps forward. His gold chakram lies flat in a circle about his neck over his iridescent breastplate jacket. "You two need to come with us."

STACIA CHIKEKE
The *Cypher* (Returning to Titan)

"Don't touch anything." A buzzing began in the back of Stacia's mind, her thoughts becoming a jumble collapsing into noise. She studied the scene of Paki's abduction. The blood-strewn walls. The destroyed workstation. The level of violence evident in the room caused her to imagine the worst.

"We have to examine the scene." Hondo placed a hand on her shoulder, meant as a reassuring gesture. The familiarity of it burned.

Stacia glared at it until he removed it.

She closed her eyes to concentrate, to tamp out the distractions of her life. That Bek was sick. That Yahya grew more distant, becoming a stranger wandering the corridors of her life. That Xola was dead. After a moment, she opened them to do her job. Activating her nanomesh suit to exude gloves, she gently scanned the blood splatter. Loneliness filled every space in her being, her truest companion, so real it took up a nearly physical presence in her life. Her mind filled with images from Xola's funeral, his body, no longer the man she knew. His large forehead no longer glistening with its constant sheen of perspiration. His skin with a waxy quality, with the vibrance drained from his hue. Leaving behind a shell, because that was all that was left, the physical remains of the man she once knew. Respected, even depended on. And now a void existed where Paki once was. All the men she'd come to trust and lean on were finding new ways to leave her. But he wasn't leaving her without her moving heaven and earth to find him first.

"Maya, are you logging this?" Stacia asked.

<Yes.>

"I'll need you to download all surveillance records for the last hour to my quarters." Stacia lowered to her knees to carefully study the base of his workstation.

<Yes.> Maya's overly formal tone was intended to not intrude on Stacia.

Not in this moment. They had a history of assuming such a tone whenever they assumed she was in emotional crisis.

In her imagination, Stacia turned Xola's head to the side, its weight heavy yet floppy in her hands. Still warm to the touch, like he could wake at any moment if she kept bothering him. His skin too rubbery, as if it might slough off in her hands. Her fingers probing for any irregularities, any clue to answer why he was taken from her.

"Captain?" Hondo risked interrupting her again.

She stilled her movement without turning to him. A measured, purposeful pause, the warning rattle of a snake, signaling that he'd better tread lightly. "What is it?"

"Are you going to want to conduct this entire investigation yourself?"

"Who else would I trust?" she stopped herself from saying. "You're here, aren't you? It's my prerogative to do an initial assessment. Is that all right with you?"

"Yes, ma'am." He swallowed hard and stepped back.

"Maya, I'll want thorough imagery of this scene. Full-spectrum analysis."

<In process. It will be downloaded to your quarters when complete.>

"Down to genetic analysis of any biological material present."

Stacia sank against the wall in a moment's respite. Still the captain, all eyes followed her, but she needed to have a moment for herself. To feel. To allow her emotions to wash over her if only for an instant. Though in that instant, she also wanted to retreat to her room, close the door, and absorb the realities that she had few if any friends left. Her thoughts drifted to Amachi. The buzzing returned as a dull roar. Her anger flared in order to quell it.

"What was he working on?" she snapped.

"I don't know, Captain. He was scanning through a shit ton of reports," Hondo said.

"Do we have a presumed assault weapon?"

"No. Probably an object of opportunity, one they took with them."

"What *do* we know?"

"That Paki is missing," Hondo said.

"Are you trying me right now?" Stacia reared toward him.

"No, Captain. I mean we just discovered him missing. We haven't had a chance to process the scene, collect any stories, or collate any data. Not even enough for a preliminary report. It literally just happened."

Stacia rubbed the bridge of her nose. After a calming breath, she blinked at him. "You're right. You're right. Raise alert status to red. Double the guards at all junctures. I want status reports every half hour."

"Yes, Captain." Hondo stepped back again.

One of Kenya's security team flashed an anxious, skeptical look to her, hoping Stacia would miss it.

She didn't.

"I want every log Paki filed, every crew member he talked to, hell, every panel he touched brought to my quarters."

"Every . . . panel?" Hondo asked.

"You get what I'm saying. I want thoroughness and excellence. One of our own is missing and may have been killed. Another may even be a murderer. I'm not resting until the appropriate party has been caught and I understand why things have unfolded this way. Which means you're not resting. None of you are. Am I understood?"

"Yes, Captain," they said in unison.

"Close down this area for investigation and then clean it up."

The aloneness stalked her, out the room and down the hallway. Swathed in a darkness, she tried not to focus on the possibility of his death for fear of tumbling into it and drowning in its waves. Stacia never experienced a death under her command before. Accidents, certainly, but not a death. The community's mood and morale already ebbed dangerously low. Her heart ached at the thought of her people going through another grieving service, so soon after Xola, with them reeling from another blow while barely recuperated from his loss. She didn't know what words to offer to her people to make things better. To give them hope. There were not enough words in any language to do that.

Stacia stormed back to her quarters. When she reached her door, she hesitated. Bek still lay in med lab, his condition worsening. The doctors now had him in a coma-like state, hoping to arrest the progression of whatever swept through him. Her heart longed to be at his bedside. Unconsciously, Stacia ran her fingers in a light play across her lips. Reminding her of the near brush from when Yahya tried to kiss her only a few hours ago. His mouth only barely missing hers because she drew back at the last moment, wanting to avoid anything too intimate.

She slipped into her quarters. And tapped her head into the wall.

<How are you doing?> The edge of formality drained from Maya's tone.

"What does my med telemetry tell you?"

<Basal temperature, heart rate, breathing all within expected parameters.>

"There you go. I'm fine."

<Checking maintenance logs for eating and sleeping times.>

"Wait . . ." Stacia wondered how much of a smart-ass protocol Maya might have written for themselves.

<Have you actually eaten today?>

Perhaps it was her imagination, but Stacia could've sworn Maya made a tut-tutting noise similar to perusing a list and being dissatisfied by it.

"Lunch. Or maybe it was dinner?"

<One meal, noted. Half a serving of jollof rice with curried stew.>

"Yes, but, I was in a hurry . . ."

<Sleep telemetry recorded from 0230 to 0345.>

"It was a rough night." Stacia hated the idea of being accountable to an entity who had access to all of her habits.

<Similar patterns marked for the previous five standard solar day/night cycles.>

Stacia sighed. "You're like the most intrusive hall monitor ever."

<What I am is . . . >

Maya's vocal unit degenerated into a smear of static.

"Don't keep me in suspense. What are you?" Stacia glanced up from her work. Maya's vocal monitors reduced to white static, until even that dissolved into silence. Like the AI had been caught in a loop, a series of misfiring, taking them off line. As if they were the object of hacking a system collapse. "Maya?"

Only silence followed. Whenever some part of ship's maintenance needed attending to, Stacia's instinct was to call for Paki. But Paki was gone. Her ship, her command, was being stripped from her one piece at a time.

✳

Though it had been only a few hours, the state of the investigation into Paki's disappearance was in disarray. Stacia had taken it for granted how much Maya aided them in their day-to-day work. They created specific subroutines to aid in making connections between cases and scenarios. Still not with the creativity of a human imagination. Maybe. Stacia mulled the idea of Maya's other possible artistic endeavors. Paki missing meant that the workload now fell on Dina and Hondo. Without his constant vigilance, the pair would work all around the problem without actually getting anywhere. Perhaps that was the entire point. Paki. Maya. Maybe this was about the investigation itself, taking out the pieces that drove it in order to slow the entire process down. All Stacia knew for sure was that she was missing something. It was foolish to imagine that she would be able to investigate as the captain. Her simply entering a room disrupted the space. Put everyone on edge. Though maybe she could use that to her advantage.

"What do we have?" Stacia asked.

As head of her security team, Kenya York was the closest thing Stacia had to a jeli. She turned slowly, setting down her probe. "I see you, Captain."

"I'm sorry. I see you, Kenya."

"Not much. Evidence of a scuffle, obviously." Kenya enacted the virtual imaging womb. Paki's chamber appeared all around them in hard light approximation. "Maya being glitchy does not help. We'd come to depend on them to help sift through the copious visual information. Not to mention trace analysis and genestream profiling. I'm still running tracking protocols tracing everyone's movements."

Stacia studied the room, capturing an image and expanding it for closer inspection to test out the womb's capabilities. She usually read only the final reports. It had been a long time since she'd been in an investigation firsthand. Her eyes drifted back to the overturned chair and smear of blood against the wall. Where a head might have tumbled against. She enlarged the screen capture of his workstation. No Code Black / Eyes Only material, but some files had been flagged. Related to the Mothership Incident, an attempted breach. No one should even know enough to go looking. On the neighboring screen, an overview of Bek's classmates' work.

Stacia wondered what connection there could be between the Mothership and her son's homework. "So it's going to be a minute."

"It's going to be a minute," Kenya repeated. Without heat or a hint of sarcasm. Only a gentle reminder.

Comfort was too strong a word, but Stacia found a measure of calm in her presence. It allowed her room to trust a little. "I had an unauthorized visitor."

"When?"

"Right before Paki's abduction. An O.E. operative. He breached my chamber using a site-to-site glyph."

"Then he's on this ship." Kenya turned from the scene. "This . . . wasn't in any report."

"Things have moved fast. I haven't had a lot of opportunity to make my logs. Besides, I'm telling you now." Stacia prepared to leave but rested her hand against the wall. "I want increased patrols."

"And a level-five security sweep." Kenya anticipated her next order. "We'll comb every inch of the *Cypher* by hand if need be. We'll find him. And Paki."

"All right, then. Carry on. You're on a clock. Let me know if you turn up anything I can move on."

✳

A group of students huddled in a corner, some freestyling rhymes with one another, dictated by the one in the center of their ring shouting news items of the day for them to opine about. A dance troupe went through their stretching exercises along the foam-cored regolith floor of the play area.

When she spotted the captain, a young lady stood up, awkward and lanky, with the light of recognition in her eyes. She sashayed over, though Stacia couldn't place her face. A brown-skinned girl with her hair drawn up. Pink and purple lights ran through it, girding her braids into place. She couldn't tell if they were strictly decorative, though she seemed too young to have a cybernetic cap.

"I see you, Captain," the young lady said.

"I see you . . ." Stacia paused, attempting to recall her name.

"Marguerite." She seemed stung. She fiddled with her Huichol collar, beaded necklace. "Pinero."

The name rang as familiar, but Stacia recalled a young girl Bek played with often, not the young woman before her. "Marguerite? Girl, when did you get so grown? I thought I had a new crew member or stowaway on board."

"Thank you. What brings you down here?"

"Can't a captain go on a walkabout on her own ship?"

"Yes, ma'am." Marguerite crossed her legs, a dancer in the rest position, as she studied the floor.

"I'm teasing. It's been awhile since I've had a chance to explore the labs. Paki told me of your new assignment. Can you show me what you're working on?"

"Yes," she said crisply, almost as if she was ready to salute. Ushering her over to a series of freestanding workstations, it wasn't hard to pick hers out. DNA strands lit up in pink and purple hues, represented in a variety of artistic styles, composition, fragmented images, cubist, dissonant color tones, the strands twisted into distorted, stylized figures. "I was experimenting with DNA sequencing as art."

"This is pretty impressive."

"My ultimate goal is actually to figure out new ways to synthesize water using whatever atmosphere composition is available. Hmm, composition . . ." Her eyes glazed over, lost in whatever song sprang to mind. "I'm not Bek. He's gifted when it comes to coding. It's like he's creating art with machine language."

Stacia didn't want to interrupt her train of thought, but was pressed. "Marguerite?"

"Sorry. The idea of DNA as music really hit me. But, yeah, what if we could synthesize water the way molecules produce proteins? That's what my pod will be focusing on."

"That sounds advanced."

"Not really. Camara Paki told us to be imaginative. The ideas didn't necessarily have to work, just be creative. Explore our ideas. No matter how wild."

Camara Paki. Stacia opted to let that slide. "I wish I had half your creativity at your age. Even now."

"Thank you."

"When did you last see . . . Camara Paki?" The word still stuck on her tongue. Stacia barely managed to get it out.

"This morning."

"Notice anything unusual?"

"Like what?"

"Anything. Did he seem distracted or nervous?"

"He was . . . Camara Paki." Marguerite shrugged, having run out of words that could more accurately describe the man.

Even if Maya was operational, even with her libraries of language codes, Stacia doubted they would have been much help. Still, Stacia had no problem picturing him. "So class was the last time you saw him?"

"Well, he left early."

"Really? To go where?"

"I don't know. He just glanced over our workstations, did that odd sniff thing he does, and booked out."

Marguerite led Stacia around the workstations. The captain traced Paki's steps, skimming the actual projects. Her true interest was in who was watching her. She didn't look over at any who gathered to watch the captain at work. She had no idea who might be watching remotely; but she knew if she kept banging on walls long enough, something, or someone, was bound to scurry from the shadows.

"By the way, how's Bek doing?" Marguerite asked.

Stacia's chest tightened at the mention of his name, like an icicle had been plunged into her. "The doctors have him resting."

"Can you let him know that we miss him?" Marguerite twisted her necklace and then straightened it. "That I miss him."

"I . . . will." Stacia recognized that look in her eye. The puppy dog eyes of the first blush of friendship deepening. She hadn't expected to encounter this, nor the idea that her son's friend was blossoming into this area of adulthood. Because that meant he was, too. But that was a path she couldn't afford to wander right now.

What did Paki find? What trail was he on? Who did he threaten? The obvious suspect, Zenith, was a mercenary in a suit. He moved only if his masters ordered him. There was a piece missing. And she needed to rattle more cages to shake something loose.

※

Stacia had been up all night. She retreated to her rondavel. Her head hit her pillow, but sleep didn't come. She curled into a ball, not bothering to toss or turn, letting the warmth from her arms seep into the parts of her she held, hoping to at least warm herself through by the time she chose to rise again. She had gone over holovids, ship's diagnostics, reports, and communication logs for Paki's investigation. She'd talked to the scientists on Titan, the Dreaming City, even on O.E. for updates on Bek's condition. She avoided staying still, on the off chance that Yahya might track her down. The thought of him left her feeling cornered. Until sheer exhaustion caused her to collapse onto her bed, even if her mind raced too much to actually rest. She was alone with her thoughts and no one to parse them with.

"Maya?" she tried again. Nothing. She'd assigned her best techs to inspect their system. Well, the best techs after Paki. Or Bek. She sent a communiqué inquiring about the status of the patrol of ships at the Orun Gate. She rolled one hand into the other, absently popping the knuckles of each finger joint before reversing hands and repeating.

Stacia wasn't one for conspiracy theories. Facts guided her. Hard, demonstrable, repeatable evidence. Invisible forces, bed partners of politics and deep entrenched business didn't interest her. She was an experienced scientist, researcher, and critical thinker. She thought her way out of situations.

She needed answers.

Her door chimed, the backup measure for when Maya was down for maintenance. She signaled for the door to open. It did. The ship's autonomic functions operated just fine. Stacia began a checklist of functions to evaluate before the figure in her entranceway fully absorbed her attention. Dina stood in there wearing her off-duty attire. Clad in a velour kaftan, she was barefoot, her toes painted metallic gold, matching her earrings and rings. "I see you, Stacia."

"I . . . see you, Dina." Leaning against the frame, Stacia half blocked the doorway. "I was about to call you."

Part of her luxuriated in the energy of the moment. Feeling desired, desiring, the tentative edge of flirting. The heady unknown of a young relationship sprouting uncertain what brand of friendship it might generate. Stacia allowed herself the moment.

In the end, Stacia succumbed to the physics of weak relationships. Weak nuclear forces were one of the half dozen forces controlling the known, visible universe. The mechanism of interaction between subatomic particles responsible for the radioactive decay of atoms; the noncontact force fields governed how the universe worked at low energies. She was at low energy, and Dina was a weak tie. Not very close with each other. An acquaintance. Someone she was familiar with rather than knew. She wondered if beyond Yahya (and Amachi), she had anyone whom she was close to rather than just cordial with. Like all weak ties, Dina wasn't really in her circle but traveled enough in them that diffuse information passed back and forth. An expanded relational network as powerful as any other, without the complication of intimacy. Weak forces made powerful connections in their own way.

"I was . . ." Whatever projection of herself Dina had wanted to display collapsed upon itself with a suddenness she wasn't prepared for. She held the portrait of herself together for several heartbeats before the cracks crept in around the edges of her face. A tidal wave of emotions crashing against the seawalls of her heart, leaving further fractures. She choked on her next words, halting, racking sobs. She reached out to grab the wall for support so as to not collapse in the hallway.

"What is it?" Stacia rushed to catch her, though Dina recovered all on her own.

"May I come in?"

"Yes." Stacia ushered her inside and fashioned a seat for her before attending her synth chamber to pour them both drinks. Leaning forward on her couch, she took Dina's hands. She doubted the woman even realized how much they were shaking. Stacia spoke softly. "Take a breath."

"I think I just needed someone to talk to." Slowly calming down, Dina's face softened in the light, her expression open and tender. Perhaps mirroring something in Stacia.

"About . . . ?"

"Hondo. He's been acting strange lately."

Stacia almost reflexively made a joke about the word *lately,* but the pain registering on Dina's face quelled all snide humor. Stacia knew she'd have to take it easy on her. "How do you mean?"

"Intense. Brooding. Wrecking shop once he gets going." Dina shifted from her seat to the captain's couch. Stacia scooted over to make room for her. The move was too familiar, so abruptly intimate it caught Stacia off guard, causing her to freeze. But only for a measured heartbeat.

"Sounds like how he usually does." Stacia couldn't help herself. She wrapped an arm around Dina. To take any sting out of her comment.

"He seems, I don't know, distracted or something." Dina folded her hands in her lap.

"He's got a lot on his plate. We all do. Maybe I should take him off the investigation," Stacia said.

"No, don't do that. It would crush him."

"Crush him?" Her words made Stacia blink hard, like she'd been swatted on the nose.

"It's taken him so long to fit in." Dina settled into the crook of Stacia's arm, which had been resting along the back of the couch. Stacia continued to comfort her. The way she would any friend.

"Only because he came at things like a bull trying to buck the past from his back." Stacia's voice remained low, trying not to break the spell of the moment.

"I know. I know. That's his way. Like how they train us in university. There's so much that's different here." Dina spent so much time being educated at O.E. schools, she still struggled with how to simply be herself. Coming from a military family, Dina claimed a long matriarchal lineage of leadership. Between that and having grown up in a religious household—not to mention graduating from LISC Corps—all she learned was a structured and rigid way of thinking. Her biggest obstacle was unlearning some of the unhealthier aspects of her training. "But the investigation, trusting him with it, means a lot. That you have confidence in him with us."

"I always had. He wouldn't be here if I didn't. I've told him that countless times. And you."

"I know. It's just, because of the investigation, he's gotten so secretive, though."

"It's the job. You both have to deal with a lot of sensitive issues. Sometimes from each other. It's strictly a security matter." Stacia shifted slightly, noting Dina's warmth. "I know the toll phrases like *Code Black / Eyes Only* or *high-level encryption protocols* can take on a relationship. So much so, I almost don't know if I'm the right person to dispense any advice on this topic. Given my lack of success."

"No, I really appreciate anything you have to say about it. I really do. It's just . . . when he runs off to his 'previous' meetings . . ."

"His what?" Stacia stiffened. Something about the phrasing jabbed her ear.

"He calls them his *previous meetings*. Like they were in the past and he didn't have to do any more. It's why he doesn't log them through Maya."

"That's cute." Stacia allowed the word to trail off as she thought. Scrambled communiqués were actually more work. The kind of effort someone would go through when they wanted to leave no official record of their transmissions. But perhaps exhaustion and stress (and Dina's warmth) made her paranoid. Or more acutely aware. Stacia extricated herself from their position, raising her glass in an offer to pour Dina a drink as she refilled her own. "It requires a . . . glyph. Internal use only."

"I hadn't heard of it." Dina gestured for another drink.

"It's restricted tech. I just had a communiqué like that earlier today . . ." Again, Stacia's words stopped short. With her meeting with Zenith Prebius. A *Prebius* meeting.

Stacia fumbled her glass, nearly spilling her wine. If her connections were correct, a cascade failure of relationships would soon follow. A failure of her community looking out for one another. Perhaps even engineering the disappearance (or worse) of one of their own. But she had to hold it together, hide her suspicions if she were to learn more.

"That kind of precaution is useful for high-level meetings if we don't want to invoke full protocols."

"I figured it was something like that." Dina seemed relieved as she reached for her glass. "It's only been going on for a few weeks."

"Yes." Stacia did not retake her seat. Not wanting to alarm Dina with her misgivings, or make her suspicious, the captain leaned against the wall. Whatever spell of intimacy had been established between them dissipated. Stacia didn't know where to put her feelings for Dina. She may have unwittingly given Hondo up. Or not so unwittingly, sensing something she didn't want to admit to. Or worse: another player set her in motion against Hondo.

The aspect of Stacia that was her heart retreated in the moment, frozen by the possibilities, allowing the part of her that was her captain's duty to take over. Her tone shifted, the icy edge of her command role girding her words. "I've had him doing a lot. Private meetings, that is. As a part of the investigation. But I will talk to him about it. Relationships always trump the work if we want a whole, healthy you. That sound all right?"

"Yes, I'd like that." Dina lowered her glass.

"Good. I look forward to my chat with him." Stacia took another drink, her thoughts fixing on Hondo. A painful sting of fear swept her up. She needed to go, right now, and collect this fool before he could do any more damage to her or her people.

18

WACHIRU ADISA
The Dreaming City

Every day our ancestors become legends
*   Stories for us to remember who we are*
Pursuing abundant life, love is hard
*   (Never afraid) To have faith, with room for doubts*
*   (Never afraid) We need to trust in us, where hope routes*
Never forget where we want to be, never retreat, never plead
As long as we have each other, we're rich, we have all that we need
To figure out the best way to serve, as guard.

There came certain leverage points, critical junctures in space and time and story, that opportunities for major changes occurred. Sometimes in a setting as simple as a meal at the Adisa family table.

"I slaved all afternoon over this," Ezeji announced, carrying in a tray of green beans. Nothing synthed, they had been grown in the gardens.

"Bro, do you even know where a stove is?" we asked.

"I know where my sister stays. And I know how to pester her to cook for me." He set the tray down in the center of the table. He held up his thumbs and index fingers to form a viewing frame before deciding he didn't like their position and shifted it down.

"You know this only means that she'll be putting this on your tab."

"She got to you, too?" Ezeji laughed that carefree laugh of his. The one that didn't care about anything past this moment. "'Sibling reparations' is not a thing. A tax for being a 'bad big brother' is straight-up abuse of her jelis' duties."

We envied him that laugh.

Our kraal had three rondavels: the central space where we relaxed, plus two bedrooms. The furniture smooth, with curvilinear designs, ran toward delicate surfaces and decorative textures. Blank spaces for furnishings that didn't have to be there all the time, like cabinets and wardrobes. The wall dissolved as our mother came in. Once she approached the table, Taiwo and Kehinde settled into her hands. With a note of formality, she paused behind the seat to our left. She watched the two of us, her posture open, inspecting us. Proud of what she saw, though her approval did not lighten the weight in our heart. We nodded to acknowledge her presence. We needed her close, to lean on her strength now more than ever. Just as much as she needed ours.

Jaha entered, setting a tray of corn bread on the table before moving to our right. Near the beginning of the period of rest, contemplation, dreaming, and healing that would be known as the Uponyaji, Jaha Dimka was already an institution builder. She very easily could have been Camara instead of Xola, but she was more interested in moving the work forward, not sitting around contemplating the next horizons. She formed the original First World board and created the Science Council. She went on to mentor Astra Black. Back then, the uniforms of the Science Police—what would eventually evolve into the Griot Circle—were gray-and-black unitards. She sucked her teeth at them, saying they made our people look like disco revolutionaries. The fundamental questions she focused on with the dream of Muungano beginning to take shape were "Who were we trying to be?" and "Who do we want to be?" So an entire cultural conversation began . . . mostly because she hated how her ass looked in the uniforms.

Not knowing where he best belonged, Ezeji waited, licking his lips in anticipation, but remained rooted behind the chair at the foot of the table. He began to pass cups around the table for each of us to take. The air was heavy with expectation. Not just of the solemnity and ritual of the dinner itself but of us. How even out of public view, our every gesture was scrutinized, dissected, our every move analyzed like game footage being broken down.

We took the head of the family table. Xola's seat. The family gathered for dinner around the table every Ojo Aiku, the Day of Immortality, with rare exception. Each child could go their own way through the week, but we came back together as the Adisa family every week. The ritual of reminder of who we were. Xola at the head, Selamault at his right side, Amachi on his left. The other seats were for guests or invited family. We always sat at the foot of the table, always facing Xola.

But Xola was gone.

We had never been completely carefree. We were aware that much of our childhood was steeped in preparation to lead. Maybe not the Ijo or even to become Camara but for wherever we found ourselves in life. The chalice felt too large in our hands, and it took several attempts before things began to feel comfortable to us. Conscious of the weight of attention on us in the moment, we cleared our throat. We closed our eyes and allowed the words to pour through us. That was our gift.

"It is said that people who lack knowledge of the past are like a tree without roots. In the spirit of remembrance, of acknowledgment, of respect, we pour this libation. We raise our cup to honor what we call God. We pour to honor the importance of family and those who came before us. We call upon our elders, whose wisdom we seek in all endeavors." Acknowledging Mom and Jaha, we poured to the north. "Asè."

"Asè." Ezeji poured to the south.

"Asè." Selamault poured to the east.

"Asè." Jaha poured to the west.

"Let us be seated." We hoped we were doing this right. Xola always had a way of making the rituals of the family meal feel natural, a story we were being reminded of and being invited into. Joining one another. We felt stiff and formal, dancing awkwardly within walls we erected to keep us from enjoying one another.

This was our first family meal without Xola.

We could picture our Pops at the other end of the table and avoided his eyes. We studied each of our family members. Ezeji with his multiringed hand clutching after a glass. All chatter and nonsense, opining on the latest pyr ball scores, his mates back on O.E., and the latest group he hoped to promote, all between sloppy bites of food. Jaha finished eating, her lithe form slipping free of her chair to fuss about unnecessarily in the kitchen, not trusting anything automated to wash the dishes. Our mother continued to eat, small and deliberate bites, well chewed before swallowing. A delicate bird bobbing about her plate. Her heavy-lidded eyes turned to us on occasion, full of worry and love, with an absence where her husband once occupied.

No masks, no pretense, they festered in their thoughts, not allowing our brooding silence to intrude. We hadn't wanted to attend a formal dinner, not yet. We wanted to just be. To hang out, enjoy family on their own terms without any agenda. But the work of community never stopped, and the Adisas had to name a new head to represent them at the Ijo. We were certainly old enough. We had the weight of expectation upon us and a position to fill.

Selamault rested her hand on ours, her touch cool and soft. "It's all right. You're doing fine."

"I'm not sure how to do this." We passed food around the table, our stomach lacking the pressure of hunger, having dined to its fill on anxiety.

"None of us do. We simply do the best we can." Selamault's voice thickened with maternal concern.

We were now the patriarch of the family. Xola's counsel was no longer available as a safety net. We no longer had the luxury to just sit at the table and call our shot when we needed to. To allow our mind to drift in the nascent melodies and rhythms that formed much of our idle thoughts. Now the table needed a head to call the family together, to see if we'd be formally accepted as head of the Adisa clan.

"Ain't no one here to judge you, baby," Jaha said. "So loosen up and do *your* thing."

Despite how much time she spent with our family, Jaha also had two children of her own. She rarely saw them, since her daughter—following in her footsteps—became a ranking member of the Science Council on Titan. Her son helped organize the Bronzeville Rebellion and continued the work of building community there. Their family reunited three times a year, once in each of their spaces.

Jaha's husband died when she was seventy. A part of the fifth wave migration from Yo, she had dropped out of high school, though she received her equivalency diploma, which allowed her to go on to university. During her career, she connected First World to other institutions, cobbling together a network that bolstered one another's work. The Thmei Academy. The Scarabys Institute. When she was ninety, she decided to go back to school to pursue a doctorate. Her thesis focused on the life of Marcus Garvey and the institutions he created. She returned to First World as a teacher.

Hakeem Buhari, the first Camara, was her elder.

"Can we eat yet?" Ezeji asked. "I'm not used to standing on occasion, and this Negus is hungry."

"Yeah, yeah. Have at it." We uncovered the rest of the dishes. Macaroni and cheese. Greens. Slow-cooked barbecue ribs. And a bottle of whiskey. All of Xola's favorites, though people were always after him to pursue the healthier diets of Muungano.

"Do we call for a formal vote to be accepted as head of the Adisa clan?" we asked.

Ezeji held his spoon hovering over the macaroni and cheese, paused mid-plunge, awaiting the answer to the ill-timed question. We motioned for him to continue. Everyone served one another food, and we pretended to not notice how Mom and Jaha exchanged uncertain glances.

"Is headship something you want?" A tentative hitch of hesitation filled Mom's voice.

"Yes. Why do you ask? Do you have doubts?" We stopped pushing greens about our plate in the illusion of eating. Our stomach panged with its own uncertainty. This was a necessary conversation, but not one we relished. Our appetite wouldn't return until its resolution.

"Not in you or your ability."

We puzzled over the curious absence in our mother's affirmation.

"Sweet baby," Jaha began her windup. "You've always been torn. Look at you and, what was that child's name?"

"Anyah." Without looking up, Ezeji heaped another serving of macaroni and cheese onto his plate. If he was aware of how all of us turned to him at the sound of her name, he gave no indication of it beyond his intense focus on the spoon clanking against his plate. Maybe he knew we weren't as fragile as everyone thought when it came to the mention of her name. Though more likely, he really wanted more macaroni and cheese.

"Yes, that's the one. You sacrificed the possibility of a relationship with her to pursue your music. That's your first love and who you are." Jaha patted our arm. "There's nothing wrong with that. You're free to pursue your gifts and passions. The people in your orbit will either fit into that or not. But you can't just 'fit' serving Muungano into a slot in your life. It consumes the slot."

"The mantle of leadership is a heavy burden." Selamault's tone turned solemn and slow, each syllable imbued with import. Her hands rested on her knees. She kneaded the flesh around them, working out a stiffness deep in her joints. The movement seemed more meditative than palliative. "One which wore on Xola, precipitating many of his health issues. But he viewed everything as secondary to the needs of Muungano. His jazz. His health. Us. Once he ascended to Camara, I became second in his life. Over fifty years of not being his highest priority." Her words, the heaviness of her heart, hung over the table. Selamault leveled her eyes at us. No pity or regret filled them. "I ask you, are you ready to make that sort of sacrifice?"

We twirled our fork in our food as we considered their counsel.

We feared that we wanted to say the words to placate the expectation everyone had for us. We allowed them to settle into us, deep into our emi, becoming part of who we were and wanted to be. We said the words—only to ourselves, the path of a journey finally coming together—the sound an empty clang in our heart. "We accept."

"We know that you do not enter into this lightly." Selamault produced a sigil. "We carry Amachi's vote by proxy. We cast our votes behind you."

We knew her face almost as intimately as we knew our own. Something bothered her. "What is it, Mom?"

"I just don't want you to be disappointed." Mom avoided our eyes. "Take some time and think about what you want."

We angled toward her, ready to press the matter, but a fluttering about our emi gave us pause. Perhaps it was only maternal concern that thickened her voice. If she'd had a vision, she would not reveal it to us.

Jaha wore an equally grave expression, as if privy to her own secret knowledge she wouldn't share. "Becoming head of the Adisa does not automatically make you head of the Ijo. We no longer live in the age of chieftains or kings. Leadership is determined by the will of the people, not bloodline. You have the rest of the families to win over."

"And you can believe the Yo ain't gonna wait on us before it makes its next move." Ezeji sopped up some sauce with a piece of corn bread. He gestured toward one of the ribs on our plate. "You gonna eat that?"

✳

What does it take to be number one is a pimp game
Exploit or be exploited is the old way, the new same
Be wary of those who want to seize power
 In wanting it, they've proven themselves lost
Ain't no victims here, no one here to cower
 Folks can speak for themselves, bossed
(Never afraid) To lead, to teach, to forgive
 Where there is repentance walked out
(Never afraid) To speak, to reach, to live
 Free of history because we're talked out
Escape the lies of those who want to leech, Truth
Heavy is the head that dares to teach, Truth
We're the only thing we should be afraid of
Willing to give up what we love for who we love

It renewed our heart to walk the corridors of the Dreaming City, to see the world the members of Muungano had built. The archways with sculptures of bronze-leaved trees. The stacked kraals. The courtyards and classrooms. This was the world we knew, all we knew. There were worlds, perhaps whole galaxies, now open to us. That we longed to explore. The burden of leadership would trap us here. We never wanted to think of our home as a cage. Home. Music. Exploration. The usual pull of a young person's heart. Whatever our decision would determine the next several decades of our life, and no matter which profound journey we would embark on, we wanted assurance from the Universe that we were on the right path.

Without thinking about it, our footsteps took us to the library. The meeting place of the Ijo. In the central chamber, Maulana sat. His chair enclosed him, a protective shell. Its tiered metal disguised armaments as art. Weapons casings, detonated ordnance scraps, the discards of war repurposed and reshaped into his seat. Even the rich draperies were canvas heat shields from low-atmosphere, suborbital jumps with netting as overlay. He shifted in his seat, a series of holovids and displays all about him. Too much visual data for an unaided human brain to take in. To our knowledge, he did not have a griot's crown or any other cybernetic enhancement. He simply enjoyed the ambiance of knowing as much as possible.

"Habari gani?" Maulana nodded without glancing over.

"Nia," we said. "We question our purpose."

"Have a seat, then. Maybe I can provide some clarity." Maulana turned his attention from his monitors. Sleep had eluded him, perhaps for days. He had that way about him when he was in one of his manic periods. Chasing down reports monitoring communications, searching for details he would know only once he found them. "I grieve the loss of Xola."

"We know. We all do."

"But someone must take his place."

"That's what we came here to discuss."

Maulana stared across the room, his attention focused on whatever dust mote, light reflection, or fleeting sound only he heard. "I'm sorry. I'm a little distracted. I was going over some files related to your father."

"Which ones?"

"All of them." Maulana stretched within the confines of his chair.

"What do you mean 'all of—'"

"Medical history. Autopsy report. Political uprisings in Bronzeville.

Briefings. Genestream analysis. Communiqués. Correspondence. Calendar. Movements."

"Hold up, genestreams are proprietary," we say.

"I have clearance. And I wanted to know if there were any deviations."

"In his locked genetic sequence?"

"Drift could happen. And there were some irregularities."

"Such as?"

"I'm still trying to figure that out. Which is why I reached out to Titan. Thing is, they recently ran across a similar kind of drift case."

"Where?" Our apprehension began to ebb. Maulana wasn't on some fishing expedition. He followed the information, making connections, tracing patterns, though sometimes they were discerned only by his particular emi.

"With a patient whose medical records they only recently sent for review."

"Coy don't play well on your face." Though with his time with the Niyabinghi and in the HOVA ranks, obfuscation was second nature, we tired of his vague evasiveness.

"Bekele Chikeke." A nervous twitch creased Maulana's jaw muscle.

"Stacia's son?"

"Yes."

"What does that mean?"

"I don't know. I only have suppositions and questions."

"Probably in that order."

"Always so clever with your words. I don't think it's a coincidence that whatever plagued Xola may have struck Stacia. Just as your mother displays some indications of the genetic drift. I'm only speculating, but if Xola was the target, whatever the means of this attack Selamault was close enough to receive some of the effects. The same, perhaps, might happen if someone went after Stacia. Those close to her might feel the effects."

"We have to warn her."

"We can't. That's all supposition and only one possible narrative."

"What's another?"

"I'd rather not say until I have more proof." Maulana's imagination always veered to the worst case. But there were few community members as ride or die as Stacia. Especially to Xola. "Anyway, I thought you'd appreciate an update on my investigation."

"We do. Asante sana." The way he emphasized the word *my,* soft but clear, left the impression that he was fulfilling some role he imagined we should be doing. "Have you given any consideration as to who would make a good candidate for Camara?"

"Are you asking if I'm considering it or if you should?"

"Both."

"Political intrigue is not your strong suit."

"It shouldn't have to be between brothers and sisters."

"You right, you right," Maulana said. "But consider this: How do you know who your brother or sister is?"

"Is this some Night Train nonsense?"

"Ignore the rumors if you want. I investigate. I gather intelligence. Just like I wonder how someone could get close enough to Xola to administer anything unless they looked like us."

"Which is why you have been checking his schedule."

"And meeting notes. Did you know he met with Captain Chikeke before she departed?"

"No, but it makes sense. She's . . . She was . . . like a daughter to him. Why? Is she Night Train now?"

"Wouldn't matter if she was. To you, they don't exist." Maulana poured himself a drink. "You so busy about 'we,' disarmed by the dream of goodness and integrity in everyone you meet, like they're going to be better just for having touched the hem of your garment or something. I see threats you're too naive to see."

"You assimilate the culture of the oppressor, coming at situations with little more than a colonized mind-set. Going into new spaces, replicating the brokenness of the past."

"That's rich considering that you propagate a worldview that still sees in terms of weusi and mzungu. Or how Muungano itself defines its members by Ugenini, Asili, and Maroon. Our own central hypocrisy when it comes to freeing ourselves from colonialist mind-sets."

"We suppose your way is better."

"It's simpler and it's honest. There are those who are of Muungano, and the rest are obroni. You're either family or an outsider. And I defend us against all outsiders. Even those who look like us," Maulana said. "Even—no, especially—O.E."

"We shouldn't be a threat to them."

"Of course we are. We stand in opposition to their entire way of life. We created new ways of being and moving. Of valuing and celebrating one another. Allowing our systems—political and economic—to grow out of our humanity. Seeking only the best for one another and our community. That's why we're a threat. And will always be seen as one. Where we go, no matter what we call ourselves, they try to exploit us; probably even enslave us if they could again. The worst mistake we could make would be to believe that a mutual dependence is possible."

"Reconciliation starts with—"

"Save your breath. I have no interest. I have no sympathy, no compassion, no interest in those who refused to confess to have had any part in committing any crime—much less the Maafa—against us. But confession depends on recognition, and they never saw us as people to begin with. We could have no social contract with those who never saw us as fully human. Coming out of the Uponyaji, when we began to see ourselves, define ourselves, that was when we became truly free. We reclaimed our dignity, took pride with no need of the validation of anyone's gaze except our own. Not begging for rights from someone else."

"To create something new on our terms," we said.

"We worked too hard to uproot every oppressive economic system and dismantle any unjust political structure. The First Lunar Ukombozi War was the necessary shock for our oppressors to release us and allow us the space and time to construct our society. Our dream. And I will defend that dream with my last breath, strength, and blood. I would absolutely take up arms to defend what we have created."

"We all would defend the dream by any means necessary."

"Do you know what your failing is?" Maulana asked.

"Please . . . do tell."

"You never see the threats around you or to those closest to you until it's too late."

He meant Anyah.

"Say that shit again." We stepped to him. "You want to play like that, then you picked the right one. We got time today."

Maulana rose. The beginnings of a grin inched across his face. His door chimed and began to open before he could respond. Jaha walked in with her strident pace, though not out of breath.

"I hope I'm interrupting," she said.

"I trust you have a good reason for barging in here," Maulana said.

"You mean some Griot Circle business. Aw, nah, baby. Maya let me know things were getting a little heated and thought I could use some company for a walk. If you don't mind me taking Wachiru off your hands."

"We think Maulana was about to have all that his hands could handle," we said.

"No worries." Maulana spread his hands, his smile broad and toothy. "We were done here. I think we know where each other stands."

"We appreciate you." We allowed Jaha to guide us out.

"And I, you, Wachiru," Maulana said to our back.

Jaha hooked her arm into ours as we strolled. A winding path of cemented regolith created a walkway around the Dreaming City library. The brilliant colors of the upinde mvua fields were unmistakable. Hedera helix climbed the nearby walls. Bowls bobbed above it at different levels, creating a floating hanging garden. Ezeji was five when he and his classmates did the installation. The goal was to create a painting using flowers as the palette. The spider plants' greenish-white flowers spilled out in a floral staircase. They had been genetically modified for their particular shade of seafoam green. The *Aglaonema* bushes lined the footpath. Both delicate and exotic, they required constant care. Taxing and exacting work, but they found that if they allowed kids room and excuse to play in dirt, they'd do it every day.

We walked surrounded by people who cared about us and about one another. Children who danced to our music, even looked up to us. Other plants—small *Chamaedorea* palms, Song of Jamaica plants—helped sweeten the air. Yet the odd combination of smells slammed us, more like sun-ripened manure. No one else offered any comment. We found out that certain genestreams reacted poorly to *Chamaedorea,* the way some people tasted cilantro as soap. It was a pretty flower, though.

"Why did you go there in the first place?" Jaha asked.

"Answers."

"To what questions?"

"We're still trying to make sense of what happened to our Pops. And the attack on me and Amachi. What if there's a plot against Muungano? So we started wondering who would have to gain from dissent among us?"

"Sweet baby." Jaha placed her hand on his arm as if comforting a hapless child. "O.E. would love nothing more. LISC leadership alone would fill my top ten guesses."

"We know. We just fear . . ."

"What?" She withdrew her hand.

"Someone closer to home."

"Who?" She stared at us, her gaze hardening into icy calculation. "Not Maulana."

"It was a thought. Sow enough discord, and his becomes the only voice . . . strong enough to hold the center."

"That's a gambit. And more of a long game than I think he's capable of pulling off." Jaha crossed her arms so hard, like she was determined to build a wall around herself. "No, say what you want about the man, but he puts community first."

So much intrigue. Thinking this was about our own exhausted us on a spiritual level. The long, yellowish spathes of peace lilies protruded, curious to sense the world about them. The red, pink, and orange arrangements of Barberton daisies lay out like a lush field on the other side of the path. The colors of the garden soothed us, allowed us to lose ourselves in our thoughts.

"That wasn't the only thing we had questions about."

"What is it, baby?" Jaha's grandmotherly drawl thickened.

"We have need of your wisdom." We bent down to cradle a flower. To brush against its feathery petal to be reminded of how delicate our creations were. "There's been a shift in Muungano. A change in its energy."

"I've felt it, too," Jaha said. "Let me ask, is it the energy you are trying to speak to?"

"What do you mean?"

"You have this burning in your belly to lead now. And to lead, you have to sway the people. And right now, a part of you fears you might not be the best voice to speak to the mood of the people."

"You think I'm afraid of Maulana."

"I didn't say that. But you know he's a strong, competing voice."

"Bayard would make a fine Camara."

"You must really not want Maulana." Jaha patted our wrist.

"You're right. His way makes us wary. It's angry. It's . . . vengeful, in the name of vigilance."

"And you want . . . what?" Jaha asked.

"We don't want it confused with justice."

Raised voices drew our attention. The open courtyard was the public space for art creation. Many spoken word poets "battled" there, pitting their verses against another. The timbre of the voices alarmed us. Jaha perked up also—slipping her arm from ours—already marching toward the disturbance before we even interpreted it as a potential problem. She shifted her pehla stick without unholstering it.

The Griot Circle were the village memory and oral historians, keepers of the nyama. Those entrusted with reciting poems or singing or telling stories that transmitted the cultural inheritance of Muungano. The record keepers, storytellers, and entertainers, the jeli tradition evolved into crisis intervention specialists, an emergency response team preferable to maintaining an investigative force, even the Science Police of First World.

The raised voices led to a shove, which was when Jaha stepped between them. The pair took quick note of her Eshu colors, recognized her as a senior jeli, and stepped away from her to their neutral corners.

"What's your name?" Jaha said.

"Kamau." Tall, his tawny complexion highlighted the scarification along the right side of his body. The etchings painted with circuitry that poets could use as AI code.

"Kamau what?"

"Just Kamau."

Jaha inspected him closer. She cupped and slowly stroked her bare chin. "Kamau, you don't look familiar to me. And I know all the regular poets around here."

"I'm down from the Belts. Hitting some of the local spots, touring the scene"—he glanced at the other man, not even a full stare, but it was enough to reignite the fire of his anger—"when this—"

"Hold on. Before we go there, he has a name, too." Jaha turned to the other man. "Who might you be?"

Short, the man's skin ran to a deep sepia, and his body still clung to its baby fat. His haptic shirt decorated in kente patterns, he was obviously a kinaesthetic artist, someone who turned sound into a felt experience. He glared at Kamau. "Obi."

"Yes, Obi Abara. Baby, I've known your momma since she was knee-high to a grasshopper. Why don't you start, and then I want to hear from Kamau."

"I was just—" Obi waved his arms halfway into some serious theatrical gesturing when Jaha cut him off.

"Aw, nah, baby. That's not how we do. We in the library square of the Dreaming City. The Dreaming City. A place we dreamt into being requiring the sacrifice of generations. Here, we create."

When Jaha turned one hundred, she asked Xola if they could stage an elder celebration, with a food festival ushered in by the pouring of libations. She specifically wanted an Ugenini lens for the activities. People arrived and, as the libations flowed, began to share their stories of her. Something she neither expected nor asked for. Stories recalling her heroism during the Lunar Ukombozi War, since many forgot her role as a general because she never spoke of it. Stories of resistance, resilience, remembrance. The experience moved her, shifted a weight she didn't know she had, and inspired her pursuit of education.

The sharing of stories became a founding principle of Muungano. The basis of using jelis as a policing force. Stories empowered people, becoming gifts created and given to one another. A revolution in thought in how we celebrated one another, all because Jaha didn't want to organize her own birthday party.

"I'll give each of you three objects to use in telling your story. Obi, like I said, you go first." Jaha stepped from between Kamau and Obi and took in her surroundings for inspiration. She ticked them off on her fingers as she said them. "The sun, moon, and stars."

Obi backed up. At first, we thought he was intimidated by the idea. Instead, he shifted into his creative space, ready to conceive and pour out a piece.

"The sun rose in the east, ready to spread his life-giving light to all, chasing off the darkness that was settling in. The moon basked in the eternal night, refusing to reflect the light of the sun or any star. Not bright enough to be its own star, the moon was determined to find an orbit centered in darkness. Not learning from the past and the rule of shadows. The moon and night failed to give way to the sun and day, the eternal order disrupted. And so it remains to this time."

"I see," Jaha said. "Kamau, I tell you what, same thing. Sun, moon, and stars."

Kamau cleared his throat. He steepled his fingers in front of him, focusing on them, before snapping to full attention. "There was a story told among my people of the time when the moon made the sun angry, though no one dared even whisper why. The moon had grown soft and content, dependent on the sun for warmth and strength. The moon saw its effect on waves and thought itself responsible for considerable changes, even impact on the planet. It confused influence with power, not realizing even its placement among the stars was dependent on the earth. The moon would never truly be free, but it was determined to please the earth no matter what. Well, the sun saw this and grew furious. It used its sharp rays to cut off pieces of the moon to learn, to plead for mercy, at which time the sun would let him go. From that small sliver, the moon would gradually grow again to become full and whole, and to truly find its place among the stars."

"Not bad, not bad," Jaha said. "We have some fine young griots in the making, wouldn't you say, Wachiru?"

"No doubt, no doubt," we said.

"Would each of you agree that there is some truth to each other's story?"

Obi and Kamau couldn't meet each other's eyes, but they ticked their heads in passing, then turned to the side away from the other as if distracted by something.

"Well, let me tell you a story. Each word in its place; none forgotten. The order is sacred, exactly as I once heard it." Jaha waited until she had all eyes on her. "For many years, the sun and moon lived on Earth with one another. Though they were forced to live in separate worlds, day for one, night for the other, rarely did they cross paths. They had found a way to live in harmony with one another. Over time, they even became friends.

"Then one day, the rains came, and water filled the earth. The sun used to visit the waters, but the waters would never return his efforts. The water said that there was no room for it at the sun's house. That if he came for a visit, he and his people would drive the sun out. The sun decided to build a very large house, for he knew that water and his friends were numerous and took up a lot of room. The sun told the moon of his plan, and together they got to work on a large new house. When it was finished, they asked water to come visit.

"When water arrived, he called out to them to ask if it was safe for him and his friends to enter. The sun and moon said yes. So water flowed in accompanied by the fish and all the other water animals. As more and more water flowed in, it soon reached the top of the sun's and moon's heads, soon filling the entire space. The sun and moon were forced to go up into the sky, where they have remained ever since. They may not always get along, but they found a way to coexist in peace. For they needed each other."

Jaha folded her arms and waited. Kamau and Obi slowly turned to face each other. They clasped wrists, mumbled their appreciation, and parted ways.

"I'm not sure all those analogies held," we said.

"Everyone's a critic." Jaha watched the young men lumber off, their beef, if not forgotten, placated for now. "They held enough to make my point.

Sometimes when a person or a community is in crisis, they simply need to be heard."

"You are a wise woman." We kissed her forehead, careful not to displace her head wrap if we valued our life.

"I need to call a meeting of the Ijo."

The more joy we express, the more they come for us
      (Never afraid) With fire, in violent chorus
They took away our homes, left us no choice
Tried to take away our hope, strip us of voice
But we built a home among the stars
      (Never afraid) First Attempts in Learning was the key
Still so far to go, we have to keep pressing for ours
      Staying true to who we are, We against the O.E.
A test, if we can live from what we've learned
Come around this fire, expect to get burned
Let there be no rift, our community will remain free
The future is a gift, what is meant to be will be.

19

FELA BUHARI
Eshu

Swimming back to consciousness, Fela swallowed back nausea. The steady rumble of the transport vehicle jostled her to full wakefulness. Even beyond her blindfold, darkness shrouded the space to where she had no sense of whether it was actually day or night. She was tired. The kind of tired where she could sleep for several days straight. The kind of tired where her muscles no longer cooperated and her mind became disoriented. Her mind drifted, allowing her to sense her surroundings. Three guards surrounded her. No way to tell how well armed they were. They sped along. Whatever vehicle they were in had no gyro stabilizers. A cramped space not designed for comfort, her hands bound behind her. The ache in her shoulder told her she'd been in this position for a while. She flexed her wrists, not wanting to draw attention to herself as she checked her restraints. Metal clamps of some sort, probably a magnetic lock.

"There's no point in pretending that you're still unconscious," a voice said. "Unless you want to remain in such an uncomfortable position."

The one thing her training always taught her was that she was going to be scared no matter what. Because she understood even more how bad a situation could turn. The key was to push her errant thoughts aside, turn her fear into something productive, and survive the situation. Fela slowly sat up. "Who are you?"

"All will be answered in good time. For now, you are our guest."

She allowed her awareness to begin to form an image of her lead captor, their presence coalescing into a featureless shadow.

"Is it a measure of your ability as hosts that I remain blindfolded?"

"True enough. Though I don't imagine that your view will improve much."

They removed the covering from her head. Her mind snapped to full alertness, gauging threat assessments, ready for any opening to free herself. Two natives, wearing gray uniforms with yellow trim, escorted her. Their skin a tincture of deep blue, as if they'd been suffocated. An unsettling series of clicks and whirs began when they were aware that she was awake. Fela eyed them with a mix of suspicious glare and curiosity. The metallic box they rode in was clean to the point of sterility, like it had never seen combat, terrain, or even much use since it rolled out from its manufacture. She'd been stripped down to her nanomesh body stocking, her navsuit armor deactivated. Her bi-olink implant still in place, enough for Maya to translate, but other functions and signals essentially cut off from her. No one could track her.

Across from her, the lead guard waited, allowing her to absorb the fullness of her situation. His image flickered. A holovid projection. A tall man with short white hair and a pale complexion, his skin the color of frost on a window. Thin, with a rugged fitness hidden beneath his façade of officiousness. His gray uniform had blocky shoulders, and a canary-colored cloth wrapped about him. His ring and pinkie fingers were fused on his left hand. A scar ran from the corner of his mouth, up along his cheek; when he turned to her and smiled, his face opened into a terrible rictus.

The vehicle slowed to a halt. The guards stood up. Fela took their measure, noting their stances. The fight about to ensue, she tensed.

"Don't," the pale man said. "I'd also be remiss as a host if I didn't inform you of the precarious position you find yourself in. You haven't even surveilled your location. Rather than start a scuffle so you can run, chance an escape, why not simply walk out? We won't stop you."

Standing slowly, the guards backed out of her way. The lead guard half bowed; his arm swept toward the exit. Not quite taking her eyes from them, Fela inched toward the door. Ducking her head, she took a tentative step out.

They approached a sprawling building. Its entrance opened into a greater structure. A phalanx of soldiers stood in formation. When she stepped from the transport ship, the troops snapped from parade rest to sharp attention.

"It's how we greet honored and respected guests." The pale man's scar sneered at her.

"With a show of strength to let her know what she was up against," Fela said.

"Come," the lead guard said. "Allow us to accompany you to your quarters."

Recalling her specialized training at the Thmei Academy—including the advanced coursework for leaders: survival, evasion, escape, resistance, improvisation—Fela collected as much intel on them and their methods as she could as they walked. She wondered whether she'd be up for this test. The building was surprisingly low-tech. Physical doors opened like ancient vaults. The occasional banner decorated the halls. The soldiers peeled off to station themselves in teams of four at every door and junction. The mazelike structure reminded her of the labyrinth used as an initiation tool into Um-lando, the Great Knowledge. Initiates had to walk through several gates in order to reach the center, performing rituals and encountering various dangers or tests before they could continue their journey forward.

Winding another corner, the pale man slowed their pace as they strode past a series of open rooms. Inside, many of the Mzisoh sat in chair-like devices. The retinue stopped at an open chamber. Its floor wet from being sprayed down. Hints of pink effluvia mottled the edges of the tiles. Something bad happened in here, and they wanted her to know how it ended. Fela took in the room, the body left on display. Tiny rivulets of blood trickled down each arm, pooling under the seat. This person had suffered. The ridge along their skull ground down. Their eyes locked open with needles. Their face locked into an agonal contortion that made them barely recognizable. Her eyes adjusted, the image's familiarity starting to coalesce in her mind.

Natan.

"I'm told he was a stubborn one. A proud one. But in the end, the body can only take so much, and everyone gives up their secrets," the pale man said.

The Mzisohs' screams echoed all the way to her chamber. She would not give her abductors satisfaction of her fear.

Fela shrugged off the guards' hands and swaggered into her cell.

✳

Time lost all meaning. It took effort to force her eyes open. Fela flopped forward, dazed and disoriented. Her hands trembled, but she wasn't cold. Or nervous. Or hungry. The vessels in her head pulsed. The air left a medicinal taste in the back of her throat. The way her thoughts churned in a sluggish morass, she suspected her hosts had dosed her with a gas of some sort.

The door jostled open, old joints straining with weight. The pale man entered, his scar taking on a near-lascivious aspect as he circled her in wary inspection. He regarded her with a long, thoughtful stare. "I have looked forward to the opportunity to chat with one of your kind."

"My kind?" Fela lowered herself into a crouch. An awkward posture, her butt braced against the wall, her knees slightly bent, she rested against the slight protrusion from the wall that served for a seat. It was either that or rest on the still-stained floor. A bar hung suspended above her.

"Human, of course. An . . . Earther, is it?" Noting her discomfort, he licked his lips, tracing the inside of his scar with his tongue.

"I am a member of Muungano."

"Ah yes. The breakaway outpost. As I said, I have been looking forward to a chat. And to see what else of our information is, shall we say, incomplete." His tone remained light and pleasant even though each word he uttered underscored an unspoken threat.

"I demand to see a . . ."

"To see a what?" He arched an eyebrow. "We have no treaty with the . . . You aren't even organized enough to be called the Earth Alliance. Nor are our peoples at war. You, my dear, are a spy. A potential terrorist captured during one of our military exercises. What rights do you presume you have? Here, you have no rank, no personhood, no name. You are little more than a disposable sack of meat. The sooner you understand that, the sooner you will understand the nature of your situation."

Fela appeared to let the words sink in. Silence settled between them, slow and deliberate, another test he formulated for her. Silences never bothered her, however, since they allowed her time to gather her thoughts. Her mind focused on the room. The door. The hallway. Guard shift changes. The number of steps to the door. The thrum of the power conduits that ran through the walls. Methods of evasion once she escaped this room. Because she would escape this room.

The door opened with the grinding creak of unoiled hinges. A woman swept in, attended by two more guards. Her blond hair, brittle from so much dye, pulled back in a bun; a mercurial smile framed by too much lipstick; white teeth, row upon row, like a shark; all on an angular face whose every muscle was taut like a painting that had been refurbished many times.

"She doesn't look like much," the woman said.

"Luckily, I believe she's under. Or else we might find out how formidable she is. As it stands, the truth crawler has attenuated to her." The pale man's face grew solemn, distant, while he studied her. Fela's thoughts became muddled, a sun's light obscured by the gentle haze of clouds. The pale man circled her twice, without her reacting to his movements. "Will you allow me to remove your restraints?"

Her thoughts dulled, Fela held up her wrists before she was conscious of her action. The gas lowered her resistance. The hostiles were either resistant or wore an unseen air filter. Fela noticed the guards, how they observed her without trying to look like they were. She didn't return their gazes, no defiant hard eyes, which seemed to satisfy them. They retreated to the far wall. The woman paced about, the sole person onstage. Once the restraints were removed, the lead guard stepped aside, and the woman faced Fela.

"Your name?" The woman scanned her. A holovid of Fela's image floated between them. Telemetric data streamed alongside the image. The woman projected another series of holovids alongside them. She checked a file, a proctor with the exam answers in front of them. She hummed a discordant melody while she perused a file.

"Fela Buhari." Barely conscious of the stiffness in her neck or the sharp pain crossing her skull, the words echoed in her ears, almost unfamiliar. Buhari was a strong name and proud family. Their house always about the safety and security of the community. It was the family she chose.

"Your place of birth?" the woman asked without glancing over at her.

"The Dreaming City. Muungano."

"Mm-hmm," the woman intoned with satisfaction, pleased with the results thus far. "What is your current mission?"

"To explore any planet on the other side of the Orun Gate that had life." This was a prime reason she'd joined the HOVA. They were the first defense of Muungano, but they were also scientists, engineers, and anthropologists. Curious minds in the guise of military adventuring.

"No, why were you in the Daedalus System?"

"Daedalus?" Fela inclined her head toward her in a quizzical manner.

The woman checked her notes. "You Muungano-ites, or whatever you call yourselves, renamed everything. It gets quite confusing to keep our intelligence on the Terran colonies straight. How many are a part of your invasion force?"

"Our expedition is comprised of a complete HOVA platoon: four squads of nine people each, thirty-six gbeto total. Plus, a medic, two rangers, and a heavy weapons unit." Fela's drone took on a lazy edge.

"Name of your jump ship."

"The *Hughes*." Langston Hughes was one of her favorite poets. *O, sweep of stars over Harlem streets, O little breath of oblivion that is night* . . .

"Name of your squad?" The woman interrupted her thoughts.

"The HOVA Hellfighters Brigade."

"What are the defense strategies for the Sol System?"

"I don't know."

"Hmm." The woman's bemused tone committed to nothing. Her manner stiffened, her words keenly articulated. A haughty tone beneath each measured word. An ache of performance filled her every moment. "Now the interesting part can begin."

Even through the mental haze, Fela wasn't afraid of the woman and wasn't sure if she was supposed to be. The woman leaned over, her face filling Fela's entire field of vision. The woman's bronze complexion had a tangerine undercoat. Severe crow's-feet not quite hidden by the makeup. Makeup. Expertly done, the skin abrasion alone made the woman's age difficult to gauge. The woman backed away from Fela as she regained her senses enough to lash out.

The woman alerted the guards, and they rushed toward Fela. The danger cleared her head. She jabbed the first one in the throat and elbowed the next, doubling them over where she delivered a satisfying crack of their jaw by her knee. But there were too many of them. One flashed a blade. They cut the nanomesh stocking, running the knife along her length. The material peeled away from her in a single sheet. The guards held her by each arm while she continued to struggle. But she stood before her adversary completely nude.

"No need for modesty. Your form does not intrigue me." The woman paraded back and forth in front of her.

Their research into the Muungano ways couldn't have been too thorough. There was no shame in nudity, so whatever psychological edge they hoped to gain from this display was lost. Fela braced herself as best she could for what might come next. The guards shackled her hands to the bar floating above her head.

"Enjoy your sleep. We'll start again tomorrow." The woman spared one last glance at her. "Or whenever we remember you next."

*

When Fela awoke, the air had a desuetude quality to it, moist and recirculated without having been scrubbed. Fela tested her restraints. The tendons along her arms screamed with each movement. She hadn't recalled going to sleep, nor felt anything approximating restfulness. Closer to her mind blacking out to find any relief from the pain. A table had been placed in her cell. Perhaps it scraping along the floor stirred her to wakefulness. Its material neither wood nor metallic, though it had the hint of a sheen. A chair placed on one side of the table, one opposite her—between her and the exit—an empty, yet expectant space.

"We have not been properly introduced. My name is Car'Annie." The woman stepped out of the shadows, placing a large pitcher and two glasses on the table. After pouring herself a glass, she raised the pitcher as she poured another to illustrate the fullness of the stream. Its cascade. The lush *whoosh* as it filled the glass. The way light reflected from it. Her show caused her to miss her target often, allowing some of the liquid to splash in front of her. Wasted water pooled on the table. Fela's eyes tracked each spilled droplet. She couldn't remember the last time she drank. Or ate. Her throat tightened.

Car'Annie raised her glass in toast to her and slurped loudly as she drank.

"I understand that you enjoy making ceramics. Pottery, mostly." Car'Annie's voice bubbled, light and familiar, an old friend catching up. Somewhere there had to be a thorough file on Fela if they had learned the hobbies she long ago gave up on finding time to focus on anymore.

"All manner of dinnerware, actually." Fela's voice cracked, a hoarse whisper.

"Interesting. Wait, I'm such a poor host." Car'Annie eased back in her seat. She tapped a control on her wrist and lowered the restraints. Fela tumbled from her perch. The muscles in her legs barely cooperated. She managed to lope to the table, her eyes focused on the water. Car'Annie made no move to stop her. Unable to feel her hands, she fumbled at the glass. Water splashed all over the table as her trembling hands brought the glass to her lips. Eventually, enough filled her mouth to warrant her swallowing. Car'Annie raised her glass to her mouth and waved her other hand in a circle for Fela to continue. "How did that start?"

"My great-grandmother was a cleaning lady for a rich woman on the other side of the town she grew up in."

"Franklin, Indiana . . ." Car'Annie continued the show of recalling her dossier.

"Yes. After the third great pandemic, work was hard to find and she took whatever work she could find. My ma-maw was a proud woman. The manner of work wasn't an affront to her dignity. She worked hard no matter the job. She'd get up early every morning, don her rebreather mask and gear, and take the bus to the other side of town. Do the woman's laundry. Sweep her floors. Wash her dishes. Once the job was done, out of her benevolence, the woman would offer ma-maw an item she'd either tired of or needed an excuse to replace. After a year of working for her, she gave my grandmother a set of dishes. A complete setting for eight people. Some of the fanciest plates ma-maw ever laid eyes on. She treasured those dishes. Every Sunday—before we called the day Ojo Aiku, the Day of Immortality—she'd set the table for her family's dinner. She passed them down to her oldest daughter, who passed them down to me."

"What did you do with them?" The woman enjoyed a long sip from her glass.

"I smashed them to bits. I had no interest in receiving scraps from the master's table." Fela smiled at the memory.

"They must've been a priceless heirloom. You couldn't have wrapped your mind around 'reclaiming' them for your family?"

"I'm sure on O.E. they'd have been worthy of display in a museum. Within Muungano, material things aren't valued for their monetary worth. That was another thing destroying them demonstrated. From their shards, I crafted my first piece. In memory of my family's tradition, my next project was to hand cast a new place setting. For eight. I made such sets for several Muungano families before I joined the HOVA."

"Just so I understand, your society centers art as its ethos, yet has no problem creating and sending out soldiers."

"History forces our hand." Fela paused to gather her strength. Her throat worked, a hard scraping without anything to lubricate the action. But she would resist this woman with every weapon at her disposal, including non-complaint. "The same story repeats whenever we established our own culture. There are those who simply won't let us be. As if our very existence, no matter how peaceful or removed from them, is an offense. So they come in, kidnap our people, build themselves up on our backs, raze our buildings, bomb us, sabotage us."

"Our history is not so different. My people call ourselves the Lei'den. Our people flourished. Yes, we fought among ourselves, but that's simply the nature of people. Then outsiders violated our space. In the name of peace and exploration. Their presence was a . . . disruption. Its only benefit was to unite our factions to rid ourselves of the invaders. And we vowed to seek them out, to defend ourselves from further incursions by taking those same disruptions back to them."

"But what of those with truly peaceful intent?" Fela asked.

"No such people exist except in fantasy." Car'Annie tapped the control on her wrist. Shackles fashioned about Fela's wrist and, as if tethered to an invisible cord, drew her to the table. The shackles dragged her the length of the table until she was completely stretched along it. "Well, this has been pleasant. Shall we get down to business?"

"I've told you all I'm going to."

"Let's go over the defense protocols again, shall we?"

"What's the point?" Fela raised her head to lock her gaze on to Car'Annie's. "Even if I knew them, once I was reported captured, my command codes would have changed, and any plans I or my team were a part of would have been adjusted."

"I believe you. I just need to be able to plead your earnestness to others." Car'Annie gestured, and a machine much like a giant mechanical spider scuttled into the room. Each leg slinked forward, a herky-jerky motion as if doubting the certainty of each step. It approached her, slow and full of menace, if a machine could be assigned intent. "This is a truth crawler. Its emissions fill the room with a neuroagent designed to lower your ability to resist. You're probably familiar with some of its effects."

The truth crawler's head appeared to be a hollowed-out ball. Two of its legs removed it from its perch and slipped over Fela's. Much like a portable scanner, it locked her in place. A pair of thin tendrils lowered from the cranial carapace, snaking into her nose. Metal arms extended from it, wrapping about her, winding down along her torso. Needles extended from the tubes. They punctured her arms.

Fela understood. This interrogation wasn't about information. It was about Car'Annie's need to vent her cruelty. But she wouldn't give her captor the pleasure of hearing her scream.

For the first hour, anyway.

20

STACIA CHIKEKE
The *Cypher* (Returning to Titan)

There was a routine to life on the *Cypher*. Those on command cycle rose for first-shift duties. Completing their morning routines of showers, room maintenance, and the donning of uniforms before they assembled for breakfast. The vessel awash with fragrances from the ship-wide maintenance performed by third shifters; the crew's duty shifts overlapped over the meal. Some gathered in small ensembles for command performance rehearsal. The idea of practicing improvisation sounded oxymoronic, but an ensemble had to spend time together. Learn one another's strengths and weaknesses; their habits and defaults, if they were to know how each would react given a key change or random riff.

Hondo bobbed along, his head flushing with exertion. Sweat dappled his forehead like he'd eaten a bowlful of ghost peppers before picking up his flute. With his penchant for spicy dishes, that wasn't out of the realm of possibility. Though not a natural musician, since he had no ear for it, he made up for his lack of gifts with a bullheaded determination. He pretended to not notice that Stacia had entered the café, but his neck seemed to buck more. Attacking each measure with a relentless fury, working his flute to within a centimeter of its life, whipping it through chord progressions to the point of ignoring scales. Anyone could practically see him counting off the beat in his head, but they had to give him points for effort.

Once his troupe ended their performance, Stacia leveled her voice at him, smooth and even. "Hondo, can I see you for a minute?"

"Yes, Captain, but I have maintenance duty next."

"I'm aware. I sign off on the duty schedules." Turning to leave, she clasped her hands behind her, the gesture reminding her of Paki. She cursed Hondo even more for sidetracking the investigation into her missing friend. "I wanted to have a sit-down with you, but if you'd rather perform maintenance . . ."

Hondo perked up to full attention, his flute still in his hands. "Nah, I'm good. I'm good."

"All right. Meet me at storage bay three." She turned back to stare him up and down. "Bring your flute."

"Really?" Hondo's face lit up. An impromptu audition with the captain meant the opportunity to demonstrate his ability for a command performance assignment.

✹

Stacia waited for him through an observation window. Kenya headed a security team posted up on either side of the storage bay entrance. As soon as Hondo walked through the door, they relieved him of his flute and searched him for any tool that might be used as a weapon. Even without sound, Stacia recognized his pantomime of protest. His pleas of confusion and innocence. She'd seen this performance too many times before. Kenya lifted a glyph for her inspection.

"Maya?" Stacia called out, little above a whisper. Not even the buzz of a garbled digital signal came in response. Only the empty space in her mind—she'd almost said emi, like so many of the mythicists would have claimed. But she acknowledged the space in her heart, its gentle ache, of missing something. The comfort of a friend. She drummed her fingers against a panel, distracting herself with its staccato rhythms while she measured her situation.

Xola dead. Paki missing. Maya off line.

The three people she would turn to first in a crisis. She might have accused herself of paranoia, but the fact remained that her main supports were suddenly taken out in a silent coup. Its architect may have overplayed his hand. She, her family, the *Cypher,* Muungano were under attack. And no one attacked her people and expected her to stand on the sidelines.

The guards left Hondo alone in the storage bay room while she waited. All interrogations were about agendas. The ground rules were simple: Hondo had secrets to keep; she had secrets to extract. To make sure he was under no illusion of who he was dealing with, she had changed into full captain's regalia. A headdress of crystals and tight woven braids, an ethereal white dress, bedecked in crystals, and a white ermine cape. By the time she entered the ad hoc interrogation room, he'd fallen asleep in his chair.

Stacia slapped the table as she took her seat. "They say only the guilty can sleep during an interrogation."

"Or the extremely tired." Hondo stirred, unhurried, stretching and yawning, his body uncoiling in the seat. She always thought of him as small, but he seemed a lot larger across the table from her. "I pulled two doubles back-to-back. You might not have heard, but I had orders to complete an investigation."

"Did you find out anything?" Stacia remained nonplussed at his casual disparagement of her. He had a sense of entitlement he believed protected him under all circumstances. She bided her time.

"I wasn't allowed to finish. I got dragged off to a cell. I mean, an interrogation chamber. Just like the police detectives used to do back on Yo. Is that where we find ourselves? Is that 'the Muungano way' now?"

The words came out of his mouth, natural, unrehearsed, and yet completely bereft of any sincerity. A con man who'd learned his mark well. The brazenness of his tone broke the last measure of faith she had of hope in him. Her words would drill down, only business. "Where were you at 0145 during third shift?"

"In bed, I hope."

"Alone?"

"The idea of community sounds great. But wasn't no one trying to warm my bed that night."

"You are pure class." Stacia side-eyed him hard enough for him to want to fix his life.

Hondo straightened in his seat. "I'm just saying."

"You see Paki at all?"

"Yeah. Right before I called it a night. You know how he does. Skulking through the hallways, walking around brooding like a storm cloud was in his head."

"Where was the last time you saw him?"

"Don't know. Dropped in for a minute when me and some of the crew were playing Tonk."

"You sure?"

"He didn't stay for the whole time, you know. Checked us out and kept it moving."

Stacia made a show of sifting through his holovid file. His life in chapters and diagrams, the dissection of a career in charts. All a person would need to read a mark, all laid out. "According to your records, you come from a very spiritual background."

"What do you mean?"

Her headdress lightly jangling as she moved, Stacia studied the anger that roiled within him. Though he kept his eyes trained on the table, it was there. In the way he balled his hands, knuckles flexed to explode the way he had gripped his flute. The purposeful blank state of his expression. So much rage.

"I have seen your story so many times I almost don't even need to look at the details of your background. You're a certain archetype. Come from one of those O.E. religious fundamentalist families. True believers. Devout. Scripture believing. Your dad worked hard, one of those self-made men. Went to trade school, became, what, a supervisor? Middle management? Work hard all day, come home to be 'the head of the household.' I bet your mom was the epitome of a different archetype. That 'submissive wife' type. Always had dinner ready when he arrived home. What do you mythicists call them? A good helpmate? You all probably went to church every Sunday morning. In time for Sunday school, morning service, evening service. Wednesday night prayer meeting. Anytime them church doors were open, your family was there. Front row. I bet your dad was one of those get-up-at-5:30-a.m. types, get his morning study of the scriptures and prayers in to start his day. And you were his son. His first-born. His pride and joy. And you had to be that perfect model. Never talk back. Never question. Never make him look bad."

He squeezed his fists so tight the skin over his knuckles became nearly translucent. Images pulled from linkage records projected like three-dimensional animations. "Don't."

"That was probably his first commandment: don't embarrass me." Stacia enlarged an image of him as a preteen. Then as a teenager. Then as a young adult. The intervening years finding him bulking up. His face thickened and hardened. His eyes, haunted. "When did he first hit you?"

Hondo turned away from her.

"Which line was his mantra? 'God had a plan for your life'?" Stacia affected a Southern preacher. "'Spare the rod, spoil the child'? No, you were too much of a straight edge. Overcompensating by being an overachiever, excelling at the things you could control. You couldn't do anything about who you were. He probably had to go with how 'you were *not* going to embarrass him or your mother with your deviant ways.' Your lifestyle, your *choices* would get you, them, most importantly, him kicked out of the church. He'd sooner kick you out of your family. That sound about right?" Stacia lowered her face into his field of vision. No matter how intently he was determined to stare at the table, he couldn't not see her. "That kind of experience, that kind of trauma might make someone wary of even the *idea* of community. To you, 'community' was code for just another cult waiting to spring its trap shut on you."

Hondo's mouth ground, but it took awhile before he uttered anything other than an unintelligible gurgle. Finally, his voice hovered little above a cracked whisper. "It's not like that."

"Then tell me what it's like." Stacia shut off his holovid file.

"I never did fit in around here." A tear welled in his right eye. An angry thing. He wiped it away out of disdain, not pain. Not sadness. Not regret. Not shame.

"What do you mean?"

"I mean, you let me in, allowed me to participate in the game of Muungano—and that's all it is, a great big dress-up game where you got to bully others and be in charge—but I was never one of you. Not really." With a brief shudder, Hondo shifted to the side, still not meeting her eyes.

"How much of that was just in your head?" Stacia leaned in close so the heat of her breath tickled his ear.

"You'd like me to believe that. That I never saw the sideways glances. Never heard the whispers behind my back. That the jokes—because everyone here is just so damn funny—were at my expense."

"So you decided to repay us by, what, betraying us?" Fashioning a chair across from him, Stacia sat down and waited for his denial. Perhaps another explosion of protest about his innocence. But his shoulders slumped. Not a lot, a barely noticeable drop, but it was like he'd released something. His fists tightened and relaxed again.

"You don't understand. People like you never do." He paused, waiting for a reflexive rebuttal, but Stacia held her silence to let him continue speaking. "Back on O.E., I got picked on. A lot. All through school. I learned early on when a group of folks wanted to exclude me, wanted to isolate me, wanted to pick on me, I needed to walk away. If they were 'too good' for me, I'd leave them alone. Better to be by myself than subject to their nonsense. And every time I left those types behind, I'd find folks like me, who also avoided them, who didn't fit in. And we'd form our own clique."

"Who's in your . . . clique?"

"What kind of friend to them would I be if I told you?"

"The same kind that claimed to be a member of this crew, I guess." Stacia hesitated, considering whether to ask—or if she wanted to know the answer to—the next question. "Was Dina a part of your group?"

"No." Hondo couldn't meet her eyes. Now the glimmers of shame began to haunt his face.

"Why not?"

"We each had our own things. I don't think she'd appreciate the nuance of where my friends were coming from."

"So, what, you were protecting her?"

"Maybe. From me. Or me from, I don't know, her seeing who I am. We all have parts of us we hide, even from those who claim to know and love us best."

"Then 'we all' have missed the point of relationships." Stacia stood up. "So does Zenith Prebius head your crew?"

Terror filled Hondo's eyes, like he'd been caught peeing in her soup. "I never mentioned . . ."

"I already know. You'd be surprised what all I already know. At most, you're just confirming." Stacia closed the series of holovids. "Now, where can I find him?"

✳

Stacia took a contingent of her finest security to the *Cypher*'s engine room. Three arms spiraled from a central chamber to the bulkhead of the ship, the containment unit of the core's kheprw crystals. The entire array was reinforced, especially the window, which allowed the viewing of the carefully curated garden of crystals and their shifting colors. Near the back was an antechamber used mostly by the maintenance crew, though rarely unless something was wrong with the isocrawl tubes.

"Priority security override: Chikekel," Stacia said. "Open this door."

With Maya still down, the command was issued to her wrist link and patched directly into the door control nodule. When the doors slid open, a man hunched over a bowl, shoveling a fistful of noodles into his mouth. Strains of classical music echoed throughout the room.

"Zenith Prebius." Stacia circled the man.

"Well, I wasn't expecting a face-to-face meeting so soon." Holding up a biscuit for her inspection, demonstrating his hands were occupied with bowl and bun rather than any concealed weapon, he continued eating. "You'll have to forgive my accommodations. I've had to prioritize secrecy over décor and comfort."

"You'll be coming with us." A muscle in her jaw clenched, her back teeth grinding against one another.

"I'm afraid I won't be going anywhere with you." His air of smugness stirred a compulsion within her to snatch his entire life.

"Maybe you didn't notice the security officers currently surrounding you. We weren't making a suggestion."

"Oh, I gathered that. But you're laboring under the misconception that I'm a stowaway or . . . worse."

"Only if by 'worse' you mean spy, saboteur, or seditionist . . . something more along those lines," she said.

"How about diplomat?" Zenith took his time sucking up a long noodle.

"What?" Stacia's mouth fixed itself to hide her shock.

Holding both hands and freezing in a "don't shoot" pose, he slowly began to lower both his bowl and biscuit with exaggerated slowness. He withdrew a sigil, activated it, and a holovid a dossier hovered in front of them. He handed his diplomatic sigil to her. "Under Article Thirty-Seven of the Lunar Ukombozi War Convention, I invoke diplomatic immunity."

"This actually looks in order." Stacia was half-tempted to temporarily disengage Maya's translation matrix to hear what language he actually spoke but reconsidered when she realized the answer would probably bore her. She handed the sigil back to him. "Allow us to escort you someplace more . . . civil so that we can chat."

"That I can do." He eyed the guards with skepticism. "However, not to cast aspersions toward your I'm sure well-disciplined and ever obedient crew, but I will need some assurances that my safety will be guaranteed."

"You carry the sigil. Until O.E. revokes your status, your safety is guaranteed. None of us are interested in starting a war over you." Camara Xola might have wiped his ass with those pieces of paper, but the convention had held the tenuous peace between O.E. and Muungano for decades. The only thing holding the delicate détente together, as there was nothing approaching relationship between them these days.

"We'll see about that."

"What does that mean?"

"Anything I have to say is for your ears only." Zenith directed his slight chin wag toward the guards.

"Then let's go somewhere . . . more secure." Stacia swept her arm toward the door.

Word had spread, and her people came out to see the spy, the possible kidnapper, paraded down the corridor. A mood swept through the crew of the *Cypher*. Stacia saw things on the faces of her crew, twisting them into an unrecognizable mob. Anger. Distrust. Many filled the hallways to catch a glimpse of Zenith. To prevent him from doing any more harm. To see the face of their attempted oppressor. To snuff that torch of hate out before it caught anything else on fire. None of her crew had firearms, and even her own security had only pehla sticks. Though rage danced behind their eyes, she couldn't help but wonder how many feigned their disgust to hide their true face of a follower.

Once they reached the antechamber, no one said anything. The silence sat between them as an accusation. Stacia backed away from him, her heart a wild drum solo of a flutter. A rising song rang in her ears, a forgotten melody. Or a missed harmony. The music had a way of sneaking up on her, a melancholy reminder. She steeled herself against it to keep from crying. "Let us have the room."

"Captain?" Kenya asked.

"It'll be okay." She turned to Zenith. "Won't it?"

"Like two old friends chatting over tea," Zenith said.

Kenya glared at Zenith, softening when she acknowledged her captain before bending toward the door. No one made captain without being able to take care of themselves.

"And your AI?" Zenith reached for a cup, pausing when security turned their batons to him at his movement. He held his arms up until they inspected the cup.

"Maya? The system is currently off line for maintenance," Stacia said without missing a beat.

"That sounds precarious for your ship. And us."

"Our AI system is designed to facilitate ease, but we aren't dependent on it. We've learned our lesson the hard way."

"Ah yes, the Morpheus Incident."

Stacia waited for her security team to leave before engaging him further. "How do you know about that? It was a strictly internal matter."

"In politics—and more importantly, in business—there are no secrets. We took great interest in the Morpheus Project. We tried to make a claim that it was proprietary tech, but its creator, Hakeem Buhari, beat us in court."

"Because he *designed* it. It was literally his intellectual property. He wanted it used for the benefit of community."

"How did that work out for Morpheus?"

"We had to . . . sunset it." The entire issue of Morpheus always saddened her. Life was life, whether they understood it or not. And as a community, they took the AI's life.

"'Sunset.' 'It.' How sanitary."

"We had no idea what it meant to regulate a self-aware AI entity."

"I'd daresay you killed it. Morpheus is what happens when our philosophical ideas about agency and identity get challenged by the application of practical technologies."

Since there were no jelis on board, Stacia played things out on instinct. One of the rules of storytelling was to keep the person talking. But she just had to make sure that he was playing her game, not vice versa. "Because engineers aren't philosophers. We like to actually build, while philosophers like to argue everything into mush."

"There's that Muungano know-it-all spirit I love so much."

"Admittedly, we don't always consider the full, even unintended, implications for what we're building."

"You can say it, you know. Admit that you don't know what you're doing. Or does that go too contrary to your Muungano sense of pride?"

"For what we were wanting to accomplish with our community, no one did. Not us, certainly not you, since you never bothered to try. How does one code an AI to maximize human flourishing? We don't even understand what consciousness is or how it develops, so we had no idea whether a nonorganic consciousness could—"

"Love?"

"Be possible."

"You overthink things. Machines don't need consciousness to be able to predict our choices. Or manipulate them. What you naively fail to consider is what happens when this self-aware algorithm doesn't share data with us? Or chooses to share it with someone else? You have a self-aware AI that's listening to us right now. Judging us."

"You don't get it, them, or us. We had to reframe the issue of AI in a human-centered way, reflecting the kind of intelligence we would like to see from any community member.

"If there was one thing we took from the tragedy of Morpheus, to the evolution of Overseer, to Maya, was that the AI was a valued part of the community. We invited them in, and they grew and developed alongside us."

"Still destined to only serve."

"Like each of us. We serve one another. That's what community is. We lost sight of that with Morpheus. What does this have to do with where we find ourselves?"

"You certainly weren't naive enough to believe that no one would want to let you control the Orun Gate. Not with your track record with valuable resources."

"That's your whole problem: the need to control," Stacia said. "You hear that it's a stable, artificial wormhole, and that represents technology that you want to declare a proprietary interest in."

"And"—Zenith held up a finger—"determine the nature of the exploration on the other side."

"I don't even understand your beef. We have been working with scientists from Titan, Mars, and, yes, even O.E. Working together, researching together, sharing our findings with one another."

"Under *your* leadership."

"That's the rub, isn't it? To you, leadership means control, and you're not comfortable with control being in 'our' hands. Why the need to have this conversation in private? None of what you've said would shock an infant among us."

"There are interests who would go to extreme lengths to wrest control of the Orun Gate from you." Zenith slowly stood up, cautiously, with no sudden movements.

"What sort of . . . extreme lengths?" Stacia watched him.

"O.E. needs resources to sustain itself. The wormhole is the gateway to untold resources. Even if a planet were deemed of no value, a creative entrepreneur could mine what was available and carve out quite a life for themselves."

"And you want to Christopher Columbus the fuck out of the other side."

"I wouldn't put it so crassly."

"History is full of such crassness." Political discussions lost all meaning. This man could dissect their difference to whatever degree pleased him, but in the end, he only described the right, left, and center of the same diffident and devouring beast.

"History is full of stories. Tiny moments that come down to a choice some-one has to face." Turning from her, Zenith's fingers twitched like he was long overdue to raise a cup of tea to his mouth. "Like Eve when she was tempted in the garden. She was presented with a simple choice."

"You do realize in this little play, you'd be Satan?"

Zenith chuckled. "I suppose that's true. The fruit, however, is a virus."

"What?" All play left Stacia's face.

He glanced over his shoulder to gauge her reaction. "Specifically, an arti-ficially created nanovirus. Your people use this . . . funkentelechy. This near-spiritual application of spirit and technology. Not all of you. I imagine some of you, not as attuned, still manage to use it, though you may require greater assists to access this ability."

Stacia rubbed her bracelet, digging her nails into her skin.

"This virus acts as a sort of carrier wave, attenuating to your funkentele-chy and corrupting it. Simply put, we hack you. In this case, hypothetically your son, Bek, may have been infected."

Stacia strained to maintain the façade of cool assessment. She set her glass down. With little more than a casual wave, she flipped the table from between them. The glasses flew through the air, shattering against the wall. Zenith barely had a moment to flinch before she reared and her fingers curled around his throat. He'd underestimated the genetic enhancements she'd had as a Mu-ungano member. And the strength of her mother-fueled fury. She snatched him by the collar and held him against the doorframe.

"Immunity," he choked out as best he could.

"We're past that. Immunity is not a shield against an ongoing crime. Es-pecially one against my family." She squeezed his throat. "Life doesn't work like that. Justice doesn't work like that."

"There's . . . a . . . cure." His eyes bulged, his skin flushed a deep shade of red.

"What?" It took several heartbeats for the words to register in her mind, but her grip loosened. A little.

"There's a cure." He was O.E. in microcosm: a jumble of half-truths and misconceptions repeated often enough to shape a measure of narrative. This man before her as much an alien to her now as if he had tentacles sprouting from his neck. Muungano and O.E. had grown so far apart in so little time, she barely acknowledged them as the same species at this point.

"You dangle my son's life in front of me? You're playing a dangerous game."

"It's the game of control. All machinations are about control. Of the research. Of the wormhole. Of access."

"So what you are attempting to present me is the choice between the life of my son and the future of my community."

"In the end, history is about choices. And its lesson is about how powerless everyone truly is."

Stacia threw her head back with the kind of laughter Ugenini folks in mzungu spaces uttered to temper their rage and prevented them from falling into the hands of law enforcement. The kind of laughter that doubled as a prayer for strength.

"And Paki?"

"He investigated places he shouldn't have. He was on the verge of unraveling the work of many of my assets. He's being kept safe, but out of play. A further assurance."

"Your . . . assets?" Stacia released her grip. "Come with me."

"Where are we going?"

"To see about your assets."

Kenya and the rest of the security team parted as she stormed out the antechamber door. Zenith trailed behind her, his steps scampering like a puppy failing to keep pace with its owner. She stopped at the docking storage bay unit that held Hondo. The door opened. Hondo looked up, his expression a frieze of pain, embarrassment, and fear of his life unraveling before him.

"Is he yours?" Stacia's voice low and measured.

"Yes. And I would request a shuttle so that we can take our leave while you consider your options. The virus might prove more unpredictable than our doctors guessed. So don't take too long." He managed to resist the urge to punctuate the statement with a supercilious grin.

"I can't ultimately, can I? Because I'm powerless." Stacia closed the bay doors again.

"Sometimes we just have to realize our place in the greater scheme of the powerful forces around us." The cybernetic interface of his left eye scanned her. His thin lips curled, hitching his still-perfectly-groomed white goatee.

"You're right." A panel lowered, revealing a window partition. Stacia punched the intercom button. "Hondo, did you know?"

"Know what?" He rose, not knowing where to direct his answer, before aiming it at the door.

"About what Prebius's offer was to me."

"I don't . . ." Hondo held his hands up and backed away from the door like he feared an angry maternal tiger was on the other side of it.

"About what Prebius did to my son." A steel, knifelike edge slipped in her voice, the way a weapon chambered a bullet. Zenith took a step away from her.

"Now wait . . . ," Hondo said.

"About what *you* helped Prebius do to my son."

"It wasn't supposed to play out like that."

"Yeah, you right, you right." A light above toggled from green to red. Stacia's finger hovered over a button.

Her grandma once told the story of how, as a child, she used to automatically move to the side whenever anyone of the mzungu persuasion approached. It wasn't until the developing idea of First World that she decided that unless they acknowledged her and excused themselves, she would stand her ground and not be moved. She dared to dream, even then, that she was just as entitled to the spaces they occupied. It was about them acknowledging her as a matter of mutual respect.

"Air lock safety protocols overridden." The automatic broadcast alerted.

"What are you doing?" Zenith asked.

"Reminding you of what powerlessness looks like." The massive doors at the rear of the cargo bay disengaged. "And that your people are not immune."

Hondo paled and ran toward the window partition separating them. He pressed his palm to it in silent pleading. The lights within the room changed from natural to a warning red. The doors began to open with the docking procedures initiated. White lights still ringed the bay door, indicating that the outer integrity field was still in place. Stacia pushed the button.

The outer field collapsed. Air rushed out of the room. Hondo's face blanched. An invisible force dragged him across the floor. He strained against it, struggling to find any purchase along the wall. His hand found a latch. He threw his arm around it. The vacuum of space sucked at him. Loose items in the room tumbled into its dark maw. The evacuating air lifted his feet from the ground. The void called to him.

Her face placid to the point of indifferent, Stacia turned to Zenith. "Let's talk about choices."

21

FELA BUHARI
Eshu

Fela lost track of how long she'd been unconscious this time. Or how many times. Her head throbbed with congestion, her throat scratchy. She coughed a few times, waiting in hopes that her sinuses would clear. It struck her that she might be allergic to the dust or some pollen native to the planet. The ludicrousness of worrying about that now made her laugh, and the sharp pain from it cleared her head immediately.

Her throat cracked with dryness, paining her to swallow, ill-fitting gears grinding together. She bided her time for the right opportunity to make her move. She memorized the guards' movements. Car'Annie raised the temperature of the room to "warm her as she slept," and Fela studied the thrum of the activated atmosphere controls. The building employed low-level technology due to the extreme conditions of the Mzisoh world. In times of war, sometimes it was better to go with simple and durable rather than risk something elementary, like sand, clogging up advanced but sensitive equipment. Her room was a simple box, the technology rudimentary, restricted mostly to shackling her. The power conduit ran nearby, though.

Fela no longer felt her arms, the muscles in them stretched to uselessness. But she needed them to do one last thing for her. She willed them to raise her. Her arms shook with the effort. She remembered all those times during training with Maulana yelling at her. *Fight for your sisters!* This time, she needed to fight for herself. Lifting herself up along her restraints, she just needed to get her mouth to its level. Her chin reached the bar, and she bit into her restraints. Her dental implants activated, the program infiltrating the nanotech protocols, causing them to disperse. She relaxed without thinking. Her body's weight yanked her arms, tearing the muscles in them further. The lights along the suspended bar blinked, a series of interruptions to its power cells, then flickered out entirely.

Fela collapsed onto the ground.

Her arms dangled at her side, all but useless. The ache in them so complete, the thought of moving them stabbed her in the soul. But she couldn't tarry long. Still wobbly, her legs threatening to buckle with each step, she limped to the door. Testing it, the handle unlatched. She'd been Car'Annie's plaything for so long, the guards had become lax. Or dismissed, with no accounting for how long they'd be gone. If they even remembered she was there.

Fela skulked down the hall. While there was no shame in her nakedness, she wanted some kind of protection, no matter how meager. She tore down one of the tapestries and wrapped it about her. Securing the curtain's sash as a belt, she tailored a sarong. The slits at the sides allowed for easy movement, and she balled the remaining cord to use as a weapon. Pausing at the first juncture, she pressed herself flat against the wall and held her breath, waiting for a group of guards to march by. Her limbs still shaky and unsteady, she didn't trust them enough to risk a fight if she could help it. In the distance, the tortured screams of some Mzisoh reverberated the wall. She ventured in the opposite direction of the shrieks.

Something wasn't right.

The halls were sparsely guarded. Unless it was the Lei'den's equivalent of third shift, the troops had been diverted. She needed to take advantage of it and gather as much intelligence as she could on her way out.

Fela stopped at a door that lacked the mass and thickness of a cell. The telltale click-clack of boot steps against the hard floors signaled a patrol headed her way. She ducked into the room. A briefing room of some sort with holovids of topographical telemetry and transcripts of chatter scrolling by midair. The transmission sources traced back to O.E. listening posts. She peeled back a layer of data to see if the Interstellar Alliance piggybacked along the O.E. signal. But there was no such carrier wave. This was a direct O.E. feed. Either they were working with the O.E. . . .

Or they were the O.E.

Fela slumped against the wall as the implications set in. This entire camp staged for their benefit. No, not the HOVA's or Muungano's: the Mzisoh's. The CO/IN couldn't have known the HOVA were coming. Or could they? The possibility raised so many questions. The O.E. having breached the Orun Gate on their own. But they had to have gained the technology somehow. They certainly hadn't leapfrogged Muungano on their own. And loaning the technology to Muungano as a joint venture maneuvered them to this place. They were being played.

The Lei'den were probably a real species within the Interstellar Alliance, the truth part of the lie. Probably the first civilization the O.E. began negotiating with. The ones who gave them the technology to navigate the wormhole. A few skin treatments here, a few prosthetics there, and suddenly the CO/IN, O.E. operatives, looked like "aliens."

She began to scan a newsfeed when a particular headline caught her eye. Xola was dead.

This was the next phase of O.E.'s machinations. A misinformation campaign aimed to drive home a narrative to the ill-informed meant to terrorize. It wouldn't work. She only needed to escape this prison.

"I see you've managed to stretch your legs." The pale guard strolled about the room.

"What is all of this?" Fela asked.

"Just a little project I'm supervising. I wanted to observe it firsthand."

"Who are you?"

"A mission, no, a *negotiation,* of this import, at this stage of the game could only be done at the highest levels. In person. Obviously, there's a great need for secrecy and subterfuge. I won't be needing this any longer. The walkabout my people know me to be on is about to come to an end. But allow me to introduce myself." The guard began to peel back his prosthetics. The pale skin gave way to a darker hue. "My name is VOP Clay Harrison."

"But you're the head of LISC."

He also stood between her and freedom. The stakes of her mission had risen so high, she wasn't cleared to even think about them. Her next move, no matter what she decided to do, would surely plunge O.E. and Muungano into war. Though since that now seemed inevitable, she might as well beat the shit out of this tool.

Fela calculated the distance between her and him. If things went south, he'd make a good bargaining chip. As if sensing her thoughts, VOP Harrison took a step backward, keeping a workstation between them.

"Actually, I've seen all I need to see. A transport is waiting for me, as I am expected back on Earth soon. Anyway, we've allowed you enough exercise for the day. Luckily, I've arranged an escort."

An entire squad of O.E. soldiers poured in from the next chamber to surround her. Several of the guards were in various stages of dress, prosthetics applied or in Interstellar Alliance uniforms as if their dress rehearsal had been interrupted.

"But . . . why?" Fela backed toward her corner to limit their paths of attack.

VOP Harrison patted his hat into place. He smiled, the languid curl of his scar nearly framing his mouth. "Any questions you have, I'm sure Car'Annie would be happy to answer for you."

With that, VOP Harrison turned on his heel and departed. The O.E. soldiers moved in to cover his exit. Their weapons drawn, her options were limited.

The soldiers fashioned shackles for her. Through the shadowed corridors, the soldiers escorted her. She searched their emi for something sinister. But they were expressionless. Blank slates. She felt something creep within her that she'd never felt among her people: fear. Her thoughts drifted to Maulana's parting words to her before she left to join the Hellfighters.

"We're free. Wherever we go, whatever we do, remember that we're free. That's what we fought to create. That's what we fight to maintain. That's what they want us to forget. People have to want to be free for the idea to spread, understand its cost. That's what O.E. never understood until the end of the Lunar Ukombozi War. Our father was there, you know, at the great standoff between our forces. His assembled gbeto spoke with one voice: that they were willing to die, down to the last one of them because they were free and they weren't going back."

"Never again," Fela said.

"This belonged to him." Maulana placed her Oya elekes around her neck.

"Maulana?" She held them out. It was the proudest moment of her life.

"He'd want you to have them."

"When they said they were free, what does that mean to you?"

"What we're doing right here. We're sitting, we're talking. We come when we want. We leave when we want. We can be who we want, share our opinions and worldviews without worry or constraint, though never without consequence. There will always be consequences for speaking freely. Freedom is a lot of responsibility, but it starts by freeing your mind."

The soldier returned her to Car'Annie.

"Did you enjoy your little jaunt?" she said in a perfect, unaffected O.E. accent.

"This plan of yours makes no sense," Fela said. "What do you hope to accomplish?"

"You don't see the big picture. Wars have been fought over lesser lies. Think of this exercise as a practice invasion. We want our people primed and ready for when the day actually comes that the real Interstellar Alliance arrive. It's all about moving our agendas forward."

"And taking back Muungano is part of that."

"Earth has to present a united front. The aliens are no different from us. They understand strength. They understand power. Together, we will be strong. Even if we have to break all of you to get there." Car'Annie stepped closer, gripping Fela's jaw in her grasp. "I'll give you one last chance to cooperate willingly."

Fela spat in her face.

"I'm sorry it's come to this." A note of genuine-sounding regret filled Car'Annie's voice. Her face awash with compassion, it hardened just as quickly, twisting into something ugly. The ease at which she feigned kindness made it all the worse. "One last performance, then. You will be given one final opportunity to speak to your people. Choose your words with care if you want your people to receive your message."

"And if I don't?"

"Your story ends the same either way." Car'Annie pointed to the ground, expecting Fela to drop to her knees. She refused. A guard stepped forward to force her down. Fela braced her stance, ready for them.

"I will say what I have to say standing or not at all."

Car'Annie waved them off and returned to her idea of an Interstellar Alliance accent. "This is a message to all who claim citizenship to Muungano. How strange it is to find so many of your agents wandering about the universe as if it all belongs to you. That you think this handful of 'HOVA' troops was enough to take one of our planets. That you, little more than an island adrift, on a vast, empty sea, would be enough to challenge us. Our people are shielded by our justice and security. What do you have to say for yourself, puppet of Muungano?"

Fela stepped forward, tall and proud, staring at Car'Annie. Only her blinking back tears betrayed any emotion.

"My name is Fela Buhari. I am now and forever will be a member of Muungano. I command a HOVA Brigade, the Hellfighters, the unit responsible for exploring the other side of the Orun Gate. You say I am a spy sent by Muungano. You can write whatever story you want of me once I'm gone. While I am here, know that no matter what you do to me, I was born free and I will always be free."

Car'Annie turned her transmission back to herself. "To their final moments, your spies demonstrate your arrogance. Your incursions bring pain to your people and death to your soldiers. Now they must pay for the policies of your nation's war machine. Your arrogance brought this upon you. You think you can just go anywhere, take anything. Well, we draw the line in the sand. If you break our borders and invade our lands, then this is the price you pay."

That was the thing VOP Harrison, Car'Annie, LISC, the Earth Firsters, all of those who clung to the "classic" paradigms, missed. Power wasn't about the ability to bend another's will to their agenda. Power wasn't about hurting others. Power was about being a shield, to protect others from harm. It didn't have to be destructive or oppressive. It didn't need to erase another's humanity. It could create opportunities. It could connect and include. And when someone was in trouble, placing herself between them and harm was her definition of a good death.

The last thing Fela heard was the sounds of blaster fire.

22

AMACHI ADISA
The Citadel

The corridors of the Citadel seemingly have an agency of their own, shifting about according to their own whims. Now you and Ishant are lost within its halls. Steeped in shadows, the great passageway stretches on without end. The soft crunch of your footfalls against the flooring marks your passage as the Niyabinghi escort you. You try to catch Ishant's face, but his gaze remains locked forward. Every part of him stays alert and ready. You pass through another support arch, another vertebra in the long spinal column of the shaft. At each juncture, another pair of guards come to stiff attention. Except they wear the royal colors of the house of Nguni. By your ancestors, you swear, even you are already starting to think of the family as royals.

The Niyabinghi halt in front of a hatch, relieving the Nguni guards who stand there. You and Ishant exchange glares. He tenses.

"Don't," one of the Niyabinghi says to Ishant. "You are outnumbered and outclassed. If we were just the Nguni guards, your gambit might be worth taking. You"—his voice raises, dangling a question while he circles Ishant in careful assessment—"have had extensive training in the Forms, though you try to hide it."

Ishant unclenches as if he'd been exposed and found wanting.

"You, on the other hand"—he levels his eyes at you with cool aplomb—"have raw talent and a lot of potential. But you're undisciplined and untrained. Probably teaching yourself, but for now you are little more than a skilled brawler."

You turn and flex anyway, ready to demonstrate the true craft of a brawler.

He holds his hands up in mock surrender, a wan smile crossing his lips. "I mean no disrespect. I only wish to illuminate your situation. If we wanted you attacked, we'd have descended upon you from the shadows before you knew we were there. You have simply been summoned for a meeting."

He emphasizes the word *meeting* to allay our concerns about this being an ambush. Or a jail cell. The Niyabinghi guard bows slightly and, with a mild flourish, directs you to the door. He remains at the door. You lower your head to enter. The room is little more than a chamber surrounding a sealed mine. Whatever vein of ore the Nguni plumbed for has been exhausted and its shaft capped off. The rocky surface—cool to the touch, nearly cold—leaves you curious if it is all that separates you from the icy vacuum of space.

Ishant inspects the room, running his hand across every uneven surface. You almost suspect that he marvels at the handiwork, the artisan expertise to shape and bevel the ore to produce the elegant sheen of the walls, drawing the beauty out of the stony outcropping. More likely, however, he's searching for any seam, any hint of a hidden exit.

"It seems we've been found out." You stare at the door, waiting for the inevitable. The rush of guards. A grand inquisitor. Lasers. This feels like the type of situation requiring lasers for a death trap.

"I don't think so." Ishant tends to end his sentences with a half chuckle, constantly amused by a joke only he got. "This doesn't have the feel of incarceration."

"Been incarcerated much?" you ask.

"Yes." He meets your eyes with an unflinching matter-of-factness that unsettles you. "This feels more like insurance."

"You enjoy speaking in riddles, don't you?" Your instinct is to fashion a chair, but nothing moves at your command. Instead, you lower yourself to the ground and draw your knees up.

"Not intentionally. Jaha says I hate the bother of words when I so clearly picture something." Ishant continues his study. Now he doesn't fake the pretense of appreciating the artistic nature of the wall. He's examining it for traps. For surveillance. For weakness.

"What are you picturing now?"

"A chamber that blocks most signals. In or out. Ensuring privacy, if you believe what our escort said about this simply being a meeting. If that's the case . . ." He keeps running his fingers along the flooring, until his face cracks with a satisfied smile, and he withdraws a small metallic shard. "There'd have to be a site-to-site transmitter."

The device sparks to life, and he drops it. Light sweeps the room; its directed beams trace the space. The scent of ozone soon follows. With a chime, another set of lights cascades the room. Tracing an image that seals the room until it appears as if you stand within an empty office. You begin to question several of your recent life choices, not the least of which is allowing yourself to be pressured into coming to Oyigiyigi in the first place. You'd rather be . . . and it strikes you that you don't know what you actually want to be doing instead. You don't pursue anything in particular in your life. No hobbies. No particular interests. You drift from project to project, buffeted by the desires of those around you and the path of least resistance. You started and stopped numerous things along the way—poetry, acting, singing—but latched on to nothing. Still, captured and locked in a room isn't on your list either.

"No chairs?" you ask.

"They must plan on a short meeting," Ishant paces the room. "It's like being summoned before the griot magistrates. Making people stand at times of occasion demonstrates power. I suspect that's also why our host keeps us waiting."

"Must you always be so cynical, Ishant?" a familiar voice says from behind them. When you turn, the image of Maulana greets you. He appears larger than usual, but it might be the projection or your angle. His face graver with the severe set of his jawline. Impeccably dressed, yet with eyes that haven't slept in days. His forehead knots into something inscrutable. His presence sends a shiver of relief through you.

"I see you, Maulana."

"I see you, Amachi. Ishant." Maulana eyes each of you in turn, though his gaze doesn't linger on Ishant for too long.

Ishant nods in response. You notice that he never relaxes his guard, even in the presence of a recognizable figure.

"Did you have the Niyabinghi kidnap us?" you ask. "This is more dramatic than I'm used to you being."

"Kidnap? No. Escort you to a secure room so that we could talk? Yes."

"Talk? About what?" You circle Maulana. His gaze tracks you from the periphery of his vision.

"The future." Maulana spreads his hands out. "What do you know of the Niyabinghi?"

"They are the personal guards of the Ijo." Your mind wants to say *the official royal guard* because the old ways die slower than anyone thought.

"True, but their order goes back much further than that. It is whispered that they were named for Niyabinghi, an orisha who became a legendary queen. Niyabinghi was the bride of Karagwe, and it was rumored that she was murdered by her husband. Her death ushered in untold horrors to his kingdom. Her essence began to possess people to be used as vessels for her vengeance. The spirits coming back to ride as passengers in the living sparked a spiritual movement.

"Once, she rode a woman named Muhumusa, an early priestess imbuing her with the power of her sabhu. Muhumusa started a rebellion against her colonialist oppressors before she was eventually captured. They held her in custody until her death. The colonizers went on to ban witchcraft, divination, and gatherings, thinking that would be the end of her threat. But ideas don't die easily.

"The bloodline of the true Niyabinghi warriors settled in the heart of Dzimba dze Mabwe. The Bgeishekatwa clan was defeated by the Shango, who adopted the rituals for Niyabinghi. They were defeated by the Kiga. Once they ruled the land, the Niyabinghi became a matriarchal power. Women who receive the Niyabinghi blessing were said to be possessed by her to become bagirwa, the high priestess governing rulers of the Niyabinghi.

"The warriors move about in secret, though our influence is always felt. The Niyabinghi Order became the oldest of the Mansions of the Rastafari; their chants became the foundation of their grounations. Rooted in their mystic ways, they developed the martial arts practice we call the Forms."

"They got high and practiced kung fu. Got it." You turn to seek some sort of look of solidarity from Ishant, but his face grows solemn and ashen. Your attention focuses back on Maulana. "Why do you give me an unasked-for history lesson?"

"I need you to understand the full scope and depth of the Niyabinghi. It's not just the royal guard of Muungano, the Ijo, or the Camara. It is its own intelligence-gathering organization."

"Who wear bright colors, announcing themselves whenever they enter a room." You scoff, but no one in the room so much as twitches a corner of their mouth.

"Misdirection. For every two members of the Niyabinghi Order you see, there are three you do not."

Maulana gestures. The wall next to you shimmers. Three agents step out as if being fashioned from it. Their camouflage nanomesh refract all light, rendering them nearly invisible. Maulana barely twitches a salute. Acknowledged, they step back, disappearing in plain sight.

"Why have you brought us here?" You edge toward the center of the room, crossing your arms since you can't sit down.

"Because you and your partner are . . . indelicate. Your method of investigation is tantamount to stomping around in mud pits before running screaming through a house."

"I don't think so." The wanting assessment of his abilities finally causes Ishant to speak.

"If we hadn't covered your trail, even the young ones apprenticing in AI programming would have tracked you."

"My encryption protocols . . ."

". . . are child's play against intelligence operations. Or military ones. And you are caught between two such operations."

"The Niyabinghi and the . . ." Your voice trails off, already knowing Geoboe plays at agendas within convoluted schemes. Planning something on a large scale. The matter settles in your mind. "The Nguni. Do they seek to sever their ties with Muungano? Become our version of the Bronzeville Rebellion that happened on Mars."

"Not quite. The Niyabinghi is working with the Nguni. We are establishing a new periphery defense system to be known as the Ring."

"The Ring? Why haven't we heard of this?"

"You simply hadn't been read in on the Ring. But Jaha sending you here, the way you two keep bumbling about, has forced my hand." Maulana displays the schematics for the array. His image flickers for a second. "The Ring will provide telemetric observations of the Orun Gate as well as monitor galactic traffic."

"You're gearing up for war," you say.

"We're being vigilant. We know full well O.E. has designs on the wormhole. Some stories have the weight of inevitability to them: Black Wall Street. Rosewood. The Atlanta, Chicago, D.C., Knoxville, and East St. Louis race riots. The MOVE bombing. The First World incursion. 'If they don't want you and me to get violent, then stop the racists from being violent.'"

"'Tactics based solely on morality can only succeed when you are dealing with people who are moral or a system that is moral,'" you say. "I can quote the prophet, too."

"Then you understand. The security council has been fortifying the Oyigiyigi mining operation for months now. Pulse turrets. HOVA staging areas. Warships constructed . . ."

"Warships?"

"We cannot face the enemy with slingshots and harsh language."

"This is not the Muungano I know." Turning to Ishant in disbelief, you throw your hands in the air.

"Don't be naive. You, like everyone else, turn a blind eye to our military operations. You're aware of the HOVA, but don't think too hard about them. We keep the HOVA separated from Muungano, always a community within the community. We don't want to remind the rest of Muungano that we are always girded for war and ready to defend ourselves. You simply rest in comfort knowing that the Muungano you know is safeguarded. With the Orun Gate, we have an asset that O.E. will not rest until they have it under their control."

"What's your interest in this?" Ishant asks.

Maulana slides his attention to Ishant with a slow and measured glare, heavy with menace, to remind him that he is barely wanted in this space. His question, however, had to be acknowledged. "I'm the civilian head of the HOVA. The Ras, though most simply call my title 'the R.' The bagirwa of the Niyabinghi has asked me to oversee this operation."

"Just so I understand," Ishant continues, "you head the Buhari clan, are a member not just of the Ijo but its security council, and you are the command for the HOVA. That's a lot of power concentrated under one person."

"You are correct. All matters of security fall under my purview. The times send us along a dangerous path. Know this: I only care about the safety and security of Muungano."

Maulana has risen quickly among the ranks of the Ijo, but that wasn't out of selfish pursuit of power or ambition. His wisdom is trusted. The Buhari name carries weight for their obsession with duty and sacrifice. You had learned much from him and admired him. You pray those fond memories don't cloud your judgment.

"Maulana." You step closer and risk sincere openness. "I have never for a moment doubted that."

A slight curl flashes across Maulana's lips. Only for a moment, but for him, it's a nova burst. "In that spirit, I would like to make you an offer, Amachi."

"What sort of offer?" You hold a breath without realizing. Only your gut tensing, like a part of you bracing for an inevitable punch, signals the fear that has dogged every parsed syllable of this conversation. Even without looking, you know Ishant positions himself to defend you against Niyabinghi swarming you from behind. Your question hangs in the air for an extra heartbeat.

"To join the Niyabinghi." Maulana enjoys the flush from your face once the words sink in. You reach your hand out to steady yourself. Your legs threaten to buckle, and you wish you could sit down, but he begins to pace about the center of the room. "Think of it this way: If you have any lingering doubts about me or my motives, you'd be close enough to directly monitor me. More importantly, you'd have the resources of the Niyabinghi behind you as you continue your investigation."

"Why me?" You wonder if you have taken a blow to the head or suffer from any aftereffects of whatever sickened Selamault and took Xola.

"Because I, too, want to get to the bottom of Xola's death. And make the responsible parties pay . . ." For a moment, Maulana's stern façade cracks to reveal the mix of pain and anger swirling underneath. It's like staring into the heart of a storm.

"May I think on it?"

"Yes, but do not take too long. It's a rare honor to be so selected." Maulana cuts his transmission. The room returns to its appearance of a hollowed-out cave pocket.

You blink as your eyes adjust. The Niyabinghi guards have vanished, as far as you can tell. You run your hands along the wall just in case. Ishant mirrors your action on the other side of the room. He shakes his head. You remain in the cave believing you can talk freely.

"What the hell was that?" Ishant asks.

"I have no idea." You shrug. "But it's nice to get job offers when you aren't even looking. It gives a person options."

"You aren't seriously considering that, are you?"

You twist the bands of your chakrams. "Actually, it's always been a dream of mine to join the Niyabinghi."

"Yet you hesitate."

"Because I know there are pieces of the puzzle missing that are keeping me from seeing the whole picture. Too many things are in motion."

Ishant slides down along the wall until he's seated. "Tell me the pieces you see."

You know his game. Another of Xola's methods. Recount what you know, aloud, to hear them, and see if you can trace any connections. Because everything is connected. There are no accidents. It's only a matter of paying attention to the moment and listening to what the Universe is trying to tell you.

"The embassy bombing on O.E., almost taking out Jaha. Xola's probable assassination. The Orun Gate. This budding Nguni-Dimka alliance. The Ring. It's all too . . ."

". . . big." Ishant's agreement only sends a stream of pinpricks down your back.

"Yeah. I can't get my mind around it. I know there's a thread that ties it all together, but I just can't find it."

"You need to clear your head," Ishant says.

"I'm going to take a Saqqara back to the Dreaming City; something doesn't feel right. Hopefully, the trip will give me time to gain some clarity. And give me a chance to talk to Selamault, get her counsel, before I have a face-to-face with Maulana."

"I will stay here. Continue the investigation, my way."

"You heard what Maulana said about your encryption protocols."

"I heard him. I also think he's full of shit." Ishant stands up and rummages through his bag, making sure he has everything. "At least on that note. I suspect that he wanted to scare me off for some reason. Which only makes me want to go back and double-check my work to see what I missed."

"Be careful." You read something in his face. "What is it?"

"I just have a feeling. Like I'm a mouse in a maze, with scientists constantly moving the walls to study how I'll react. Constantly detailing me or moving me to dead ends, wasting my time. Someone has moved at every turn to slow this investigation down. Taking out leaders only set the stage for war."

"Who benefits from Muungano girding up for war?" you ask.

"I don't know. But that's the question, isn't it?"

"I can stay and back you up." You rest a hand on his shoulder. He tenses at the contact, but doesn't retreat.

"No, it's okay. I got this. Here." Ishant slips a glyph into your palm. "I'll do a site-to-site with you when I learn something."

✳

Space is a vast graveyard of all the ships wrecked and stripped along the way to building the outposts. Testament to the desire to dream and build. The opportunity to carve a new path for ourselves. The cost of freedom. The solar sails of your Saqqara glide your ship through space, skimming the void, riding the waves of starlight at speeds approaching sublight. Leaving you at peace to acknowledge the throbbing in your temples you call your racing thoughts.

You marvel at the vastness of space, yet are able to traverse from the outer rim of the Oyigiyigi to the lunar settlement of the Dreaming City in days. You dutifully close your eyes to ignore the displays and translucent screens of information. You snuggle into your seat to allow your thoughts to drift.

You can't help but replay your conversation with Maulana, noting his tone and the way his eyes kept washing over you as if unconsciously assessing your faults and weaknesses. And the Nguni. As you parse the implications of Geoboe's proposal and innuendo. You come up with all manner of witty comebacks or things you wished you'd said rather than be so caught off guard in the moment and falling silent.

Too much time on your hands gives your mind too many opportunities to reminisce. To wonder what could have been or have the conversations you always wished you could have. Your path veered away from the Orun Gate and, more important, Titan. To resist the temptation to detour from her mission and connect with Stacia. To discuss the unsaids and unspokens between you. To find a place of closure that will allow you to move on.

Beeping jars you out of new mistakes you're thinking about making. The displays begin to fritz, the way an outside signal might interfere, overriding all communication channels and transmissions. The image of Commander Fela Buhari fills your monitors, her face in close-up. The defiant purse of her lips in close-up while an offscreen voice recites charges. You sit at rigid attention. Your mind doesn't register what it's processing. Attenuating the signal for a clearer image, for volume, more out of reflex, the need to do something. You yell at the image. You remember calling Fela's name, though language sounds strange in your ears over the inchoate noise of your rising fear and rage. Her captors shown briefly. Your thoughts paralyze, at turns angry, grieving, and terrified, racing at how Maulana might respond after the pronouncement of her guilt. The end of their propaganda speech still echoes as blasters erupt and Fela's body collapses.

You can't move. Your mouth agape as the image fades. Your belly empties and tightens, your soul in a deep clench. And your heart breaks for Maulana. You run your hand over the controls, not sure you're ready to replay the broadcast. But you know all of Muungano has begun parsing the footage to begin studying it for information. Because you need to provide answers to Maulana, facts for him to move on. All hands on deck because the drumbeats of war rise in a chorus.

But none of your instruments respond.

Your flight pattern veers horribly off course, your Saqqara caught up in the gravity of Mars. Its red surface rises on your horizon, looming through your window. You try to adjust the pressure from the sails to your thrusters. Nothing responds to your commands. The Saqqara plunges through the planet's atmosphere. Turbulence buffets the ship. The power flickers, intermittent lifelessness. The controls overload, the navigation system freezes. You attempt to reboot the entire system.

The Saqqara careens madly through the sky. You lose any sense of equilibrium or direction. The ship barely clears a ridge of mountains. A tract of desert plains stretches out before you.

You brace as best you can as the ground rushes toward you.

23

MAULANA BUHARI
The Dreaming City

"My name is Fela Buhari. I am now and forever will be a member of Muungano."

The broadcast cut across all signal and linkage channels, almost as if it circumvented, or utilized, Maya to hijack my systems. Wanting me to see Fela's last words. Her execution. The universe will remember her name.

Only the dull flicker of the broadcast illuminates my room. Silent except for the disembodied crackle of Fela's last words. Shadows creep about its edges. The darkness bears witness to the cold umber, that nameless kind of rage that numbs me and threatens to explode from every cell in my being. Unmoving in the dark, I watch my sister's last moments. I play the transmission over and over. A frozen dagger plunging into my heart each time I watch the broadcast. I force myself to study each second, never turning my eyes from it, searing her face into my mind. The images will find me in my sleep or every time I close my eyes anyway. Her gentle face. The light in her eyes fading under the barrage of blaster fire. My brave, brave girl.

"No matter what you do to me, I was born free and I will always be free."

I'd put off getting dressed, stalking my rondavel naked, from one end to the other in a mindless pace. Detached, my mind a fugue of anger and despair. A hungry, devouring thing that draws me in its inescapable gravity. I only barely want to venture out and do so only because the Ijo need to be briefed. Eventually. And there's no guarantee I'd find the will later.

My door chimes. My joints creak in protest. My muscles unlock, slow and painful with each movement as I stir from my position. I've lost track of how long I sat in that position. I don't remember the last time I ate. Or when I last bathed.

Her two spheres orbit above her head. Selamault stands in my entranceway like the most regal of aunties ready to pick a much younger me up for church. A deep, abiding sadness wells in her eyes. A knowing sympathy radiates from her, like an inexorable tide, threatening to carry me along with it. I can barely meet her eyes.

"I see you, Selamault Adisa."

"I see you, Maulana Buhari. May I come in? I don't want my presence to add to your burden."

"No." My heart answers before my mind does. I want to be left alone with the darkness, my fury, and my hatred. I want to nurse the festering wounds curled up in the dark corner of my soul. I want to plot and lash out. I want their worlds to know my pain. Yet . . . I also want someone to hold me and tell me that everything will get better. "I mean, come in. I . . . wouldn't mind the company of another."

"If it's no bother, I'd like to sit with you." Her voice, soft and calm, soothes a balm on my raw, burning pain, as if my every nerve lies exposed and set aflame.

"I think I'd like that." *Like* doesn't sound as if it was the right word, a foreign concept voiced aloud. I'm not sure I'm supposed to *like* anything anymore. I'm not supposed to see or hear or taste or feel any part of life anymore. Fela is gone.

We sit in silence. Time loses any meaning again. We're just two people adrift in the silence of mourning. Communicating and sympathizing loss without the need for words. Sitting because our legs might not be able, be ready, to bear us up. Focusing on our loss without distraction, brought low by the sudden unexpected absence in our lives; yet hoping to find comfort, strength, and faith in our journey together.

"I always meant to come see you after Xola's passing." I break the easy quiet between us. Not wishing to ruin the peaceful space we've carved out, but now finding myself again needing the comfort of her voice.

"I know. And no offense, I did not miss your company." Her smile rueful, a bittersweet thing without malice. I arch an eyebrow for her to continue. "In the many rituals of grief, I had no shortage of company for the first few days after his passing and send-off. Conversations obliged to begin with 'Sorry for your loss.' Community wrestling with their own sense of loss while I struggle to figure out how to respond to this conversational reminder of my pain. Underneath the exchange, you know they fight the temptation to treat you like you have a disease they might catch."

"The thing is, I've caught it." I hunch over.

Selamault softly pets my back. "I know. Grief isolates because the sadness is the only part about it that anyone knows. It's complicated. And strange. I think about the happy times with Xola. His ridiculous jokes. And I laugh. Then wonder if I'm allowed to laugh. And part of me fears with every exchange that I'll never be able to talk about the funny memories again without making everyone around me uncomfortable. So I have to navigate spaces filled with pitying head tilts, averted eyes, and everyone treating me as if I am fragile. While acknowledging that I, in fact, am."

"I'm not fragile. I'm angry." Shifting in my seat, the words—bitter and sharp—cause me greater discomfort than I thought. A window to my pain I'm not prepared to have.

"You're both. We all are. This is the journey we're on. That we've always been on. Navigating the history of pain, anger, unfairness. Our family torn from us in ways we didn't expect. Grief isn't just one thing. A process compounded by the fact that the Universe won't allow you room to grieve in peace, because your loss was shrouded in horror, played out for all to see."

The silence settles between us again. There is a wisdom in it because in the face of such tragedy, suffering, and loss, there's nothing to say. No words to bring true comfort or solace. Only presence for the journey of grief.

Taiwo and Kehinde whir above her, their orbit buzz near her ear, drawing her attention. She inclines her head toward me, and I know it's her turn to break the silence.

"Communities can be transformed by loss. My loss comes with wrestling with Xola's legacy, the footprint he continues to leave in our lives. Your grief, our loss, comes with decisions to be made."

Then it dawns on me the reason for Selamault's appearance on my doorstep. "I see. That's why you're really here. To check the temperature of my thoughts. To make sure I react as Ras Maulana, the R, not Maulana Buhari, bereaved brother."

"I came because someone in my community hurts with a particular kind of pain I can speak to with an expertise few others can." Selamault grows quiet, taking stock of her words and heart, which is her way. "And, if I'm completely honest, to seek your counsel as well as offer guidance."

"My counsel on what?"

"Do those events not strike you as having the deliberation of calculation?"

"Oh, it has definitely occurred to me. As the R, we referred to it as a *suspected decapitation strike*. First the attempt on Jaha. Then Xola 'dies' under questionable circumstances. Now my sister, head of an elite military division on a covert operation. It's the most frighteningly logical scenario."

"Then I only ask you to pause long enough to ask who would provoke us so? Why antagonize the people of Muungano, if not to galvanize us to rash action?"

"There is a lot to consider and too much to do." I lower my head under the weight of the long nights ahead of me.

"You don't have to be the one to do it."

"If not me, then who?"

"You are not irreplaceable. None of us are. We are part of a community. If you, as a leader, have not mentored those who can step into your place, you have failed in your duty. Have you failed?"

"No." There are several I have groomed to replace me. Or could step into the role of Camara. Though I do not trust Bayard and Wachiru clings to na-ive ideas of community, Jaha would be fine. At least until Amachi has a few more years of experience under her. But my dream, my hope, had been Fela.

And my soul aches with a fresh stab of pain.

"All I ask is that you take the time to deal with your grief. Don't take on additional burdens during this time. Your place will be here when you are ready. We value your counsel, but we value a whole you more." The twins swerve in a wide berth, signaling that Selamault is about to stand. Rising, she steps toward the door but stops short. She rests an easy hand on my shoulder, and I feel her sincere love and concern for me. "I appreciate you."

"I appreciate you." Once the exit reseals behind her, I return my attention to the frozen image of Fela. I can feel parts of me breaking off like shards of crystals trying to reflect itself. The dissolution of grief. I struggle, my thoughts devolving into the internal chaos of white noise.

Fela's eyes stare at me from the display. Fixed and intentional. I continue watching the transmission, studying her eyes. They speak to me; I need only to discern their message.

"No matter what you do to me, I was born free and I will always be free."

I rewind and begin the process again. Rewind. Rewatch. Rewind. Re-watch. Rewind. Rewatch.

"My name is Fela Buhari. I am now and forever will be a member of Muungano."

I know every twitch of her face. I have committed every tremble of her cheek, each defiant flare of her lips, and down to knowing each blink of her eyes to memory. My mind latches on to the details, my emi stirring as if it might discern a pattern in her final moments of terror. Some might call me desperate. Or on the verge of some shamanistic break. But I know it's there. A sequence coalesces from the flutter of her eyes. Leaning closer, I rewind and rewatch. Her eyes blink out a message. One intended for me. Underneath the notice of her captors, her head still clear. Using even her last opportunity to communicate intelligence back to me. The R. Her brother.

O.E.

Her last message to me. O.E.

O.E. still vociferously denies any part in the bombing of our embassy. They claim it to be the work of terrorists. Pretending we are ignorant savages incapable of discerning the obvious events around us. If a person tells you who they are, reveals it to you repeatedly in their actions, one would be a fool to ignore them. I am no fool.

"You think you can just go anywhere, take anything. Well, we draw the line in the sand. If you break our borders and invade our lands, then this is the price you pay."

We are under attack from within and without.

They will pay the full price of my pain.

※

I attended my first Ijo meeting when I was six years old. Though officially only the leadership met, all members are welcome and encouraged to attend because every Muungano member has a voice. First brought by my parents and later ferried by my curiosity, I had no idea what was going on. All of these adults, tall as trees, talking, relaying big ideas, and telling stories. The stories were my favorite part. I had no idea that the meetings weren't about the leaders getting together to decide issues crucial to the future of Muungano but were themselves training sessions, allowing any member the opportunity to study the process under the mentorship of Ijo members. The Ojo Aje, the Day of Profit, meeting of the Ijo typically set the cultural priorities of Muungano. There were the usual report-outs from different committees and the breakout times for individual kraals to have opportunities to handle housekeeping matters and other issues that arose. Most attendees deferred to the elders of the Ijo to hear reports and, to be honest, to keep the meeting moving along. Allowing everyone a voice came with the cost of the meetings sometimes dragging on for hours even with the simplest agenda. This was also where conflict transformation occurred, the true test of living in community: when parties who had issues with one another had the opportunity to voice their issues and allow community input to help resolve them. We used djemaas for our conflict transformation, how our disputes were worked out in public. Collective self-criticism. I admired every member of the Ijo; knew I wanted to be one of them as soon as I found my voice.

Today, we gather to voice our anger.

"This marks the first time Muungano has been directly attacked since its inception," I begin.

"What about the terrorist threat Astra Black thwarted?" Bayard always has to interject, probably in the belief that we wouldn't know how to think or feel without his guidance. No matter how well intended, his is a heavy hand when it comes to shepherding others. Overbearing and smothering, an insecure parent needing to demonstrate their authority. His overprotective concern can't help but lead to a slow erosion of agency.

"Back then, we were still First World," I say.

"Blacktopia!" someone cries out, their call met with cheers and a smattering of laughter. The spirit of Xola remains alive and well in the space.

"Exactly. Out of it we dreamt the experiment known as Muungano into being."

"At a cost." Bayard seems determined to challenge me at every turn. To not allow me to get into a rhythm of my words. I don't know where this sudden need to press me comes from, but we have urgent matters to attend to that we can't just pray away. My glare and silence wait him out. He eases back to allow me room to speak.

"There is always a cost when we establish our communities. The Maafa, the Great Disaster that was our holocaust, was our first and more terrible lesson. The lingering history of atrocities inflicted on our people, beginning with our enslavement. Continual, unrelenting, the Maafa ignited a system of the negation of our humanity, one that morphed as the times changed. Physical persecution, legal disenfranchisement, economic redlining, all institutionalizing suffering for economic gain. Adapting itself like an ever-evolving creature set loose upon us, determined to track us, with capitalism as the slave masters' hunting dogs." My pain resonates with them without me needing to hammer it. My words peel back the scars left by a history of attacks upon us playing in our collective unconscious. "The Maafa extended through lynching through Jim Crow through delayed civil rights through a police state through the Lunar Ukombozi War. Which brought us to the Uponyaji. At the heart of the

Uponyaji was the reality that in order to heal, people needed to tell their stories, their truths, which required people to hear them. To critically examine the past to understand our social structures and where we found ourselves. To never forget the lessons we learned and the healing we experienced. We came together—Ugenini, Maroon, and Asili—as one weusi people. We shared our stories. We poured out our pain, and we dreamt of a better future—this present we call Muungano—together."

"Where are you going with this, Maulana?" Bayard brays, but the way he studies the room to find his constant cynical interruptions unsupported deflates him.

"We remember, but that was then, and this is now. We cannot let an attack against us stand." I pound the dais. "We must respond in kind."

"O.E. has issued a blanket denial of any involvement in the matter of Fela's death." Swathed within a hoodie, Wachiru points with his index and pinkie fingers. His eyes distant, preoccupied with the latest data feed.

"Her *execution*," I correct. Her loss will not be made more palatable to digest with petty euphemisms.

"They have also warned that they will move to protect themselves," Wachiru says.

"They provoke us with impunity, then cry the victim when they fear we might retaliate. They push us toward war but don't want to be seen as the aggressor."

"What I'm saying is that we agree. We have to do something, but we shouldn't be rushed to act rashly." Heads bob in agreement, caught up in the easy rhythm of his voice. Wachiru is both every bit his father's son and cut from a different cloth entirely. Though he probably doesn't think so, I admire the young man he's grown into. I just find his naivety dangerous. "We simply don't know enough yet. We must broaden our investigations. We have to be . . ."

". . . measured? We're past the point of that kind of response. Precision is a luxury never afforded us. Even exact strikes count many of our bodies as collateral damage. We're always acceptable losses in some people's eyes. How many times must they take one of our own before we find the courage to act? We can't allow them to strike us again while we wait on our investigations. We know enough and suspect even more. Anything less than treating O.E. as a serious, ongoing threat risks Muungano. And anyone who drags their feet in action, a coward."

Wachiru's eyes snap to full wakefulness then. I have his attention, stirring the well of his anger. Good, he should get mad. They all should.

"Now hold on, Maulana. We understand your loss and pain . . ." Sensing the percolating fight, Bayard defaults to his peacekeeper mode. He steps between us as if blocking our direct line of sight with each other will still the bubbling rage.

"You understand nothing." I snap louder than I intend, but those with ears need to hear. "I hurt, yes, because *we* hurt. *We* have been attacked. *We* lost Xola. *We* lost my sister. *We* grieve loss after loss after loss. And *we* are angry."

"Maulana." His face softening, Wachiru composes himself, a note of genuine concern creeps into his tone. "Are you well? Should you even be here right now?"

"I have no place I need to be more." Because there will be no body to grieve over. Fela died alone and unburied on an alien world. I will not participate in any empty rituals that deny that. I pinch the bridge of my nose. "We have some decisions to make."

"Yes, we do. We cannot neglect our calling as professional dreamers. We dreamt of a better community. We dreamt of being better neighbors. We dreamt of correcting inequalities. We dreamt of correcting injustices." Wachiru paces about the dais. Confidence exudes from him, an artist performing at a standing-room-only venue. "We have a proverb: 'If you hate someone, please hate them alone. Don't recruit other people to hate them with you.' Too long we dined on hate, been force-fed inhumanity, and absorb all of the casual brutality that comes with the crime of having been born weusi. We should also fear what we might become in our retaliation."

"And I fear what we might become if we don't retaliate." A few members of the Ijo nod alongside me.

"As I stated," Wachiru begins, leaving a space for the words *before we lost your sister,* "we need to isolate O.E. Starting with sanctions. Freezing our diplomatic relations. We should also extend our formalized alliance with Mars, not just Bronzeville. And we need to fortify our borders."

"Your plan remains nice." I dive back in, not allowing time for his ideas to land, much less take root and bloom. "But we have to do what is necessary before we can do what is nice. There is a debt that has been incurred. Do we extend grace, mercy, and forgiveness when none has been asked for?"

"We have to release the bitterness and anger that clouds our vision." Wachiru's eyes narrow, almost in a silent plea to me.

"We can do that and pursue justice. Some of us have the stomach for it." I pause to let the barb bite deep. I want his, all of their, full attention. "We will not be handling this as if we are cultural ambassadors. We will not be handling this with grace, poise, and dignity. We will blow the shit out of each and every last one of those O.E. motherfuckers." A smattering of cheers erupts. More and more heads nod. A susurrus of whispers begins rippling like a building tide within the Dreaming City.

"We think you made your position quite clear." Bayard raises his hands to still the conversation. But he is no Xola. Lacking such gravitas, he moves to bang at the dais several times until he regains the room's attention. The conversation pauses, more out of surprise than anything else. Bayard's face contorts into something this side of disappointment. He knows he's lost them and any hope to be their voice. "Let us adjourn to consider the matter further among the security council."

The full Ijo adjourns. Wachiru and I lock eyes again, our gazes never breaking while our fellow members disperse around us. The security council starts to reseat themselves in a more intimate arrangement. Selamault places her hand on my shoulder, breaking Wachiru's and my cold war.

"We have need of your counsel in regard to your role as the R. Are you up for that?" she asks.

"Always."

"We need Ras Maulana, whole and healthy. We will not put a meeting's experiences over your well-being. One of your aides can update us."

"No, Selamault. I can continue." Out of sheer concern for me, Selamault might have benched me. Xola damn sure would have without hesitation. She sees that I need this, to do the work, in order to move forward. But I'm aware enough to know that if I lead the charge, take point on the work, they would have to unite to force me to step aside. Even now, Selamault wavers. "Though may I suggest Jaha lead the meeting."

Selamault acquiesces.

Striding toward the dais, she adjusts her headdress. Jaha's dress whirls about her, an iridescent black with reds that streak through it like comets against a starless night. Gold bands wrap her neck, accentuating her ceremonial chakrams. She presses her hand to my shoulder and squeezes it. I raise my hand to pet hers before she releases her grip.

"We agree with both you and Wachiru, in that our first order of business must be the fortification of our borders." Jaha consults her notes. "The Dimka move to immediately suspend all trade talks with O.E."

"That hadn't happened immediately after the bombing?" Bayard asks.

"We still had operations in motion that took time to wind down." Her eyes, hard pinpricks, sharpen at his implied criticism. He's done stepped in it for real. "Speaking of some of those operations. Where do we stand on the Ring?"

"The Ring stands fully operational," I report. I shove a series of holovids to each of the security council representatives' displays. Full schematics, capabilities, and projections. "The Nguni are making the final preparations before bringing it fully on line."

"That's much faster than we anticipated," Wachiru says.

"Circumstances have forced us to move faster than we anticipated." I level my eyes at Jaha. At her insistence, I read in both Amachi and her obroni cultural attaché. Jaha is not one to be denied, especially when she is right. She upticks her chin in my direction. "I do wonder in light of recent events, if we ought to reconsider our position in regard to the Orun Gate."

"How so?" Selamault asks.

"It poses an extreme security risk."

"And it's one of our chief assets," Wachiru interjects.

"That's 'Yo' thinking," I say in the slang of his generation. "It was never ours."

"We control the space around it."

"That's like saying we control a star. It merely is while we are in proximity to it. The question before us is: What level of threat does it represent?"

"That doesn't hold. It's an artificial wormhole, one that wasn't built by us. But we now have the technology to be able to utilize it. We aren't about giving up assets that can benefit the entire community," Wachiru says.

"As does O.E. As do its original creators. Who could come through at any time and we'd never know," I remind him. "This asset is proving to have too steep a cost."

"You personally authorized an exploratory HOVA unit to post up on the other side," Wachiru said.

We see how that worked out, I can almost hear him say.

"One whom we've lost contact with." I pause. My silence allows them to picture Fela's last words in their minds. One of my assistants rushes in. She whispers in my ear. "What? On screen."

"What are we looking at?" Selamault stands.

"A new problem." I gesture to enlarge the image. "Have the Nguni bring the Ring fully on line. An unauthorized ship is on a collision course with the Orun Gate."

24

STACIA CHIKEKE
The *Cypher* (Returning to Titan)

The human body was not designed to survive the vacuum of space. People were little more than bags of water with a thin layer of flesh to try to keep everything inside all in place. Under low pressure, the remaining air trapped within the lungs expanded, ripping the soft tissue. Water in other such tissues of the body vaporized, causing them to swell. Luckily, human skin was designed to remain a tight seal.

Hondo's eyes bulged with knowing panic once the hangar doors began to open. The air rushed from the bay, the whoosh of escaping air buffeting him on its escape. The call of space tore at him.

"In the vacuum of space, the gas exchange of the lungs continues, but results in the removal of all gases from the bloodstream." Stacia spoke in the disturbingly calm monotone of a bored professor giving a familiar lecture.

In desperation, Hondo wrapped his arm around a bar, holding on to his wrist with his free hand. He wouldn't explode as so many movies might depict. Gas expelled from his bowels and stomach. Nor would any depiction of simultaneous vomiting, urination, and defecation make an attractive portrait. After that, photons and other radiation would savage him.

Held in place by Kenya and the security team, Dina screamed, her words reduced to incoherent noises.

"You'll be able to hold on to the bar for about ten seconds, maybe fifteen, before deoxygenated blood reaches your brain and you lose consciousness. Then you'll tumble into space, where you can survive for up to a couple of minutes. Don't hold your breath or inhale deeply; it will only make it worse. Ironically, you have to fight against your instinct to survive in order to live longer. If only a few minutes."

"Stacia!" Hondo cried out. "You don't have to do this!"

"You conspired to kill my son," Stacia whispered.

"Stacia . . ." Hondo's grip started to falter, his flesh giving way in centimeters.

"You conspired to kill my son!" She slammed her palm against the observation window.

His protests stilled as ice began to coat his tongue. His body relaxed, growing limp. His grip slackened. His body tumbled toward the open bay doors. Almost as if he had fallen into darkness, an undifferentiated shape among the shadows swimming about.

Stacia's mouth opened and closed in voiceless frustration. Angered by her inability to utter anything, she heard another voice. The voice of Xola. *This is not our way.*

Stacia hit the emergency override button, and the integrity field reestablished around the *Cypher*'s bay. The outer doors began to close. Hondo's unconscious body tumbled to the ground. Stacia turned around, greeted by the drawn horror etched on the faces of everyone in the room. She fixed her face into a stone thing and met each and every one of them in the eye. Her stomach twisted, souring with a distant ache. She pointed in the general direction of Hondo.

"Get that piece of garbage treated and placed into confinement." Stacia spun on her heel, ignoring Dina's wails, to glare at Zenith. "There's one thing you need to understand about me: don't ever think you will make me powerless. When I enter a space, I am the power. Kenya, escort this one to my quarters and station security there. No one goes in or out without my authorization."

Kenya gestured, sending her people to escort Hondo to med lab one for treatment and a thorough examination, while she took Zenith into custody.

Stacia needed time to calm down.

The corridors of the *Cypher* felt alien and unfamiliar. No longer home. Word traveled quickly in tight communities. There were few secrets in Muungano. Every person she passed averted their eyes, afraid or ashamed. Needless cruelty was not the Muungano way. The crew did not know what to make of her, how to approach her. It was only a matter of time before someone screwed up the courage to confront her. Usually that person was Paki.

Stacia turned the corner of the hallway in time to witness Dina shove Kenya.

"Say that shit again," Dina demanded. From the frenzy in her eyes, she indeed was ready to throw hands. So she obviously wasn't thinking straight.

Kenya allowed Dina her outburst and the shove. She was nearly a hundred years old. Kenya had a distinguished career in the HOVA, receiving commendations for her role in Operation Obatala, before transferring to the *Cypher*. With all of her genestream engineering to become a gbeto, she had nearly a half meter and a couple of dozen kilograms on Dina. "You were the one sleeping with him. It's fair to ask if you were an Earth Firster."

"You just saw how the captain dealt with one of them." Terror filled Dina's voice, that much was obvious. Unless she had a background in theater, she was hurt, confused, and lost. Not knowing what to believe about Hondo or their relationship. What to think of her friends. Of Stacia herself.

"Exactly. Which means the rest of you might have to be more careful." Kenya loomed over her in silent intimidation.

Not backing down, Dina stepped so close, Kenya had to feel the heat of the rage on her breath. "Insinuate that I am a traitor to our family one. More. Time."

"I'm not insinuating anything. I've been pretty clear."

Dina locked eyes with her. She balled her fingers with a suddenness and fury that might have caught another off guard. Kenya yankadi-ed out of the trajectory of the punch, turning to catch her hand just behind her wrist, locking it. She applied just enough pressure to catch Dina's full attention.

Dina struggled, each flex causing her greater pain, while she tested for any give in the guard's grip. There wasn't any.

"Dina, stand down. If there are any more in league with Hondo, I'll ferret them out," Stacia said.

"What gave her license to fix her lips to call me a conspirator?" Dina jerked her arm free.

"I only asked the question." Kenya stood at attention.

"Here's a question for you." Stacia angled her head toward her, leaning in for a stage whisper. "Where is Paki?"

"Captain?"

"A member of your crew, an elder of our community, has gone missing. We have no idea where he is. How is that investigation coming?"

"That's what I was coming to report on when I saw this." Dina waved her uninjured hand in front of them. She produced vidsheets. When she brought the digital broadsheet into reading range, a simple message filled each screen. IN-STEAD OF AGITATING FOR WAR, WE SHOULD BE OPPOSING IT IN EVERY POSSIBLE WAY. WE WILL BE AMONG THE FIRST TO FEEL THE CONSEQUENCES OF WAR. TOLERANCE IS A VIRTUE THAT DEPENDS UPON PEACE AND STRENGTH. All Earth First propaganda.

"Where did you find them?" Stacia asked.

"In a cargo hold. I'm trying to find the vidlogs for the area, see who may have been meeting there, but Maya hasn't been operating efficiently."

"Are they still off line?" Kenya asked.

"Yes." Dina did not otherwise acknowledge her. Turning to Stacia, she added, "*Glitchy* might be the better word."

"Is that your technical diagnosis?"

"It's like she's been infected with a virus," Dina said. "Captain."

"A . . . virus?" Stacia glanced toward med bay. Too much of that was going around lately to be a coincidence. "What kind of virus infiltrates a quantum system?"

"I don't know, Captain."

"Well, find the virus and purge it from their system. Bring me back Maya."

"Yes, Captain," Dina said.

"And you." Ignoring Dina's passive-aggressive overuse of her title, Stacia returned her attention to Kenya. "Find Paki. Turn this entire ship upside down if you have to. But find our elder."

"Yes, ma'am." Kenya strode off, not quite in a huff.

"And remember: We are still a family. There will be no more accusations," Stacia said without apology. "We will root out our problems a different way."

"No more air lock solutions. Got it." Dina didn't hide the disrespectful sneer to her voice.

It was Stacia's turn to allow her some latitude. "Dina, I had no choice."

"You had plenty of choices, Stacia." Crossing her arms, Dina refused to meet her eyes. Her tone remained cold. "Last on that long list, which should have started with 'Ask Hondo some questions,' was 'Torture Hondo with an air lock.' He deserved better. We deserved better from you."

"You're . . . right. I'm sorry."

"Sorry? You didn't spill juice on my prom dress. You nearly took a man's life because you were mad and scared." Dina threw the vidsheets against the wall and walked the opposite direction. "I . . . I just can't with you right now."

Stacia knew all too well what it felt like when something fundamentally broke in a relationship.

Some days it was as if she carried deep in the core of her being a little child version of herself. One who had been rejected, hurt, misunderstood, and abandoned. A collection of assorted childhood wounds she thought healed, feeling broken beyond repair, and losing all hope of becoming whole. The remnants left over from having been raised elsewhere, coming late to the ideal of Muungano with its denizens speaking love and truth so fully into her life as she bloomed into an adult. This shadow child, her internal ogbanje, retreated so far within her, she thought it had disappeared. But in her dark times, those quiet nights of the soul full of doubt, her nagging negative voices, nursed enough to cling to life. Left her lost in a sea of pain wondering where her God, family, and friends were. Afraid to be around anyone for fear of burdening them with all of her anger and sadness and baggage; leaving her a walking contagion of sorrow and disappointment. She wanted to withdraw, to hide, by herself in a cave, where she could bleed all over the place without the possibility of anyone seeing, reaching for, or comforting her. But because of her duties, she had to go through the motions of living. Dragging herself from one crisis to the next; the pain of others a distraction if not exactly a balm for her own.

Heading to the bridge, Stacia veered off at her quarters. The rondavel was dark, the light not adjusted by Maya. Looming silence had settled on the space. No Yahya. No Bek. No Maya. Now no Dina or Paki. Only interminable quiet. Leaning over her toilet, she vomited.

It took a solid five minutes of body-racking spasms until her system emptied itself.

When Stacia came out of her bathroom, shaky and bone weary, she tugged at the hem of her vestment, straightened her cape, and decided to head to the med bay.

Her heart broke a little when she saw Bek in the isolation unit. Resisting the urge to scoop him up right then and there to retreat to her quarters where she would hug and kiss and hold him back to health. Before she could make her way to Bek, a few doctors scurried to seal off a room. She glimpsed the still form of Hondo being attended to. By the time she reached Bek, Yahya half jumped, startled to wakefulness in the seat next to him.

"I see you." Stacia wrapped an arm around him.

"I see you." His voice cracked with exhaustion. Wiping the sleep from his eyes, he rested his arm along her shoulder.

"How is he?"

"The same. His symptoms seemed to have plateaued." Yahya lowered his voice. "There are rumors that . . . Hondo is here because of you."

"The rumors are true." Stacia took his hand. "Yahya, I need you to come with me."

"I need to be here. One of us should be." Glancing about the room, Yahya drew his hands away. He must've truly been in a dark place, missing the note of concern in her voice that would have had the man she had partnered rushing to her side.

Stacia wasn't in the mood to be his emotional punching bag. Nor to punch. Him, at least. "You didn't hear me. It's important."

"As always, you didn't hear *me*. I'm staying here." Yahya rose fully engaged, ready to spar for no other reason than to prove his rightness. Or win the competition of who was the better parent. "Unless you're planning on dropping *me* out an air lock next. That seems to be your new method of dealing with people who disagree with you."

"It's about Bek. I . . . know what's wrong."

"You . . ." Yahya jumped out of his chair. "Tell me. No, tell the doctors."

"Not. Here." Stacia glanced around. Nervous doctors stared at her. Pursing her lips in an aborted attempt at a smile, she hoped it was close enough to allay them.

"Stacia . . ."

"Keep your voice down and come with me." She locked her eyes on his. He might have missed the gentle pleading in her voice before, but he dared not ignore the steel in her tone now. "You have to hear this for yourself."

His eyes tracked her, failing to recognize her, his gaze glowering at an impotent glare.

"Please." Stacia lowered her voice. The woman he had partnered would have held out her hand, inviting him along. She might have allowed the tear that threatened to well in her eye to form, perhaps even fall. All the captain she was now could do was tilt her head toward the door and begin walking.

When they reached her quarters, Kenya and her security team stiffened.

"Any problems?" she asked as they parted for her.

"He's been quiet. We've checked on him once an hour." Kenya stared straight ahead. Not meeting her eyes for fear of being asked about progress on the investigation. Luckily, the captain had more pressing concerns.

"Good." Stacia summoned an entrance.

"He who?" Yahya asked.

"Meet him for yourself."

They were barely in her quarters before they saw Zenith rifling through her cabinets as if he were at home.

Finding a suitable cup, he synthed tea as if they hadn't entered. "Two sugars and light cream."

Walking past them, he delicately sipped at the cup. A series of holovids danced across his display. "I hope you don't mind. I got bored and hacked into what's left of your system."

"I mind." Stacia sat down across from him.

"Who is this?" Yahya remained standing.

"Yahya Chikeke. Zenith Prebius."

"A pleasure." Setting down his cup and saucer, Zenith stood and extended his hand.

"Shut up and sit back down," Stacia said. "Keep your hands to yourself, where I can see them."

"Rude." Zenith kept his hands out for inspection before taking his chair again.

"Who is he?" Yahya remained wary, now approaching cautiously, bracing to pounce at any threatening gesture from the stranger. "I know every member on board, and we've had no declarations of any ship docking."

"He's the reason Bek is sick."

"What?" Waves of confusion and anger crashed over Yahya's face.

"Tell him," Stacia said.

"An unreasonable set of circumstances has forced us into a place of unreasonable actions," Zenith began by way of introduction. Catching her eye, he said, "I suppose I'd best dispense with the preliminary pleasantries before I find myself on the wrong side of the air lock bay doors."

Yahya glared at Stacia. She crossed her arms, unable to bear the weight of his scrutiny. Zenith repeated the details of the true nature of Bekele's condition. Yahya absorbed the news, his face contorting with each turn, before settling on unfettered rage.

The first punch sent Zenith tumbling over the coffee table. Yahya landed on top of him before Stacia could react. Or, more precisely, wanted to react. When the third heavy punch landed, Stacia summoned the strength to intervene to stop him.

"Yahya, you can't." She hooked her arm under his and locked her hand into his back to hold him in place.

"You can send motherfuckers out of an air lock, but you won't allow me to beat the living shit out of him until he cures our son?"

"Hondo was his motherfucker!" Stacia shouted. "This one has diplomatic immunity."

"I don't care." Yahya shook, anger and adrenaline coursing through him like a drug ready to send him into overdose.

"But I have to."

Yahya struggled against her one last time. With no give to her grasp, he relented. Releasing him, she helped him to his feet, allowing Zenith room to scramble out of range to nurse his wounds.

"You have to tell the crew," Yahya said.

"To be fair, I was rather hoping to keep this matter between us. A closed loop, as it were." Zenith dabbed his lip.

"Shut up, Zenith," she said. "The news will tear them apart."

"No, them thinking their captain acts rashly is tearing them apart."

"But . . ."

"They are angry and scared and don't know who to trust. Not even you. Without an explanation, you've broken their sense of security and have taken away their ability to choose."

"Like I did with you."

"I never said—"

"Let me have some time to think about my next moves." Stacia fashioned a chair. Neither of the men dared to move. Eventually, Yahya crept toward her, his hand landing lightly, testing a spot on a nearby couch to see how she'd react to his proximity. With a slight nod for consent, he edged into the seat, but allowed the silence to bloom between them.

Zenith continued to tend to his injuries. The cut above his eye released a thin trickle of blood, and a bruise blossomed on his left cheek. Straightening his jacket and tie, he retreated to his overturned chair. His hands shook, steadying themselves once he retrieved his cup and saucer.

Tracking Zenith's movements from the corner of his eye, Yahya was the first to break the silence. "It's got to be a trap. They want you to go through the wormhole too badly. And then there's the matter of how we are supposed to get a galactic cruiser past Oyigiyigi, Titan, and Mars without notice or question."

"And even if we could," Stacia's voice sounded like she spoke to no one in particular, "our ship isn't even fitted with jump gate navigation technology. We'd be flying blind and could end up anywhere."

"That won't be an issue. If I may?" Zenith pointed to his satchel. With diplomatic immunity, no one was allowed to inspect its contents.

Stacia nodded. "Slowly."

Yahya braced, still searching for an excuse to pummel the man again. Zenith withdrew a strangely ornamented and grooved glyph.

"What is that? Looks almost like a glyph."

"Next-gen prototype. Quantum based." He set it on the table between the three of them, not risking any possible direct interaction.

Leaning forward, Stacia examined it closer, wishing Maya were back on line to help her analyze it. "Give us time to consider it and examine this."

"Don't take too long. We heard a rumor that some among the Ijo would like nothing more than to seal the wormhole."

"I will take as long as I take." Stacia stood to depart. Yahya trailed after her. Once the door closed behind them, he went on.

"Stacia, you can't seriously trust that—"

"Get some rest. It's going to be a long couple of days. And I could use your clarity. I'll station myself at Bek's side until you return."

Yahya's stance softened; his eyes held something close to affection. He bowed and headed down the hallway.

The med bay prohibited fashioning since it might interfere with their systems. So when she arrived at the med bay, she dragged a seat over to Bek's side. Before taking a seat, she hovered over her son, brushing back his hair. A thin sheen of sweat dappled his forehead.

"It's been a long time since I've been able to sit with you like this. You're getting so big now. So grown. Too grown for your mother to fuss over." She eased back into her seat. "Your father's a good man. I know you know that, but can I tell you a secret? Part of me never thought I deserved a good man, much less would find one. I know why. I don't talk about my daddy much. You never met him. He was a good man, too. Driven, focused, yet broken in other ways. The way too many of our visionaries and architects were. We create a mythology about our founders, even the everyday geniuses around us. Romanticizing that to be the kind of person who makes such a singular impact in their field, they have to be broken. It's a lie, one to excuse how they treat others because we need them to create, do what they do.

"My father was Khamaal Besamon. He was one of the first graduates of the Thmei Academy. He came up alongside his mentor, Hakeem Buhari, and Dona Jywanza, two of the cofounders of what would become First World. Hakeem was a brilliant man, but a war waged in his mind all his life. He struggled with shamanistic ways, but that way of seeing was also part of his brilliance.

"Hakeem designed a system he called Morpheus. It was the AI system that ran all of First World. To hear it told, it was also a bit of a pain in the ass, as

Hakeem based its personality matrix on his own. Hakeem had the inspiration of Uponaji from the beginning, believing that a time of healing should be our starting place as a new, free community. But then the Astra Black incident and the Lunar Ukombozi War delayed his plans.

"Now Khamaal was a brilliant scientist, too. He was the chief architect of the Science Police, believing that the path to chart our new way forward rested in the pure ways of science. He was a little naive, believing that anything could be pure when it involved people. He recruited your auntie Jaha in his first class of officers. You should see the holovids. She was so young and beautiful. The thing about my daddy was that he loved the work. He was always about big ideas. The future. He believed in all the possibilities the Universe had to offer.

"Sometimes he failed to see the people in it.

"Khamaal wanted to design our first research ship. He drew inspiration from stories he'd read about the 'wheel of God.' The wheels within wheels from Ezekiel 1:19 . . . He loved the image of that, each spoke being a manifestation of some attribute of God. And he set out to design a great plane of wheels within wheels.

"Despite what O.E. media would have people believe, he and his team constructed the great wheel. Their propaganda took root because it was easier for O.E. to believe that 'aliens' designed it rather than us. It soon became known as the mothership. Khamaal fitted it with his then experimental protophobic force drive and commenced testing. Naive to the reality of the power shift his groundbreaking work represented and ushered in. In that moment, our very existence became a threat, never more so than when we were free and flexing the power of our imagination.

"Even you understand that when a superior technology presents itself, one that a neighboring sovereign nation cannot overcome, that nation will believe its security compromised. The nonreality of the threat doesn't matter, only the idea of it. The warmongers among them believe their first priority is to protect and secure its members. By destroying the technology.

"With its initial launch, the mothership drained most of the power from First World, and its flight path sent it careening toward Earth before it winked out of existence. Lost in time, as it turned out. But our scientists didn't know that then. They worked feverishly for hours, days, weeks, attempting to track the ship. And then one day, the mothership returned. Muungano scientists found a way to bring it back to its correct time. If there were such a thing.

People and events simply here, where they were supposed to be when they were supposed to be there. Locked its orbit on the far side of the moon, in a state of partial phased reality. Our scientists were nearly drunk with all of the telemetry data recorded by the ship. Rumors swirled that the ship jumped back in time. To 1929. February 1942. September 17, 1985. The more they learned, the more First World declared the data proprietary.

"Throughout all of this, Khamaal focused on his work. Lost in it. It's easy to find refuge in your work when things get hard. Perhaps guilt drove him, since his simple curiosity created enemies against First World. Perhaps his numerous breakthroughs required his constant attention. Perhaps he sought escape from my mother and me because relationships are hard, especially if you don't do them well.

"As you can probably imagine, all of this only fueled O.E.'s paranoia of us, stoking their fears that we plotted against them. They came to believe that it was only a matter of time before we unleashed the destructive force of our military might. Because history has told us that was what they would have done.

"Their first test of us came with the terrorist attack thwarted by Astra Black. In the course of dealing with the incursion and their subsequent sabotage, we had to sacrifice the mothership. One might think that with the threat of the superior weapon removed, tensions between the powers would ratchet down. But those events only started the dominoes that led to the Lunar Ukombozi War.

"Sometimes it takes fire and blood to birth a dream.

"Out of that, Muungano was born. All because Khamaal Besamon had a choice of whether or not to launch his ship into the unknown. When the Orun Gate was discovered, everyone assumed we had perfected our technology. Making all the wrong people nervous. History has a way of teaching us what's going to happen."

Stacia ran her fingers through Bek's hair and stared out the port window. There were so many stars out there.

＊

Stacia left the med bay, taking the most circuitous route possible, not consciously avoiding most of her crew. Looping around the outer level of the *Cypher,* the interplay of the ship's artificial gravitational fields and her nanomesh suit sent a weird charge along her skin. The way children played with static electricity. She focused on her thoughts, allowing herself the space to feel everything going on within. Attempting to sort through the tangle of her emotions, achieve a measure of clarity. Or at least a path to move forward.

"Any word on Maya?" Stacia stepped onto the command deck.

"It almost looks like someone used a narrow-band harmonic keynote to disrupt our systems." Dina did not raise her eyes from the series of holovids displayed at her station. "The compression sequence of the backup modules in engineering nearly overloaded our memory core. The systems will take some time to repair. Its amplifier fed directly into the kheprw crystals' containment unit. Or some modulating signal that has Maya caught in a sort of internal loop. They are still active, just not responsive. Like they are, I don't know, out of phase."

"Entanglement." Stacia advanced on one of the holovids. "Shit, I hadn't considered it."

"Considered what?"

"It's all about potentialities. Think of the universe as musical and how we're simply here to learn its song. When we're improvising, if I know the next note is the right tone, it opens up possibilities for the note that comes after it. The same is true at the quantum level. The more certain the momentum of a particle, the more possibilities emerge for it to be in a multitude of positions. It's the basis of quantum computing."

"I still don't understand." Dina scooted away from her workstations. Her demeanor still cool. Professional, but her curiosity had been stirred.

"A quantum entity is neither wave nor particle but has both attributes at the same time." Stacia's voiced drifted off, working her theory out loud, no longer conscious of Dina. "If Maya's experiencing a, I don't know, feedback loop of sorts, they've already gone through the Orun Gate. We've already gone through the Orun Gate."

"No, we're—"

"We are here. Maya is here. And there." Her decision had already been made. Now she needed to make it. "Never mind. You were saying Maya is out of phase."

"Yes." Dina's quizzical stare didn't venture to inquire further. "They are in there, simply not responding. All systems are functioning and responsive. They simply won't talk. I can't help but imagine they are like a traumatized child huddled in a corner, refusing anyone's contact."

"Needing a reboot." Stacia wanted to ask after Hondo, but this was the most Dina had spoken to her in a tone approximating respectful. She opted not to push things and allow Dina space to chart her own timetable to forgiving her. With no guarantee she ever would. "Can you patch me through for a ship-wide communiqué?"

"Whenever you are ready." Dina raised an additional display to obscure the sight line between her and Stacia.

Stacia ignored it. Instead, she closed her eyes and inhaled. Following her long exhalation, she waited for the broad linkage signal and began to speak. "This is your captain speaking. It has been my privilege to serve you for the last several years. Though, with recent events, I don't know if I continue to deserve that honor. I want to explain my actions. And to, well, give you a choice as to whether you want to continue to have me serve you."

All work on the command deck ceased. Dina cleared all of her holovids. Stacia could only imagine that similar scenes took place all around the ship in that moment.

"As some of you know, my son, Bekele, has been sick. He has a degenerative neurological condition that none of our doctors here, on Bronzeville, or on Titan could diagnose or even tell me the origins of. Yesterday, an . . . operative from LISC informed me that a virus had been administered to my son by agents within the Earth First movement. In . . . anger, I brutalized a member of our crew who I discovered was a conspirator in that movement. Those actions, while they felt righteous in the moment, are not the Muungano way. LISC operatives continue to dangle the life of my son as incentive for me to order our ship through the wormhole to secure his cure. As Bek's desperate parents, I will." She held out her hand. Yahya joined her. "We will."

"I understand that my actions have appeared rash, but I am not. Any who do not wish to explore on the other side of the Orun Gate are free to take the shuttles and return to Titan. We want the committed, the unequivocal, on this ship because we don't know what we'll face. Or when we will return. But we need to be united if we are to pursue this course. Those who wish to depart need to report to docking bay five for disembarkment. That is all."

*

Stacia led her security team to the docking bay. Zenith stood in front of about twenty members of her crew. Brought up on a medi-cart, Hondo refused to meet her eyes. A few Ugenini and Asili dotted the sea of mzungu and other obroni faces. No matter, they were all obroni to her now. Earth First. Night

Train. Whatever they called themselves or were called, they were outsiders who no longer would walk among them.

"Not going to blast us out the air lock, are you?" Zenith asked.

"To be fair, I only air locked Hondo a little." A mirthless smile crossed Stacia's lips. "I could be talked into going all the way if all of you don't get the fuck off my ship."

"Is being so judgmental part of the Muungano way?"

"How badly do you want to test me right now?" Stacia asked.

"Then I'll leave you with a gift." He tapped the console embedded in his wrist. "Check the compartment you first found me in. Do a resonant-level scan. I have reason to believe your missing crewman might be there."

"Security," Stacia locked her gaze on his, unwavering, "to cargo bay seven. Sweep using a resonant-level scan and report."

Seconds ticked by. Stacia refused to break her stare with Zenith, noting the eminent punchability of his too-pleased-with-himself face.

"Paki secured. Unconscious, but vitals appear strong," Kenya's disembodied voice said.

"Take him to med bay one."

Zenith interrupted her before she could ask. "Tesseract field. They're all the rage with O.E. security these days."

"Get. The entire fuck. Off my ship."

"Until we talk again, Captain." Zenith tipped an imaginary hat at her and disembarked toward the crowded Saqqara.

"No, not you. You're coming with us." Stacia wagged two fingers. Two other members of her security team sidled up to either side of Zenith and restrained him.

He struggled, albeit a vain effort. "This is unacceptable. I have . . ."

". . . boarded the *Cypher,* my command, without permission. Threatened my family and disrupted my crew. You dangled a cure out here. We'll need you to verify it. If this scenario conflicts with your diplomatic immunity, we'll straighten out the misunderstanding when we return."

"My superiors . . ."

". . . will note my logs about how we didn't discover you until after we went through the Orun Gate. You were so good at hiding. Tesseract fields and all."

"None of that will withstand scrutiny," Zenith said.

"Probably not. Still, you're coming with us. If you don't like it, you should have considered that before fomenting an insurrection on my ship. Find him some suitable quarters."

Her security officer approached the man, who shrank away from her touch.

Zenith held his hands up. "Wait, how long do you plan on keeping me?"

"How long do you think?"

"I'm the prisoner. I can't decide when I go free."

"That's the difference between you and . . . us." Stacia watched her ex-crew begin to board the ship. A pang nagged at her heart. She had to admit to herself that she actually felt some sort of way about so many of her people leaving. Twenty of the hundreds on board still seemed like too many. Too many folks to be welcomed and treated as family but to be ultimately working against the interests of the community. One in particular drew her attention.

Hondo nursed a sprain in his wrist. Dina pushed her way through the gathered crowd. When he spied her, his mouth opened, but no sound came out. Not finding the words to ask her to join him. She held up her hand in a tentative wave goodbye. Not finding the words to want to leave the ship. Silently, he boarded the waiting shuttle, followed by several others. Stacia watched the ship clear the *Cypher*. She prayed that she was acting in the best interest of the community, not simply placing her son's life above all others'.

*

On the command deck, Stacia wrapped her long braids within an Ashanti-patterned sheath. Unable to get comfortable in her seat, she crossed her legs. She leaned slightly forward, not anxious but with focused attentiveness. Her bracelets slid down the middle of her forearm. She tapped the console of her wrist and whispered the word *Maya,* hoping the AI might respond. But only silence hung in the air. "Dina, plot a course taking us through the wormhole."

"Yes, Captain." Dina kept the stiff formality between them like a shield, but she was still on board. Still part of the *Cypher*'s family. A tremulous note of fear filled her tone. "The *Morrison* and the *Baldwin* have vectored into an intercept course. Those are warships."

"Warships that transport HOVA Brigades." Stacia neared the view screen.

"We're not going to win a firefight with them."

"We're not going to engage in a firefight with our own in the first place."

Stacia left no room for doubt or misinterpretation in her command. "Open a communication channel."

Maulana Buhari's image popped up as a holovid. The signal had been directed at the ships, which meant a command override was in place and the situation was under a Code Black / Eyes Only lock of the R.

"I . . . see you, Maulana." Stacia's voice remained even, not betraying a hint of surprise.

"I see you, too, Stacia. What are you doing?" His holoimage stood and approached her viewer. In the background, the Ijo's security council watched on. He now occupied the seat Xola once filled.

"I need to cross the Orun Gate."

"You aren't authorized."

"I know. But I have to go. The life of my son depends on it." Stacia drew up her files. "Transmitting my Code Black / Eyes Only report to you now."

The *Morrison* and the *Baldwin* sped toward them. The distance between them shortened. On an intercept vector, no weapons lock was detected. But they were also still out of range.

"I'm sorry for the situation you find yourself in. And rest assured, these interlopers will be dealt with. But be that as it may"—Maulana looked up from scanning the report, fixing his serious and intense gaze on her—"we can't allow you near the Orun Gate. We just voted to seal the wormhole."

"You can't. Once you seal the gate, no one from the other side can return."

"The *Hughes* has been . . . lost. The *Morrison* and the *Baldwin* were on their way to Titan for a full debrief when we received the alert of your intended course."

"Well, we're going through."

Maulana's face filled her entire view now. "Stacia, I can't allow that."

"Then you'll have to decide whether or not you want to fire on your own."

"Don't test me—"

"I appreciate you, Maulana." Stacia cut off their communication channel.

"Stacia," Dina said. "The *Morrison* and the *Baldwin* are closing in fast. They're almost within weapons range."

"We won't fire on our own." Stacia leaned over her to check her telemetry readings. "And they won't fire on us."

"That's a big gamble."

"It's no gamble. We aren't threatening them or community. And neither are they. We can't settle differences between us by raising weapons at one another. We are either a community or Muungano is a lie that deserves to be exposed. Now we're going through. Full forward." Stacia took her seat and secured herself for what she knew would be a bumpy ride.

"The *Morrison* and the *Baldwin* are coming about."

"Keep an eye on—"

"We have a weapons lock!" Dina whirled around. "They've launched missiles!"

"What?" Stacia shouted. "Hard to port. Deploy deterrent. Increase thrust to maximum. I don't care if you exceed safety protocols."

"Quantum payloads detected." Dina double-checked her scans. "Correction. Their weapons have locked on to the Orun Gate."

"Are they insane? Can someone calculate the effects of a quantum payload on the wormhole?"

"No one knows the full effect," Dina said.

Paki would, Stacia kept to herself. "Damn it. Can we beat the missiles to the gate?"

"It's going to be close."

"Shields to maximum." Stacia closed her eyes in silent prayer. "Brace for impact."

The *Cypher*'s approach triggered the opening of the Orun Gate. A swirl of light and a vortex of energy, it carved a hole into the space-time fabric of the universe, creating a window to another side of the universe. Stacia nodded, and Dina steered the ship into the wormhole's event horizon just as the missiles struck. The explosions shuddered the *Cypher*. Sparks erupted from consoles. The main cabin lights darkened. Emergency lights flicked on, illuminated the doors and walkways. All about them, bulkheads slammed into place, cordoning off the decks in preparations for breaches. The detonation destabilized the event window of the Orun Gate. The cosmic maw simply collapsed.

All signals within the gate, including the *Cypher*'s, ceased.

25

ISHANT SANGSUWANGUL
The Citadel

"They're good. Oh, they're real good." Mumbling to himself, Ishant half snorted at a joke only he heard and redoubled his efforts. Various nodes ran through the bulkheads of every structure in Muungano. The nodes were like nerve clusters, the systems mimicking biological nodules. Peeling back a layer of his bioplastic arm, he had plugged into an AI node. From there, he ran his encryption protocols. "I got you now."

No matter what Maulana said, Ishant knew he hadn't been tracked. He couldn't tell Amachi how he knew. The Dreaming City used one level of encryption protocols. The Niyabinghi and the HOVA used another. Ishant had designed the next generation. No one else had it. That was the basis of his fellowship. Hakeem Buhari had always been a hero of his.

Ishant backed out of the junction nook. Drawing his cloak about him, he clung to the shadows, tracking the quarry he couldn't identify. This would serve as his command post. The spy had to still be here on Oyigiyigi. Ishant tracked the comings and goings of all ship traffic. And their cargo. And the passengers. One figure and their cargo moved about the station like a duppy among shadows.

Basically, he tracked an absence.

If fifty people disembarked from a ship from the Dreaming City, but only forty-nine were on the manifest, his data ghost was present. Whoever they were, they were good. Moving in crowds, hiding in plain sight. Then came the other complicating factor: Whatever phantom ripples they left in their passing—unaccounted for manifests, gen-ident sigils, and so on—were being systematically erased. As if a digital encryption worm followed them. Ishant had designed similar things that allowed him and Jaha to arrange clandestine meetings off the books, but the sophistication of this one was still intelligence-grade.

Ishant brushed back his shock of white hair, which had a habit of flopping across his forehead. He took a deep breath and hoped that the stims he took wouldn't wear off soon. He hated working alone as much as he liked, even needed, to work alone. He wondered if he should have had Amachi stay. She proved to be more capable than he'd first assessed her to be. She had calm and poise, not easily ruffled when encountering the unknown. All useful skills in his work.

Nguni guards became alert as he rounded the corner from the nook. Ishant's palms moistened with anticipation. They eyed him with casual suspicion, as an out-of-place alien among them. In the way. A nuisance. Impure. But he needed to get to the docking bay.

"This is a restricted area." A guard stood at the rear entrance of the bay. "Ident sigil."

"Here."

"A diplomat? Of Muungano?" The guard looked him up and down as if he were small. Or nearly unwanted. "Is this what the Ijo have come to?"

Ishant's extensive training kept him from rolling his eyes. Or from having anything sarcastic or offended registering on his face. "May I proceed?"

The guard allowed him to pass. With a measured nonchalance, Ishant walked along the raised corridor. The mining gangplanks gave him a great view of the bay. Scanning the scene, a crowd of Muungano members milled about the area. Day cycle must have neared. Or dusk. He'd lost all sense of time, always a risk with the way he threw himself into his work, reminded once again of time's artificial arbitrariness. All he knew was that he was tired, that he probably hadn't slept for untold cycles because that wasn't his way. Once he'd been given a job that needed to be done, he'd see it straight through to completion. Only Jaha had the presence to remind him to do the little things, like sleep.

There, he thought, thumbing through the generated data stamps. A member passed a checkpoint and soon afterward, their metadata on the transit logs disappeared. He withdrew a Black Caesar, a device used to pirate link streams. He tagged the ghost's metadata with a marker and programmed the Black Caesar to alert him to any disappearing data logs. Ishant scrambled along the passageway. The data tag wouldn't last long. Like any good stream worm, it wasn't designed to last long since ones with longer half-lives were more easily detected. Ishant hurried toward the lower hall, hoping the agent wouldn't lose him in all of the splitting passageways of the mine.

The hallway split into a service corridor, like the isocrawl corridors on a research ship, which ran parallel to many of the shafts. Ishant hesitated. There was no reason for anyone to take them except for service workers. Unless the agent knew they were being tracked.

A strange scratch echoed from down the passageway. Ishant rested his hand on the wall panel, which provided a sense of reassurance. He swept down the hall, thankful for the poor illumination. Again the wall braces appeared every ten meters or so, with the dark walls devouring the light and deepening the shadows. In the distance, a wary shadow bobbed, nearly a heat shimmer in the wan light. Silently, Ishant advanced on the figure. He skirted the jutting rocks and slipped farther into the tunnel. Whoever it was headed toward one of the refinery chambers.

Ishant never gave too much consideration to things like a cover or blending in, often using his mzungu appearance to his advantage. Eyes glided over him, never lingering in detailed study. He'd offer up an awkward smile if anyone met his eyes, but they'd note his color and place before moving on. No one would've been able to pick him out of an O.E. lineup.

The crowd thickened as he neared the corner. A group of drummers performed. A man carted a stall through the crowd, displaying his handcrafted statuettes. A row of food courts roasted a variety of meats or warmed stews or roasted breadfruit. Many of the miners stopped to watch or gather in circles to catch up with one another. Chatting, laughing, and enjoying one another like a rush hour intersection of pedestrian traffic. The congestion swelled without complaint as more food artisans and musicians showed up to demonstrate and share their work. The chaos of a night shift.

Ishant kept a close eye on his ghost. They'd be slowed down by the crush of people, a shoulder-to-shoulder throng, over fifty people between them. If he wanted, Ishant could sidle to within a meter of them and not be noticed. The ghost shuffled forward, with the occasional furtive glance to track their surroundings, surveying any reflective surface or incongruent sound. The ghost couldn't just use the Niyabinghi cloaking tech. The Niyabinghi could easily track him, as cloaked agents were active duty and they had to know where and how they were positioned. Ishant opted to hang back.

The ghost moved off the main strip along a quieter, more residential road. The rough-hewn kraal full of open doorways and neighbors gathering on porches. Older ladies sat younger ones between their knees, drawing a comb through their hair, with the occasional scoffs at the yelps of the more tender-headed. Ishant's mind raced, his curiosity tripping him up, overruling the cautious part of his brain so that he could figure out what the ghost was up to.

His arm went numb. A projectile of some sort struck him. His cloak absorbed the brunt of it. Had it been a heavier charge, Muungano doctors would be standing over his corpse, examining the hole in his chest. Ishant turned. Blinking rapidly, almost excited to get into a tussle, he'd offered up his face as if anticipating being hit.

Lij Matata Okoro was happy to oblige.

Matata half stumbled toward Ishant before jerking upward, thrusting his right arm out. Ishant dodged the blow, but that gave Matata the room to do what he really wanted: draw a weapon from the folds of his Basotho blanket. Matata shifted to the left, locking his arm in a grip. His other hand removed his belt, a feint within a feint. With a flick, the length of the belt hardened into a doubled-edged panga the length of a staff.

Ishant dodged the savage arc of the blade's swing. Without thinking, he leapt on Matata's back, wrapped one arm around his neck and pressed his forearm against the back of his neck. Matata thrust the blade through Ishant's side. Howling in pain, Ishant held on, cutting off the Lij's airway. Matata bucked once, twice, trying to twist the panga edge upward through more vital organs, before his body finally stilled. Matata's unconscious weight dropped to the ground, taking Ishant with him, the blade still lodged in his side. Ishant couldn't risk their discovery. He didn't know who his allies were and, more important, who Matata was here to meet. He activated the commlink.

"This is Ishant. Code Black / Eyes Only Uhlanga protocols." He hoped citing a classified program would catch the attention of the right ears. "Triangulate on my signal. I have the package."

A dull ache radiated from his side. He rolled over a little to ease the pressure. He was so tired. He needed to close his eyes for only a moment. Get just a little rest.

＊

"Have a seat." Jaha's careful scrutiny tracked Ishant as he shuffled into the room and plopped onto the chair across from her. The chair's high back didn't change, though the rest of the seat adjusted to his body. A decanter waited on the table between them. After waving his hands about in a nonsensical gesture calling for her assent, Ishant began to pour a glass for each of them.

"What is it?" He glanced at the label.

"Old." She took her glass. "And free, so what do you care?"

"Fair point." The scotch burned with familiarity when it hit the back of his throat. Ishant closed his eyes and enjoyed the rush. "This tastes expensive. That can only mean you're about to read me in on a complicated job."

"Sweet baby." She patted his arm. It had the comfort of his grandmother's touch. "The most complicated you've ever had."

Ishant poured another glass. "What's the job?"

"You know the saying 'All my skinfolk ain't kinfolk'?"

"Not really. I've heard people repeat it, but never really understood it."

"Let's just say that just having the right skin color is not a guarantee of anyone acting in the collective best interest of our people."

"Sometimes I wonder if that's how people see me." Ishant took a long, slow sip of the brown liquid.

"As what?"

"An infiltrator within Muungano spaces. A traitor from outside of them. Because I chose to live and work here, I am forever consigning myself to be an outsider."

"Yeah, that's all on you, baby." Jaha raised her glass to him.

"What do you mean?"

"You do that to yourself. You're so insecure, you push yourself harder and dive deeper into every aspect of the work than anyone ever asks you. I've told you that you don't have to keep proving yourself. You belong. That's the whole point of Muungano: to create a place where you belong well before you believe."

"You took a chance on accepting me, bringing me in." Ishant cradled his glass with both hands, staring into its liquid contents like it held the secrets of life. "I just want to do right by you. I don't want to screw this up."

"We take that risk anytime we enter a relationship. But make no mistake, buddy. I'm gonna let you torture yourself and do all sorts of extra shit. There's a lot that needs to be done, and if you need to work your angst out that way, I'll let you." Jaha spun slightly in her chair, swirling the oversized glass. She never raised it to her lips.

"I took an oath when I began my fellowship on Muungano. The work of dismantling supremacy. To fighting against oppression and injustice. By any means necessary." Ishant swallowed another finger's worth of the whiskey. The effects began to hit him, and he decided to switch to sipping mode. "But sometimes I wonder if this is my fight."

"What do you mean?"

"My family's from Thailand."

"And you don't carry the burden of our ancestors." Jaha set the glass down. "You don't feel the mission in your bones. Like you have to do it to survive. To breathe."

"Something like that."

"What do you carry?" Jaha folded her arms like a bored bird of prey waiting for the show to begin.

"I . . . don't know. I want the liberation of all people. I want to be part of a mission greater than myself." Ishant held his glass up, in sudden fascination of the way light glinted from it. In due course, his attention returned to her. "Here's what I believe in my heart: working for the greater good of your people is the path to fighting for the greater good of all people."

Jaha grinned, a smile so wide it revealed each of her pearled teeth. "I'm glad you see it that way. Not everyone does. That's what I want you to investigate: some of our own may be working against us."

"I'm not comfortable making that judgment of which Ugenini, Maroon, or Asili were . . . the right kind."

"Shit, no one's asking you to do that. We've always had disagreements on that score. Last thing we need is someone outside the family trying to make that judgment." Jaha spun one of her historical images charts. It landed on an image of Duke Ellington playing at the Sunset Terrace on Indiana Avenue. A wistful thing flitted in her eyes. "There were always those who believed that all we had to do was dress right, speak right, and act right—try to fit in better—to have society recognize our humanity. As if holding on to our culture was us self-inflicting our oppression. It didn't advance our cause any. We were some of the best-dressed lynched folks."

"Where is all of this coming from?"

"Fears. Whispers. Suspicions. Always keep your eyes open. Make sure to always be about the work of community. That will tell you who is true or not."

"Okay." From her face, he guessed at what she was trying to warn him of.

"I have a mission for you," she began. "You'll be traveling with Amachi Adisa . . ."

*

Darkness pressed in all around him. A pressure built on his chest, making it hard for him to catch a complete breath. The shadows clawed at him, wanting to drag him to greater depths. His consciousness swam in the night, a disembodied spirit searching for any glimmer of light. His eyes cracked open to the slimmest of parting. The daylight dragged him the rest of the way to full wakefulness. Escaping the haze of the memory of pain and the muddle-headedness of medication.

"How's the side?" Lebna hovered over him, his face far too close. "The weapon did not pierce anything vital."

"I consider every part of me vital. And prefer it intact." Ishant slid out from under the man's stare, attempting to sit up. A dull yet deep ache notched in his side. The Nguni doctors did good work. The wound had been sealed and would heal nicely. It would still be a day or so before he'd feel 100 percent, though Ishant chided himself. He couldn't afford to be so careless in the future. "Who are you?"

"Lebna Dimka, we met at—"

Ishant shook his head. He hated being unclear, his mind not sharp and alert. He tried again. "No, I mean why are *you* attending me? Are you also a doctor?"

"No, just a jeli. Like my aunt."

"I know. I work for your aunt." Ishant ignored his claim of being "just" a jeli. "Just" a griot would not have been read in on a Code Black / Eyes Only protocol.

"I know. She speaks highly of you."

That news pleased Ishant more than he was ready to admit. "You should let your soon-to-be father-in-law know. I didn't receive the warmest of receptions."

Lebna shifted with unease. Ishant couldn't tell if it was the impending marriage or the man who made him uncomfortable. "Now that we have the space to do so, Geoboe clings to many of our ancient ways."

"What does a jeli need with a cultural attaché?"

"What we in the Griot Circle love most: to be trusted with nyama and learn a new story." Lebna swiped his wrist. A holovid of Matata being detained in an empty room coalesced in front of him. "Who's this?"

"A person of interest in the matter of Xola's death."

"How 'of interest' is he?" Lebna inclined his body, inviting and honest, no intelligence-level-bullshit answer.

"My chief and only suspect," Ishant said.

"Ah." The answer seemed to satisfy Lebna, which meant he confirmed what the griot magistrate already knew. "Then he will not enjoy the comforts of home."

"I have no doubt. And there is much we don't know." Ishant read something in Lebna's face. Jaha often spoke about reading a person's emi, but his rational mind wasn't able to make that intuitive leap yet. Still, he recognized concern, a shadow the man didn't wish to share. "What is it?"

"My friend, there's no easy way to tell you this." Lebna gestured for Ishant to take a seat.

"Just tell me, then." Ishant backed onto the bed, sitting without realizing it.

"It's Amachi. Her Saqqara crashed."

"What?" Ishant heard the words and understood them, but he asked out of reflex. As if buying time for his mind to process the information.

"Her transponder showed her going dark while on the far side of the Mars colony. In the barrens outside of Bronzeville."

"Is she . . . ?"

"Presumed. So no recovery mission has been mounted, especially since no one has been able to triangulate her precise location. Scout ships have been dispatched to scour the area. I just wanted you braced for the worse."

"Asante sana." Ishant lowered his eyes to hide his jumble of emotions. He'd failed another member of the Adisa family, whom he'd pledged to serve.

"If you are up to it, I'd like to have you sit in on his interrogation. Keep Matata off guard and off balance."

"Yes, of course. Just no strong-arming him." Needing the distraction if nothing else, Ishant gathered his things. "He may have to go before the Ijo security council to face the full measure of Muungano."

"Coerced confessions do no one any good. We want the truth. This isn't O.E."

They entered the chamber together, the entryway barely having a chance to re-form before Lebna took the seat across from Matata. Ishant didn't take the other seat. He walked behind Matata, settling in along the wall, just out of his peripheral vision.

"My name is Lebna Dimka, griot magistrate for the Griot Circle of Oyigiyigi."

"I know who you are. Both of you. I'd be terrible at my job if I didn't," Matata said. "Why have I been taken into custody? To detain a Niyabinghi in the course of their duties, well, the repercussions may be quite severe for your agency."

Lebna remained nonplussed and unmoved by the implied threat. "We're here because special circumstances demand a certain level of response."

"What kind of circumstances?" Matata slid his eyes toward Ishant as if not wanting to lose track of him.

"We've had surveillance on you for some time," Ishant said.

"Oh?" Matata grinned smugly. "I take no offense. I am a handsome man. I'm quite used to the attention."

"Yet you've kept a low profile here," Ishant said. "Almost like a ghost."

"Is that a crime now? I am a member of the Niyabinghi. Low profile is part of the job description. What we do doesn't allow for a lot of outside distractions."

"Yet even among you fellow members, you are a bit of a cypher." Lebna swiped at his wrist to examine a data cache.

"I'm private. Again, a habit shaped by the job," Matata said.

"To a fault. You don't allow anyone in. No one knows you. That works against what we're about as a community."

"I want to keep my professional life isolated, to not let it bleed into the personal. Else it muddles the waters and undermines my performance." Matata leaned back in his seat, his legs in a near sprawl. Relaxed. Too relaxed. He was an experienced Niyabinghi, but his body language was that of a man without a care. One biding his time. Ishant wondered who was in control of the room.

"I get it," Lebna reiterated. "Do your job well and get home."

"Exactly." Matata both lowered his head and angled his gaze up at Lebna, waiting for more. Taunting him.

"Compartmentalized."

"Exactly."

"It's almost like you have two lives."

"I wouldn't say that."

"I would. In one life, you are Lij Matata Okoro, dedicated member of Muungano and agent of the Niyabinghi."

"And in the other?" Matata moved within a low-lying cloud of smugness that clung.

"That's what we want to find out," Lebna said.

"I don't know what you hope to get out of me."

"The truth."

"Assuming I'm lying." Matata took pains to not cross his arms. That would be defensive. Right now, as far as he was concerned, they played along to his script.

Ishant had seen enough. It was time for him to change the game up. "Or hiding something."

"Or that." Matata turned from Ishant with a lingering disdain. "I've had the same training as you. This buddy cop team-up wouldn't confuse a toddler. I can probably beat all of Maya's biometrics and withstand drug treatment. Even torture."

"It won't come to that." Ishant shifted farther to the side opposite Lebna.

Matata had to angle his body to keep both of them in his sight line. "Why not?"

"Because you want to tell us. You want to rub our noses in it."

Matata paused, studying Ishant in cautious reassessment. Ishant might not be able to read a person's emi, but he was adept at body language. Something he just announced to Matata alarmed him. Now aware of this, the man would try to send false signals with his body language, careful glances, shifts in positions, and tics of the face designed to tell a counternarrative, but Ishant was a skilled story reader. And Lebna a gifted storyteller.

"What would an obroni know of telling our stories?" Matata ventured, hoping to put Ishant on the defensive.

"I've studied your people. The history. The philosophy."

"The talking points. I can practically see Xola's hand up your ass, shaping your words." Matata's lips tightened in a rueful purse.

"Its philosophy is the grounding principle of my life." Ishant stretched the wrist of his artificial arm. With a surreptitious flick of his finger, he initiated a file request on Matata.

"Then you are a fool. This place is a lie."

"And yet you're there and I'm here."

"No, I mean Muungano. It's built on a lie and has become a lie."

"This will be good." Ishant folded his arms and angled away from him, forcing Matata to lean forward in pursuit of his full attention. Anger, perhaps a hint of betrayal, fueled him. Blinded him to his training. Whatever hurt he felt ran deep. And personal.

"Make fun of me all you want, but in your heart, that's what you're afraid of. That this, all this you've pledged your life to, is too good to be true. And it is." Matata jabbed his finger into the table. "You ain't free. You've never been free. You're more chained now than you ever were on O.E., and you don't notice your situation because the chain holders look like us. We walk around 'seeing' one another and 'appreciating' one another. But you can't even come and go as you please. Everyone's in one another's business. You can't make decisions on your own. It's life by committee."

"That's accountability to community." Lebna stirred, reciting the lessons of instilled Muungano training.

"It's chains by another name." Matata spared him an unsympathetic glance.

Lebna shifted uneasily again, undue defensiveness crept into his voice. "Call me what you want. It's truth you can't handle. Trying to tell me who I am. I'm my own man. I'm not oppressed."

"You made it." Not allowing Matata to distract and derail him, Ishant allowed a touch of mocking to accentuate his tone. He'd encountered this archetype before. The kind who believed in exceptionalism. The self-satisfied accomplished who believed because they succeeded, everyone who didn't was guilty of whining or playing the victim. That somehow the systems in play designed to specifically hold people back were an illusion. Rooting their stories in themselves, they wielded the language of their oppressors as their weapon.

"Damn right, I did."

Ishant swiped at his data caches and reports. "You studied at the Thmei Academy. Were one of their brightest stars. The way I heard it, you weren't as good with relationships. Had a way of burning bridges wherever you went."

"That's how they spun it," Matata said.

Ishant splayed out the holovids. Matata's history within the Thmei Academy. Bouncing back to O.E. Reconnected in Muungano after a brief stint in the HOVA. Joining the Niyabinghi. Rising quickly and with a favorable word from Xola, his attachment to Jaha.

"This doesn't look like spin," Lebna said.

"The facts were simpler: I outgrew them." Matata stood up, careful not to move too quickly and earn a pehla stick response. "The Muungano rhetoric sounds good for a minute, but the lifestyle becomes claustrophobic, and they give you no choice but to get out."

"Back to O.E. Where you bounced around looking for a cause—" Lebna began.

"No," Ishant said. "Looking for a master."

Lebna and Matata both turned to him.

"I can't be controlled by nobody. I have the power in my hands. You have no sense of self, so you push this collective bullshit. Afraid to think for yourself. I'm here to do it for myself, by myself. I never looked for no handouts.

If I wanted it, I went and got it. You preach complete reliance, and anyone who disagrees you call names and exile from the community. But I'm a free-thinker you can't silence, and now I'm here to break the chains."

"Look here, Grandpa Moses, we get it. You want to make O.E. great again," Lebna interjected.

"You laugh, but that's the point. There are threats out there we haven't considered. Muungano is so busy spitting on its 'oppressors,' it doesn't know how to ally with those who are ready to give us power. To face what's coming, we have to stand together as one people. Earth, Mars, and Muungano."

"Ah, a reintegrationist. I should've known." Lebna tossed his hands up and threw his head back in exaggerated exasperation.

"Only with the reintegration being on my terms." Matata's voice rose with the concern of not being taken seriously.

Ishant shrugged. "Listen to how you talk. 'I' this and 'my' that. Never 'we,' as if you were never a part of Muungano. But for all of your 'freedom,' you still found yourself gravitating to Xola. Then back to O.E. With your résumé, you were an asset to many organizations. You sound good . . ."

"Articulate." Lebna found the page Ishant now worked from, falling into his conversational rhythm. He was very good. Such a talent. Who warranted an eye being kept on them.

"You look the part . . ."

"Clean shaven. I daresay respectable." Lebna nodded in mocking agreement.

"But you destroy community everywhere you go," Ishant said.

"Poison."

"You look like us and sound like us, but you weren't one of us."

"Night Train." Lebna delivered the blow with a smooth aplomb.

"You've been played and probably don't even realized how they've used you as a highly trained sleeper agent inserted into Muungano society to sab-otage." Ishant moved in, not giving Matata a chance to reel from the accusa-tion, much less defend himself. And assassinate.

"How long have you waited to strike? Years? Decades?" Lebna's words hung in the air, a cold accusation.

"Were you ever one of us?"

"'Us'? There was never any 'us.'" Glaring at Ishant with focused intensity, Matata nearly knocked the seat out of his way. "Look at you, then look at me. Yet somehow you get to be 'us' and I'm . . ."

". . . on the outside looking in," Ishant said.

"Fuck. You." Matata sucked his teeth and turned away. Surrendering to the voices in his head, he settled his breathing enough to sit back down. "You got me up here, another one of your boogeyman stories. Night Train? Really? That the best you can do?"

"You're right. All we have are suppositions and coincidences." Ishant displayed his reports. "An O.E. agent sent to kill the Muungano Camara. After a bombing of our embassy, injuring a high-ranking member of the Ijo security council, forces security protocols and redeployments. A withdrawal to the Dreaming City. Allowing you proximity to the Ijo members. A high-ranking military leader on a sensitive mission gets exposed and executed. And now the Camara's daughter suddenly disappears. It all points to two words: *decapitation strikes.*"

"Wasn't me. But that's a good story." Matata crossed his arms and looked away.

"You're good." Lebna turned to Ishant. "But the Night Train program, I'm sorry, always had the ring of a fairy tale for spies. Do you know how good an agent would have to be to pull that off? To rise through the ranks of the Niyabinghi to get that close? To fool Jaha, Selamault, and Xola while in proximity? Not a Thmei Academy washout. As much as I want to close this investigation, I'm not trying to get a clearance on some proxy."

"Proxy?" Matata sneered.

"That's all you've ever been. Look at your track record. A cutout for other people's beliefs, all in the name of sounding like your own man. You are an empty suit," Lebna said.

"You barely exist," Ishant said.

"But here's what we know about our suspect. He's a member of the Niyabinghi. Served in the Dreaming City. Among the personal escort of the Ijo."

"I'm telling you, there's no record of him. No gen-ident. No Maya file. Not even holovid beyond what were captured since we apprehended him. Even then, there's no match within our database or any shared with Titan, though we're still waiting on O.E."

"O.E.?" Matata asked with the thrum of apprehension.

"Let's just say we have back channels. Some that even they aren't aware of," Ishant said.

"Do they have similar back channels?" Lebna turned to him.

"That's what we're here to find out." Ishant enlarged the files in front of Matata. His movement, prior to the bombing. Being recalled to the Dreaming City. The movements of a data ghost, tracked by being invisible. Then fleeing to Oyigiyigi once Amachi dogged his trail. "All of my collected data is right here. What story would you have us read?"

"It's simple, really," Matata began in a low, not-quite-resigned tone. "We need to bring Muungano to the table. But you all are so damn proud. Self-sufficient. Don't have to take anything from anybody. Doing things on your terms or your timetable. Calling yourselves 'free' when all you are is arrogant. Blind as Xola. You can't see your need for others, even against an overwhelming threat."

"The unknown is not a threat," Lebna said.

"Now you're just being naive. Oyigiyigi. Bronzeville. The Dreaming City. All of Muungano has to reunify. Partner with LISC. One way or another, you'll be brought to the table so that we can form a united Earth alliance. That is the only way we'll be strong enough to face the coming storm."

There it was: the story Matata wanted to tell. Young, smart, ambitious, he got caught up in O.E. and their games. Never understood that he swam with sharks. The kind that would use him for their own ends before leaving him to be devoured. If they didn't devour him themselves. Ishant shut off the images. They had all they needed. Only a few loose threads remained.

"Weaning ourselves from supremacist and colonialist thought, ways and ideas so deeply entrenched it might take several lifetimes to truly liberate ourselves from. So that in becoming free of our oppressors, we don't carry on the work of our oppressors." Lebna's tone was a low, sad thing, full of pity. "Did you have a hand in Fela's execution?"

Matata sank into his seat, neither defeated nor defiant. "No."

"Did you play a role in Amachi's crash?"

"No."

"Were you a part of the terrorist plot to blow up our embassy?"

"Yes."

"Did you kill Xola?"

Matata reared up, both hurt and angry at the accusation. "No."

"Would you even know if you were used as the weapon?" Ishant turned his back to him. "We're sending you back to the Dreaming City. They'll know how best to deal with you."

Lebna stood up and stared at Matata one last time. "Nanny fe Queen."

Lebna escorted Ishant toward the door. They shuffled out of the room without a sound, leaving Matata without any sense of community or belonging.

"You did well in there," Lebna said once the door sealed behind them.

"The evidence you gathered, your final report has all been sent to Maulana. What will you do next?"

"My job here is done. I need to return to Muungano to aid in the search for Amachi."

Lebna brushed his shoulder, halting him in his tracks. "I have an offer from Maulana."

"What's that?" Ishant lingered, not freeing himself from Lebna's touch.

"To join the Niyabinghi."

"What?" Ishant's eyes widened in amazement. "No obroni has ever been a member of the Niyabinghi."

"You'd be the first."

"Why me?" Ishant glanced down at Lebna's hand.

Withdrawing it, Lebna backed up half a step, but was still well within Ishant's personal space. "This affair has shown us a few blind spots that we have."

"The Night Train?"

"That's part of it. We need well-placed operatives of our own. Is that something you'd be interested in?"

"Yes. Right after we find Amachi," Ishant said.

"I'm afraid your asset training would take precedence. And deployment beginning immediately."

"What's the rush?"

"You already have an assignment," Lebna said.

"What's that?"

"To return to O.E."

26

EPYC RO MORGAN
Eshu

Epyc Ro saw her first dead body during the Montes Caucasus conflict of the Lunar Ukombozi War. The O.E. ambush made little sense other than to send the message that every square meter of First World was going to be contested. By the time the skirmish was over, she'd lost two people. O.E. forces lost nearly two dozen, about what she'd predicted, considering her people knew the lunar ridges like the backs of their hands. Epyc Ro replayed the horror in her mind. People being blown to bits. The fervor of bloodlust. The violence, desperate and brutal, she had to inflict. And endure. She feared for her humanity.

"There is the person I was, the person I am, and the person I want to be." She *wondered about her future, her hoped-for self. If she had served her people.*

"You need to make peace with the fact that they are all the same person," Robin *said.*

"How?"

"Let them continue to be in conversation with one another. Never forget the mother and scholar you were, the warrior you have to be now, and . . ."

"And what?" Epyc Ro asked.

"The proud leader in Muungano you will be." Robin slung her Busta over her *shoulder and walked away. "You survived. That was service enough for today."*

When Epyc Ro came across the body, she knew it was her kill. Even in the heat of the moment, she remembered this figure coming into her sights and her squeezing the trigger. The body was positioned exactly as she imagined they would have fallen. Their arm draped over them, still clutching their rifle. Half their face sheared through by her pulse blast. No neat hole, more like a small fist cored its way through an eye socket and out the back of the skull. The inside of the helmet caked with scorched blood. She never became hardened to the loss of life. The arbitrariness of violence, the way war inflicted its brutality on bodies. Each death representing the snuffing of dreams, hope, and potential. Every casualty had a human face and a human cost.

Only this time it was a friend.

The Interstellar Alliance left Fela's body in a ditch for the Hellfighters to find. The setting sun pooled deep pockets of shadows in Fela's face. The scene had been staged for their benefit, as a message. A warning. The way Confederate monuments were once erected to declare the future they hoped for and worked toward. Epyc Ro couldn't bring herself to look at her commander in the face. Each of the HOVA had seen combat and knew its cost. Had cradled the dead of innocents. Friends. Enemies. The rest of the team studied her, took their cues from her in something akin to blank empathy, both allowing her a heartbeat to process the moment and offer their silent presence as support. Their calluses hadn't shielded them to complete indifference, only provided the armor to protect their remaining humanity. This was always the true test.

Once the shock and disbelief wore off, grief gave way to rage.

"Damn." Taking off her helmet, Robin dropped to her knees next to the commander's still form. "Damn, damn, damn."

"They just left her out here. In the open. Like she was trash not worth sweeping up." Anitra stood apart from the rest of them, never comforted by the power of presence, but always ready to comfort. But her internal engine revved, steadily hyping herself up, ready to storm the gates of the refinery herself. Slowly, she moved behind Robin, a gray curtain cordoning off her grief display. "Someone's gonna die. Bad."

"Bad as fuck," Epyc Ro cosigned in a whisper. The well of their grief drew her back into their circle. Huddled in shared condolence, allowing themselves the moment to fully absorb and feel their loss, since the realities of combat rarely granted such moments.

Ellis waited at a distance. Still reeling from the loss of Natan, they resonated with the idea of loss of one of their own and the grief the HOVA suffered. But this was the HOVA's time and understood that they had to find a measure of comfort with one another. Ellis simply needed something to do with their hands. They stood on point, on lookout, to allow the team room to mourn. Chandra remained in prophet mode: silent, listening, searching for patterns in whatever chatter she scanned. Determining intentions, probabilities, calculating locations and movements among the enemy's assets. She took the full measure of the scene, storing all the information in a catalog of carnage.

"Permission to wreck some shit?" Anitra crouched low, her navsuit caked in dirt and dust, baked in the terrain of the planet. She turned to study the encroaching ring of their faces.

"You got a plan?" Epyc Ro asked. Epyc Ro ached under the weight of guilt and failure. One by one, she took stock of the Hellfighters' wounds.

"I just said *wreck some shit.*"

"In Jesus's name," Robin said.

"I feel you, but . . . nah." Epyc Ro stood up—not having realized she'd sat down—struck by the sheer pointlessness of it all. The faces of her people, full of questions and doubt, looking to her with expectations. Their unit was diminished, no longer whole, and teetered on collapsing into a hole of grief and hurt. "We need a plan. We can't just act out in anger."

✳

Theirs was the first deep-space mission into uncharted territories. They knew there would be casualties. They would not always have the opportunity to mourn and retrieve their dead, but when they could, they would. Each gbeto carried with them their own burial disk. A flat disk of green metal. It was Epyc Ro's duty to attend the body. Igniting glow orbs to illuminate the cavern space. She held a moment of silence for her friend. The solemn ritual began with her removing her Oya elekes beads. She completed a scan of Fela's remains, genetic sequencing to confirm gen-ident, telemetry for autopsy records. The disk pack rose, glowed like a low-orbit sun, and reduced her body to ash and collected her remains.

When her duty was done, Epyc Ro consoled herself in the corner. She strung the sacred beads between her two hands like a necklace cat cradle. The silence was cold comfort in the moment. She had her people to take care of, not to mention getting Ellis and his crew to something approximating safety. Above all else, she was tired. A weariness she couldn't give into.

Robin shoved a plate in front of her. "Your belly sounds like it's mumbling the 'I Have a Dream' speech."

"Thanks." Epyc Ro couldn't remember the last time she ate.

"What's the plan?"

"I am the perfect balance of ratchetness and righteous anger." Anitra followed her in and plopped down on a large rock next to them.

"I know you are. We all are. Now that we have taken care of our own, we need to find those responsible."

"We start with what we do best. Infiltrate and disrupt." Epyc Ro allowed Fela's elekes to fall from her fingers into a pile. She shoveled in a mouthful of food. Slowly, her jaws stopped chewing, fearing that any further movement of her mouth would cause her to taste more of whatever assaulted her tongue. It tasted like bare feet that had run through a field and then danced in manure for good measure.

"Yeah, it'll make your breath smell like six months of bad decisions, raw ass, and garlic," Robin said, "but it's all we got."

Epyc Ro stabbed at her food with listless enthusiasm. She had the distinct feeling that a moment had passed. That same longing for the good old days, which could never be recaptured. She had achieved a measure of peace with the idea that she'd never get to lead her HOVA Hellfighters unit. Not the way she wanted. She replayed the events in her mind since planetfall. Her challenge of Fela's presence. The ambush. The Mzisoh. The Lei'den. The firefight. The *Hughes*. Fela's capture. Their failed rescue. Fela's body. She searched for any lesson to help in a future skirmish.

"It's not your fault." Robin rested a heavy hand on her shoulder.

"I don't think you're in a position to understand or judge what I'm feeling!" Epyc Ro snapped. Lowering her head, she added, "I'm not entirely sure either."

The last few days were a crucible, refining a process she was already on. All the people she knew, grew up with, and cared about were on the other side of the Orun Gate. All that remained of the family she chose were the three women in the room. Those relationships were life for her, but they were changing. She was changing. The woman they knew, she was sloughing off, an unwanted skin in search of something new. She didn't know who she'd be at the end of her journey, only that she had to let go of their expectations and be open to who she'd become. And part of her was terrified at the prospect.

"Well, if you don't mind company, I don't mind walking alongside you while you figure things out." Robin sat down next to her. "It's all over your emi. The blame. The guilt."

"We failed. I failed. Our mission, our community . . ." Epyc Ro's voice spiraled into something dispirited.

"Don't do this to yourself, Ro. We can't afford to lose you, too."

"We've lost our ship and any way to return home. And now I'm in charge of a collection of walking wounded."

"Is that what we are?" Robin asked.

"No, I meant—"

"I know what you meant. And I don't care. No one planned for this scenario. But we adapt. We improvise. We pay attention to the moment. That's how we get through. That's the Muungano way."

"There were some aspects of Muungano's ways that were steeped in traditions that now made little sense once we find ourselves so removed from the context of a story." Epyc Ro stabbed at her plate of food. "They ossify, the old ways becoming outdated ideas; the rituals little more than empty gestures."

"What do you propose?"

Epyc Ro stared at the HOVA insignia on her shoulder. "Maybe it's time for a new way of doing things. Perhaps it was time to withdraw from the entirety of it."

"What, like quit Muungano?"

"No. The HOVA."

Epyc Ro took out her panga blade and sliced the HOVA insignia from her navsuit. She cradled it in her hands. "The *Hughes,* Muungano, our way of life, were all gone. The HOVA Hellfighters are no more. For what comes next, I don't think I'll be able to live up to the Muungano ideals. I will have to find a new way home."

She tossed the patch into the campfire flames. Robin watched the patch blacken and shrivel before pulling out her own panga and cutting off her patch. By the time she tossed hers into the fire, another landed on top of it. When she looked up, Chandra rubbed her head and back to comfort her.

"What're y'all doing?" Anitra wandered over.

"Stripping ourselves out of the HOVA," Robin said.

"I'm down." Anitra took off her mesh shirt and tossed it in the flames.

"Shit, Anitra, we just burning our HOVA patches." Robin snatched it from the fire, swatting out any sparking flames.

"When I commit, I commit." Anitra slipped the smoldering mesh back on.

"If we're not HOVA no more, who are we?" Robin asked.

"I don't know yet," Epyc Ro said. "We need to reclaim our independence. Find out who we are."

"A name change, then. Something calling who we're meant to be into being. Name what we want to manifest in the world."

"Is there going to be a ritual? You know how we love a good ritual," Anitra said.

Epyc Ro set her plate down. Her hand brushed the elekes. She stood and signaled for Robin to join her. Using both hands to cup the beads, she presented them to Robin.

"Cap'n?" Robin asked.

"Each set of elekes have to go through a process before they are received.

These beads were made with love and passion. By someone who intended them for Fela. She's no longer here, but we carry her with us." Epyc Ro raised the disk pack. "I am keeper of her remains. But I need a second to carry her spirit with us. We have been through the fire. We continue her journey alongside her, into the darkness, possibly into death. But we travel together, as sisters. Will you accompany your sisters?"

"I will." Robin received the elekes.

"Who will accompany each of us? To aid and guide. To be pillars and examples."

"Well . . . shit. I do." Anitra took Robin's side.

<Yes.> Chandra rose to move next to Epyc Ro.

Epyc Ro felt the resurgent music in her breast, a melody that played out to her fingertips. A renewal, of purpose and being, with her sisters. And with it came a new perspective.

"I don't know if the moment's past or nah, but the real question I have is: Do I get to blow shit up?" Anitra asked.

"We're going to take the fight back to them, commandeer an Interstellar Alliance vessel, and . . . ," Epyc Ro said.

". . . get the hell off this planet," Robin finished.

"Exactly. And heaven help anyone who gets in our way."

"So we about to become space pirates?" Anitra asked. "I'm down as fuck."

❋

Eshu's desert had a dangerous beauty to it. Its sands a strange shade of yellow, sprayed about with a child's enthusiasm. Harsh, hostile, a barren stretch punctuated by bursts of mountains or gorges. The occasional trail of vegetation on arid landscapes. Ominous clouds obscured the moon, reducing the mountains to stark shadows. The road leading up to the facility remained abandoned, dark and empty as a corpse's eye. A bloated tick on the desert skin, the refining facility sat, fat and still.

No matter how she strained to hear, Epyc Ro heard only their own haggard breathing. The rear of the facility bustled with activity. Ships loaded and boarded, the Interstellar Alliance forces scrambling to move out despite their advantage. Only a skeleton crew patrolled the area. At its rear, smaller ships launched into space with regularity. The Interstellar Alliance prepared for complete disembarkment. They wouldn't be leaving for long. Having taken the full measure of the Mzisoh, they would call for support forces to occupy and strip-mine their world. She couldn't leave the Mzisoh alone against this enemy.

"Something isn't right," Epyc Ro said.

"Trap?" Robin asked.

"No, that's not the vibe I get." Epyc Ro mulled over the possibilities. The road remained deserted. No creatures stirred. No insects chirped. The checkpoint posts were abandoned. A solitary guard strolled this side of the building.

Chandra's sensor sweep turned up little by way of security. <It's simply not a good situation. Look at the way they are bunched up. The camp is thick with patrols.>

"Picking our way through the patrols is going to be a bitch," Epyc Ro said.

"Being a bitch is what we do best," Anitra said.

"There's no way we can get in, explore the terrain, and get ghost without raising an alarm. We'd never make it back to the extraction point," Robin said.

"I don't see the problem. It looks like a brief run and we're free," Ellis said.

"Yeah, but you're barely out of whatever passes for diapers around here. So your opinion don't count." Anitra glanced back at them. "I'm just fucking with you, big dog."

"A single soldier could slip in unnoticed and wreak havoc, opening a door for a small group." Epyc Ro kept surveying the target. "Anitra, you up."

"I'm on it." Anitra slid her navsuit helmet into place and hopped over the barricade of stone down the rocky slope.

"We can't just wait here." With the impatience of youth, Ellis's loyalty was to their family, their tribe, not either of these two invading interlopers, be they ally or enemy. "We should've gone in all at once."

"This is our show and we're waiting on Anitra to clear a path for us." Epyc Ro turned to them, her voice not inviting debate. She needed to be straight with them. "The only reason this mission is remotely viable is because the Interstellar Alliance is pulling up stakes. Otherwise, we are outgunned, outmanned, and outmaneuvered. But our biggest advantage is they lack heart. That's been shown in every encounter. So you'll do things our way or you can leave."

"Anitra can't go it alone." Something more than concern thickened Ellis's voice.

Epyc Ro stared at them, managing not to roll her eyes in annoyance. Her mood and focus left no room for adolescent pining.

"She'll get us in. You've obviously not seen an Anitra in the wild." Robin summoned the holovid feed of Chandra's drone tracking Anitra's movement. She started narrating the action in a low baritone. "Observe how she approaches the guard. Notice how she slides up to them unseen and unheard. How she takes out the first guard before the other even knows there's a problem."

The silent projection showed Anitra grabbing the nearest alien, covering their mouth, and dragging them into the shadows to subdue them. Even had the sound been available, her fluid movements would've produced no noise. Robin continued her narration.

"Once the remaining guard notices her, only because she wants him to, she gauges their interest in what Ugenini scientists refer to as *some of that smoke*. The guard goes against all notions of common sense, trying to get big on her, then attempting to grapple with her like they're a church deacon who likes to grip hands way too tight in a handshake."

Anitra opened her arms as if inviting an embrace. For a moment, the guard puffed up but quickly opted to throw a blade at her.

"An Anitra shifts into a mode commonly referred to as *a'ight then*. She's mad now. You can tell by her new posture and, well, that gesture in particular, that she's just asked him to 'do that again.' And"—Robin paused—"yes, notice how she proceeds to take her shoe to beat him into unconsciousness. A now-successful Anitra prepares to wave us into position."

Anitra scurried about, planting charges around the facility and some of the parked vehicles. Positioning herself away from their entry point, she climbed up an embankment of stones and set up her nest. Little more than a shadow, Anitra motioned to the enemy positions. Sweat poured down her despite the nanomesh filter layers, her DMX-3000 ready to engage the enemy. She opened fire. Pulse charges erupted, stirring the camp. It was time for their game faces to be put back on.

"Follow me." Epyc Ro waved them forward.

The chaos provided excellent cover for Epyc Ro and her team to move in unnoticed. The trail ran over rough terrain with chunks of shale protruding with its razored edges. They negotiated the steep embankment, with Epyc Ro slipping several times along the scree, but reaching out to steady herself. The rest of the squad darted around the perimeter. Despite the cuts and scrapes on the way down, they maintained noise and light discipline. All the hastily constructed adjoining structures and buildings, spare towers and hangars, formed a simple shell. The larger buildings grouped around an open square in a pattern her mind registered as familiar. By the time they reached the door, the unit stacked up in breach formation behind Epyc Ro. On her count, they rushed in, their loud assault designed to startle and panic. As Epyc Ro, Robin, and Ellis entered, Chandra remained in cover by the entrance to direct drone strikes to guard their rear. They swept down the hallway to reach the hangar bay. Weapons hot, they cleared the corridor and adjoining rooms with each step. Epyc Ro watched for reinforcements. Robin set charges at each juncture. They would bring an end to this chamber of horrors.

They rounded a corner and stopped short. A wide room brightly lit with floating screens filled with data streams and linkage holovids on display. In the wide array of an interrupted work space, the afterimage of Fela's assassination vanished.

"This what we here for?" Epyc Ro asked.

<Yes.> Chandra jacked in, scanning and copying data as fast as she could.

Two Lei'den CO/IN soldiers, led by a woman in white, streamed into the room. She canceled several projections with a sweep of her hand. She was the kind of woman who rolled up to a party, drink in hand, not quite realizing she'd crashed a church service. Everyone froze. She stared at Epyc Ro with the nonplussed tilt of her head, taking in the scene with languid interest. Her sleeves rolled up, she drew herself up, slow and stiff as if nursing an aching bruise. Her fist raised to halt any fire from her team.

Hesitating just enough to allow her curiosity room to roam, Epyc Ro raised her fist. Matching the woman's demonstration of calm and control. Besides, trusting her team's weapon discipline, she strode toward the woman knowing that her people had her back should anything untoward go down. The tension percolated but didn't rise to the timbre of an awkward silence. Just two women out for a night on the town with their friends, waiting to see if anything interesting jumped off.

"You got what you need?" Epyc Ro kept her weapon trained on the new figures.

<Clearance codes and anything else I could scan before she activated her data worm to erase everything.>

"I don't believe we've had the pleasure. My name is Car'Annie." She extended her hand.

Running out of patience, Epyc Ro wasn't in the mood to play any games. "Are you the one in charge?"

"In a way. Your merry band of misfits is to be commended. You've made quite a mess of our operation." Car'Annie swept her platinum-blond hair out of her face, a woman used to her looks easing her way through life.

"So you were the one who orchestrated our commander's murder." A level of menace filled Epyc Ro's voice so thoroughly, even her own people took half a step backward.

"Times of war make for a testing of a people's moral compass." Car'Annie bristled. "I suspect there's only one way for this encounter to end."

"I suspect." Epyc Ro tightened her grip on her talon.

Car'Annie withdrew a hand weapon. She whirred and shot the guard on her right and then the left before dropping the weapon and raising her hands before the bodies hit the ground. "I'm a defenseless prisoner now. If I'm to be tried, let me be judged. If your way is indeed superior to ours."

Epyc Ro's mouth twisted with disgust. "Those were your own people."

"They were. Now it's just me." Car'Annie smirked as if hearing a joke only she got. "We could be allies."

The entire setup disturbed her. Epyc Ro waved her people in closer. "What were you hoping? We'd 'capture' you, you embed yourself in the alliance, and you would deliver a pocketful of misinformation to distract us."

"I hate me some fake-ass allies," Robin said.

"Don't get me wrong." Epyc Ro cleared the weapons from the dead soldiers. "In some ways, I respect how the CO/IN units do their business. Come out of nowhere, strike hard. No fucks to give."

"And disappear when you're done. I like a tidy operation," Robin added.

Epyc Ro patted Car'Annie down for more weapons, glyphs, or data skimmers. "You know what our merry little band of misfits have in common?"

"Oppositional defiance disorder?" Car'Annie asked.

"We don't let rules—don't matter if they're orders, theology, or laws—keep us from doing what's right. Your CO/IN units are filled with soldiers who may swear allegiance to the Interstellar Alliance. And more than a few who simply like being cruel." Epyc Ro signaled for Chandra to do a scan for implants. After studying the woman in grim appraisal, Chandra waved Robin over.

"You dress up your outlaws in pretty-sounding rhetoric, but deep inside, you know we're the same way." Car'Annie tracked Robin's movement once the gbeto gathered her complete attention by producing her panga blade. Robin jammed her blade into the woman's left scapula. Chandra directed her incision. Car'Annie grunted without further comment. Satisfied, Robin fished her finger into the wound and removed a data fiche, little more than a thread, but it could relay her position and other data. Chandra handed it to Epyc Ro.

"Maybe, but we don't revel in what we do. We're simply good at it." The captain held the strand up to her eye. "We'll have to do this the hard way."

"That's the way we do," Robin said.

"Chandra, you got her?" Epyc Ro said.

Chandra glared at the woman before fastening Car'Annie's hands behind her back with fashioned cuffs.

"Your continued resistance is only hurting what could be the new stellar federation," Car'Annie said.

"Look here, man-bun Becky," Robin said. "You done earned the look from Chandra. That was the look that said, 'You got one more time, then I will kick you straight in your sunken place.'"

"Let's get out of here," Epyc Ro announced.

They doubled back down the hallways they came. The corridors began to look the same. Epyc Ro could think only of the torture rooms of the other housing unit. The echoes of screams scratching at the back of her mind. She slowed as they neared their exit.

"It doesn't even matter if you kill me. CO/IN units are ready to sacrifice anything for the sake of their mission," Car'Annie said.

"You ain't worth the wave your voice travels on," Epyc Ro said. "Anitra, you got us?"

"You know it," the disembodied voice said through Chandra's commlink. "You look mighty good through the lens of a twenty-five-times zoom. You have a group of fine folks converging on your position."

"I figured as much." Epyc Ro crushed the data fiche under her heel. "Can you do me a solid and welcome these fine folks to our party?"

The nearest three Lei'den guards to their position dropped under Anitra's sniper fire. They scrambled for cover, scanning for the position of the sniper. Anitra's EVM doubled as her camouflage, rendering her invisible to all manner of sensor telemetry. The soldiers had little concept of how her DMX-3000's AI operated in perfect tandem with her instincts to guide her shots.

A few moments later, explosions ripped along their landing strips. Flames shot into the sky, a barreling conflagration, taking out the few remaining vehicles on their side of the building.

Epyc Ro smiled. Debris pelted her face. She turned to figure out the source, when another volley of shells rippled the tarmac. She turned to Chandra. Her mouth moved, but no sound came out. Epyc Ro feared that her hearing might be fading. Chandra gestured to the side. A wide beam of light pierced the thick darkness. The next explosion knocked Epyc Ro from her feet. Darkness washed over her.

Chandra's face came into focus above her. Her cheeks smeared with blood. The heavy machinery near her obscured by a halo of smoke. All sound rushed at Epyc Ro at the same time. A wall of noise buffeting her from all sides. The world lost its equilibrium in a staccato burst of volley weapons.

Chandra placed a hand on either side of Epyc Ro's head and shrank her signal field.

Signals screamed at one another. Epyc Ro had been caught in Chandra's channel scans. She'd been overloaded with signal bursts, and her containment field lost integrity, allowing Epyc Ro in for a moment. That was what her world sounded like at all times.

Her team had taken several hits. Nothing directed or focused. Just scattershot fire, but the enemy had gotten lucky. Once the explosions lit up their positions, it was easier to lock on to them.

"This plan's gone to shit. Go, go, go!" Epyc Ro yelled.

"Captain, I'm hit." A large shard of metal protruded from Robin's calf. Blood mixed with the dirt beneath her.

"Hang on." Epyc Ro charged toward her. She leapt over a burning hedge of metal and slid into position next to her. She checked Robin's wound. With no time to be gentle, she ripped the shard out. Biotelemetry indicated nothing too damaged. She sealed the wound with a field pack, used to numb and fill wounds before re-sheathing her nanomesh. "We gotta go."

Robin struggled to her feet. Testing her leg with her weight, she nodded before Epyc Ro could ask her about how she felt.

Anitra stood tall, off to the side, firing at incoming troops. Charge fire spit up all around her, but she refused to duck or seek cover. A madwoman laughing hysterically. Flames backlit her. She laid down cover for Ellis to guide the Mzisoh across the bay.

"They're still coming at us from all sides," Robin said.

"Death blossom?" Epyc Ro asked.

"I hate that you get so excited by that prospect."

"Anitra, keep our guest in your scope. Chandra, you want to lay down the beat for us to dance to?"

Chandra launched suppression fire as Epyc Ro and Robin charged toward the remaining soldiers. A weapon in each hand, the pair continued to fire. Once they neared the center of the opposing troops, they slammed against each other. Their arms interlocking as they moved, they spun back-to-back in a tight circle while continuing to fire a constant barrage in all directions. Bodies dropped. No time to think. Or aim. Only move and fire, hoping that this deep into the enemy's ranks, the designated shapes were all hostile combatants. Epyc Ro and Robin locked in a choreographed ballet of talon fire and rhythm. A spiral of limbs and a single beating rhythm. At the empty whir of their drained batteries, they glanced about. What few Lei'den troops remained were in full retreat. Anitra dropped a straggler without a single shot, causing the rest to scurry away faster. She climbed down from her perch. Handing Epyc Ro, Robin, and Chandra their EVM units, her eyes fixed on Car'Annie with an uncanny precision that dared the woman to break eye contact. Cold and still. Closing one eye partway, Anitra squinted, training Car'Annie in her weapon sights.

"Quit looking at me like that!" Car'Annie squirmed under the unsettling weight of being in the gaze of someone trained to extinguish her life without a second's thought. "You can judge me when you've faced the things I've had to face and done better."

"Nah, we'll judge you now." Epyc Ro shoved her forward. "We'll need your authorization to board the ship."

The ship wasn't the size of a Muungano research ship. More freighter than battle cruiser, it was larger than several combined Saqqaras or drop ships. A long, slender cylinder, its molybdenum-like alloy was both lighter and strong. The corrugated molybdenum shielding, sheet armor plating, didn't gleam in the dim light. Powerful engines, warship grade, formed the bulk of its underside and rear, its design appeared to favor quick takeoffs and jumps.

"I . . . ," Car'Annie began her protest.

"Does she have to be conscious to provide it?" Anitra asked.

"We'll find out shortly." Robin closed in on her.

"Fine." Car'Annie opened the door. "What are you going to do with me? You've got what you want."

"Nothing," Epyc Ro said.

"Nothing?" Robin and Anitra turned toward her.

"She's right. We aren't in a position to judge her. Anitra, could you finish the cleanup of the base?"

Anitra punched a code into her wrist comm. Explosions erupted all around the compound. Ellis's troops climbed down from the desert basin, guided by the light from the pyres of machinery. The cloaked figures scurried quickly, not wanting to be caught exposed in the open and sensing that their journey neared its end. Mothers clutched their young to them, stilling the scared mewls as much as possible. Mzisoh soldiers stripped the bodies of the fallen Interstellar Alliance soldiers of any weapons and gear.

"Let's pull out. We have a ship to commandeer," Epyc Ro said. "Ellis, get your people somewhere safe. The CO/IN may be gone for now, but they may regroup and return in force. I don't want your people nearby when they do."

"Captain?" Ellis wiped caked dirt from their forehead, leaving a thick gray grime. "I don't have a patch, but if you'll have me, I will go where you go."

"We have no idea where we're going." Epyc Ro sensed a lingering hesitation, which filled her with caution.

"Yes, but your travels will take you out there." Ellis pointed to the stars. "I want to be a part of that."

"Are you sure?"

"No." Ellis gestured to his people. "My home is here. But my heart, my heart wants to explore."

"All right, come on, then," Anitra said. "That's as sure as any of us ever get anyway."

"What about her?" Robin pointed toward Car'Annie.

A group of Mzisoh soldiers neared. Their hoods lowered over their foreheads, leaving little more than slits exposing their eyes. The stained cloaks made dark under the glow of the moon. For the first time, Car'Annie's face lost its veneer of calm control. Each Mzisoh face bored into her, their hate and anger a near tangible thing buffeting her. She backed away from them, stopping once she bumped into the captain.

Epyc Ro shoved Car'Annie out and slammed the door behind her. "Let's go."

Epyc Ro and Robin took the flight seats and strapped themselves in. Epyc Ro's eyes adjusted to the faint green illumination of the instrument panel. After a moment of study, she intuited a feel for the layout of the instrumentation. Not too different from the ships she trained in as a part of the HOVA's joint military exercises with the O.E.

"Not a lot of room in the cockpit," Epyc Ro said.

"Ain't we got a better name for this than that by now?"

"It's too small to be any use, though I bet the designers thought it was huge in their hands."

"Cockpit it is." Robin scanned the motherboard. "Controls look standard."

"It does," Epyc Ro hunched over them. "Go through prelaunch sequence."

The engines primed, the ship loomed over the gathered Mzisoh, its wings casting a shadow over them. The ship took off with a powerful rush. Careening upward in a tottering trajectory, their flight course rocked in fits and starts as Epyc Ro and Robin got used to the navigation system. The wings began to retract as the ship entered the upper atmosphere. It banked over the horizon, ready to leave the planet behind them.

"How's it look back there?" Epyc Ro asked.

"This thing's awkward as hell. It was designed for lots of cargo. All sorts of bays."

"Transport ship?"

"A well-armed one. With powerful engines, though it maneuvers for shit," Robin said.

"Everything has a trade-off."

"We have a go. I have . . ." Robin rechecked her instruments. "Five CO/IN ships. Three of them warships."

Their ship climbed through Eshu's atmosphere. The larger vessel withstood the buffeting of the atmospheric forces much better than the *Hughes* did when it dropped them. The orangish sky gave way to night. And with that, they found themselves back in space. As soon as they did, their viewer filled with images of starships.

Epyc Ro expected the firing to start immediately. A barrage of laser blasts or whatever weapons the Lei'den's CO/IN forces used. Their cruiser exploding in a ball of fire and scattered debris. The story of the HOVA reaching its violent end.

"They expecting us?" Anitra shouted from the rear.

"Or investigating the party favors you just shot off down there," Robin said.

"Quantum drive operational?" Epyc Ro asked.

"Yes. Not as good as our protophobic engines, but . . ." Robin continued to run diagnostics, familiarizing herself with the systems as she went.

"We can do upgrades later."

"This drive might be better suited for combat. Especially close range." Anitra ran her hand along some power conduits.

"Yeah, we don't seem to have much of a choice on that front. Weapons systems?" Epyc Ro settled into the captain's seat.

"Magnetic rail guns," Robin said.

"Shit," Anitra said. "We bump into the only species who doesn't use energy weapons or some other futuristic shit?"

"Lasers are off line," Robin said.

"Well, at least we have them." Epyc Ro activated the thrusters. "Prepare for a jump. Chandra, begin the calculations and forward the protocols to Robin for my countdown."

"What? We have to clear the atmosphere. And at the rate they're closing in, it's not going to leave a lot of room for error," Robin said.

The ships orbited Eshu, their velocity already in sync with the rotation of the planet. They weren't going to outmaneuver them by launching in the opposite direction. This was a battle of math. Their orbit elongated into an ellipse, needing it to stretch out to detach from orbit. Then they could punch the quantum drives. But Eshu needed to be at the aphelion for such a maneuver to work. They needed to buy some time. Every second counted.

"Then double-check your math." Anitra strapped herself in. "You'd better carry the one or some shit. Twice."

<Destination?> Chandra began her calculations. If she was frantic, scared, or nervous, her affect didn't betray her.

"Anywhere but here," Epyc Ro said.

"Coordinates entered. On your command." Robin punched in the course.

"Deflectors on maximum," Epyc Ro said.

"Why are our deflectors ever *not* on maximum?" Anitra asked.

"To conserve power," Robin said.

"Look, I can chip in on the power bill if it will keep the shields up all the time!" Anitra yelled.

"On my mark," Epyc Ro cried out. "Put us on an intercept course."

"Cap'n?" Robin asked.

"We testing out these rail guns?" Anitra asked.

"Now's as good a time. Don't target. We don't want them detecting a weapons lock," Epyc Ro said.

"What, I'm firing by hand?"

"We'll get you in close enough for good shots. We only need to buy some time." Robin checked her scanner, but glanced over her shoulder to say, "Think of them as a really long DMX."

<Communication coming in. They want our ident code.>

"Open a channel."

"Cap'n?" Robin glanced at her.

The grim set of Epyc Ro's jaw was her only response.

"Channel open, it is." Robin opened the comms.

"Identify yourself," a voice demanded.

"This is Captain Epyc Ro Morgan. Formerly of the Muungano HOVA brigade known as the Hellfighters. Back on O.E., our unit was named for the famed Harlem Hellfighters, a regiment of the New York national guardsmen. They were one of the most decorated units and were given to the French infantry. They spent more time in combat than any other American unit in World War I. However, before then, in Alkebulan, there was an all-female military regiment of the Kingdom of Dahomey called the Mino. One of their battalions was known as the Reapers. Do you want to know who we are? That is who we are now. Anitra, introduce us properly."

The shots burst in a wild spray. To her mind, everything moved in slow, sweeping arcs, their positions splayed on monitors and view screens, until they passed up close and personal. Anitra continued firing a rapid succession of shots. The patterns appeared curved since the ballistics were fired from a position they were no longer in. Projectiles peppered the outer hull. Targeting nothing, hoping that something in the hailstorm would hit something vital or pierce the hull. Shut down a vital system or rupture something for rapid decompression. The CO/IN ships now reminded her of long caskets.

The CO/IN ships veered off in evasive action, swinging around to target their ship. The Reapers' whole ship shook. Nothing good happened when equipment functioned like that. They'd taken a few hits. The lights fluttered in indecision whether to wink out or not. A faint smell of fire wafted for an instant before internal suppression systems snuffed it. The ship spun in an attempt to keep the heaviest shielding in front of their weapons fire. The crew lurched about, the gravitational system already taxed, sending Robin bouncing against the floor and walls. She rose, still clutching Fela's elekes.

Their new course cleared out more space for the Reapers' ship to maneuver. Chandra shouted something indistinct. But she was shouting so Epyc Ro knew. The CO/IN had a ship full of computing AI. The Reapers had Chandra. Epyc Ro would take that bet every time.

"Mark!" Epyc Ro shouted.

Robin punched the command. A thrum shot through the ship. She felt the acceleration of the engines. She swore she felt the sensation of moving forward, but knew it was an illusion of motion. The universe slowed down. As the ship lurched, space elongated. Light bent, space shimmered. Before they could gather their bearing, another vibration coursed through the ship. Almost a counterwave. The stars reconfigured about them. They were in a new sector. Anitra retched in the corner. Ellis held her hair back.

"Any sign of the ships?" Epyc Ro asked.

"No pursuit. Yet." Robin adjusted the restraints on her seat, which protected them from the intense gravity. "Reapers, eh?"

"You like the designation?"

"I'll miss the HOVA Hellfighters."

"So will I." Epyc Ro stared out the view port. "But I look forward to seeing what story the Reapers will write."

"You need a shower." A smile creased Robin's face.

"Six showers!" Anitra yelled from her amen corner.

"And sleep," Robin said.

<And then what?> Chandra asked, and she and they all turned to their captain.

Epyc Ro stared into the blackness of her view port. So many stars, so much potential. She chewed on her lower lip. Her crew had to adjust. Learn who they were and what they were going to be about. They had to mourn. They had to heal. It would be a long, difficult journey. "We regroup. And once we're ready, we take the fight back to the Interstellar Alliance . . . and finish what they started."

Epyc Ro sat back in the captain's seat and took in the sweep of stars.

27

MAULANA BUHARI
The Dreaming City

The Ijo chamber thrums with the gathered crowds. Folks fill all the available seats and stand in the aisles, crowding the entrances. The energy radiates across the Dreaming City. The assembly is live-linked, the holovid of the events data-streamed everywhere in Muungano.

The crowd in the library assembly chamber bustles with the kind of intense energy reserved for matters of high occasion. Only two times have I heard tell of its murmurs reaching such a crescendo echoing throughout the entire Dreaming City like this: the signing of the treaty ending the Lunar Ukombozi War and the choosing of Xola for the first Camara of Muungano. The chatter's a mix of excitement and nervousness. Whorls of people gather in factions to negotiate their votes in informal caucus. What cannot be picked up is the nervous murmurs among the debates.

Wachiru waits with a group of young men, Ezeji among them, near the central table. The low-floating light globes illuminate them with a backlit tinge, making them appear like poorly rendered projections. They whisper, drawing up a game plan. Selamault studies her son. Worried about the toll leadership might take on him. She passes me without comment and makes her way to the table. I suspect the reason for her silence. When she meets my eyes, she turns away, confirming it.

I am to be the next Camara.

As a Black Dove, of the line of oracles, the Libyan Sibyls, Selamault has seen it in her visions. Though she'd said nothing to me, I can tell from the way she avoids eye contact whenever we encounter each other. I will need her on my side. Now is the time to be building relationships. I cannot serve my people alone.

Surveying the room, the role of Camara comes down to me and Wachiru. I take the dais lightly and read the room. The people are—we are—tired of waiting. We have no interest in bowing and scraping our way to appeal to O.E.'s better angels. We are Muungano. We are strong. And it is time the universe hears that.

"Who should be the voice that speaks to them on behalf of Muungano?" Selamault said. "It's time. Then let us be about the business of the community."

And the room stills to something close to silence. There is a power to the silence, a reverence of the moment.

"Freedom is what it means to be human." Bayard steps up, making his play right off the top.

The voice of any member of Muungano may be heard in the Ijo. His entry, though not entirely unexpected, complicates matters. A debate between Wachiru and myself represents two clear, distinct paths. Bayard is the voice of compromise. Those unwilling to make a clear decision could find him the safe option. I am many things; safe is not one of them.

"That was the message we took, that core tenet, had to be central. Understanding that evil is systemic and that no matter what binds us—a destroyed civilization, cruel leaders, or the tyranny of technology—can be a means of oppression.

"Either we aren't completely there yet, we have to continue to be vigilant and ready to fight injustice. We have to see where God is at work and join in. Continue the fight for liberation of people. I simply cling to a hope, an ever-future hope, of justice and freedom."

"The stories that shape your faith would have us be patient, ever looking to tomorrow, for us to find justice and freedom. That day was yesterday," I say.

"We are a people of faith. And a people of stories. The overarching story always resonated with us. How an ancient people rose up to decry oppressive powers. Brought out of slavery in an exodus, only to wander in a desert for generations. When they found their promised land, they were exiled in a land not their own. Stripped of their language, their culture, and their God. Always living in hope of a future exaltation. Too many want to return to Egypt rather than enter the promised land. True freedom is more than creating a comfortable life within the systems of oppression."

"Speak plain, Bayard, or quit speaking," I say, not hiding my bored impatience with his pontifications.

"You lack the necessary spirit to speak for us. You are in a dark place, and your voice would threaten to carry us all there with you."

"Our battle is not yet over. I fear it has just begun." I turn to the Ijo. "Our liberation, our awakening, our restoration are all a part of our journey from colonization. And at its heart, colonization is an act of violence that only understands violence . . . and may require violence to throw off its shackles once and for all. I'm not saying that I want war, only that we should prepare for it."

Wachiru approaches the dais. He lifts his chin, the casual kind of quick tick he used when he performed to make sure his voice reached every corner of the room. "Muungano is about a culture. What we use to maintain our social fabric. Who we are as a people. Our beliefs. Our ideas. Our work continues. We impact the spaces we're in. Model agency for others. When other communities face challenges, where do they turn? To us. We're ambassadors of a better way. And we need to live up to that."

In him, I hear his father's voice. But the time for Xola has passed. "You advocate for respectability in a time of war."

"That's not what we said. We're about building relationships as our primary strategy. First, we need to reestablish relationships with one another. The very idea of a Night Train should be ludicrous. We should be able to talk to and reach our own. Second, we establish authentic relationships with other communities. All other communities. No one should be off the table. In the face of challenges, we can't lose sight of the fact that we do transformative work. War is easy. Transformation, now that's the motherfucker right there." Wachiru bobs to his own internal beat, almost unaware of the chorus of approvals he receives.

Waiting for the cries of support to die down, I circle the table before speaking again. "Relationship on their terms I have no interest in. We do not long for them or their ways. They want us to be reasonable. To seek the values . . . of their dream. Values they aspired to, but never lived out. What they actually want is to not be knocked from their place of comfort. They want convenient discourse. But to have any discourse, there'd have to be a meeting of the minds. But if one starts from a place of our dehumanization, halfway doesn't make us whole. To believe otherwise is the way of dreamers and madmen."

"Which do you call me?" Wachiru asks.

"I call you what you are: not ready." Mindful of who he is and what he represents, I near him. "In fact, I'd go so far to say that you are the voice Muungano needs to walk us into the future. One day. However, today—right now—the community requires the voice of experience and . . ."

". . . wisdom?" Wachiru doesn't hide his sarcasm.

"Pragmatism. We've done things the Adisa way for a long time. Where has that gotten us?"

"You walk a dangerous path. Yours are not the Muungano way."

"Ways change. Do not make the same mistake O.E. does thinking that our way of moving through the world being different marks us as weak. We change with the times and the circumstances." These are uncertain times. The only way through is by carving to the heart of their doubts. Expose their fears for what they are: chains. "I don't have Wachiru's gift of reading people's sabhu or Bayard's for probing the spirit, but my emi knows the way of battle. There are difficult choices to be made in the coming days. Sacrifices we will have to call on our people to make as we move forward. We need the voice of righteous anger, not that of a legacy dilettante who'd rather play music than lead his people."

"Maulana." Selamault's cautioning tone rings like a warning shot. One I choose to ignore.

You failed Fela. You failed all of us, I hear Wachiru say.

I keep digging at Wachiru. I know beneath his calm façade, the peace he holds on to through his music, there is anger. And doubt. And pain. "Someone more interested in being an overseer and dancing for other people's entertainment."

Wachiru shoots up, ready to throw hands. Jaha steps between us. She fashions her pehla stick into a staff and stamps it once. I smile, a muscle memory testing itself.

"That is quite enough," Selamault says. "Maulana, that was uncalled for, out of line, disrespectful, and unbecoming of one who claims to want to serve our people."

"I'm . . ." I face Wachiru. His anger rages in pure reflection of my own. Disapproving frowns crease many a forehead. It was a gamble, I tell myself. That they needed to see my spark, the same energy I'd keep to confront O.E. and LISC. The voice in my mind quiets, more than satisfied. But I teeter on losing the room and whatever ground I've gained. No, that's a political calculation. I grieve for him and all he's been through. Hurt is the language we speak too well. "I make no excuse for my passion. But . . . I stand before you completely ashamed. You did not deserve that."

Wachiru's stance softens, but only slightly. "You're not in a good place. You are far from whole. All of us are. But we can't let that take us down dark roads."

"My righteous anger gives me a clarity. And yet I also know how to heed the wisdom of my elders." I bow before Selamault. "I will serve with the strength of our culture. I am many things, but I'm not a foolish man. I'd be foolish to want to lead without Wachiru's tempering voice. I'd be foolish to want to lead without the spiritual counsel of Bayard. I'd be foolish to want to lead without the institutional memory of Jaha. I'd be foolish to want to lead without your wisdom, Selamault. I'd be foolish to want to lead without the blessing of this council.

"All we want is to live free and in peace. We are just so tired of waiting. We are tired of being attacked, shouldering the brunt of atrocities, because we dare want to exist. We are tired and impatient and we say, 'No more,'" I say without heat or venom, only the pride Muungano instilled. In each of us. "Muungano was founded by those who turned their backs on the past and sought only the future. It was not enough for us to leave O.E. That was just our immediate escape from the grip and machinations of the enslaver. But we cannot forget those who were left behind. We did a disservice to them. We explorers of the future, carving out a new frontier of thought and culture, did not reach back to bring others to our shores. We left them in exile." I meet Bayard's eye in acknowledgment. "Our work is not done until each and every weusi, each and every citizen on O.E., is free. Freedom must be inclusive as well as indivisible. The ways of O.E. no longer matter to us. Their look does not cause me to avert my eyes. The sound of their voice does not cow me in terror. Their presence does not bother me. Everyone in Muungano is a revolutionary. Our ideas are the revolution. But if need be, if O.E. needs reminding, we have not forgotten the ways of war, especially in the defense of our own. Our home. Our way of life."

Something shifts in Wachiru. He reads the energy of the room. Fixing his mouth, he steps down from the dais. The wave of cheers and chanting begins in earnest.

Maulana. Maulana. Maulana.

✸

The gbedu drums' rhythm pulses in my temples. I request for Selamault to accompany me out to the gathering of the full Ijo, through the pressing crowd, down toward the central corridor. Hands stretch to reach me, greet me as their brother and friend. Their Camara.

Bayard takes center stage. "May I have your attention."

"You have my attention!" the crowd cries out in response.

Bayard moves with a stiff formality, offering a vague genuflection before Selamault and Jaha. "We call upon our elders, whose wisdom we seek in our endeavors. I ask your permission to commence."

"Granted," Jaha says and strikes the ground once with her staff.

With a slow nod, Selamault gives her assent.

With both hands, Bayard raises the kikombe cha umoja. The ornate cup glints in the light. "To the Creator of all things great and small, we show our reverence for the original source of our life."

"Asè," the crowd responds. Their unified cry washes over me, pinpricking my skin.

"We give thanks to the Motherland, Alkebulan, cradle of civilization. And to Muungano where it has brought us."

"Asè."

"We call upon our ancestors and their indomitable spirit, for these fore-bears are the foundation of our families. Immortalized in our thoughts, we call them by name." Bayard turns to the assembly to await their roll call.

Sojourner. Martin. Haile. Barack. Ira. Malcolm. Nanny. Maya. Harriet. Huey. Shaka. Frederick. Marcus. Zora. Hampton. Castile. Langston. Rosa. Adam. Elijah. Nat. Booker. August. Nelson. Samora. Jomo. Kwame. Julius. Cudjoe. Astra. Hakeem. Daisy. Angela. Xola.

They call upon many ancestors in the moment. The name, the memory, chokes in my throat, my lips barely able to shape the word without any sound. "Fela."

The gbedu drums continue to pound in my mind.

"We remember our struggle and those who have struggled on our behalf." Bayard dips his hands in holy water. Once cleansed, he lights small incenses filled with sage.

"Asè," the people say.

He again raises the kikombe cha umoja. "We call upon our family and ask that they be with us in our thoughts. 'He who is not taught by his mother is taught by the world.' We show our children the importance of family. For they represent the promise of tomorrow."

"Asè." The crowd's tone lowers to a prayerful murmur.

"And by what name do we call our new Camara?"

"Maulana Langston Buhari, son of Hakeem and Tiamoyo Buhari," I an-nounce.

"We cast libation to the north, the south, the east, and the west." Bayard pours out the kikombe cha umoja to each of the cardinal directions. Pausing, he meets my eyes without rancor and steps aside, allowing me to present myself.

"Asè. Asè. Asè." I raise my arms.

Selamault walks over, and I drop to my knees before her. My assistant brings over the headdress I designed and presents it to her. Elaborately grooved horns with a central conical blue coiffure that rises from the two faces on the mask. A veil of beads to curtain the face. It depersonalizes the man behind the mask and points to the office. According to some, it also protects onlookers from the danger of casting their eyes directly upon the divine presence of the oba. Selamault places my headdress upon me. When I rise, I am Camara of Muungano.

"Long may you serve," Bayard says.

"Asè! Asè! Asè!" the Ijo cry out.

✸

From the time of my selection—though not official—through my appointed confirmation day by the Ifa oracle, Selamault, I have chosen to withdraw into seclusion, retreating for the Ipebi ritual of isolation. Though Muungano no longer adheres to the government of kings, royal seclusion is a tradition among my people. Meditation in isolation should be a new tradition for any accepting the mantle of Camara or any senior leadership position.

I'd stripped my living space of all unessential furnishings, with only Maya for company to train me in my people's history, customs, and traditions. Incense burned at all times. I prayed to my ancestors, spending quality time with them. I ate only food prepared in traditional ways, if one allowed for synthed meat. Because this was a time of cleansing, I refused to see even the closest members of my family, even as I considered the community's next steps.

Besides, I saw Fela every time I closed my eyes.

On the seventh day, the beating of gbedu drums signals my return from Ipebi. I never understood Camara Xola's careful shuffle before. Despite his infirmities, his walk should not have been affected. But the slow steps, the slight stoop, all hinted at the weight of his office. The dignity and grace required to shoulder it. As I dress, the symbology of the occasion serves as reminder for who I am now. The loose-fitting, wide sleeves of my white-and-red handwoven robe. Its interlaced patterns, triangles divided into smaller triangles, forming the sacred triangles of Alkebulan. The way the diamond patterns repeat continuously, illustrating the continuity and balance to life. To eternity. My bead-embroidered headdress has the image of a bird sculpted on top of it. A beaded veil shields my face, the world obscured by a thin partition, a reminder of the distance required to see clearly. Free from the constraints and entanglements of a single relationship.

Fela's image sears my mind.

An alarm siren clangs from outside my chamber. I dart out of my room and race to the source of the disturbance. The Green Zone lies only a few meters down the hallway. The air sweetens with every step in its direction. I pause at the outer rim of the entryway. My senses on fire in ways I don't understand. My thoughts gallop. My emi attenuates to a peak. Without reason, I whirl.

A panga blade misses me by centimeters. My robes flutter when I lunge to the side and grab the wrist holding the blade. I bend it and use it to control the body of its bearer, drawing him into my knee. A little more pressure and I could snap his wrist in several places.

"Drop it." My eyes flashed with anger. My tone is clear: I would issue this command only once.

The blade clatters against the fused regolith floor. Niyabinghi agents arrived in time to collect the blade and detain the man. A contingent of guards has not been assigned to me yet. Though I have little need for security since I am the one who trained them. I study the man. A nondescript weusi with flat features and dusty complexion. A haughtiness buoys his spirit. A pride fills his eyes. He's a martyr waiting for his moment.

"Why did you attack me?"

"Don't act innocent now. We know you plot with the aliens. You may have stopped me, but you can't stop us all." He fidgets, a performer buying time to remember his next lines. No matter, I have what I need.

Night Train are here.

"Take him into custody. We'll deal with him and his brethren later."

News of the attack on me circulates. Selamault meets me at the chamber entrance. "Are you harmed?"

"No, though it wrinkled my outfit more than I would have liked for a state occasion."

She is not amused. "You know what you need to do."

I nod. I need to call an emergency meeting of the security council.

28

WACHIRU ADISA
The Dreaming City

Maulana had not been Camara for an hour—the sounds of the feast still in full roar—before he summoned us to the Ijo table. By the time we reached him, he sat at the head of the table. Veiled by the mask he refused to remove, a faceless judge. The full Ijo had been assembled.

"Muungano is impacted by the perception that we're engaged in conflict." Maulana's voice strained with a thin melody because of the veil, as if he spoke through a reed. Only he could pull off such an outfit. Because while it stayed this side of pompous, each piece was a dedication to the story of his people. He felt and lived that shit to his bones.

"Perhaps we should adjourn to a more private space," we suggested.

"We shouldn't start the habit of hiding uncomfortable words from each other. We'll all be the stronger for it. Hard words were exchanged between us. Before anything festers between us, let us get all lingering matters out in the open so that we can deal with them. Let us begin our conflict transformation."

The djemaas, the palaver for conflict transformation, was a way to build sustainable peace between parties. Xola loved them, partly because he simply loved drama, but mostly because they represented opportunities for people to be real and raw with one another. The way Xola conceived it, conflict was a springboard to further develop people and character. "People development work takes time and effort," he often said, and it became the heart of building the Muungano alliance. Without it, there was no real community. The sessions could drag on. He let people put their sides out there, all the things bothering them, any which way they wanted to tell it. Then came the probing questions designed to elicit the true heart of the issues. Then any affected parties were encouraged to speak their piece, to share stories of each party, and to reflect back to them how they were seen by the community that loved them. Only then did the dialogues begin, identifying hurts, determining acceptable goals, adding new perspectives. Disembedding the conflict from where it was and—by shaping a series of tasks—embed it elsewhere. He brought the parties to the table with the goal of withdrawing from the conflict, so they could work out their own self-sustaining process to move forward. Xola used humor to make everyone relaxed and remind them that we all wanted the same thing.

"I don't have time for your shit," Maulana began. "Muungano doesn't have time for your shit."

"Camara." Bayard lowered his voice. Since the Camara himself was a part of the conflict, at least one other Ijo elder needed to be present. We could only guess at the strange combination of emotions he might be experiencing in this role.

"No. Time. We gird ourselves for war, and no one can afford to be distracted by our nonsense. Bayard, ask the questions."

"How do you feel about Wachiru?" Bayard asked him.

"I love him like a son." Maulana faced us. Though his face remained hidden, he paused. His voice betrayed him with the hint of a crack he quickly recovered from. "I respect the work he's done. I'm proud of the man he's grown into and look forward to see what he'll do in the future. I need him to keep challenging me at every turn to check my course."

"Wachiru?" Bayard asked.

Caught off guard by the candor of his admission, we falter before following suit. "Maulana is an example of the man we want to be. Honorable. True. Honest about his flaws, yet always striving to be better. Never afraid to fail in the name of trying to love the people in his life the best way he knows how."

"What don't you like about each other?" Bayard asked.

Holding up his hand to halt the answer, Maulana's face rotated to us. The beads of his veil rustled with the movement. "This is Muungano. We have one another's back or we have nothing. If you can't live with that, you know where the door is."

Maulana turned his back, dismissing us. The entire room held its breath. Respected and charismatic, he did not care about being liked and would never be accused of coddling anyone. But he was a real one and could always be counted on to speak true and direct. Though the Ijo remained in session, we adjourned to the next room with Bayard.

"What the hell was that?" Bayard asked.

"Welcome to Maulana's expedited conflict transformation. Are we good?" We extended our arm.

"Yeah, we good."

We clasped arms. The grasp felt real. Bayard's emi light and genuine.

"Xola would have handled that different." *Better,* we wanted to say.

"But Xola's not here." Bayard came around to our side of the table, sitting on its edge. "Look, Maulana's new to this and hasn't found his footing yet. It's our job to help him develop into the leader he's meant to be."

With that, any residual tension left the room. Even toward Maulana. Our thoughts drifted to the work of Muungano and the new spaces where we found ourselves. We needed to figure out where we fit in to support the work. By the time we returned to the antechamber, the raised voices indicated that the meeting was already well under way.

"In light of the attack on Maulana, the actions of sealing the Orun Gate seem all the more prudent," Jaha said.

"Or all the more rash. We have no idea the factions in play," Geoboe said, a flickering holovid image. He could not be bothered to make the trip from Oyigiyigi.

With the posture of resigned dignity about him, Maulana made his way to the dais. In the midst of the raucous debate, the scrape of his boots was oddly audible. He patted the air to regain control of the room. Now that we had reentered, he waited for us to find our seats. The assembly drew back, also taking the opportunity to sit down.

"You started without us?" we asked.

"It wasn't like that." Jaha glanced at Maulana. "It was all friendly chitchat and such, usual premeeting small talk. That . . . escalated."

"I called this meeting in order to brief the security council first," Maulana said.

"I see you have learned and grown." Selamault smirked, reminding him of his grandstanding when he became head of the Buhari family.

"Well, allow me to recap." Maulana shifted, an acknowledgment of Selamault's words, but also figuring out how he wanted to present himself to the Ijo. He was finding his way. "The R received a final transmission from Captain Chikeke before I sealed the wormhole. It was her full accounting, copies of her logs, of the events on the *Cypher.* The activities of the new LISC ambassador, Zenith Prebius, though careful parsing of her report suggests that he and the Earth Firsters may only be sometime allies. But her confirmation of Night Train agents, the fact that they managed to even infiltrate her ship, disturbed me most of all. I had their Saqqara detained at Titan, at the O.E. embassy there. The Niyabinghi are handling their questioning, processing, and immediate deportation back to O.E. They will not step foot on Muungano soil again. There would be a reckoning. All accounts will be settled."

The briefing stretched on for hours to cover the totality of where we found ourselves. The *Cypher*. LISC and Earth First and the matter of this unknown virus. The status of the *Morrison* and the *Baldwin,* stationed at Titan. The status of the Ring. The status of the investigation of the bombing of our embassy on O.E. Fela. The *Hughes*. All the HOVA Hellfighters lost on the other side of the Orun Gate. The tracking of Night Train operatives to Oyigiyigi. Matata. The disappearance of Amachi. The community was under assault from all sides.

"Which brings us to how best to handle O.E. and LISC. Let's open a direct communication with the head of LISC."

The full Ijo fell silent while the image coalesced to life.

Clay Harrison, the VOP of LISC, perched behind a grand oak table. The backdrop of the Indianapolis downtown behind him, with its orange skies and thick haze obscuring the iconic Monument Circle. A scar seared his face, creating an echo of a grin, no matter the face he made. A broad-shouldered, slightly oversized trench coat draped over a louche, tailored, white corporate uniform. Rendered with satin sashes and gilding his ecclesiastical vestments, his outfit specifically designed to remind everyone of his former title of reverend. His mask filtered O.E. air, which always smelled of freshly poured asphalt.

"I have only recently returned from a walkabout, or else I would have been the first to call to congratulate you after your official installment as the new Camara of Muungano. Xola was a great leader and had a gentle way of holding everyone around him into account. He will be missed." With only a few of the security council of the Ijo visible in his feed, VOP made eye contact with as many people in the room as possible, ever assessing his audience. His eyes lingered on us and then Maulana's mask, making a mental recalculation.

"Yes, he will be," Camara Maulana said.

"I hope we can begin your time in leadership by continuing the rich dialogue Xola and I shared." VOP bridged his fingers in front of his face, his voice heavy and breathy through the filter of his mask.

"Xola was a once-in-a-lifetime gift. It's too bad that gift was taken from us prematurely." Maulana's posture changed. An angry edge sharpened his tone. Lacking patience and having the need to prove himself, he allowed VOP to bait him with his timbre.

"Yes." VOP's voice held the hint of uncertainty, reading something akin to a trap in Maulana's tone.

And we began to wonder if this would be our role now. A spectator, shut out of the game, whose counsel would go largely ignored.

"You should know who I am. I am Maulana Langston Buhari, the new Camara of Muungano. Son of Hakeem and Tiamoyo Buhari and grandson of Hakeem Buhari, one of the cofounders of First World."

"Yours is a long and proud lineage." VOP's voice rose, turning the statement into a question.

"Yes. And I say all of that to confirm to you that I am not Camara Xola Adisa." Without quite turning from him, Maulana seemed to side-eye him. He needed to be careful. He wanted to project strength and confidence, but he approached the precipice of coming across as a person struggling with his role and thus overcompensating.

"I understand that." VOP lowered his gaze. The man appeared to age several decades. A web of fine lines crept about his eyes with the heavy creases in his face.

"I don't think that you do. My name is Camara Maulana Buhari. As Camara, I am much like your title, the Voice of the People. But . . . I am also not the leader as you understand leadership. The Camara of Muungano understands that all have a voice here, that in any given moment, any can speak. Even now, you speak before the entire Ijo." Maulana stepped aside to allow VOP the view of the full Ijo. Seething with anger and uncertainty, he didn't know how far he could push VOP. Or how far VOP could afford to appear pushed.

"That's . . . unusual. When Xola and I spoke . . ." The scar along his face twisted into a languid sneer.

"Again, you seem confused. *My* name is Maulana Buhari. Camara Adisa tended to keep your conversations to a smaller circle. He was always interested in the comfort of the person he was talking to. What you need to understand is that how a Camara operates is up to their discretion. Xola was taken from us. In his place, I now have the privilege to serve."

VOP shifted in a series of careful calculations. For a few heartbeats, only the strained huff of his breathing could be heard. Finally, in a measured cadence, he spoke. "I called to ensure that our relationship got off on the right foot. To remind us that our two powers face great challenges moving forward. Not the least of which is this 'Interstellar Alliance' and the threat they represent."

"Indeed, we face threats on all sides. Some much closer than an Interstellar Alliance on the far side of a now-sealed wormhole."

"Sealed? We had reports of an energy discharge from your sector . . ."

"Reports? I'm sure your observation array produced clear, up-close footage of us launching our quantum payload. You should be sifting through firsthand accounts now. The Orun Gate represented a security risk to all of Muungano. One I could not in good conscience abide for the sake of my people."

It was a delicately woven trap. The more VOP Harrison protested his innocence, the more the Ijo—all of Muungano—would believe his complicity. Because history had demonstrated time and time again exactly how O.E. would act in light of the Orun Gate. Maulana did not need to wait for evidence. Just like he understood—probably never doubted—that he would be the next Camara. He understood that he could do the things we could never do. And somewhere deep within, we understood that, too.

"That was a unilateral decision. One that should have been done in consultation with your allies." VOP rose from his chair, his pleated trousers flowing with his sudden movement.

Camara Maulana smiled, VOP now having been unsettled out of his gamesmanship. "Allies? We have no allies when it comes to the internal security of Muungano. Also, we are wary of allies who plant agents to infiltrate us."

"That's quite the accusation. What proof do you have?"

"The kind that has us choose to seal our borders and cut off trade relations as the cost of violating our sovereignty." Maulana gathered his robe and stood. "You should be receiving several of your ambassadors and other operatives any day now, assuming you haven't heard from them already."

Maulana didn't turn to any of us. Did not involve us in the conversation. We were all silent props, a background at best, of his show. He didn't see the openings VOP tried to extend to him. VOP shouldn't be underestimated. No matter how depleted, he possessed a fleet of ships and the resources of an entire planet. Much of which we still depended on for our survival, despite his talk of cutting off trade. VOP knew that. A toddler knew that.

"You sound like you want to take us to the brink of war." VOP chose his words carefully.

"Someone, an enemy perhaps in the guise of an ally, certainly brought us here. To paraphrase a prophet, we will not be a defenseless people at the mercy of a ruthless and violent racist mob. Since self-preservation is the first

law of nature, we assert our right to self-defense. By any means necessary."
Anger flushed Maulana's neck. Despite the mask, a vessel bulging like a snake
attempted to crawl to his head. He realized his overreach.

Both men seemed so desperate.

Composing himself to buy time to think, VOP took his time returning to
his seat. "It . . . saddens me that this kind of overreaction will set the tenor of
our relationship."

"In the name of setting the proper tenor of our relationship, let me be can-
did. We suspect agents, wittingly or unwittingly, work to further the aims of
our oppression, and we stand prepared to defend ourselves against it. Here's
what we suspect: Someone, an enemy perhaps in the guise of an ally, had a
hand in taking Xola from us, the people who loved and revered him. We suspect some of our allies are not working in our best interests. Someone, an enemy perhaps in the guise of an ally, sent agents who looked like us to sabotage
and weaken us. Those events directly—again, let me be clear, directly—led
to me becoming Camara.

"Xola is gone. Someone has seen to that. If you wanted a different tone
to the relationship, perhaps a true ally would have better seen to his care.
Perhaps someone took his ways or ours for weakness. Or softness. Now
everyone—allies and enemies in the guise of an ally alike—has me to deal
with. Being mistaken for weak or soft will not be made. Now we await the
inevitable call to arms. We stand ready. My name is Maulana Buhari. Camara
of Muungano."

Camara Maulana cut off the transmission to O.E. Projecting strength and
calm, he turned to address the full Ijo. "There is a time to tear and a time to
sew. Now is a time to tear."

✳

The Dreaming City was no longer home. We had no place here. We needed
to figure out who we were and who we were going to be. To rediscover the
song of our heart and move us to even create music again. The door chimed.
Waving our cousin in, we packed the last item into a slingpack.

"What are you on?" Ezeji plopped onto the couch he fashioned, like he
was listening to a poet who made zero impression on him.

"Heading out."

"To where?"

"We don't know." We paused at the truth of that realization. "Yet."

"I've been wanting to chop it up with you for a bit. You've been keeping an awful low profile around here the last few weeks. Hardly even know you around." Ezeji occupied his attention with a shelf that was now blank.

We stopped working and gave him our full attention. After a protracted silence, we said, "We don't want to be a liability to the Adisa name."

"What's that smell?" Ezeji sat up and sniffed about. "It smells like straight-up CAP."

"It's obvious the people want someone like Maulana to speak for them. We don't want to get in the way of that."

"Maulana spanked that ass, now you want to get ghost?" His tone kept light, but Ezeji sat up, his emi both troubled and concerned. He pressed his lips together, having more to say but knowing he wasn't going to say them in the best way.

"Look, it don't work like that. With Xola gone, we thought our role was to fill in for him. However, community chose another voice—Maulana—to speak for it."

"You leaving is the last thing anyone, Maulana included, wants."

"We know that. On one level. On another, we took it as a sign that we weren't ready. That we needed to grow, to challenge ourselves. We want to find . . . me . . . in all of . . ." We gestured to the room, but meant all of it. The Dreaming City. Muungano. "This. We believe the next stage of our journey lies away from the Dreaming City. Somewhere we have room to explore."

"That's deep. You don't know where you're going or what you're going to be doing. It sounds to me like the next stage of your journey is homelessness." Ezeji walked over to us and extended his arm to clasp ours in support. "Sounds fun. Can I come?"

"Nah, your place is here." We clasped his arm and drew him into our embrace. "We submitted your name to stand in our place. Head of the Adisa family."

"What?" Ezeji backed up a step.

"We both have new areas of opportunities to explore. This journey will be good for you."

✳

The Dreaming City did not have a spaceport. Not the way O.E. considered them. The outer band was almost an open-air market, filled with song and dance and the great smells of outdoor cooking. It led into an interior of tunnels, the walls and floors still a curated art experience, but there was a somberness to its tunnels and docking stations. It was a place of transitions, where people could lose themselves in the in-between spaces. We approached the recently docked Saqqara. Members disembarked, and others prepared to embark. A flood of people streamed in from O.E. Those leaving were going anywhere except there. A figure stiffened when we came into view. Jaha hefted her own slingpack.

"What are you doing?" we asked.

"Going with you," Jaha said.

"Your place is at Maulana's side," we said. "He will need your counsel and ability to get shit done for the next phase of Muungano he is building."

"I pledged myself to be at *your* side, not in Maulana's leadership circle. Besides, this is no longer the Muungano I know. And I fear it will be even less recognizable as time moves on."

"We don't know what we're getting into." People passed by, close but not bumping into us. We want her to grab our hand, draw us into an embrace and hold us in the Dreaming City.

Jaha rubbed our back. "Where you go, I go."

We glanced about the docking bay one last time. Inhaling sharply, we boarded the Saqqara, bound for wherever it was heading. The ship wasn't as crowded. The tension of the past few weeks had dampened the spirit of travel. Especially away from the Dreaming City. We were able to secure the seats near the rear of the Saqqara. The closest passengers to us were several rows ahead.

"We have a long trip ahead of us. What do you want to do first?" we asked.

"Let me tell you a story." Jaha engaged a virtual imaging womb. The hard light sealed off our row, and it appeared as if the two of us sat around a campfire. "Each word in its place; none forgotten. The order is sacred, exactly as I once heard it . . ."

29

AMACHI ADISA
Mars

Your last conscious memory was your Saqqara plunging into a crater. You can only surmise that it and you are now buried deep within it. Your ship has twisted into a sarcophagus of crumpled molybdenum and carbon nanotubes around you. All consciousness brought for you was the press of darkness and pain so ubiquitous you didn't know where it ended and you began. You know your life ebbs from you in uncounted trickles. Clawing to stay awake, you are desperate not to be drawn into the all-consuming darkness awaiting you. Too wounded to move, you can no longer feel your toes. In your mind, your fingernails rake against the encroaching darkness that you slowly slide into. A part of you already knows and begins to accept that you're fated to die here. Cold and alone.

✳

You don't quite make it back to consciousness. Your mind—maybe not even it, perhaps only a corner of your emi—becomes aware that hands unwind metal, creating just enough room to free you from the jutting struts pinning you. Those same hands gently lift you from the wreckage. They examine your wounds, checking the extent of your injuries. Your breath comes in thin gasps. You don't know how much air you have left. Fitting a mask over your face, the hands slough you onto a board of some sort. A cool spray of air washes over you. You inhale sharply; the exertion wears you out. You recall the sensation of being dragged as the night calls to you again.

✳

You awake to a rhythm of dull aches pounding across your body. But they are only the distant thuds of wounds that have been tended to. A fire dances in the center of the cavern. On the other side of the flames stands a robed woman.

"You're up. Good." The woman's voice is both calming and reassuring.

And familiar. The first thing that comes into view was her black robe, dusty and ragged. Red tail feathers have been woven into the base of her white hair, which has been shaved into a mohawk. Gold elekes rope her neck, bright against the sepia color of her skin. Her large brown eyes seem comfortable penetrating a person's soul.

"Where am I?"

"My home." The woman stokes the fire. Her hand wraps around a glass filled with a milky white liquid that smells of overripe fruit.

"You live in a cave." You try to sit up, but muscles you didn't know you possessed scream in protest.

"Wherever I am, I am home." She smirks. You can't tell if it is at your failed attempt to sit up or the cleverness of her answers.

"Who are you?"

"That is the nature of my journey. Constantly interrogating who I am. But you may call me Nehanda. Nehanda Jywanza."

"Jywanza?" Despite the pain, you force yourself up. When you study her face, you see the family resemblance. Pain rips through your side. Tears well in your eyes, but you're happy to feel anything. "Any relations to Selamault?"

"My sister. Your aunt."

"I never . . ." You don't know how best to finish that sentence. "It is good to meet you. Thank you for saving my life."

"Don't thank me yet. You face dark days ahead."

You measure her words, searching them for any hint of threat. Her emi is closed off to you. She's like reading a shadow. You reach for your chakrams.

"No need for weapons," Nehanda says without looking at you. With a casual flick of her wrist, two chakrams form in the space between you and her. They spin about, crossing back and forth like the belted kraals of Muungano, except whirring like manic blades before evaporating. "That is, unless you are the weapon."

"What . . . are you?"

"Ah, now there's a better question. I am Iyami Aje."

"One of the sacred mothers."

"An elder of the night. You are to begin your training as an agoze, a disciple in the journey of becoming an ologun." No one can choose to initiate the Iyami Aje. The witches choose whom they wish to initiate. "Only if you are interested in taking on your true role as a beacon of hope for your people if they are to weather the coming darkness."

"I don't know what I want or where I'm supposed to go next. I have no past, and in my present, I've given no thought to my future."

"That is as it should be. The past, the present, and the future often collide with one another," Nehanda said. "You have but a single destiny to fulfill: your own."

The fire dances in the night, blowing in an unfelt breeze while Nehanda begins her night song.

Fela Buhari
Rank: Commander
Complexion: Dark and brooding
Hair Status: Bald (though always in need of a shave)
Born: The Dreaming City, Muungano
Special Note: Recent graduate of the Thmei Academy.
Campaigns: None.

Anitra Gouvei
Rank: First Lieutenant
Complexion: High yella with freckles
Hair Status: Braids
Born: Mars colony, Bronzeville
Skills: Named the Tananarive Due Endowed Professor in the Humanities
at Spelman College; sniper, her weapon of choice being the DMX-3000
rifle.
Special Note: Has a strange fascination and hatred of Kappas.
Campaigns: Returned home after the Shango incident; officially has 144 kills
attributed to her; played a leading role in the Bronzeville rebellion.

Robin Townsend
Rank: Sergeant
Complexion: "Highly melanated"
Hair Status: Afro puffs
Born: Titan outpost, Arkestra
Special Note: From the secretive lineage known as "the Keepers of the Belt."
(Also, do not call her RowTow.)
Skills: Studied at the Thmei Academy; combat specialist with knives; minor in
surgery. She nicknamed her modified talon Busta.
Favorite Quote: "I will cut a bitch."

Epyc Ro Morgan
Rank: Captain
Complexion: Blackity black black
Hair Status: Bantu knots
Born: First World outpost
Special Note: Rumored to be a descendant of rebel leader Astra Black.
Skills: Accomplished pilot; combat and tactical specialist.
Campaigns: Operation Bumba; Operation Obatala; the Yemaya Campaign; the
  only known survivor of Operation Hellwalk.

Chandra Elle
Rank: Second Lieutenant
Complexion: Mocha latte
Hair Status: White mohawk (earning her the designation "the militant Ororo")
Born: Indianapolis, Indiana, O.E.; emigrated to lunar outpost First World.
Skills: Communications specialist.
Special Note: Silent Negro.
Campaigns: [classified].

GLOSSARY

agoze—initiates to ways of sorcery

Aje—a woman who wields myriad arcane creative biological, spiritual, and cosmic powers

akata—wild cats

Alkebulan—the Motherland

Asante sana—"Thank you very much"

Asè—the power to make things happen

Asili—natives of Alkebulan

bagirwa—revered priestess, spiritual head of the Niyabinghi

balafon—a kind of wooden xylophone or percussion idiophone

Basotho blanket—a distinctive form of woolen tribal blanket traditionally worn by Sotho people and unique to the Kingdom of Lesotho

bembe—a drumming party to call down orisha into the body of an initiate

Black Caesar—a device used to pirate link streams

Black Dove—a line of oracles, the Libyan Sibyls

boerewors—a type of sausage

CAP—current aspirational phase

chakram—a gold band that lies in a flat circle about the neck; when activated, it becomes a bladed weapon

djemaas—from North Africa (à la palavers of West Africa)—disputes worked out in public; collective self-criticism

ekpu—ancestor figure

emi—spirit

fashioning—manipulation of nanobots into objects

funkentelechy—the use of emi to direct nanobots for fashioning

gbedu—big drum

gbeto—soldiers/hunters

glyph—site-to-site transmitter

Griot Circle—policing force, story investigators

Habari gani—"What's the news?"

HOVA—military of Muungano; name taken back when O.E. was thrown into religious wars just after the Mars colony was established. O.E. referred to gbeto as "God's army" and Jehovah is another name for God

Ijo—governing body of Muungano

Ipebi—ritual of isolation

Iyami Aje—a Yoruba term of respect and endearment used to describe a woman of African ancestry who is considered to be an Aje. No one can choose to initiate as Iyami and only Iyami can choose who they will initiate as Iyami

jeli—griot officer, court musician

jeliya—griot's ancient art, handlers of the nyame

kanaga masks—worn primarily at dama, a collective funerary rite for Dogon men whose goal is to ensure the safe passage of the spirits of the deceased to the world of the ancestors

kanzu—shirt

kaross—cloak made of sheepskin, or the hide of other animals, with the hair left on

kheprw crystals—minerals mined from lunar strata as well as the asteroid belt; used to fuel Muungano starships

kikombe cha umoja—unity cup

kizungu—language of the wanderers (English)

kraal—village

kreef—crayfish

Lij—head of a Niyabinghi Order unit; translates as "child"; serves to indicate that a youth is of noble blood

linknet—personal data streams

LISC—Liberation Investment Support Cooperative, the corporate entity running the Original Earth government

Maafa—the Holocaust of Enslavement

Maroons—descendants of Africans in the Americas who formed settlements away from slavery

Muungano—means "Togetherness" in Swahili. Centered on the terran moon whose capital is called the Dreaming City, Muungano extends to include Bronzeville on the Mars colony, to Titan guarding the Orun Gate, to the distant Oyigiyigi mining outpost.

mzungu—someone with white skin

nanomesh—suit like a second skin interface between wearer and their nav-suit/nanobots for fashioning

navsuit—combined nanomesh and exoskeleton (military grade)

Negus—derived from the Ethiopian meaning "to reign." The title has subsequently been used to translate as "king."

neoniks—the generation fascinated with the late twenty-first century era as part of what they called the Remember Revolution

Ngwenya Mine—named for the oldest mine on earth

Niyabinghi Order—honor guard of the Ijo, taken from the gathering of Rastafari people to celebrate and commemorate key dates significant to Rastafari throughout the year

nyama—the spoken/sung word and the power that storytelling releases

Nyamakalaw—handlers of nyama (civilian head of the Griot Circle)

obroni—outsider

ogbanje—changeling spirit

orisha—deities

Orun Gate—the name of the nearest wormhole

Oyigiyigi—a series of asteroid belts and the mining colony; named for the orisha's eternal rock of creation

panga—daggers

pap—a thick porridge of finely ground corn

PAW—public ass whipping

pehla sticks—charged batons; griots weapons

phase suits—combined nanomesh and exoskeleton (civilian grade) to control nanobots for fashioning

Ras—civilian head of the Niyabinghi Order; is a rank of nobility equivalent to duke, though it is often rendered in translation as "prince"

Reapers—named for a subset of the Mino, the female fighting units who fought with meter-long straight razors

rondavel—home

sabhu—the language of the soul

Saqqara—ship named for the Saqqara Bird; a bird-shaped artifact made of sycamore wood, discovered during the 1898 excavation of the Pa-di-Imen tomb in Saqqara, Egypt

sosaties—a traditional dish of meat cooked on skewers

synthed—synthesized

Thmei—the Egyptian goddess of truth and justice

Tjwala—a potent home-brewed beer

Ubuntu—"humanity" or "I am because we are"

Ugenini—children of the diaspora

Uhlanga—according to the Zulu, it is the marsh from which humanity was born; code for Muungano's secret panspermia program

umbidvo wetint sanga—cooked pumpkin leaves and peanuts

Umoja—"unity" in Swahili

upinde mvua—rainbow (Swahili)

Uponyaji—a time of healing

wazungu—the plural of mzungu, people with white skin

weusi—blackness

yankadi—a slow and mellow dance

Yo—the generic term for the O.E. or its mentality or systems

ACKNOWLEDGMENTS

With a book like *Sweep of Stars,* the first in the Astra Black trilogy, it's hard to know where to begin with whom to thank. Except, well, at the beginning.

This journey all started with drinks in New York City with editor Diana Pho, who pressed me about what I was looking to write next. I pitched an idea on the spot, a novelization of a story I was writing for Mur Lafferty (yeah, I wasn't even done with the story yet). Then into the hands of my then agent, Jen Udden, the idea went. She then pushed me into all sorts of uncharted areas in terms of how I write stories (and do business!).

I feel like my thanks will look a lot like baton passing, because the would-be story bundle then passed to new (to me) editor Will Hinton and new (to me) agent Stephanie Kim, who would see the project over the finish line.

All that said, I wouldn't be anywhere without the inspiration of the Kheprw Institute: our founding elders (Imhotep Adisa, Pambana Uishi, and Paulette Fair) as well as some of our frontline folks (Diop Adisa, Leah Humphrey, Alvin Sangsuwangal). Others will have to wait for Book Two or else I'll be here all day, though I do need to give a special shout-out to another group of organized neighbors, The Learning Tree.

Speaking of folks who continue to inspire, push, and challenge me, I can't help but thank many of the local artists around me: Stacia Murphy, Sibeko Jywanza, Ro Townsend, Robin Jackson, Anitra Malone, Chandra Lynch. All the folks who help imagine a better world.

I wouldn't hear the end of it if I didn't thank Bella Faidley, Rianna Butcher, and my other student dreamers from the Oaks Academy Middle School.

I'd also like to thank the many editors who have published stories of mine that led up to me writing this novel: Jason Sizemore, Bill Campbell, Scott Andrews, Susan Forest, Lucas K. Law, Mur Lafferty (for the story I *did* finish), Lynne and Michael Thomas.

I'd be remiss if I didn't thank the friends who were my cheerleaders along the way. Anthony Cardno. Wayne Brady. Jerry Gordon. And I know I'm forgetting some folks, but luckily there will be Book Two. . . .

A special thank-you to Rodney Carlstrom and Will Johnson.

An even more special thank-you to Chesya Burke.

And the most special thank-yous to my mom and my sons, Reese and Malcolm, and my wife, Sally.

I couldn't make this journey without you.